Praise for *New York Times* bestselling author
Phillip Margolin

AFTER DARK

"Exciting . . . whiplash plotting. The reversals and
revelations are many and diabolically clever. . . . No legal
thriller fan, once hooked, will wiggle free of the story
line . . . before reaching its utterly surprising, and
surprisingly dark, conclusion."—*Publishers Weekly*

"Margolin's . . . tale is worth the telling, and readers will
be hard-pressed to anticipate the action as they lie awake
with *After Dark*."—*People*

"Rips along like a carnival ride."—*The Oregonian*

"Opening *After Dark* ignites a fast-burning fuse that races
to a dynamite ending. . . . *After Dark* exposes the drama
and suspense that are often shrouded by judicial robes.
Beyond any reasonable doubt, Phillip Margolin has
presented his best case yet."—*BookPage*

GONE, BUT NOT FORGOTTEN

"It's the next *Firm*."—*Entertainment Weekly*

"Best fiction book of the year? Easy. *Gone, But Not
Forgotten* keeps the twists and turns coming at breakneck
speed."—Larry King, *USA Today*

"Part *The Fugitive*, part *Silence of the Lambs*."
—*Us* magazine

"One scary story . . . It takes a really crafty storyteller to
put people on the edge of their seats and keep them there.
But Phillip Margolin does just that."—*Chicago Tribune*

"A suspensefully conceived chess game of a novel."
—Clive Cussler

Please turn the page for more praise
for the novels of Phillip Margolin. . . .

THE LAST INNOCENT MAN

"Jam-packed plot . . . [Margolin] shows us . . . the difficulties of lawyers as people practicing in a system of justice which is the same for the guilty and the innocent . . . and exposes the costs paid by a conscientious lawyer in the coin of human feeling."—*The Washington Post*

"Fast-paced . . . a thriller . . . a cut above most novels of this genre."—*The Sacramento Bee*

HEARTSTONE

"I was somewhat reminded of *In Cold Blood,* but in some ways, I think this is a better book. . . . It's fascinating reading—the classic 'page-turner'—and I admit to being stunned and shocked at the unexpected ending."
—Dorothy Uhnak, author of *The Investigation*

ALSO BY PHILLIP MARGOLIN

After Dark
Gone, But Not Forgotten
The Last Innocent Man
Heartstone

THE
BURNING
MAN

—

PHILLIP
MARGOLIN

—

BANTAM BOOKS

NEW YORK TORONTO LONDON
SYDNEY AUCKLAND

This edition contains the complete text of the
original hardcover edition.
NOT ONE WORD HAS BEEN OMITTED.

THE BURNING MAN
A Bantam Book / published by arrangement with Doubleday

PUBLISHING HISTORY
Doubleday edition published September 1996
Bantam edition / July 1997

ISBN 0-553-57495-7

Published simultaneously in the United States and Canada

Bantam Books are published by Bantam Books, a division of
Bantam Doubleday Dell Publishing Group, Inc. Its trademark,
consisting of the words "Bantam Books" and the portrayal of a
rooster, is Registered in U.S. Patent and Trademark Office and in
other countries. Marca Registrada. Bantam Books, 1540
Broadway, New York, New York 10036.

PRINTED IN THE UNITED STATES OF AMERICA

OPM   10 9 8 7 6 5 4 3 2 1

For Bart C. and his parents,
Phillip and Kaye,
who never gave up hope.

ACKNOWLEDGMENTS

Some of the events in *The Burning Man* are similar to incidents that actually occurred in a murder case that I handled many years ago, so I want to make it crystal clear that no character in this book is intended to represent a real, live human being. This book is peopled by fictional characters whose personalities and motivations I invented for the purpose of entertaining my readers with a make-believe tale.

Some very real people helped me in the writing of *The Burning Man*. I want to thank Judy Margolin, Bart Reid, Dr. Donald Trunkey, Dr. Stanley Abrams, Robert Palladino, Detective Patric Montgomery of the Oregon State Police, Dr. Benson Schaeffer and my friend and fellow writer Dr. Michael Palmer for sharing their technical knowledge with me.

The comments of Jay Margulies, Pam Webb, Vince Kohler, Susan Svetkey, Larry Matasar, Jerry, Joseph, Eleonore and Doreen Margolin and Norman and Helen Stamm, who were kind enough to read my first draft, were greatly appreciated.

I also want to thank the dynamic duo of Lori Lipsky and Elisa Petrini, the world champions of tag-team editing, for riding to my rescue, Estelle Laurence for her careful copy editing, and everyone (and I mean everyone) at Doubleday and Bantam Books.

Finally, I never get tired of thanking Jean Naggar and everyone at her agency for taking such good care of me, and Doreen, Daniel and Ami Margolin for putting up with me.

PART ONE

———

CRASH AND BURN

———

CHAPTER ONE

1

On the day the gods chose for his destruction, Peter Hale ate his breakfast on the terrace of his condominium. The sun was just beginning its ascent above the city of Portland and a bloodred aura surrounded the flat, black silhouette of Mount Hood. The dark metropolis looked like an ink-black carpet crisscrossed by Christmas lights. A poet would have savored the sunrise for its beauty, but Peter enjoyed the advent of day for another reason. He believed that Galileo was wrong when he imagined an Earth that revolved around the sun. In his heart of hearts, Peter knew that the sun that was slowly rising over his city revolved around him.

A crumb from his bran muffin fell onto the leg of Peter's gray Armani trousers. He flicked it off, then took a sip of the café latte he had brewed in the espresso machine that graced the marble counter of his designer kitchen. Peter lived in the condo, drove a fire-engine-red Porsche and pulled in a high five-figure salary as a fourth-year associate at Hale, Greaves, Strobridge, Marquand and Bartlett. The salary did not cover all his expenses and Peter was a bit overextended right now, but he never had any trouble obtaining mortgages, car loans or things of that sort since everyone knew he was the son of Richard Hale, one of the firm's founding partners and a past president of the Oregon State Bar. With all this, Peter was not a happy camper.

The living room drapes moved. Peter looked over his shoulder. Priscilla padded across the terrace wearing only an oversized Trailblazer T-shirt. She was a flight attendant with United. Peter had dated her on and off for a few months. Most men would have killed for such a lover, but Priscilla was talking about "commitment" with increasing frequency and Peter was finding it more and more difficult to avoid discussions of the dreaded "C" word.

Priscilla bent down and kissed Peter on the cheek. Peter's head moved slightly and she sensed the rebuff.

"Boy, are you a grouch this morning," Priscilla said, straining to keep the hurt out of her voice.

"Yeah, well, I've got to get to court," he answered brusquely.

"How is the case going?"

"Great for Sir Richard. Not so good for me."

Priscilla sat across from Peter. "What's wrong?" she asked.

"The same damn thing that's been wrong since I made the mistake of going to work for my father."

Peter did not try to disguise his bitterness. It felt good to vent his anger.

"Last night, right after court, Sir Richard informed me that he would be cross-examining all of the defendant's important witnesses and giving the closing argument."

"Your father has let you try some part of the case, hasn't he?"

"He's let me examine a few insignificant witnesses. That's about it."

"Oh, Peter. I'm so sorry. I know how much you've been counting on being lead counsel."

"Yeah, well," Peter shrugged, "I should have known better. My father just has to hog the glory."

Peter looked out toward the sunrise, but his thoughts

4

were turned inward. When his father asked him if he wanted to work at Hale, Greaves, Peter had imagined serving a brief apprenticeship followed quickly by a succession of major cases in which he would act as lead counsel, winning multimillion-dollar verdicts and establishing his credentials in the legal community. It had taken four years serving as Richard Hale's vassal to bring him to his senses. He had worked on *Elliot v. Northwest Maritime* from day one and he knew more about the case than his father ever would. If his father would not let him be lead counsel in *Elliot,* he had little hope of being lead counsel in a major case in the near future. He had to get out from under his father's influence. If necessary, even leave Hale, Greaves. A new start with a new firm might be the answer. He would seriously consider a move when the Elliot case was over.

The senior partners in Hale, Greaves, Strobridge, Marquand and Bartlett looked out from corner offices on the fortieth floor of the Continental Trust Building at the rivers, towering mountains and lush green hills that made Portland, Oregon, so unique. Though the skyscraper was new, the firm's quarters were decorated with heavy, dark woods, polished brass fittings and fine old antiques, giving the place an air of timeless quality.

At precisely 7:30 A.M., Peter entered a small, windowless conference room where he and his father met before court every morning to review the witnesses who would testify that day and to discuss any legal issues that might arise. Peter's father still had the same massive build that helped him win second team All-American honors in football and an NCAA wrestling championship at Oregon State in 1956. He owned a full head of white hair and his craggy face was outfitted with a broken nose and a cauliflower ear. Richard Hale practiced law the way he played sports, full steam ahead and take no prisoners. This morning, Peter's father was striding back and forth in front of a low credenza in his shirtsleeves,

5

a phone receiver plastered to his ear, muttering "Jesus Christ!" at increasing decibel levels each time he made a turn.

Peter took off his suit jacket and hung it behind the door on a hanger. He noted with distaste that his father had flung his jacket onto a corner of the long conference table where it lay crumpled in a heap. Richard loved playing the humble, hulking man of the people in front of juries and he thought that the disheveled clothes helped his image. Peter could not imagine wearing a suit that had not been freshly pressed.

"When will you know?" his father barked, as Peter took several files from his attaché case and arranged them in a neat pile.

"No, goddamn it, that won't do. We're in the middle of the goddamn trial. We've been in court for two weeks."

Richard paused. His features softened. "I know it couldn't be helped, but you don't know Judge Pruitt."

He paused again, listening intently. Then, his face turned scarlet with anger.

"Look, Bill, this isn't that difficult. I told you I needed the goddamn things two weeks ago. This is what happens when you wait until the last minute.

"Well, you better," Richard threatened, ending the conversation by slamming down the phone.

"What's up?" Peter asked.

"Ned Schuster was in a car wreck," Richard answered distractedly, running his fingers through his hair. "He's in the hospital."

"Who?"

"Schuster. He's supposed to testify today. Now, Bill Ebling says they can't get the papers to court because Schuster had the only copy."

Peter had no idea what his father was talking about. He glanced down at his files. There was one for each witness and none was for a Ned Schuster. When he looked up, his father was leaning against the wall. His face was as pale as chalk and he was rubbing both sides of his jaw vigorously.

"Dad?" Peter asked, frightened by his father's ashen pallor and the beads of sweat that suddenly bathed his face. Instead of answering, Richard grimaced in pain and began rubbing his breast with a clenched fist. Peter froze.

"Heart attack," Richard gasped.

Peter snapped out of his trance and raced around the conference table.

"I need to lie down," Richard managed, as his knees sagged. Peter caught him before he hit the floor.

"Help!" Peter screamed. A young woman stuck her head in the door. Her eyes widened.

"Call 911, fast! My father is having a heart attack."

When Peter looked down, Richard's teeth were clenched and his eyes were squeezed tight. He continued to rub his chest vigorously as if trying to erase his pain.

"Hold on, Dad," Peter begged. "The medics are coming."

Richard's body jerked. His eyes glazed over. The two men were sprawled on the floor. Peter held his father's head in his lap. He was concentrating so hard on his father that he didn't notice the room filling with people.

Suddenly, Richard's eyes opened and he gasped, "Mistrial."

"What?"

"Get . . . mistrial . . . Must . . ."

"Don't talk. Please, Dad. Save your strength."

Richard grabbed Peter's wrist and squeezed so hard his fingers left raw, red impressions.

"Must . . . Mistrial," he managed again.

"Yes, I will," Peter promised, just as someone called, "Let me through." Peter looked toward the doorway. He recognized the older woman who was pushing through the crowd as a nurse the firm had hired to assist in working up personal injury cases. A moment later,

Peter was standing on the far side of the conference table as the nurse tried to save his father's life.

The idea of Richard Hale dying sucked the air right out of Peter. He slumped onto a chair just as two medics rushed into the room with oxygen, a stretcher and a portable IV. Peter's mother had died several years ago after a long illness and her death had been expected, but Peter saw his father as a mountain that would last forever. When he looked up he could not see his father through the crush of medical personnel who surrounded him. What if Richard didn't pull through? he asked himself. Peter's heart beat so rapidly he had to will himself to calm down. The anxiety attack passed. He opened his eyes and saw his briefcase and his files. The trial! Peter looked at his watch. It was almost time to go to court. Suddenly, the people in front of the door were backing away and the medics were rushing out of the room with a stretcher that supported his father. Peter wanted to follow them to the hospital, but someone had to tell Mrs. Elliot what had happened and ask Judge Pruitt for a mistrial. There was no way he could see his father now anyway. Peter knew he would probably have to stay in the hospital waiting room for hours before the doctors could tell him anything.

Peter stepped out of the conference room into the hall. It was empty. Everyone had followed the medics to the elevator. Peter walked away from the crowd and left the offices by a back door that opened near the men's room. He was trembling and flushed. He went to the rest room sink and splashed cold water on his face. Then, he leaned forward and looked at himself in the mirror. His brown, blow-dried hair was a mess, his shirt was rumpled and his tie had been wrenched to one side. Peter took out a pocket comb and wet it. When his hair looked presentable, he tucked in his shirt and straightened his tie.

Peter examined himself again. He saw a man whose genetic inheritance from his mother had softened the sharp features his father had contributed. Peter had his

8

father's intense blue eyes, but he also had his mother's smooth, high cheekbones. His nose was straight instead of craggy and his lips were thinner than Richard Hale's. At five feet ten, one hundred and sixty pounds, he was slender and wiry with none of the bulk or height of his father.

Peter straightened up. He felt back in control of himself and the situation. There was nothing he could do for his father now. Richard would be unconscious or drugged for hours. Peter decided that he would quickly explain what happened to the judge before going to the hospital. Certainly, Pruitt would grant a mistrial under the circumstances. No judge would require the trial to go on when the lead counsel had been stricken with a heart attack.

Peter took the elevator to the lobby. The courthouse was only a few blocks away. As he rushed toward it, an unsettling thought suddenly occurred to him. Mrs. Elliot was suffering terribly. He could see how hard it was for her to sit through her trial, both physically and emotionally. If a mistrial was declared, Mrs. Elliot would have to suffer through a second trial. In a second trial, the defense would have transcripts of Mrs. Elliot's witnesses and would know all of their strategy. Delay always helped the defendant when the plaintiff had a strong case. And the plaintiff's case was almost finished. Only two short witnesses remained.

Peter paused inside the courthouse doors. Lawyers, litigants, policemen and clerks swirled around him, the noise from dozens of conversations formed a constant din, but he was oblivious to the crowd. Was his father thinking clearly when he told Peter to ask for a mistrial? He had been in unbearable pain. Did his father really want to abort the case when it was going so well? Would Richard even remember his order when he recovered from the trauma of his coronary? Peter was certain that following his father's wishes was not in Mrs. Elliot's best interest, but the thought of disobeying Richard Hale's command terrified him.

Peter realized that he was trembling. He took a deep breath and willed himself to calm down. A lawyer's first duty was to his client. Why, then, had his father told him to ask for a mistrial? It took a moment for the answer to dawn on Peter. Richard Hale had no confidence in Peter's ability to take over the case.

Peter's fear gave way to a sense of outrage. He squared his shoulders and strode across the lobby toward the elevators. By the time the elevator doors opened, Peter was ready to go to court. He would show his father just how good he was. He would win *Elliot*. Then, he would place the multimillion-dollar judgment in front of Richard Hale, irrefutable proof that he was ready, willing and able to step up to the big time.

Alvin Pruitt was a cadaverous jurist with a military crew cut, beady, bloodshot eyes and sunken cheeks that always seemed to be covered by gray stubble. He was foul-tempered and ran his courtroom like a Marine barracks. By the time Peter walked into court, he was ten minutes late and the judge was furious.

"I hope you have a good explanation for your tardiness, Mr. Hale."

"I do, sir. There's been an emergency. May I approach the bench?"

Pruitt frowned and searched the room beyond Peter.

"Where is your father?"

"That's what I want to tell you," Peter answered, as he pushed through the low gate that separated the spectators from the area before the bench.

Pruitt beckoned Peter forward, then addressed the attorney representing Northwest Maritime and their driver.

"Mr. Compton, you'd better get up here."

Peter paused at the plaintiff's table to say hello to his client. Nellie Elliot was a washed-out woman who had been worn down by poverty, the untimely death of her husband and the grueling task of raising five young children when life added a final insult by putting her in the path of a Northwest Maritime truck. Now, Mrs. Elliot was a wheelchair-bound quadriplegic and her lawsuit was worth millions.

"What's wrong?" Mrs. Elliot asked. Since the accident, she could move only her head, which bobbed toward her left shoulder as she spoke in the halting, slurred speech that was another product of the defendant's negligence.

"I'll fill you in after I confer with the judge," Peter answered with a reassuring smile.

"Well?" Judge Pruitt asked impatiently.

Peter spoke quietly, so his voice would not reach his client.

"Your Honor, my father had a heart attack just as we were leaving for court."

Lyle Compton looked stricken and the judge's hard-bitten demeanor disappeared. Both men had known Richard Hale for more than twenty years. Though Judge Pruitt was brusque with all who appeared before him, he had the highest regard for Richard. Richard and Lyle Compton had been friendly adversaries in countless courtroom battles.

"Is he going to be all right?" Pruitt asked with genuine concern.

"I don't know."

"Well, I'll adjourn court and we'll reconvene tomorrow so you can bring us up to date," the judge said.

Peter had been afraid the judge might try to stop the trial on his own. "There's no reason to adjourn," he said, hoping he did not sound as anxious as he felt. "I won't be able to see my father for hours."

Judge Pruitt's brow furrowed. He looked at Peter as if he was certain he had misunderstood him.

"You don't plan on continuing the trial, do you?" the judge asked.

"Oh, certainly. After all, our case is almost over and there's Mrs. Elliot to consider. It would be awfully hard for her to go through a second trial."

"Yes, well that may be, but your father is lead counsel," the judge said.

Lyle Compton was short, bald and rotund. He usually had a disarming smile on his face. He represented insurance companies for a living, but he was sympathetic to plaintiffs and was fair and charmingly nonadversarial until he was forced into the courtroom.

"Peter, it wouldn't be right to make you continue this case," Compton said with sincerity. "Mrs. Elliot has a right to be represented by the best. If you move for a continuance or a mistrial, I'm not going to object."

Peter kept control of his facial expression, but he was seething. He believed Compton was trying to sucker him into moving for a mistrial so he could save his case. And that crack about Mrs. Elliot deserving the best . . . Peter's heart hardened. He would show Compton what it was like to really go up against the best.

"I appreciate your concern, Mr. Compton, but I'm prepared to continue."

"Do you feel that you're ready to do that, Mr. Hale?" the judge asked. "You've never been lead counsel in a case this complex, have you?"

"No, Your Honor, but I worked on this case from the beginning. I prepared the witnesses, wrote the pleadings and the legal memos. In all modesty, I believe I know the ins and outs of Mrs. Elliot's lawsuit as well, if not better, than my father."

"Is this what your client wants?" the judge asked.

"I haven't had an opportunity to confer with her. She doesn't know what happened."

Judge Pruitt looked troubled. "Well, why don't you take a few minutes to confer with Mrs. Elliot. But before you do, I have to tell you that I think you're making a big mistake if you go ahead. You should be with your father in the hospital. I know you're thinking of your client's interests, which is commendable, but I can't imagine how you're going to be able to focus on this case without knowing that your father has pulled through."

12

Peter felt a brief flash of elation. The trial was going to continue and he was going to try it by himself. Then, as Peter walked over to his client, a moment of self-doubt assailed him. Aside from his mistrust of Peter's abilities, was there some other reason why his father had ordered Peter to ask for a mistrial? Peter remembered how upset his father had been just before his heart attack. What had that been about? Some witness and some papers. As Peter sat down next to Mrs. Elliot, he tried to review everything he knew about the case. He could think of no witness who needed to testify other than the two who were scheduled for this morning and no papers that had to be introduced.

Before he could consider the matter further, Mrs. Elliot swung her wheelchair so she could face Peter.

"Where's Mr. Hale?" she asked fearfully.

Peter promptly forgot about the mystery witness and said, "Mrs. Elliot, I want you to stay calm. I have some news for you that may be a bit disturbing."

"Plaintiff rests," Peter declared in a voice that conveyed to the jury the confidence he felt in his case. His last two witnesses had been terrific and Peter could not conceive of a juror who was not convinced that Nellie Elliot should be awarded millions to compensate her for the negligence of Northwest Maritime's driver.

"May I confer with Mr. Hale for a moment?" Lyle Compton asked Judge Pruitt.

"Why don't I send the jury out for lunch, Mr. Compton. As soon as you're finished talking to Mr. Hale, you can make any motions you may have. We'll start the defense case after lunch."

"That would be fine, Your Honor."

When the jurors were gone, Compton motioned Peter to join him out of earshot of Mrs. Elliot. Peter felt he was on top of the world as he crossed the courtroom. During a phone call to the hospital, he had been assured that his father would make a full recovery, and he was on the brink of winning his first million-dollar verdict.

"Peter," Compton said in a low voice, "I'm prepared to recommend a settlement of 1.5 million. I think that's a fair offer."

Peter's chest swelled. Compton was on the ropes and he knew it. The offer was a last-ditch attempt to save his client the several million dollars more Peter was confident the jury would award.

"Sorry, Lyle, but I don't think that's enough."

Compton seemed uneasy. "Look, Peter, I feel very uncomfortable about the way this case is proceeding. You shouldn't have continued to try this matter. You're too inexperienced."

"Oh," Peter replied, fighting hard not to smirk. "Why don't we let the jury decide that."

Compton looked down. He took a deep breath and exhaled.

"I probably shouldn't do this, but I don't want to take advantage of you. I respect your father tremendously and, because of that, I feel compelled to tell you that you have problems with your case. Under the circumstances, this is a very good offer."

Peter wanted to laugh in Compton's face. Problems with his case, indeed. Did Compton think he would fall for this transparent attempt to prey on the insecurities of a young lawyer trying his first big case? He felt great seeing one of the best insurance defense attorneys in the state squirming like a worm on a hook.

"Lyle, I appreciate your concern, but it's no go."

Compton looked distraught. "All right. I tried, Peter, but I have a client, too."

As soon as the lawyers were back at their respective tables, Mrs. Elliot asked, "What happens now?"

"Mr. Compton will probably move for a directed verdict. It's nothing to worry about. It's routine. The defense always does that after the plaintiff rests. He's going to argue that we haven't produced enough evidence to let the case go to the jury. He has to make his record."

"He won't win?" she asked anxiously.

"Of course not," Peter answered with a confident smile. "To rule against us, the judge would have to find that there is no reasonable interpretation of the evidence that could support our position. It's an almost impossible burden to meet."

"I have a motion for the court," Compton said, sounding almost apologetic.

"What is the basis for your motion, Mr. Compton?" Judge Pruitt asked.

"Your Honor, plaintiff's complaint alleges that Northwest Maritime is a corporation registered in the state of Oregon. It is in paragraph one of the complaint."

Peter looked down at the pleading that had been filed a year and a half before to formally put the case before the court. Mrs. Elliot's complaint alleged that Northwest Maritime was a corporation doing business in Oregon, that a truck driven by one of its agents had caused her injury and that the driver was negligent in the way he drove. It was a simple, straightforward court document.

"Our answer denied each and every allegation in the complaint," Compton went on. "When a defendant does that, it becomes plaintiff's duty to prove each and every allegation in the complaint. I kept track of the evidence and I submit that Mrs. Elliot has failed to prove the existence of the corporation."

Peter did not hear anything else Compton said. It was as if the engines on a plane in which he was flying stopped suddenly and the plane began plummeting downward at a dizzying speed. Peter had assumed that his father had entered the corporate documents on one of the occasions he had been in the law library researching legal issues. Now, it looked as if the evidence had never been produced.

Suddenly, Peter remembered Ned Schuster, the mystery witness who had been in the accident. The man who was bringing the documents his father was so upset about, right before he'd had his coronary. They must

15

have been the documents that would prove that Northwest Maritime was a corporation. That's why Richard had implored Peter to move for a mistrial.

". . . to dismiss the case against Northwest Maritime and grant a directed verdict for my client," Compton concluded.

Judge Pruitt looked very upset. He turned toward Peter, who was rereading the complaint as if, somehow, he could will the words to change. This point that Compton had raised was such a little thing. A technicality. Everyone knew Northwest Maritime was a corporation. It owned huge buildings and declared its existence from immense signs with fat red letters. The missing document was so small. A notarized paper that took up no space at all.

"Mr. Hale," the judge stated quietly, "I've been expecting this. The answer does deny the existence of the corporation. That does put the burden on you to prove your allegation regarding the corporation. This morning, I looked up the case law in anticipation of this motion."

"The . . . the driver. Mr. Hardesty. I believe he said . . ."

Judge Pruitt shook his head. "No, sir. The question was never put to him."

"But Mrs. Elliot? What about her?" Peter asked pathetically. "If you dismiss the case against Northwest Maritime, only the driver will be left and he doesn't have the money to pay for Mrs. Elliot's bills. She's paralyzed. You know Northwest Maritime is liable."

Peter stopped. The judge could not look him in the eye and Lyle Compton looked sick, like a child who has played a successful practical joke and now feels guilty about it.

"Mr. Hale," Judge Pruitt said, "there is nothing I can do in this case. You did not prove that Northwest Maritime is a corporation. No reasonable jury could conclude it was from the facts in evidence and the jurors may not go outside the evidence produced in court. If I deny Mr. Compton's motion, he will appeal and the court of appeals will reverse me. They have upheld motions of this sort in seven reported cases I have found. My hands are tied."

Judge Pruitt turned toward Lyle Compton and Peter sank onto his seat. His head was spinning. He had no idea what he should do. He thought he might be sick.

"I'm granting your motion, Mr. Compton. A verdict will be directed for Northwest Maritime. The case against Mr. Hardesty will proceed."

Peter felt the wheels of Mrs. Elliot's wheelchair bumping against his chair.

"What is it? What is it?" she asked, her slurred voice trembling with panic and fear. With each repetition, Mrs. Elliot grew louder and more strident and everyone in the courtroom looked at Peter to hear the answer he would give to this poor, crippled woman who would not receive one cent for the anguish and horror she had been through. Peter wanted to answer her, but he could not speak. He could only sit, eyes staring straight ahead, as his world went up in flames.

2

After court, Peter staggered back to Hale, Greaves in a daze. Martin Strobridge was one of the most eloquent attorneys in the state of Oregon, but he was struck dumb by Peter's account of his attempt to try *Elliot v. Northwest Maritime*. When Strobridge recovered his senses, he issued an order that no one was to tell Richard what had happened for fear of sending him into another cardiac arrest. Then, he suspended Peter from all his duties at the firm until a committee reviewed his conduct. Strobridge had no idea how grateful Peter was for the opportunity to stay away from the firm where he

17

would be the object of derision as soon as the office grapevine spread the news of his disgrace.

Peter drove directly from his office to the hospital. He was allowed into the intensive care unit for only a few minutes. Richard's doctor assured Peter that his father's condition was not serious and that Richard would be out of the hospital within the week, but the shock of seeing his father hooked up to IV drips and blinking machinery was as great as the trauma of losing *Elliot*. Though he had never seen him play, Peter's image of his father always involved football. He thought of Richard Hale as a man of boundless energy who crashed through lines and smashed into opponents. The Richard Hale who stared at him with heavy-lidded eyes was old and frail and his speech was barely coherent. Peter tried to smile. He made a few feeble attempts at conversation. Then, he stumbled out of his father's room before his allotted time was up, grateful that the drugs his father had been given prevented him from thinking clearly enough to ask about the outcome of the Elliot case.

In the intervening days between his debacle and the inevitable summons to the offices of Hale, Greaves, Peter hid in his apartment trying to imagine a scenario in which his life would go on as before. Thankfully, Priscilla had flown off to some unknown destination leaving him alone with his despair. Peter knew that there would have to be some consequences for his actions, but by the time the phone call came requesting his appearance at the firm Peter had created a fantasy in which he apologized and promised to never do anything so foolish ever again, and all was forgiven.

On one of Peter's visits to the hospital, his father had asked about *Elliot* and Peter had answered that everything was taken care of. As soon as he entered his father's massive, corner office on the day he was summoned, Peter knew that someone had finally broken the news of Peter's disgrace to his father. The man who

18

slumped down across from Peter behind the vast oak desk was tired. He studied Peter with weary eyes. He had lost weight in the hospital and his ruddy complexion was now pasty. After a moment, Richard shook his head slowly and sadly.

"Sit down, Peter," Richard said, indicating a high-backed leather chair. Peter sat.

"I never imagined that it would come to this."

Peter wanted to protest, to defend himself, but there was a lump in his throat the size of an apple and he could only look down at the polished desktop.

"You wanted to be lead counsel in a big case. That's why you did this, isn't it?"

Peter nodded.

"I know how much you resented me for denying you your chance." Peter looked up, surprised. He had no idea he was so transparent. "But I could not permit it."

Richard sighed. He looked defeated.

"I've tried to fool myself about you, Peter, but what you've done has forced me to face the truth. You are a highly intelligent young man. I have your scores on IQ tests to prove it. But you have never lived up to your potential. You didn't apply yourself in high school, so I had to use my pull to get you into a good university, where you partied for four years, achieving grades that were so low that I had to call in every chip I could find to get you into law school. Then I did the same thing to get you a job with this firm, hoping against hope that you would finally change into a responsible adult.

"In part, I blame myself for your failures. I know I wasn't around as much as I should have been when you were growing up, because I was working so damned hard to build this firm. And when I was around, I tried to make up for my absences by spoiling you rotten. With the wisdom of hindsight, I see now that you would have been better off getting through life without so much of my help. Maybe, if you had been forced to deal with failure, you would have developed the toughness, the moral fiber . . ."

Richard's voice trailed off. He closed his eyes and rubbed the lids. When he opened them he looked sad and resigned.

"Well, it doesn't matter now. Regardless of who's to blame, you are who you are and that is why I could not let you try *Elliot*. I know you possess the intelligence to be a good lawyer, but you are lazy and self-centered. You have always taken the easy way out. You have never given one hundred percent of yourself to anything. For you, trying *Elliot* was an opportunity to show off your trial skills and gain advancement in the firm, but this case was Mrs. Elliot's life. Your arrogance and your thoughtlessness have deprived that poor woman of the money she needs for medical care and her children. You have destroyed her future and her children's future and, the saddest thing for me, as your father, is that I don't believe you care."

"Dad, I . . ." Peter started, but Richard shook his head.

"There is nothing left to say, Peter. Mrs. Elliot will sue this firm for malpractice and I will have to tell her lawyers that you disobeyed my direct order to ask for a mistrial, that you misled Judge Pruitt so you could have your day in the sun and that your conduct was a blatant example of malpractice. Naturally, under the circumstances, you can no longer remain here. As a favor to me, the firm will give you the option of resigning. That, however, is the last favor you will ever get from me."

Richard leaned forward. He rested his elbows on the desk and clasped his hands.

"It pains me to say this, but I must be blunt with you, for your own good. This may be your last chance to be saved. I've thought about what I am going to say long and hard and I hope and pray that I'm doing the right thing. First, I've changed my will to disinherit you. Second, I will never give you another penny. You have not earned the way you live. From now on, you must live according to what you earn."

The words hit Peter like a hammer and he could only stare, openmouthed. His father was turning his back on him, his law firm was taking away his job. Not one more penny, Richard had said. How would he meet his payments on the Porsche and the condo? How would he pay his debts? And the will. Disinherited, Richard had said.

"Dad," Peter managed, "I know I was wrong. I'm sorry. I . . . It's just . . ."

Richard shook his head. "Save your breath, Peter. I love you, but I can't stand the sight of you anymore. You have no idea how hard it is for me to admit to myself that my only child is a failure. I had such high hopes for you. But you let everyone down. Me, the firm, Mrs. Elliot."

"You can't do this. You can't cut me out of your life."

"No, I can't. I'm going to give you one, last chance to make something of yourself."

Peter collapsed with relief, feeling like a hiker lost for days in the forest, near death and bereft of hope, who suddenly hears the voice of his rescuer.

"Anything, Dad. I know I was wrong. I'll do what you want."

"You're not going to like what I'm about to propose, but I see it as the only way out for you. If you can prove to me that you are a responsible adult, I will reconsider my decision to disinherit you. To that end, I've spoken to an old friend, Amos Geary. Amos and I go way back. We played football together at Oregon State and we were once partners. He has a practice in Whitaker, a small town of about thirteen thousand in eastern Oregon, and the contract to provide indigent defense for Whitaker County and several other small counties around there. His associate just quit. He's willing to give you the job. It pays seventeen thousand to start."

Peter could not believe his ears. He'd been to Whitaker to take depositions, two years ago. There were four streets in Whitaker. When the wind blew, you couldn't see the buildings for the dust. If it wasn't for the college, which was packed with Future Farmers of America, there wouldn't be any life at all.

"I won't do it," he said, shaking his head from side to side.

"Then, we have nothing more to say to each other."

Peter stood up. He'd had enough.

"That's where you're wrong." Peter's voice shook and tears welled up in his eyes. "You may have nothing to say to me, but I have plenty to say to you. You call me self-centered. You are the most arrogant son of a bitch I've ever met. You call yourself a father. You were never a father to me. Mom raised me. You put in appearances and made rules. And it sure is no surprise to me that you think I'm a failure. You let me know how little you thought of me every chance you had when I was growing up. My grades were never good enough. I never put out enough at sports. Well, I'll tell you this, no one could live up to your standards. All-American, high school valedictorian, first in your law school class. How was I supposed to compete with a god?

"But I tried and you never gave me credit for trying. And now, when I was ready to show you what I could do in court, you stepped on me, every chance you could. You're afraid to admit how good a lawyer I am. Well, I'll show you. I'll get a job with another firm. I'll make partner and Hale, Greaves can kiss my ass."

Richard listened to Peter's tirade calmly. When Peter was through, Richard asked, "What firm will give you a job after the stunt you pulled? They all know what you did. You're the talk of the Portland legal community. How are you going to get a job once your potential employer talks to us? I will tell you flat out that no one here will give you a recommendation."

Peter's bravado disappeared. He knew that what his father said was true.

"You may not believe me," Richard said, "but I do

love you. You have no idea how it hurts me to cast you out. But I have to do it for your sake. Go to Whitaker. There won't be any temptations for you there. Learn to stand on your own two feet and live within your means. Learn how to be a good lawyer. Learn to be a man."

CHAPTER TWO

The sun was a blistering disk that mercilessly baked the brown dirt covering the vast expanse of wasteland east of Whitaker. There were no clouds to compete with it in the pale blue and unforgiving sky. The young Oregon state trooper was grateful for his Stetson and fervently wished for a breeze that would cool him down and create a cloud of swirling dust thick enough to obscure the thing that lay among the sagebrush halfway down the gully. When Dr. Guisti's vehicle appeared, shimmering in the heat like a toy trapped in a bubble of molten glass, the trooper was intentionally standing with his back to the thing. One long look before radioing for assistance had been enough.

The trooper knew it was disrespectful to think of the young woman as a thing, but she no longer resembled any woman he had ever known. The creatures of the desert had feasted on her flesh, the elements had had their way with her, and something else had been at her. Some person whom the trooper also had trouble thinking of in human terms.

A group of students from a geology class at Whitaker State College on a field trip with their professor had found the body. They huddled together while members of the Major Crime Team took their statements. The young trooper noticed that they too averted their eyes from the gully, even though there was no way they could see the body from where they were standing.

The City of Whitaker had a sixteen-person police force. The county sheriff's office was even smaller, with one under-sheriff and five deputies. On those rare occasions when a major crime occurred, it was investigated by a Major Crime Team, which consisted of a detective from the small Oregon State Police office headquartered in Whitaker, the Whitaker County sheriff, or his designee, a member of the Whitaker Police Department and police from neighboring Blaine and Cayuse counties. Since the body was found outside the city limits of Whitaker, and because the Oregon State Police had taken the initial call, the team had designated Detective Jason Dagget of the Oregon State Police as the officer in charge.

Dagget had summoned a forensic team from the Oregon State Crime Lab to the scene and they were working the area around the body. Then he called Dr. Harold Guisti, a tall, anorexic man with a florid complexion who had practiced family medicine in Whitaker for thirty years and contracted with the state medical examiner to perform autopsies in Whitaker, Blaine and Cayuse counties. The doctor's battered Range Rover bounced to a stop in front of Detective Dagget. The detective went around to the driver's door. Dr. Guisti stepped out. A sudden wind blew dust in the doctor's eyes and spread his thinning gray hair across his partially exposed scalp.

"Where's she at?" Guisti asked, as soon as the wind died down.

"In the gully. We think she was killed somewhere else and dumped down there. We haven't found much blood. She's also naked, but there are no clothes."

Guisti grunted, then stepped over the lip of the gully, cautiously edging sideways down the wall far enough away from the body so that anything he dislodged in his descent would not foul the crime scene.

"How was she killed?" he asked Dagget, who was following behind.

"She was butchered, Harold. Plain and simple."

Guisti had been hoping that the woman had been shot or poisoned, because there had been another body discovered in an outcropping of rock two months ago, naked and butchered. Guisti believed the weapon used was a hatchet of some kind. He was hoping he would not come to the same conclusion when he examined this young female, because he did not want to think about what that would mean for the people of Whitaker, Cayuse and Blaine.

PART TWO

A FINGER
EXERCISE
FOR HELL

CHAPTER THREE

1

Surrounding the City of Whitaker was farmland made green by irrigation systems that tapped into the Camas River, but beyond the farms, hot, dusty winds blew tumbleweeds across vast flatlands that were broken only occasionally by high, brown hills. As Peter drove through the desert, he felt his spirit burning up and crumbling slowly to gray ash and he entered the City of Whitaker as empty as the arid land that encircled it.

Peter spent his first night in Whitaker at the Riverview Motel, which was clean, quiet and actually had a view of the Camas River. After breakfast, Peter walked from the motel to the offices of Amos Geary. He was exhausted from tossing and turning all night in strange surroundings as his emotions shifted from boiling rage at the injustices that life had heaped upon him to feelings of fear and utter despair as he struggled with the very real possibility that he might have lost forever the love of his father.

The walk from the motel took Peter through Wishing Well Park, which ran the length of the town between High Street and the Camas River. There was a wistful beauty in the slow-moving Camas, but Peter found the town as dry and uninteresting as the wastelands that surrounded it. The biggest bookstore was the Christian Bookshop; you could easily find a store that fixed saddles but none that made café lattes and the town's only movie theater featured wholesome family entertainment. Peter thought of Whitaker as a finger exercise for the architect who designed hell.

City center started at High and First where the courthouse stood. Peter turned up First Street to Main. Running parallel to Main Street was Broad Street. Elm, the street farthest from the river, started commercial, then curved through a pleasant, tree-shaded, residential section of town until it arrived at the campus of Whitaker State College. On the other side of the college was the hospital.

As Peter walked, he saw battered Ford pickups in the parking spaces and noticed more cowboy hats than he had seen all of last year in Portland. When he reached Main and Fourth, he checked the slip of paper with Geary's address. On both sides of Main were old, two- and three-story brick buildings. Peter saw Dot's coffee shop, B.J.'s beauty salon and an orange-and-black Rexall sign, but no law office. Then, he glanced up a story and saw AMOS J. GEARY, ATTORNEY-AT-LAW painted in flaking gold letters on a second-floor window. Peter backtracked and found a narrow doorway between the beauty salon and the coffee shop. The door opened directly into a cramped stairwell. Dingy, green linoleum was secured to the stairs by dented brass runners. It creaked underfoot as Peter climbed to the second floor.

The hall at the top of the stairs was dark and musty. Geary's name and profession were painted in black on a door to the left of the stairwell. The door stuck and Peter had to push hard to get it open. A middle-aged woman with hennaed hair was sitting behind a desk working at a word processor, the only item in the reception area that did not look as if it had been purchased in a secondhand store.

Two issues of *Field and Stream* and a dog-eared copy of *Sports Illustrated* lay on a low Formica-topped end table next to a couch made of cracked, red imitation leather. A ceiling fixture lit by a dim bulb and a little sunlight that managed to work its way through the dirt-covered front window conspired to cast a dull yellow glow over the room. Peter could not help comparing this antiquated dump to the elegant offices from which he had so recently been evicted. The memory of the plush carpets, brass fixtures and polished woods made his stomach seize up in rage and frustration. It just was not fair.

The woman looked up when the door opened and stared at Peter through glasses with thick, black plastic rims.

"I'm Peter Hale. I have an appointment with Mr. Geary for nine."

The woman eyed him suspiciously.

"You're the young man who's going to work here, aren't you?"

"Yes, ma'am."

"Well, take a seat. Mr. Geary's not in, just yet. But I expect he'll be along any minute. He has court at ten."

The secretary-receptionist went back to her work without another word. Peter was shocked by her abrupt dismissal, but decided against reprimanding the woman. She'd probably be typing his work and it did not pay to alienate what appeared to be the only support staff in the office.

Peter sat on the couch. After a while, he looked around the reception room. Except for some cracks in the ceiling plaster, he did not see anything he had not seen the first time he looked. Peter glanced at his watch. It was nine-fifteen. He decided to check out the *Sports Illustrated*. It was nine months old but Peter thumbed through it anyway. He was finished skimming it by nine-thirty and was deciding whether to read an article on a Peruvian boxer or start on *Field and Stream* when the door to the law office opened.

Amos Geary's face was a beet-red matrix of busted blood vessels. What was left of his unkempt hair was a dingy gray and he had compensated for its loss by growing a shaggy, walrus mustache. His bloodshot eyes were lost in folds of puffy flesh. Geary was as tall as Peter's father and looked twice as heavy. His stomach sagged over his belt and the buttons on his shirt looked as if they were about to pop. Peter was wearing a tailored gray pinstripe suit and a tasteful maroon tie. Geary was wearing an awful aquamarine tie spotted with stains that matched those on his rumpled brown suit. Peter's facial muscles twitched with the effort it took to hide his distaste.

Geary studied the young man from the open doorway, mentally reconstructing his face with his mother's features deleted and his father's expanded.

"Peter Hale, I presume?"

"Mr. Geary?" Peter asked hesitantly while he studied Geary's sagging jowls and bulbous, red-veined nose. Geary shifted his battered briefcase and extended his right hand. It was sweaty and Peter withdrew his own after a light touch as if he feared he could contract alcoholism from the brief contact.

"How was the drive?" Geary asked, ignoring the slight and Peter's discomfort.

"Fine," Peter responded, flinching slightly as Geary's alcohol- and mouthwash-drenched breath hit him full in the face.

"Glad to hear it."

"Don't forget you have court at ten," the secretary reminded Geary.

"What case, Clara?"

"*Judd.*"

"Oh, lord. Not *Judd,*" Geary answered, turning his back on Peter and trudging down a dark and dingy hall.

"Follow me," Geary called over his shoulder. Peter trailed his new boss to a poorly lit office that stank of stale smoke. Geary tossed his briefcase on top of a mess of files and papers stacked atop a battle-scarred, wooden desk. Peter sat on a straight-backed chair in front of the desk. While Geary rummaged through a dilapidated gray metal filing cabinet for the *Judd* file, Peter looked around the office. On one wall, among diplomas and certificates attesting to Geary's admission to various state and federal bars, was a black-and-white team photo of the 1956 Oregon State football team. Geary caught Peter looking at it.

"I'm in the front, kneeling down. Your father's behind me on the right. I opened holes for him for four years and I've got cleat marks on my back to prove it," Geary said with a brusque laugh.

Peter forced a smile. He was not in the mood to listen to an old drunk wax nostalgic about the man who had exiled him to this big zero. Then, he noticed a framed law degree to the right of Geary's OSU diploma.

"You went to Harvard?" Peter asked, trying not to sound incredulous.

"Class of '59. Does that surprise you?"

"Well . . . Uh, no," Peter said, flushing because Geary had read him so easily.

"It should. A Harvard man stuck out here in the boonies. But, then, you're stuck here with me, aren't you?"

This time, Peter flushed from anger. Geary found the *Judd* file and slumped onto a slat-back chair behind the desk.

"Your father told me everything when he asked me to hire you. To be honest, I was against it. Not because I was unsympathetic to Dick's attempts to save your soul. I just didn't want to put my practice at risk while your father was fighting for your salvation."

"If you didn't want me here," Peter asked resentfully, "why did you agree to hire me?"

Geary folded his hands behind his head, leaned back and studied Peter without rancor.

"I owe your father a great debt. Supervising your stay in purgatory will take a little off the top. But I made it clear to Dick that I'll drop you like a hot coal if you fuck up. I have a sense of honor, but not a shred of sentimentality. Do we understand each other?"

Peter nodded.

"Good," Geary said. "Now, let me tell you the facts of life in Whitaker. There are fifteen lawyers in private practice in this county. Five of them work at Sissler, MacAfee and Petersen. They handle every insurance defense case in Whitaker and the five surrounding counties. Those boys make the big bucks. The other ten attorneys, including yours truly, do not. We fight over the scraps. There's the occasional personal injury case. One good old boy runs his four-by-four into some other good old boy's four-by-four. I write wills, I handle divorces. If it walks through the door and it doesn't take a lot of expertise, I'm your man.

"Then, there's crime. Crime does pay, only not for the criminals. You're probably wondering how I can afford these palatial digs. Well, I'll let you in on the secret. About fifteen years ago, the state decided to contract out indigent defense and I was firstest with the mostest. I've had the contract for Whitaker, Blaine and Cayuse counties, ever since. It pays my overhead and makes me a small profit. It's easy money and I aim to keep it. That's where you come in. You're gonna become the Perry Mason of Whitaker County."

Peter was gripped by deep depression. He had not gone to law school to muck around in the swamp called criminal law. Real lawyers sued for millions or handled massive business deals. On a scale of one to ten, with ten being the most prestigious type of legal practice, criminal law was a minus seventy-two.

"I hope my father didn't misrepresent my qualifications, Mr. Geary," Peter said hesitantly. "I've never handled a criminal case."

"Peter, we're not talking crime-of-the-century. We're talking shoplifts at JCPenney, driving while stupid. Most of these cases will plead out and the rest could be handled by Forrest Gump. Your dad told me about some of the cases you've tried on your own and some of the ones you've second-chaired. I'd say that you're

34

probably one of the most experienced attorneys in town, right now. So, don't sweat the small stuff.

"Now, here's my plan," Geary said, fishing through his desk until he found a cigarette. "Your office is next door." A plume of smoke blew across the desk and Peter held his breath to avoid breathing in the foul, cancerous discharge. "The walls are paper-thin, so we don't need an intercom. Settle in. Read through the twenty case files on your desk. Keep a copy of the Criminal Code at your right hand, a copy of the Constitutions of the United States and the state of Oregon at your left, and a copy of the Oregon State Bar Criminal Law Handbook within easy reach. If you have any questions, try not to bother me with them. I'm very busy."

Peter looked stunned. Geary grinned maliciously.

"Welcome to the real world, son. And have a nice day. Now, scat. I have to go to the ninth circle of hell to fight the devil for Elmo Judd's soul."

2

Whitaker State College was founded as an agricultural school to service eastern Oregon in 1942, but had since developed a decent liberal arts program. The older, brick buildings surrounded a quadrangle at the center of the campus and were covered with ivy. The legislature had funded an expansion program in the late fifties and, again, in the early eighties, and a school of business, the football stadium, a new athletic facility and a block of two-story, brick dormitories were among the newer-looking buildings that spread out from the hub.

In the shadow of the business school was a large blacktop parking area. Shortly before 10 P.M., evening classes ended and the faculty and off-campus students emptied into the lot. Christopher Mammon drove a dull green Chevy when he did not want to attract attention. Tonight, the Chevy was parked as inconspicuously as possible in the shadows of a large oak tree on the edge of the lot because there were two kilos of cocaine in separate Ziploc bags under the driver's seat.

The Chevy was a normal-size car, but Mammon was so massive that there was barely room for Kevin Booth in the front seat. Mammon's body was so large it approached the grotesque. At a flabby two hundred pounds, Booth had been big enough to play high school football, but alongside Mammon's enormous lats, awesome thighs and mile-wide chest, he appeared to be one dimensional.

Booth looked over his shoulder through the rear window as he had several times each minute since Mammon parked. After a few seconds, Booth twisted forward and drummed his fingers nervously on the dashboard.

"Where is that bitch? She said nine forty-five and it's after ten."

"Relax, man." Mammon's eyes were closed and he sounded bored. Booth could not believe how calm Mammon was with this much dope in the car. Of course, Mammon was always calm. When you were that big only King Kong could raise your blood pressure. If they were arrested and went to jail, Mammon would be the king of the beasts in a jungle filled with wild animals. Booth would die in prison, prey for the lowliest of meat-eaters.

"There's something about that cunt I don't trust," Booth told Mammon, as he looked anxiously over his shoulder again.

"You don't trust anyone. That's your problem," Mammon said, opening his eyes and lifting his huge head from the headrest.

"If this deal gets fucked up, Rafael is gonna be really pissed," Booth said, more to himself than Mammon. Booth could not decide who scared him more, Mammon or the slender man with the lifeless eyes who supplied Booth with cocaine.

36

"That's why you should be glad I'm dealing with your buddy, this time."

"But what if the bitch doesn't show?"

"She'll be here," Mammon assured Booth, a hint of menace creeping into his voice. "She knows what would happen to her if she let me down."

Booth imagined the things Mammon would do to punish the blonde if she crossed them. Then he imagined what Rafael might do to him if the sale did not go through. One of Rafael's mules had dropped off the two kilos at Booth's house early this evening. Booth's part in the transaction was turning over the cocaine to Mammon and giving the thirty thousand the girl was bringing to another of Rafael's mules. Objectively, Booth was only a go-between, but Booth had vouched for Mammon.

"What if she goes to the cops?" Booth asked anxiously. "She's been acting squirrelly lately."

Mammon sighed. He switched on the dome light. Then, he took a mirror and a razor blade from the map holder on the driver's door and handed them to Booth. Mammon opened one of the Ziploc bags and dipped a slender coke spoon into the bag. Mammon held the spoon over the mirror. Booth fixed on the white powder, hypnotized by it.

"I need some peace and quiet, Kevin. If you promise to shut up, I'll let you have a little nose candy."

Booth's brain told him it was dangerous to use in public. It was also a form of suicide to use any of Rafael's cocaine before the deal went through, because Rafael would weigh the dope if it was returned. Booth thought about turning down Mammon's offer, but his need overcame all objections and he leaned forward greedily as the white powder cascaded onto the mirror to form a small mound. Booth separated the white powder into several thin lines, then rolled a ten-dollar bill tight and inserted it into his nostril. Using the bill like a straw, he sucked up the coke, then leaned back to enjoy the rush.

Mammon returned the razor blade and the mirror to the map holder and turned off the dome light. He started to close his eyes when a voice next to his ear said, "Freeze," and he turned slightly to his left to find himself staring into the barrel of a gun.

CHAPTER FOUR

1

Peter spent his second morning in Whitaker looking for a place to live. After lunch, he went to the office. As soon as he opened the door, Clara Schoen thrust a case file at him.

"Mr. Geary called from Blaine County. He'll be there all day. He wants you to interview this man at the jail."

"The jail? Where is that?" Peter asked nervously, as pictures of drooling psychopaths and perverts danced in his head. He had never been to any jail.

"It's a block from the courthouse," the secretary told him, shaking her head.

Peter opened the file. On the right side was an order appointing Amos Geary to represent Christopher Eugene Mammon. Beneath the order was a complaint filed by the district attorney charging Mammon with possession of a controlled substance: cocaine. Peter cleared his throat.

"Uh, Mrs. Schoen, what exactly am I supposed to do with Mr. Mammon?"

"How am I supposed to know what you're supposed to do? Am I a lawyer? I just do the typing here, Mr. Hale. Didn't they teach you what to do in law school?"

The narrow, concrete room in the Whitaker jail where attorneys met their clients was about the length of a dog run and doubled as the jail law library. It was poorly lit, cold in winter and stifling hot in summer. The so-called library consisted of two handmade wooden bookshelves containing a one-volume edition of the Oregon Criminal Code, a one-volume edition of the evidence code and a worn set of Oregon Supreme Court and Court of Appeals cases. A high window with thick, escape-proof glass let some light into the room. The rest of the light was provided by two bulbs that hung from the ceiling in wire cages.

Peter sat on a metal folding chair in front of a rickety wooden table with his back to the far wall, nervously waiting to meet his first criminal client. His fingers were drumming a solo on Mammon's case file when the door to the interview room opened. Peter stood. A guard stepped aside and all the light from the hall was obliterated by the man who filled the doorway.

"Knock when you want me," the guard said. Then, Peter heard the lock on the thick metal door snap shut, trapping him inside the overheated coffin of a room. Christopher Mammon moved under one of the caged lightbulbs and Peter sucked in a breath. He was used to large men. His father was large, Amos Geary was large. But Christopher Mammon was bizarre. Curly black hair hung down over his high, flat forehead and cascaded over his massive shoulders. Tufts of hair stuck out of the collar of an orange jail-issue jumpsuit that was stretched taut across his gargantuan chest. The jumpsuit had short sleeves and Peter could see snake and panther tattoos rippling along Mammon's forearms and biceps whenever he moved. About the only parts of Mammon that were not grotesquely big were his cold blue eyes, which were narrow and focused like a predator's, and his ears, which were tiny and delicate.

"Good afternoon, Mr. Mammon. I'm Peter Hale, the

attorney the court appointed to represent you," Peter said nervously, holding out one of Amos Geary's business cards. The card disappeared in Mammon's hand. He examined it, then examined Peter.

"If you're my lawyer, why isn't your name on this card?" Mammon asked in a voice that was velvety smooth and very scary. It was the sort of purr that might issue from a hungry leopard while it was deciding what part of a staked goat to eat first.

"Well, actually, the court appointed Amos Geary. He'll represent you, if we go to trial. I work with him. In fact, I've just started. My cards are on order," Peter babbled, managing a tiny smile he hoped would convey his perfect harmlessness and the fact that he should be considered a friend and not dinner.

"I see," Mammon said, returning Peter's smile with an ominous glare.

"Mr. Geary is in Blaine County this afternoon. He wanted me to conduct the first interview. Why don't you sit down and we can get started."

Peter sat on his folding chair and took a pen and pad out of his attaché case. Mammon remained standing. Clara had placed an interview form on the left side of the file. Peter scanned some of the questions on the form, then, without looking up, he said, "There's some background information I'll need. Can you give me your date of birth?"

Mammon tilted his head to one side and read the interview form upside down.

"Can I see that?" he asked, pointing at the form.

Peter hesitated, then took the form out of the file and handed it to Mammon. Mammon studied the form for a moment, then slowly ripped it into tiny pieces.

"If Geary's my lawyer I'll talk to Geary and not some flunky."

As Mammon let the pieces of the form flutter from his fingers like a mini-snowstorm it suddenly occurred to Peter that he was locked in the interview room and there was only a flimsy wooden table separating him from a very dangerous wild animal.

"Yes, well, I'm an experienced attorney and anything you tell me is confidential. I'll only talk about our conversation to Mr. Geary," Peter told Mammon in an attempt to steer his client out of the world of ultraviolent kung fu flicks and graphic slasher movies.

"Just how experienced are you, Peter?" Mammon asked.

"I've been a lawyer for four years."

"And how many criminal cases have you handled?"

"Well, none, but, uhm, I have tried many complex legal matters and I . . ."

Mammon held up his hand and Peter stopped talking. Mammon rested his hands on the table and it buckled. Then, he leaned across the table until his face was inches from Peter's.

"You just lied to me, didn't you, Peter?"

Peter turned pale. His voice caught in his throat and all he could manage was, "I . . . I . . ."

Mammon held him with his eyes for a moment. Then he went to the door and pounded on it. The locks snapped open and Mammon walked out of the room. It took a moment for Peter to realize that he was still alive.

2

Peter's only other visit to Whitaker had been spent humiliating and browbeating a local attorney and his client. After the deposition, Peter had celebrated at the Stallion, a bar popular with the students at Whitaker State, where he met a nurse named Rhonda something whom he fascinated with his description of the devastation visited on his adversary. The next morning, Rhonda had written her name and phone number on a piece of motel stationery before she left for the hospital. Since the Stallion provided the only good memory Peter had of Whitaker, it was here that he ran as soon as he escaped the jail.

"What am I going to do?" Peter asked himself, as he started on his second Jack Daniel's. He could not endure another encounter with a Mammon-like individual. It was out of the question. But what was his alternative? Being a lawyer was all Peter knew and no one except Amos Geary would offer him a job after the Elliot fiasco.

Peter longed for his condo, now owned by a Merrill, Lynch exec who had gotten it at a fire-sale price because of Peter's sudden descent into poverty, and his Porsche, which he had been forced to trade in for a used Subaru. He wanted a job of which he could be proud. Most of all, he needed to reclaim his dignity. But his material possessions, his job and his dignity had been stripped from him. He was, he thought bitterly, as big a failure as one could become.

"Peter Hale?"

Peter looked up and found a tall, solidly built man in a business suit staring down at him.

"Steve Mancini," the man said. "We went to law school together."

"Right!" Peter said, breaking into a smile.

"Mind if I sit down?" Mancini asked as he slid into the booth across from Peter.

"Hell, no. What are you drinking?"

"No, no. It's on me. I'm half owner of this joint."

Mancini signaled for a waitress.

"You live in Whitaker?" Peter asked incredulously, unable to fathom why any sane person would choose to live in a town without one decent clothing store.

"Live here and practice law here. But what are you doing in Whitaker? I thought you went to work for your father's firm. Are you out on a case?"

"Uh, yes and no," Peter said, stalling for time. There

43

was no way he was going to tell Mancini the truth, but what could he say?

"There you are," a woman said, and Peter looked over his shoulder into a pair of hazel eyes that had no room for him and were filled with Steve Mancini. Standing next to the beautiful brunette was a rugged-looking man with the broad shoulders and thick forearms of someone who labors for a living. He had curly black hair, a bushy mustache and blue eyes and he was grinning widely at Steve.

Mancini stood and kissed the woman on her cheek. Then, he took her hand.

"Pete, this is my fiancée, Donna Harmon, and her brother, Gary."

A law school memory of Steve Mancini and a pretty blond wife made Peter frown for a moment, but he caught himself and said, "Hey, congratulations."

"Thank you," Donna answered with a satisfied grin.

"When is the wedding?"

"We're tying the knot in a few weeks," Mancini answered, as he ushered Donna into the booth and sat beside her. Gary slid in next to Peter.

"Do you have the tickets?" Gary asked.

"What tickets?" Mancini asked deadpan.

Gary looked panicky. "My football tickets. The season tickets. You . . . you didn't forget my tickets, did you, Steve?"

"Don't tease him, Steve," Donna said sternly. "Of course, he has them, Gary."

"Here they are, buddy," Mancini said, pulling an envelope out of his suit jacket.

Gary Harmon's face lit up and he started to grab for the tickets.

"What do you say first, Gary?" Donna asked gently.

Gary looked confused for a second and Peter examined him more closely. The guy looked normal, but he was acting like a kid.

Gary's face suddenly broke into a grin and he said, "Thanks, Steve."

"Hey, guy, you're welcome."

Gary took the tickets and examined them as if they were a priceless work of art.

"So, Pete," Mancini asked, "what brings you to Whitaker?"

Peter had hoped that Mancini had forgotten the question, but the arrival of Donna and Gary Harmon had given him time to invent an answer.

"I'm working for Amos Geary."

"Geary?" The expression on Mancini's face registered disapproval. "I never pictured you as the type to practice small-town law. I thought you were aiming for a partnership in a megafirm."

"Yeah, that's what I thought. I was working in my father's firm in Portland. Hale, Greaves. But I got tired of the rat race and Dad's an old friend of Amos. They played ball together at Oregon State."

Mancini forced a smile and he and Donna congratulated Peter on his new job.

"How did you get to Whitaker?" Peter asked to divert Mancini's attention.

"Didn't you see the trophy case when you walked in?"

"Well, no, I . . ."

"Then, check it out when you leave. In my senior year, I quarterbacked the Stallions to the NCAA Division II title, Whitaker State's only national championship in any sport."

"Tell about the run, Steve," Gary begged, leaning forward eagerly.

"You've heard this story a million times," Donna chided her brother.

"But I haven't," Peter said, hoping that Mancini would not press him further on his reason for being in Whitaker if he could keep him talking football.

"Looks like you're overruled," Mancini laughed. He put his arm around Donna and leaned back in the booth.

"It was the fourth quarter. Texas A&I had a three-

45

point lead and we were backed up on our own six with less than a minute on the clock. I was supposed to hand off to Rick Sandusky, but the son of a bitch slipped. I turned back toward the line, only to be confronted by three of the biggest human beings I have ever seen. Their eyes were red-rimmed, steam was coming out of their nostrils and I could see that they were dying to commit an act of extreme violence on yours truly. That's when I was inspired to make one of the greatest runs in football history. You can find a wall-size photo of me in the Whitaker gym galloping the last ten yards before the end zone. In this town, Pete, I'm an immortal.

"After graduation, most of the class gravitated to the big city, but people remember me here. I've got a great practice, I'm big in the Chamber of Commerce and," Mancini added, puffing up his chest, "my ship may soon be sailing into the dock."

"Oh?"

"Yeah. Bend has the inside track on the next Winter Olympics and I'm involved with some guys who are building condos just fifteen minutes away from Mount Bachelor."

"How long have you been in town?" Donna asked.

Peter decided that Steve's fiancée was every bit as good-looking as the wife he remembered.

"This is my second day," he said.

"Have you found a place to live?"

Peter shook his head. "I'm still at the Riverview Motel."

"We can't have that," Donna said, turning to her fiancé. "Can't you help him, Steve?"

"I think so. I own a few rental properties near the college, if you're interested."

"I've got my own house," Gary said proudly.

"You shouldn't interrupt, Gary," Donna reprimanded her brother gently. "Peter and Steve are talking."

Gary stopped smiling. "I'm sorry," he apologized, looking down at the table.

It suddenly dawned on Peter that Gary Harmon was retarded. Peter shifted a little toward the wall. Gary looked harmless enough, but Peter had still not recovered fully from his encounter with Christopher Mammon and he felt uncomfortable sitting so close to a person whose behavior he could not predict.

"Gary just moved into his own home and he's working as a janitor at the college," Donna explained. "He's very excited. It's his first job."

"Oh, yeah," Peter said, trying to be sociable. "Do you like your job?"

Gary frowned and considered his answer. "It's hard, but Mr. Ness says I'm doing good. He says I work real hard."

"Well, that's great," Peter answered lamely, at a loss for anything else to say.

"I think I might have a place for you," Mancini said. "It's furnished and only three quarters of a mile from town, not too far from my house."

Mancini took out a business card and wrote an address on the back. Donna looked at her watch.

"We'd better go. Mom's expecting us."

"It was good seeing you," Mancini told Peter. "Give me a call after you look at the house. I'll take you out to lunch and give you the lowdown on Whitaker. And, since you'll be living here, I'll send you an invite to the wedding."

Mancini followed Donna and her brother out of the bar and Peter ordered a pitcher of beer and a burger with everything. He felt a little better. At least he knew someone in town. Peter remembered Steve Mancini as a real party animal. If there was anything going on in this hopeless burg, he would know about it.

When Peter finished eating, he suddenly remembered the last name of the nurse he had spent the evening with the last time he had been in Whitaker. It was Kates. Rhonda Kates. He decided to go back to the motel and give her a call.

On the way out of the Stallion, Peter looked in the trophy case. There was Mancini's helmet and cleats, a program from the championship game and a photo of Mancini's famous run. Fame and fortune, Peter thought wistfully. Steve Mancini certainly seemed to have it all.

CHAPTER FIVE

At six-thirty on Friday morning of his second week in town, Peter awoke in the house he was renting from Steve Mancini, then ran four miles through the quiet streets of Whitaker. The houses Peter passed were not split levels or indistinguishable tract homes. They were old, wood frame houses with gables and front porches that stood in yards rimmed by white picket fences where swings hung from the thick, gnarled limbs of ancient oaks. In the half light of early morning it was easy to imagine the glow behind the curtained windows was cast by an oil lamp and that the rickety garage doors would open wide, barn style, to reveal a horse and buggy.

After his run, Peter showered, dressed for court and brewed a café latte in the espresso machine he had brought with him from Portland. He drank the latte with his breakfast at a rickety wooden table in his post-age-stamp-size kitchen. Amos Geary had been dragging Peter around Blaine, Whitaker and Cayuse counties so he could meet the D.A.'s, judges and court personnel. Geary had not let Peter handle anything by himself but Peter was starting to realize that criminal law was not that difficult. After breakfast, Peter walked to the courthouse to watch Geary handle the preliminary hearing in Christopher Mammon's case.

Criminal complaints in felony cases were lodged in the district court, but only a circuit court had jurisdiction to try a felony. There were two ways to change the jurisdiction of a felony case to the circuit court: A grand jury could meet in secret and hand down an indictment or a district court judge could hold a preliminary hearing in open court and order the case bound over to circuit court. District attorneys loathed preliminary hearings because they gave defense attorneys the opportunity to hear the state's case and cross-examine the state's witnesses. It was very rare to hold a prelim in cases as serious as Mammon's. Amos Geary had been shaking his head about the development all week, but he was not going to look a gift horse in the mouth.

The four-story courthouse was the tallest building in Whitaker. It was a square, no-nonsense edifice of gray stone and it stood at the end of High Street across from Wishing Well Park. The office of the district attorney was on the top floor above the two circuit courts. The administrative offices and the traffic court were on street level. Misdemeanor cases and certain preliminary matters in felony cases were handled in the district court, where the preliminary hearing for Christopher Mammon and Kevin Booth was to be held.

Peter walked up the central staircase to the second-floor courtroom and found Steve Mancini standing in the hall talking to the cutest thing Peter had seen since moving to Whitaker. Peter figured her for five two at the most. She had curly red hair, freckles that made her look like a high schooler and a body that was definitely not adolescent. Just looking at her made Peter feel all mushy and downright lascivious at the same time.

Mancini waved Peter over. "You're here to help Amos with the prelim, aren't you?"

"Yeah. He wanted me to sit in," Peter said, fighting to keep from staring at the redhead.

"Then, you should meet Becky O'Shay, Whitaker's

most vicious prosecutor. Becky, this is Peter Hale. Watch out for him. He's a big-city lawyer who's moved to the sticks to prey on innocent young things like you."

O'Shay looked up at Peter and he swore she was gazing into his eyes with something more than polite curiosity.

"Pleased to meet you, Peter," she said. Her voice sounded like the trill of clear water rushing over smooth stones in a mountain stream. O'Shay extended a tiny, delicate hand. Peter took it and felt a jolt of electricity.

"Time to go, boys and girls," Mancini said.

"Are you involved in this case?" Peter asked him.

"I'm representing Kevin Booth, the co-defendant."

O'Shay entered the courtroom and Peter watched her walk to the prosecution's counsel table. When he tore his eyes from her, he saw Christopher Mammon sitting with Amos Geary at the defense table. The two were chatting as if they were old friends and Geary did not seem the least bit intimidated.

To Mammon's right was Kevin Booth. Mancini's client was a mess. His jumpsuit sagged on him, his dirty black hair was uncombed and pimples dotted his pale skin. The contrast between Booth and Christopher Mammon was amazing. Although they were facing sentences that would keep them in prison for eons, Mammon looked as if he was going to fall asleep, while Booth's prominent Adam's apple bobbed up and down from fright and he could not keep his hands still. When Mancini sat beside him, he jumped.

Peter edged behind Mammon and Geary and sat at the end of the table. His boss looked up at him with bloodshot eyes.

"Good morning, Mr. Geary," Peter said.

Before Geary could reply, the bailiff rapped his gavel and District Court Judge Brett Staley, a short, balding man with thick glasses, ascended to the bench. Becky O'Shay told Judge Staley that Earl Ridgely, the district attorney, was on vacation and she was handling the preliminary hearing. Then, she called her first witness, Jeffrey Loudhawk.

A dark-complexioned man with high cheekbones and straight black hair was sworn in. He was wearing the uniform of a Whitaker State campus security guard. After some preliminary questions, O'Shay asked Loudhawk if he had seen either of the defendants on the evening of May 22.

"I saw both of them."

"Tell Judge Staley how you came in contact with them."

"Yes, ma'am. I was patrolling around ten o'clock when I noticed the defendants seated in a car at the far end of the parking lot."

"Was the lot crowded?"

"Yes, it was. Classes were just letting out and there were a lot of students milling around and a large number of cars."

"What was it that attracted you to these two gentlemen?"

"The dome light came on suddenly and I was able to see into the car. Something about Mr. Booth looked odd. When I came closer I saw a rolled, ten-dollar bill in his right nostril."

"Why did that attract your attention, Officer Loudhawk?"

"I've attended seminars on narcotics cases run by the Oregon State Police and I know, from my training, that addicts use rolled bills as straws to assist them in snorting cocaine."

"What did you do after you saw Mr. Booth with the bill in his nose?"

"I radioed for assistance using my walkie-talkie. Ron Turnbull, a fellow security guard, arrived and we approached the car. I went to Mr. Booth's side and Officer Turnbull went to the driver's side."

"Then, Mr. Mammon was driving?"

"Yes, ma'am."

"What did you observe when you reached the car?"

52

"Mr. Mammon was sitting behind the wheel of the car with his head against the headrest. Mr. Booth was in the same position in the passenger's seat with his eyes closed."

"Where was the ten-dollar bill?"

"I found it on the floor of the car on Mr. Booth's side."

"What happened next?"

"Officer Turnbull told Mr. Mammon to freeze and I did the same with Mr. Booth. They both complied. I looked across Mr. Booth and saw, in plain view, a transparent, plastic Ziploc bag filled with a white powder."

"Where was this bag?"

"Halfway under Mr. Mammon's seat on the driver's side."

"Did you see anything else that your training led you to believe was associated with narcotics use?"

"Yes, ma'am. I saw a mirror in a map holder on the driver's side."

"Why did the mirror interest you?"

"I know from my training that users of cocaine will prepare the drug on a mirror before snorting it."

"What happened after you saw the bag of powder and the mirror?"

"I asked Mr. Booth what the powder was. He said he didn't know. I accused him of snorting cocaine and he denied it. Then, I placed both men under arrest and radioed the Whitaker police for assistance. When the police arrived, I turned over the prisoners, two bags of cocaine, the mirror and the rolled bill."

"Nothing further."

Peter thought the case against both men looked open and shut. Geary asked a few perfunctory questions of the witness, but his heart was not in it. Then, it was Steve Mancini's turn.

"Officer Loudhawk, how far from Mr. Mammon's car were you when you saw Mr. Booth with the bill in his nose?"

"It's hard to say."

"Several car lengths?"

"About six."

"And you saw no mirror when you observed Mr. Booth with the bill in his nose?"

"No, sir."

"Out of curiosity, was a test administered to Mr. Booth to determine whether or not there was cocaine present in his blood?"

"Not that I know of."

"No further questions."

Booth leaned over to Mancini. He was upset.

"Is that all you're asking? Why didn't you make him say he didn't see me with any coke? He's lying. They planted the dope and the bill. Call him back."

"Calm down, Kevin. Let me do my job."

"But he said he saw me snorting coke."

There were beads of sweat on Booth's forehead and his eyes were dancing everywhere.

"Will you shut up? I've got to concentrate and I can't do it with you whining in my ear."

Booth chewed on his lip for a moment. Then, he said, "Okay. I'm sorry. I just don't want to go to jail for something I didn't do. I'm innocent. This is all bullshit. I didn't even have that bill in my hand."

"Right, Kevin, I believe you," Mancini answered sarcastically. "Now how about letting me listen to this witness."

Miles Baker, a chemist with the Oregon State Police, finished testifying about his qualifications. Then he explained how he determined that the substance in the two bags was cocaine. Geary did not cross-examine.

"Mr. Baker," Mancini said, "the evidence log lists several other items that were turned over to you, including a ten-dollar bill and a mirror. Did you test the bill and the mirror for traces of cocaine?"

"No, I did not."

"Thank you. No further questions."

"The state rests," O'Shay said.

"Any witnesses for the defense?" the judge asked.

Geary shook his head.

"No witnesses, Your Honor," Mancini said, "but I have a motion for the court."

"Very well, Mr. Mancini."

Peter could not imagine what motion Mancini might make. If he were the judge, he would have both defendants breaking rocks on Devil's Island by now. Peter guessed that Mancini was putting on a show to make Booth think he was earning his fee.

"I move for dismissal of the charges against Mr. Booth," Mancini said. "The state has accused Mr. Booth of possession of a controlled substance. Now, there was a controlled substance under Mr. Mammon's seat in a car registered to Mr. Mammon, but there has been no evidence connecting Mr. Booth with that controlled substance. Officer Loudhawk never said he saw Mr. Booth with cocaine and nothing was done to determine whether Mr. Booth had ingested cocaine, although this could have been accomplished with a simple blood test. I don't believe probable cause exists to bind over Mr. Booth."

"What was he doing with the ten-dollar bill up his nose?" the judge asked with a straight face.

"That is for the state to explain, Your Honor. He could have been cleaning his nasal passages, he may enjoy the aroma of American currency. I don't know. But there is certainly no evidence that he was snorting cocaine with that bill. According to the officer, you do that from a mirror. There is no evidence that the mirror and the bill tested positive for cocaine."

Judge Staley frowned. He was lost in thought for a moment. When he addressed Becky O'Shay, he sounded concerned.

"What do you have to say to Mr. Mancini's argument, Miss O'Shay?"

Peter gazed at the prosecutor. He was certain she would respond with a brilliant argument. Instead, all she managed was, "Mr. Mancini is being ridiculous,

Your Honor. It's obvious that Mr. Booth was snorting cocaine."

"Why is it obvious? There is no evidence that there was cocaine on the bill or the mirror, the cocaine was under Mr. Mammon's seat, the car is registered to Mr. Mammon and Mr. Booth denied using cocaine."

"He had the bill up his nose," O'Shay repeated in obvious frustration at her inability to counter Mancini's argument.

"That's not illegal conduct in this state, no matter how disgusting it may be. No, Miss O'Shay, I'm going to have to grant Mr. Mancini's motion."

O'Shay looked as if she wanted to say something else, but she slumped onto her seat instead. Peter thought she looked adorable. He wanted to rush across the room and console her. Instead, he studied Christopher Mammon, expecting him to go insane with rage because his co-defendant was free and he was not, but Mammon sat passively as Judge Staley addressed Steve Mancini's client.

"Mr. Booth, don't think you have me fooled one bit. I know damn well you possessed and used cocaine on the evening of your arrest, but we are a country of law and one of our most fundamental rules of criminal procedure is that the state must prove its case with evidence, not conjecture. If the state can't do that I must set you free, no matter what my personal feelings might be. So, I am going to dismiss the case against you. But that doesn't mean I'm going to forget your face. You better not come before me again, young man. You've had your break. If I ever see you again, I will make certain that you go to prison for a long, long time.

"As for you, Mr. Mammon, this court finds probable cause to bind you over for prosecution in the circuit court on the charge of possession of a controlled substance. You will be released, Mr. Booth. Guard, you can take Mr. Mammon back to jail."

Amos Geary took a long drag on a cigarette and trudged toward his office. The old lawyer was short of breath and he walked with effort. Peter hoped he would make the three blocks to the office without collapsing.

"What did you learn from this morning's outing, Mr. Hale?" Geary wheezed.

"Uh, well, I saw how a preliminary hearing works."

Geary shook his head. "You saw an aberration. Ninety-nine times out of one hundred, the judge binds over the defendant. I don't know what got into Brett this morning."

"Steve was pretty amazing. I didn't know he was that good an attorney."

"You know Mancini?"

"We went to law school together."

"Hmm," Geary said.

"What does that mean?"

"Watch yourself. Mancini's an opportunist."

"Why do you say that?"

Geary took another drag on his coffin nail. "Has he suggested that you invest in Mountain View?"

"Is that the condominium deal?"

Geary nodded. "He's tried to get every lawyer in town to invest, except me. He knows I don't have a pot to piss in."

"Steve seems to think those condos will make him rich."

"Oh, they will. *If* Bend is awarded the Winter Olympics. That's a big if. If Bend doesn't get the Olympics, Steve just might end up in my tax bracket. I just hope he doesn't sucker Jesse Harmon into putting up some money."

The name sounded vaguely familiar and Peter asked, "Who is Jesse Harmon?"

"He's one of the most successful farmers in the county. Mancini wasn't divorced more than a month when he put a move on Donna Harmon, Jesse's daughter."

Geary drew on his cigarette and they walked on together in silence. Peter was not surprised that Geary was trashing Steve, especially after the way Mancini had shown him up in court. Geary never had a nice thing to say about anyone. Peter decided that Geary was just a sour old fart who, like his father, could not stand seeing a younger man succeed.

Peter's thoughts turned to Becky O'Shay. He wondered if she was seeing anyone. Peter had gone out with Rhonda Kates again. She was okay, but O'Shay was really interesting.

"The D.A. sure was bent out of shape when the judge swallowed Steve's argument," Peter said.

"Rebecca doesn't like to lose."

"How long has she been a prosecutor?"

Geary stopped in mid-stride and looked at Peter. Then, he shook his head in disgust.

"I know exactly what you're thinking. Forget it."

"Forget what?" Peter asked innocently. Wearily, Geary shook his head again.

"That cute little thing has every young buck in three counties panting after her, but I'm going to give you some advice, which I assume you won't take. Stay away from Rebecca O'Shay."

"What's wrong with her?"

"Did you see that Tom Cruise movie where he plays a vampire?"

"*Interview with the Vampire?*"

"That's the one."

"Sure. Great flick."

"Remember the little girl vampire?"

"Yes."

"Rebecca O'Shay was the model."

CHAPTER SIX

1

His mouth was dry and he could barely breathe. She was so beautiful. He knew if he touched her she would be soft like a rabbit. He wanted to close his eyes and stop his ears to make time move faster, to bring her to the moment where she would take off her clothes, but he was afraid he would miss that moment if he shut his eyes.

He heard a sound on the path that went past the girls' dormitory. Instantly he was down, hidden by the bushes. Two girls passed, chatting about a boy one of them was dating. They giggled. When they were gone he rose up slowly, until his eyes were level with the sill.

Where was she? He could not see her. She was gone. Please don't let her be gone, he prayed. Then the bathroom door opened and his heart stopped. Her jeans were off. She was holding them in her hand. Tossing them on the bed. Her legs were bare. He licked his lips and undid his zipper. Please, please, he prayed.

She walked to the chest of drawers and took out a shorty nightgown. Suddenly, she remembered the window. She turned and only his quick reaction saved him from discovery. He heard the blinds go down. No, he screamed silently. It wasn't fair. He had been here so long, waiting forever, worshiping her while she studied. Praying so hard to see her naked. And now this.

Suddenly, he noticed a wedge of light and adjusted his body. Praise God. There was a slit. A gap between the edge of the venetian blinds and the window ledge. He peeked into the room and was rewarded by a vision of a goddess with long blond hair.

She began unbuttoning her blouse slowly, as if she knew he was watching. Maybe she did know. Maybe this was for him. She would strip slowly, tantalizing him, then she would walk to the window, raise the blinds and ask him in.

He was hard now, working himself with his fingers as her blouse came off. Breasts, he thought. He could feel his body tensing as his excitement grew with each quickening stroke of his hand. The moment was now. She reached behind to unhook her bra. Now! He felt his body tremble. Now! His eyes shut tight, his teeth clenched in ecstasy as his back began to arch.

Then, a deep voice said, "Well, well. What have we got here?" and fear and shame engulfed him.

2

Rhonda Kates was dying to see the romantic comedy playing at the Whitaker Cinema, so she and Peter caught the early show then ate dinner at an Italian restaurant on Elm. Rhonda lived just on the other side of the campus near the hospital. It was a beautiful June evening and they walked the mile or so to the theater and back. Rhonda had to get up early, so Peter only stayed for a while. Before he left, Peter promised to call, but he was not certain he would keep his promise. He liked Rhonda, but there was something about Becky O'Shay that fascinated him. In fact, Peter had called O'Shay earlier that day, but she was in court and he lost his nerve and called Rhonda instead.

Peter was starting to examine what there was about Becky that attracted him when he heard a commotion. A small crowd was watching two men struggle in the bushes under a window at the side of the women's dormitory. Peter pushed his way to the front of the crowd and saw Jeffrey Loudhawk, the campus security guard who had testified at the preliminary hearing, wrestling with a man who was thrashing around and wailing incoherently. The high-pitched, keening sound issuing from the captive was eerie and unsettling. Then Loudhawk jerked the man around and Peter recognized Gary Harmon.

"What's going on?" Peter asked just as Gary made it halfway to his knees. Loudhawk was a large, muscular man, but it took all his strength to bring Gary back down to the ground.

"Gary, don't fight. You'll only get hurt," Peter said.

Gary turned his head toward Peter's voice as soon as he heard his name.

"I'm Steve Mancini's friend, Peter Hale," Peter told Gary.

Gary stared at Peter, wide-eyed. He looked terrified.

"You know this guy?" Loudhawk gasped, grateful that Gary had stopped struggling.

"He's Gary Harmon. I met him through a friend. What did he do?"

"I caught him peeping in a girl's room."

"Don't tell Mama," Gary pleaded, his voice rising.

"You're Jeffrey Loudhawk, right?" Peter asked.

"How'd you know my name?"

"I work with Amos Geary. I heard you testify at that prelim the other day. The drug bust."

"Right."

"I don't suppose you could cut Gary any slack? He's retarded. I'm sure he didn't mean anything by what he did."

"It's not my call. I radioed for backup before I ar-

61

rested him. You'll have to work it out with the Whitaker police."

"Could you wait to write this up until I talk to them? Gary is working at the college. If you report him, it will probably cost him his job."

"It should," Loudhawk answered indignantly.

"Well, yeah. Normally. But he seemed real slow when I was with him. Like a kid. I mean, listen to him now."

All during their conversation, Gary had been weeping and moaning. Loudhawk took a hard look at his prisoner. Then, he said, "Okay. I'll wait to see what the police say."

"Thanks. Thanks a lot."

Peter rushed home then drove to the police station while the police transported Gary. Peter knew he had to tell someone what had happened, but the way Gary was carrying on he knew he couldn't tell Gary's parents or his sister. It was almost twelve, so he decided not to call Steve Mancini right away. Peter figured he would wait at the station until he knew what was going to happen to Gary. If the police let him out, Peter would drive Gary home, then tell Steve what happened in the morning.

When Peter arrived at police headquarters, Gary was being interrogated. Peter told the officer at the desk that he was Gary's lawyer. A few minutes later, an officer escorted Peter to the back of the building. The door to the interrogation room was opened by Sergeant Dennis Downes, a jovial, thirty-four-year-old, who wore his hair in a crew cut. Downes, an avid outdoorsman, had moved to Oregon four years before for the hunting and fishing. He was roly-poly, which made some people believe he was soft, and he always smiled, which led some people to think he was dumb. Downes did not try to dispel either impression. As a policeman, he found it was an advantage to have people underestimate him.

The interrogation room was covered with white acoustic tile and the only furniture in it was a long wooden table and a few straight-backed chairs. A large, two-way mirror covered a section of one wall. Gary Harmon was seated at the table across from a uniformed officer. He had a Coke and a half-eaten hamburger in front of him, but he did not look hungry. Peter could not remember ever seeing anyone who looked so ashamed.

Downes dismissed the other officer. When the door closed, Downes asked, "Just what is your interest in this, Mr. Hale?"

"I'm a friend of Steve Mancini. We went to law school together. Steve is engaged to Gary's sister. He introduced me to Donna and Gary. I just happened to be on campus when Gary was arrested and I recognized him."

"Well, Gary here is damn lucky he has you as a friend." Gary hung his head. "I should throw the book at him, but I'm gonna let him go."

"That's awfully nice of you, Sergeant."

"Gary's folks are well respected. I don't know 'em that well, but I sure don't want to embarrass them." Downes turned his attention to Gary. "And you shouldn't either. You hear me?"

"Yes, sir, Sergeant Downes, I'm real sorry." Gary's eyes watered. "I'll never, never do that again," he said, wagging his head back and forth for emphasis. "I promise I'll be good."

"Your promise doesn't mean anything to me, Gary. It's what you do that counts. Think of what this would do to your folks if they found out."

Gary looked alarmed. "You won't tell 'em, will you?"

"I should, but I won't. How would your mother feel if she learned you were creeping around the girls' dorm like some sex pervert?"

Gary started to cry.

"That baby stuff won't solve anything."

Gary wiped his forearm across his eyes and sniffled. Downes turned to Peter.

"You better have a talk with this boy. If this happens again, he'll be seeing the inside of a cell."

The front door of Gary's tiny cottage opened into a small living room. To the left was a narrow kitchen. A yellow, Formica-topped table was next to the stove and served as a dining area. A short hall led off the living room to the rear of the house. The bathroom was on the left side of the hall and the bedroom was across from it on the right. The beauty of the house was that it was small enough for Gary to take care of and it was within walking distance of the college.

Gary opened the front door and turned on the living room lights. The room was neat. He cleaned it every day, just like it said on the "To Do" list his mother had taped to the refrigerator door.

"You want a Coke?" Gary asked, the way his mother had taught him.

"Sure," Peter answered as he surveyed the room. On the walls were a seascape and a farm scene Donna had picked out. There was a sofa against the wall that faced the front window, two armchairs, an end table by the sofa, a standing lamp and a television.

Peter heard the refrigerator door open. He wandered down the hall to Gary's bedroom. Pictures of Stallion players and Stallion banners and posters covered the walls. Gary smiled when he saw Peter looking at pictures of the football team.

"We're going all the way this year," Gary said as he handed Peter the soft drink.

Peter sat on the bed. This room was also neat. Peter found the "To Do" list taped to the closet door.

"Your mom write that up?" Peter asked, pointing to the list.

"Yeah. Mama didn't want me to forget nothing important."

Gary suddenly thought of something.

"Are you gonna tell my mom what I done?"

Gary seemed pretty contrite. It looked as though Downes had done a good job of scaring the hell out of him. Sometimes, with a kid, that's all you needed to set him straight, and Gary acted more like a little kid than an adult.

"I should tell your folks, but I'm not going to."

"Thank you."

Peter took a sip of his drink. Gary did the same.

"You sure fucked up tonight. What were you doing looking in that girl's window?"

Gary hung his head and mumbled, "I don't know."

"How would you feel if you found some guy peeping in your sister's window?"

Gary did not answer.

"You wouldn't want that, would you?"

"No."

"You have to think about things like that."

"I will, honest. I ain't never gonna do that bad thing again."

"You better not."

They sat in silence for a moment while Peter drank his Coke.

"Do you date?"

Gary shook his head sadly. "I can't get no girls to like me that way."

"Hey, don't run yourself down. You're a good-looking guy."

"I'm dumb. When the girls find out they don't want to be with me."

Now it was Peter's turn to be embarrassed. He felt sorry for Gary.

"Any girl that doesn't want to be with you because you're not smart isn't worth being with. And you shouldn't be ashamed of your intelligence. Being smart is just luck. And being smart doesn't mean you're nice.

"Now, stop feeling sorry for yourself. You'll find the right girl some day. Meanwhile, you can't go around doing what you did tonight. Do you understand that? If Sergeant Downes wasn't such an okay guy, you'd be in jail and your picture would be all over the front page of the newspaper. The next time you get the urge to do something bad, think of how your folks and your sister would feel if everyone in Whitaker found out about it."

Peter stood up and put his empty can on Gary's dresser.

"I'm going now. We both have work in the morning and we need our sleep. Do I have your word that this won't happen again?"

"Never. I swear."

3

After Peter drove away, Gary carried the soda cans into the kitchen and put them in the garbage. He checked the "To Do" list and was pleased to see he had done everything he was supposed to. Then, he locked the doors and turned out all the lights.

Gary changed into his pajamas, said his prayers and went to bed. He thought he would fall asleep right away because he was exhausted from the night's excitement, but as soon as he closed his eyes he saw the blond girl from the dorm in her bra and panties.

Gary opened his eyes quickly. He didn't want to see that girl. That was bad. But sure enough, when he closed his eyes again, there she was. To make matters worse, his penis was getting hard. Gary opened his eyes again. He was scared. He didn't want to think about dirty things, but he did want to go to sleep. How could he sleep if he saw that girl every time he closed his eyes?

The magazines. No, he did not want to do that tonight. What would happen if Mom came into his room and found him with those magazines? But he did want to sleep. What should he do?

Gary tossed and turned. He felt sick. Finally, he got out of bed and opened the closet. The magazines were way in the back on a top shelf stuck under some sports

66

magazines where Mom would never find them. He took out his favorite and opened it to the centerfold. That girl was blond, too. Just like the girl at the dorm. Gary made believe that she was really in his room. He closed his eyes and took the magazine into bed with him. He imagined he was married to the girl in the magazine. When he touched her, she was as soft as a bunny and, best of all, she liked him to touch her and, when he did, she didn't laugh at him.

PART THREE

THE SUPERNATURAL MIND

CHAPTER SEVEN

Gary Harmon always felt important when he went to the Stallion because Steve Mancini was one of the owners. When he walked in the door, Steve's trophy case was the first thing he saw. The bartenders, the waiters and the waitresses knew Steve was his friend and they treated him well. If Steve came in when Gary was there, he would buy Gary a beer, even though his parents said he wasn't supposed to drink alcohol. Steve would wink and say it was their secret.

The table where Gary was sitting was on a raised area that overlooked the bar. Below Gary, couples danced frantically to the music of a raucous band. Tonight, Gary felt even more special than usual about being in the Stallion because Steve and Donna were getting married tomorrow and he was the best man. Arnie Block, one of the bartenders, had given him a free drink and so had several other people. In fact, Gary was drunk when he spotted Kevin Booth frantically scanning the faces at the crowded tables for Christopher Mammon, who had ordered Kevin to meet him at the Stallion at ten-thirty.

Gary and Kevin Booth were both graduates of Eisenhower High. Gary remembered Booth as one of the few students not in the special education classes who would talk to him. Gary forgot that Booth paid attention to him because Gary was one of the few students at Eisenhower that Booth could bully.

"Hey, Kevin," Gary yelled over the music as Booth walked by. Booth stopped at the sound of his name. "It's me, Gary Harmon."

Booth had no time to waste on a retard, but all the tables were taken and he had no idea how long it would be before Mammon showed up.

"How's it going?" Booth said, sitting down without asking.

"It's going great! Do you know Steve Mancini?"

"Sure. He's my lawyer."

"He is?"

"Yeah. Why?"

"Steve is my friend. He's gonna marry my sister tomorrow."

"Congratulations, man," Booth said as he scanned the crowd again, then looked back toward the door just as Mammon walked in. Kevin stood up and waved. Mammon saw him and headed up the stairs.

"Hey, my man," Mammon said, clapping Booth on the shoulder as he sat down at the table. Gary looked at Mammon with awe.

"Who's your friend?" Mammon asked Booth.

"Oh, this is Gary Harmon, a guy I knew in high school. Gary, this is Chris Mammon."

"It's nice meeting your friends, Kevin," Mammon said sarcastically, "but we have business to discuss."

"Do you know Steve Mancini?" Gary asked with a big smile.

"What?" Mammon asked, as if he could not believe that Gary had the temerity to address him.

"Steve is my friend," Gary said proudly. "He's marrying my sister tomorrow. I'm gonna be the best man."

"Why the fuck should I care?" Mammon snapped.

"It's okay, Chris," Booth said nervously, afraid Mammon would erupt into violence. Then, he whispered, "Gary's a retard. He don't mean anything."

Mammon thought about that for a moment. He had to get rid of Harmon and he had an idea. The body builder spotted what he was looking for at the bar.

"Your friend's getting married tomorrow?" Mammon asked, feigning interest.

"Yeah. At the church. I'm gonna wear a tuxedo."

"Hey, that's great. But what are you doing here? Why aren't you at Steve's bachelor party?"

"What's that?" Gary asked, his brow furrowing.

"You ain't never heard of a bachelor party?" Mammon asked, nudging Booth with his elbow.

"No," Gary answered, embarrassed that, once again, other people knew things that he did not.

"Where you been, Gary? That's the party your buddies throw for you the night before you get married. There's plenty of drinking and you tell stories and there's always a special gift for the groom-to-be," Mammon concluded with a lewd wink.

"What kind of gift?"

Mammon leaned toward Gary and, in a confidential whisper, he said, "Pussy."

Gary flushed. "Steve wouldn't go for a party like that."

"Why not?" Mammon asked with exaggerated concern. "He ain't queer, is he?"

"Oh no. He's a regular guy. He got me season tickets to the Stallion games."

"Then, what's he got against pussy?"

"Steve's a lawyer," Gary answered proudly.

Mammon and Booth cracked up. Gary laughed, too, because the others were laughing, but he did not know what was so funny. Steve was a good lawyer.

"You're not telling me that lawyers don't get laid?" Mammon went on when he stopped laughing. "I bet he'll get laid on his honeymoon."

Gary blushed. He did not like to think about anyone having sex with his sister.

"It's sure too bad there ain't no bachelor party," Mammon said, shaking his huge head.

"Hey!" Mammon said, as if he'd just had a sudden thought. "Just because Steve is a stick-in-the-mud doesn't mean you can't have your own bachelor party."

Gary looked confused. Mammon slid his chair next to Gary's and put his arm around Gary's shoulder.

"Don't be too obvious," Mammon whispered in Gary's ear, "but look over my shoulder at the blonde at the end of the bar near the door."

Gary turned slowly. A slender woman with straight, shoulder-length hair, wearing tight jeans and a Whitaker State T-shirt with a rearing stallion on it, was talking to a short brunette. Her emerald eyes sparkled when she laughed.

"Now, Gary, I'm a little jealous. That woman has been giving you the eye since I sat down."

Gary looked at her again. "Nah," Gary said nervously, "it wouldn't be me."

"Who else, buddy? You're one good-lookin' stud."

"She wasn't looking at me," Gary repeated stubbornly, hoping Mammon was wrong and terrified that he was right.

"Kevin, did you notice that blonde giving Gary the eye?"

"Yeah, Gary," Booth said enthusiastically, "she's hot for you."

"You a fan of the Stallions football team, Gary?"

"Yeah!"

"Well, my man, if I was a stud like you, and a woman like that was giving me the eye, I'd strike hard and fast like a Stallion linebacker."

"What . . . what do you mean?"

"Get on down there. Check it out. Odds are you'll be inside that tight squeeze before I can finish my beer."

Gary felt sick with excitement. He knew he could never have a girl like that, but Mammon seemed so certain.

"You got someplace to take her?" Mammon asked.

"I got my own house."

"I bet that place rocks from morning to night, right?"

Gary did not answer. Mammon's arm tightened around his shoulder and Mammon's breath felt hot against his ear.

"You do know how to pick up girls, don't you?"

"Sure," Gary answered, because he was too embarrassed to tell the truth.

"Then you know you have to go down there and ask her if she wants a beer. Now she'll say no at first. These bitches always play hard to get. You insist, though. Women like guys who won't take no for an answer. Be forceful."

"I don't know. She really don't look that interested in me."

"Are you kidding? Shit, man, she's creamin' over you."

"That's true," Booth chimed in, anxious to get rid of Gary so he could find out what Mammon wanted with him. "She definitely wants it."

"And she wants it from you," Mammon said, lifting Gary to his feet. "Now, you aren't a fag, are you?"

"Oh no. It's just . . ."

"It's just nothing, my man. And you know what? I'm jealous as shit, because you're gonna be sleeping with your ears between those silky thighs tonight. Go on."

Mammon gave Gary a push toward the stairs. Gary walked down them slowly, twice looking over his shoulder at Booth and Mammon, who waved him on. He was sick with worry, but he could not disgrace himself by turning back. What would the guys think if he could not score with a girl who was giving him the eye? And if he did score with a girl that pretty, it would really be something. Maybe he would even ask her to come with him to the wedding.

There was an empty space next to the blonde at the bar. Up close, she was even better-looking. Gary stood there for a moment, but the girl did not seem to notice him. Finally, Gary worked up the courage to talk to her, but the words caught in his throat when he tried to speak. Gary swallowed. Then, in a quivering whisper, he asked the girl if she wanted a beer, but the noise in the bar was so loud that she did not hear him.

Gary felt nauseous. It had taken all his courage to make this attempt and he was too frightened to try again. He looked back at Booth and Mammon. They were doubled up with laughter. Mammon waved at him to go on. He turned back to the girl and tapped her on the shoulder, pulling his hand back as soon as he touched her. The girl stopped in mid-sentence and turned toward him.

"Can . . . can I get you a beer?" Gary managed.

The girl flashed a smile that barely disguised her annoyance. "No thanks," she answered quickly in a tone that made it clear that she was used to being hit on and didn't like it. When she turned back to her friend, Gary looked at the table for help. His friends were laughing again. Why would they laugh like that? He wanted to run away, but he remembered what Chris said about being persistent. He tapped the girl's shoulder again, a little harder. The girl turned around. She looked angry.

"What do you want?" she asked.

"I like you and I want to buy you a beer."

"Thank you, but I'm talking to someone, okay?"

"I can buy her a beer, too."

"Look, I don't want you to buy me a beer. Neither does my friend. Take no for an answer, okay?"

"I like you," Gary repeated lamely.

The girl looked at the ceiling and rolled her eyes. Gary cringed with embarrassment.

"Ch . . . Chris said you want me to buy you a beer," he stuttered.

"Who?"

"Chris. My friend," Gary said, pointing toward the table where Mammon and Booth were still laughing. The girl saw them and figured out what was going on.

"Go tell your friends they were wrong and leave me alone."

"You . . . you don't like me?" Gary asked, hurt and confused.

"Are you an idiot?" the woman asked incredulously. "Didn't I just tell you . . ."

Gary's hand shot out and grabbed the girl's tee shirt. "I ain't no idiot," he yelled.

The girl staggered backward, startled by Gary's sudden rage.

"Don't call me no names," he shouted in her face.

"Let me go," she screamed, as she tried to pull out of Gary's grip. Gary yanked her toward him.

Arnie Block, the bartender closest to the commotion, turned when he heard the girl scream. At the end of the bar farthest from the front door, another attractive blonde in a Whitaker State tee shirt and jeans was sitting across from Dave Thorne, the other bartender. The girl was wearing a silver medallion around her neck. It had a cross embossed on it. The girl fingered the medallion while she sipped a beer. Thorne was working on a drink order when Arnie shouted to him.

"Dave, call Steve. Tell him Gary's causing trouble and to get over here."

Dave looked down the bar, then grabbed the phone on the shelf behind him. He made the call. When he hung up, he noticed that the blonde with the medallion was watching two men who were walking toward the back door that led into the rear parking area. One of the men was big and flabby. The other looked like a professional wrestler. The girl looked very frightened, but Thorne had no more time to think about her because Gary was shaking the other girl by both shoulders.

"Say you're sorry," Gary screamed. "Say I ain't no idiot or I'll . . . I'll kill you."

Arnie Block reached across the bar and grabbed Gary around the neck. Gary shrugged him off.

"Let her go, Gary," Arnie yelled. This time, Gary realized who was talking to him and his grip relaxed.

"She said I was an idiot," Gary pleaded with the bartender. Block found a clear space and leaped the bar.

"She shouldn't have said that, but you can't shake her. Can't you see she's scared?"

Gary looked at the girl. She was breathing hard, and she was near tears and very frightened. Gary released the girl and she staggered into the bar, upsetting her drink.

"I called for Steve. He's really pissed," Block said, as Dave Thorne pushed through the crowd. "You'll be lucky if you don't get arrested."

Gary's eyes widened as he remembered what would happen to him if he was arrested again. He would go to jail and it would be on the front page of the paper. Mama would read it and it would kill her.

"Dave," Block said, turning away from Gary, "take care of this lady. Make sure she's all right."

When Block turned back, Gary was streaking for the door. Arnie shook his head as Gary raced into the night. He made no attempt to stop him.

Dave Thorne took the blonde and her friend to an empty booth. Arnie brought over a glass of brandy just as Steve Mancini walked in. He was wearing a suit, but his shirt was open at the collar and his tie was pulled down.

"What happened?" Mancini asked the bartender.

"Gary got a little out of hand with that girl."

"The blonde?" Mancini asked, looking in the direction Arnie was pointing.

"Yeah."

"What did Gary do?"

Arnie told him.

"Jesus. Where is he?"

"I don't know. He took off as soon as I said you were coming over."

"That dumb fuck," Mancini said, absentmindedly running his fingers through his hair. "All right, all right. Damage control," he muttered to himself.

"I'm gonna talk to her," he told Block.

Mancini walked over to the booth. The blonde looked up. Her makeup was smeared and she looked frightened.

"I'm Steve Mancini, one of the owners. Can I sit down?"

The girl nodded and Mancini slid into the booth across from the women.

"Are you all right, Miss . . . ?"

"Nix. Karen Nix. I'm just shaken up." She shook her head. "He just went crazy. I thought he was going to hit me."

"But he didn't."

"That's only because the bartender stopped him," Nix said, anger flaring in her eyes. "Do you know what he said? He threatened to kill me. I'm calling the cops as soon as I find out who that creep is."

"I wish you wouldn't," Steve said.

"Are you kidding? He's a lunatic. He might hurt someone else."

"I don't think so. Gary says the first thing that comes into his head when he's angry. He doesn't mean what he says."

"You know him?"

"I'm getting married tomorrow and Gary is going to be my best man. He's my fiancée's brother. Normally, he's a sweet kid, but he's retarded and . . ."

Nix's hand flew to her mouth.

"Oh, my God. That's why he got so angry."

Mancini looked puzzled.

"I feel terrible," Nix said. "He wanted to buy me a drink. I thought he was hitting on me. I told him not to bother me a few times, but he persisted. Then, I called him an idiot. That's when he went crazy."

"That explains it," Mancini said. "Gary is very sensitive about his intelligence."

"I feel awful."

"Don't. You had no way of knowing and Gary should have known better, but he's like a little kid . . ."

"You don't have to say anything more. I'm not going to call the police. If I'd known I . . ."

Nix paused. She looked toward the table where Mammon and Booth had been sitting.

79

"Is something wrong?" Mancini asked.

"Gary told me that a friend told him I wanted him to buy me a beer. He pointed to a table on the landing. There were two men sitting there. They were laughing. Maybe they put Gary up to this as a joke. You know, taking advantage of him."

"Are they still here?" Mancini asked.

"They're gone, but I'd know one of them anywhere. He was gigantic, like a body builder. Just huge. And he had tattoos on his arms."

Mancini scowled. "Did Gary mention any names?"

Nix thought for a moment. Then, she brightened.

"Chris! I'm certain that's what he called him."

A flicker of fear shaped Mancini's features for a moment. Then it was gone. Nix reached across the table and touched his forearm.

"Mr. Mancini, you don't have to worry. It looks like Gary was the butt of a practical joke. I shouldn't have called him an idiot, anyway. And I don't want to spoil your wedding day."

"Thanks a lot, Karen." Mancini looked at his watch. "Look, if it's all right, I'll leave now. I have some work at my office I'm wrapping up."

"You go ahead."

"You're terrific. I'm leaving word with the bartenders. Anytime you're in, the drinks are on me."

"Oh, that's not necessary."

Mancini held up his hand. "Not a word. You've been very understanding. Not everyone in your position would be."

At the other end of the Stallion, Dave Thorne was making up a drink order for a waitress. The blonde with the medallion was no longer on her stool. Thorne assumed she had left while he was up front, but he turned around to give the waitress her order and saw the blonde walking out of the front door behind Steve Mancini.

.   .   .

80

Christopher Mammon led Kevin Booth out of the Stallion while Gary Harmon was screaming at Karen Nix. The muffled music from the bar rumbled in the night air. Fear tightened Booth's gut when Mammon stopped in the darkest part of the rear parking lot.

"It's great seeing you out, Chris," Booth said, trying to sound sincere. "What's your lawyer think will happen with your case, now?"

"Geary's an old drunk, but he seems to know his stuff. He's not too encouraging, though."

"That's too bad."

Mammon shrugged. "Shit happens."

"So, Chris, what did you want to talk about?"

"We have a problem, Kevin."

"What's that?"

"Rafael wants his thirty thousand dollars."

Thirty thousand was the amount that Mammon was supposed to pay for the two kilos of cocaine the police seized when Booth and Mammon were arrested.

"That's not my problem," Booth answered nervously. "You made the deal with Rafael."

"I agree with you, but Vargas sees it differently. He says you set up the deal, so you're responsible for the money."

"That's not fair. I introduced you as a favor. You should have told him it wasn't my fault."

"Oh, I did, Kevin. Unfortunately, Vargas says you and I both owe him the money and he doesn't care who pays."

"You still have the money you were going to use to buy the dope. Give it to him."

"No can do. See, I represent people. These people put up the money, but they won't pay it over unless they get cocaine for it. These people I represent are not big on charity."

"Well, I don't have thirty thousand dollars. And I shouldn't have to come up with money your people owe. I'm gonna tell that to Rafael."

"I wouldn't do that. He was very angry with you,

81

Kevin. He said for me to tell you not to call him unless you had the money. He seemed very serious. Of course, you know Vargas better than I do. Maybe he was just funning."

Booth knew Rafael Vargas well enough to know that he was only rational part of the time and that he was very violent all of the time. If Rafael said "don't call" Booth was not going to risk it.

"There is a solution to our problem," Mammon said.

"What?"

"My people are still interested in buying a very large shipment from Vargas and Vargas wants to deal with them. I'm too hot to be involved because of the arrest, so I thought up a plan that helps my people and helps you make it up to Rafael."

A wave of nausea passed over Booth. Christopher Mammon was a sadist and a bully. Since Mammon arrived in Whitaker six months ago, Booth had never seen him do anything for anyone without an ulterior motive. Whatever Mammon had in mind, it could only mean trouble for Kevin Booth.

"You're going to do a favor for my people and Rafael. If everything works out, we'll both be off the hook for the thirty thousand."

"I don't want to be involved, Chris. I was lucky to beat my case. You heard what that judge said he'd do if I was arrested again."

The smile left Mammon's face and a wall of ice formed behind his eyes. Booth stopped talking and licked his lips.

"This is my ass, too," Mammon said in a voice heavy with the threat of dire consequences. Booth felt like a small child in the presence of a stern and punitive father.

"I just . . ."

"Kevin," Mammon said softly, "don't be afraid. You can handle it."

"I'm not the right guy, Chris. The cops are gonna be watching me."

"You're small potatoes, Kevin. The cops lost interest

in you the minute your case was dismissed. Besides, there's no risk. All you have to do is hold some product."

"Chris, please. I don't want to go to jail," Booth pleaded.

Mammon stared hard at Booth. Then, in a low, slow voice, he said, "There are worse things than jail, Kevin. Besides, you don't have a choice. I've already assured Vargas that he can count on you."

"Aw, Jesus. Call him back."

Mammon placed a hand on Booth's shoulder near his neck and applied a little bit of pressure. Booth turned white.

"If you do as you're told, you won't go to jail and you'll be off the hook for the thirty grand."

Mammon squeezed a little harder. Booth dropped to his knees on the asphalt. He tried to pry Mammon's hand off his neck, but the iron fingers would not budge.

"On the other hand," Mammon said quietly, "if you fuck this up for me, you'll wish you were in jail."

Booth gritted his teeth and twitched and wriggled in pain.

"Please, Chris."

Mammon released Booth and he tumbled onto the asphalt. Mammon let him lie there for a moment. Then, he reached down and pulled Booth to his feet as easily as if he were a child.

"I'm sorry I had to do that, but I'd rather hurt you a little now than have to hurt you a lot later, because you failed to understand how serious I am. My people and I want this done and Vargas wants it done. I don't want to have to pay out any of my money to square this. Now, do I have your promise that you'll be a good boy?"

"Sure, Chris. I'll do what you say."

Mammon smiled. "I know you will."

"What . . . what do I have to do?"

"Just sit tight. You'll be contacted soon. I don't think

it's a good idea for us to be seen together from now on, so don't call me or try to see me."

"Okay," Booth assured Mammon, eternally grateful that he would be rid of Mammon.

Mammon started toward his car. Then, he stopped just as a man walked by the far end of the Stallion heading toward the side parking lot. Mammon turned toward Booth, who was only a few feet from him.

"One more thing, Kevin. Don't even think of running."

Booth did not answer. He was shaking from fright. Mammon turned back toward the lot. A light at the far end of the building illuminated a slender blonde in a Whitaker tee shirt and jeans. The blonde paused under the light and headed toward the side lot. She called to the man Mammon had just seen. Mammon squinted. He knew that girl. He wondered what she was doing.

CHAPTER EIGHT

1

Two stone pillars at the end of High Street farthest from the courthouse marked the main entrance to Wishing Well Park. A wide path between the pillars led to the wishing well, which had been built in 1972 as a memorial to the men of Whitaker County who had given their lives in the Vietnam War. From the wishing well, the park expanded into a large recreational area with a marina, baseball diamonds, a playground, a band shell and a series of hiking trails.

It was only one mile from Oscar Watts's house to the wishing well, but Oscar was a neophyte in the world of physical fitness and the two-mile round trip of alternate jogging and walking was pure agony. Oscar worked as a bookkeeper at the JCPenney on Broad. Though his doctor was always chiding him about his weight, Oscar was never troubled by the fact that his belt was lost in overlapping rolls of fat. He loved to eat, and he didn't really need to be physically fit to add up columns of numbers. Then, Oscar had a stroke and his doctor gave him a solemn lecture about blocked arteries, sky-high cholesterol counts and saturated fats. Now, instead of spending each morning consuming stacks of his wife's fabulous maple-syrup-and-butter-soaked hotcakes,

Oscar spent his mornings gasping in agony as he struggled along the hiking trails of Wishing Well Park.

Head down, feet dragging, mouth open and gulping for air, Oscar trudged ahead on legs of lead. When he looked up, the wheezing jogger saw the wishing well wavering like a ghostly beacon in the half light of dawn, reminding Oscar that his self-inflicted torture was half over. He was one hundred yards from the well when he spotted the object at its base. He was fifty yards away when he realized it might be human. Oscar stopped running and leaned forward, resting his hands on his knees, straining for a better look. Sweat obscured his vision. He ran his forearm across his eyes. Could that be a woman? It was hard to tell. Whatever sex it was, the person was curled around the base of the well, knees almost touching the red brick and hands and arms tucked out of sight, as if the person was sleeping. She could be sleeping, Oscar thought hopefully, as he crept toward the well.

At twenty-five yards, Oscar started to make out the dark stains that had soaked into the long blond hair and puddled at the base of the well. He wondered if he should call a cop now or take a closer look. Oscar didn't want to jump to conclusions and look like a fool. He decided to check things out. It was the last time Oscar thought about food for a long time.

2

Earl Ridgely could hear the gentle rush of the river from where he was standing. The summer air smelled of fresh-cut grass and roses. Morning dew shined his scuffed, black leather shoes. It was the type of balmy July day that made Ridgely wish he were lazing in a hammock sipping from a cold glass of sangria. Instead, he was sweating in a business suit, just inside the perimeter set up by the forensic experts from the Oregon State Crime Lab as they studied the body huddled next to the red brick wishing well.

Ridgely was a slender man with thinning straw-colored hair, tortoiseshell glasses and a thick mustache. A local boy who graduated with distinction from Stanford, but was smart enough to attend an in-state law school because he wanted a career in politics. Ridgely was forty and at the tail end of his second term as Whitaker County D.A. A spot on the circuit court bench would be opening up soon. A good friend from law school was the governor's legal adviser and Earl had been assured that he would soon be taking his first step up a ladder that he hoped would end at the Oregon Supreme Court.

As he approached the body, a young policeman wearing latex gloves was delicately holding up for Sergeant Dennis Downes's inspection a thin metal chain at the end of which dangled a medallion. Downes had been selected by the Major Crime Team to be the officer in charge because the crime being investigated was within the Whitaker city limits. The team was composed of the same men who had viewed the body found several weeks ago in a gully in the wastelands at the border of Whitaker County. The method of murder and the type of victim were sufficiently similar to put every one of these seasoned professionals on edge.

"Should I bag this?" the officer asked.

"Where'd you find it?"

"In the bushes by the entrance."

"Better do it," Downes decided, even though the bushes were a distance from the wishing well. The officer walked away with his find.

"Morning, Dennis," the district attorney said.

"Mornin', Earl."

"Any idea who she is?"

"Not yet, but she's got to be from the college. Looks the age and she's wearing a Whitaker tee shirt."

"Does she have any ID?"

"If she had a purse or wallet, we haven't found it."

"Then, let's get her picture on TV and ask the *Clarion* to run it on the front page of the afternoon edition."

Downes jerked his head toward the body. "Like that?" he asked, wanting to be certain he understood Ridgely.

"Of course not. If she can't be cleaned up, have King make a sketch."

Downes looked relieved. Ridgely didn't blame him. He had taken only one quick look at the corpse, but it was enough to leave him light-headed. People died unnatural deaths in Whitaker County, but the dead were usually the victims of auto accidents and farming mishaps. This girl's skull had been split, exposing the brain and drenching her long blond hair with blood that had soaked into her clothes and spilled onto the ground in such quantities that even the careful forensic experts were stained by it. The girl's face had been lacerated by chopping blows, creating open wounds that also bled profusely.

Ridgely spotted Dr. Guisti bending over the corpse. Guisti straightened up when he saw the D.A. approaching.

"Was the murder weapon a hatchet?" Ridgely asked when they were far enough away from everyone else so they could not be heard.

"I can't say for certain, but I will say that there are enough similarities between this crime, the murder in the gully and the murder in Blaine for me to say they are either the work of the same person or a very good copycat."

"Any signs of sexual activity?" Ridgely asked. The first two women had been raped before they were killed.

"I won't know until I examine her, but I'm guessing no. The other women were naked. She's got her clothes on. The first two were murdered in a location different from where they were found. I'm guessing the killer abducted the other women and held them for a while, but fouled up the abduction here and had to kill her."

"I don't like this one bit, Harold. What you're telling me is that we've got a serial killer in Whitaker County."

"Looks like it."

"Well, shit. I don't have the personnel to investigate something like this."

"You'd better figure out how to do it quick. I started doing a little reading on the subject after we found Emily Curran in that gully. One thing's for certain. Our boy has tasted blood and, according to the literature, once he's taken a liking to the killing, he's not going to stop."

3

The Mancini-Harmon wedding reception was held in the dining room of the Whitaker Elks Club. A long table stocked with hors d'oeuvres, salads, desserts and a selection of roast beef and fried chicken stood against one wall next to the bar. A band played in front of a large dance floor on the opposite side of the hall. The guests chattered noisily at tables covered by white-and-red-checkerboard tablecloths. Peter was refreshing his drink at the bar when a finger poked him in the back.

"Hi, Peter."

Peter turned too quickly and a splash of gin and tonic slopped over the lip of his glass, wetting his hand. He jerked his hand back reflexively and some more liquid jumped out of the glass.

"Having trouble holding your liquor?"

Peter looked down and found Becky O'Shay observing him with a bemused smile.

"Don't you know better than to sneak up on a person

like that?" Peter asked, annoyed that Whitaker's prosecutorial pixie had made him look foolish.

"Just practicing what I was taught in law school," answered Becky, her grin widening. Peter laughed, too, even though he was upset. He couldn't help himself. O'Shay was just too cute to stay mad at.

"Are you a friend of the bride, the groom or both?" Peter asked.

"Steve. How about you?"

"Steve. We went to law school together. Where do you know him from?"

"Oh, here and there," O'Shay answered enigmatically. "Steve tells me you worked at Hale, Greaves before moving to Whitaker."

"Why did he tell you that?"

"I asked him," O'Shay answered with a mischievous grin. Then, she cocked her head to one side and asked, "You're related to Richard Hale, right?"

"He's my father."

"I'm impressed. He must be great to work with."

"Dad's a trip, all right."

"Isn't Whitaker a little dull after the big city? Hale, Greaves must be such an exciting place to practice."

"Dull is what I wanted after four years in the rat race," Peter answered tersely, keeping to the story he told everyone.

"What else did Steve say about me?" Peter asked, secretly pleased that O'Shay was interested enough to pump Steve about him.

"I said you were a pervert and an incurable womanizer," Steve Mancini answered, draping an arm across Peter's shoulder. "How are you two getting along? Had enough food, enough booze?"

Mancini looked dashing in his tux, but his eyes were bloodshot and his speech was a little slurred.

"Congratulations, Steve," O'Shay told the groom.

"You're a lucky guy," Peter added. "Donna looks great."

"I think so," Mancini said.

"What have you got planned?" Peter asked.

"Portland, tonight and Sunday. Then, a week in Hawaii."

"I could live with that," Peter said.

"I need it. I've been breaking my ass on Mountain View."

"Is that your condo deal?"

"Yeah," Mancini said, flashing a smile that looked a little forced. "We're almost there, but I have to stay on top of everyone to keep the momentum going. Then, I've got two cases set for trial early next month. I almost put off the honeymoon, but I couldn't disappoint Donna."

"Forget about business, will you," Peter said. "Loosen up. This is your wedding."

"You're right," Mancini said as he took a scotch from the bartender and swallowed half of it.

"You need an associate to take some of the pressure off you. Why don't you put Donna through law school?" O'Shay joked.

"Donna? A lawyer?" Mancini answered derisively. "Not a chance. Besides, she's going to be too busy with the little Mancinis to have much time for anything else."

"What's this about little Mancinis?" asked Donna, who had a middle-aged couple in tow. She looked radiant in white.

"I was just telling Peter and Becky about our plans," Mancini said, as he gave Donna a kiss. Donna blushed with pride.

"Steve, I want you to meet Bob and Audrey Rosemont," Donna said. The Rosemonts and the newlyweds wandered off.

"They make a great couple, don't they?" Peter said.

"They sure do," O'Shay answered without enthusiasm. Then, she added, "I hope Donna's driving to Portland."

"I just had an idea."

"Oh?" O'Shay said, returning her attention to Peter.

"I've been told that you can get a great steak at the

Range Rider. Want to help me find out if the rumors are true?"

"How would I do that?"

"By accompanying me to dinner tonight?"

"I don't know if that's such a good idea."

"I can assure you that the idea is brilliant," Peter said, flashing her his best smile.

"Look, Peter, this is a small town and we're adversaries. How would it look if a juror in one of our future cases remembered seeing us together on a date?"

"Ah, come on, Becky. I've spent most of my evenings staring at my TV since I moved to Whitaker. I'm going stir-crazy."

While O'Shay considered his proposal, Peter sucked in his cheeks, hunched down and made himself look pathetic.

O'Shay laughed. "Oh, all right. If you're that desperate."

Peter straightened up and grinned.

"Great," he said. "I'll pick you up at eight-thirty and I'll treat you like a goddess."

"You'd better."

Gary took two more shrimp from one of the silver platters on the massive table that held the hors d'oeuvres, then wandered down the line and put another chicken leg on his plate. Next, Gary spotted something wrapped in bacon near the cold cuts. He liked bacon with pancakes, but this bacon looked as if it was wrapped around liver. Gary did not like liver. He wondered if it would be okay to eat the bacon and throw out the liver. He wanted to do the right thing. He did not want to embarrass Donna and Steve. After all, he was the best man.

Gary remembered his part in the ceremony and smiled. When Steve drove him to the church this morning, he told Gary that he looked handsome in his tuxedo. Gary wondered if there had been a girl in the church who thought he was handsome. That would be something. Gary looked around the crowded room to see if any girl was looking at him. He did not see any, but he did hear a lady with gray hair tell another lady with gray-streaked brown hair about a body that had been found by the wishing well. Gary walked over to listen.

"Eric thinks this killing might be connected to the girl they found in the gully and the other girl who was murdered in Blaine," the gray-haired lady said.

"Oh no."

"Eric saw the body. He said it was awful. The killer used a hatchet. Her head was almost chopped off."

"I remember when you could walk anywhere in town, any time of day," the other woman said with a shake of her head. "It's getting so I'm afraid to go out at night."

"That girl was at the Stallion last night," Gary said.

The two women looked at Gary. He smiled, proud to know something they did not.

"Hey, Gary, you look great," said a big, balding man in an ill-fitting brown suit. Gary recognized Eric Polk, a Whitaker policeman, whom he had met at several Elks Club functions.

"Hon, we got to go," Eric said. "It's one-thirty and we're expected at the kids' at two."

Wilma looked at her watch. "I had no idea. I'm going to have to leave, Mabel. It's Kenny's third birthday."

"Is that grandson of yours three already?" Mabel Dawes asked.

"Looks five, he's that big," Eric said proudly.

"Donna looked lovely, Gary," Wilma Polk said, as she, her husband and Mabel Dawes walked away. Gary's chest swelled with pride. His sister was beautiful. So was that girl at the Stallion who had been mean to him. Mrs. Polk said the girl's head had almost been chopped off. Gary thought of the hogs he had butchered on his family's farm. They would squeal and get all excited on the way to die. A picture of a mean girl all tied up and squealing came into his thoughts unbidden. For a moment, it was like it was really happening. Gary's mouth was dry and he started to get hard.

If the mean girl was tied up in his room, he could ask her why she was being mean to him. No, not his room. Mom would find her when she came to clean. But some place. He could put her someplace where no one could find her. Only he would know where she was. And she would have to do what he said. She would have to kiss him if he wanted and learn to love him. That was the most important. Love him like Donna loved Steve. Love him for ever and ever.

4

Marjorie Dooling's shoulders shook convulsively each time she sobbed into her boyfriend's shoulder. Tommy Berger held Marjorie and tried to comfort her. Dennis Downes waited patiently. He understood the shock Marjorie experienced when she saw Sandra Whiley's face, because he had experienced the same feeling that morning in the park.

"I'm sorry," Marjorie apologized, trying hard to stop her tears.

"You take your time," Downes answered compassionately. "Do you want some water?"

Marjorie nodded and Downes poured some from a pitcher he made certain was on his desk before he brought her back from viewing the body.

Marjorie sat down. "I'll be okay," she managed after taking a few sips. "It's just . . ."

She shook her head, at a loss for words.

"What made you call the police?" Downes asked, giving the girl an easy question to distract her from her grief.

"I saw the sketch on the front page of the afternoon *Clarion*. It looked so much like Sandy."

Downes nodded. "You two share a dorm room?"

"No. We live in a boardinghouse near the campus."

"Did you worry when Sandy didn't come home last night?"

"We, uh, spent the night at my place," Tommy answered.

"When I got back to the room this morning, Sandy wasn't there," Marjorie told Downes. "I figured she was studying or something."

"When was the last time you saw her?"

Marjorie looked at Tommy.

"About ten-thirty," he said. "We all went to the Stallion."

"Tommy and I wanted to leave. We offered to drop her off at the house because we came in Tommy's car, but she wanted to stay." Marjorie's eyes teared again. "If she'd only come with us . . ."

Downes waited patiently while Dooling gathered herself.

"Sergeant Downes, I was wondering . . . When they found Sandy, was she wearing a necklace?"

"Why do you ask?"

"Sandy always wore a medallion around her neck. A Crusader's Cross. It would be for her mom. I know she'll want it. Sandy's grandma gave it to her and it was her lucky piece."

Sandy Whiley wasn't wearing anything around her neck when the first officer arrived on the scene, but it seemed to Downes that one of the officers had found something resembling the jewelry Dooling had described. He would check on it later. For now, the medallion was evidence and would have to be held until the killer was caught and convicted.

5

Business was usually slow at the Stallion at four in the afternoon, and the stunning summer weather was keeping all but the staunchest regulars outdoors. Dennis Downes spotted Arnie Block and Dave Thorne chatting behind the bar as soon as his eyes adjusted to the darkness inside the tavern. Downes was in uniform and the bartenders stopped talking when he sat down.

"Hi, Sergeant," Block said. "The usual?"

"Not today, Arnie. Were you and Dave on duty last night?"

"Yeah. We were both here."

Downes took out a photo of Sandra Whiley that Marjorie Dooling had given him when he followed her back to the boardinghouse.

"Do you remember seeing this girl in here?"

Arnie studied the photo. "She looks familiar, but I don't know if she was here last night."

Thorne frowned. "It could be . . . Yeah. Her hair was a little longer, but I'm sure . . ." He took the photo from Block and brought it closer.

"See that medallion around her neck? She was playing with it at the bar. It's definitely her."

"When was she in?"

"It had to be around eleven. In fact, I'm sure of it, because I remember seeing her leave shortly after the fight broke up."

"What fight?" Downes asked.

"Oh, it wasn't anything. Gary Harmon was yelling at a woman. Arnie calmed him down."

"What's with the girl?" Block asked.

"We're trying to trace her movements. She was murdered sometime after she left the Stallion."

"No shit!" Thorne said, looking more closely at the photograph. "Hey, she's not the girl they found by the wishing well?"

Downes nodded.

"Jesus. A couple of customers were talking about that earlier. We thought it might be the other one."

"What other one?"

"The woman Gary was hassling. I saw the sketch in the *Clarion* and it looked a little like her."

"What happened?"

"Do you know Gary?" Arnie asked.

Downes nodded.

"Then, you know he's a little slow, and he'd had one too many. He tried to hit on this girl. She shot him down and he didn't take it too well. He grabbed her by her tee shirt and yelled in her face."

Arnie shook his head.

"What kind of tee shirt?" Downes asked, remembering the way Whiley was dressed.

"Uh, a Whitaker State one. The one with the rearing horse on it."

"Was she wearing jeans?"

"I think so."

"And you thought Gary might have killed this girl?" Downes asked.

"Not really," Block said with a laugh to show how ridiculous the whole thing was. "Gary just gets excited sometimes and acts like a kid. I mean, he did threaten to kill her, but no one took him seriously."

CHAPTER NINE

1

Dennis Downes was normally an easygoing guy, but the possibility of busting the only serial killer in the history of Whitaker County had him on edge. Seated next to Downes in the passenger seat of their patrol car was Bob Patrick, whom everyone called Pat. Pat was tall and thin with wiry muscles. His face was narrow and pockmarked and his eyes were close-set, making him look scary and mean. Pat wore his hair long and greasy in an Elvis Presley, fifties' duck's-ass style that was a little intimidating because it was so weird. Everything about him screamed "tough cop," which was why Downes brought him along. Pat was as psyched up as his partner.

"Jesus, Dennis, I think you're definitely on to something here," he said, as Downes drove toward Gary Harmon's house. Following them was another patrol car with two more officers.

"It's got to be him," Downes responded confidently. "I talked to Karen Nix at her dorm around six. She and Whiley aren't twins, but they're the same type. Blond, long hair, slender. And they were both wearing jeans and that Whitaker tee shirt with the horse.

"The way I see it, Harmon has this fight with Nix. He stays mad like a little kid would and broods about the put-down. Then, he gets a weapon and waits outside the Stallion for her. The door opens, out walks a blonde. Only it's the wrong one. He follows her, waits for his chance . . ."

"And kills her, just like he threatened."

"There's something else. A few weeks ago, Harmon was arrested for peeping a coed's room at the dorm."

"Hot damn."

They turned the corner and Gary's house came into view.

"We've got to be careful with this," Downes cautioned. "Everything by the book. Lots of 'Please' and 'Thank you.' The bathroom, if he's got to pee. Coke, if he's thirsty."

"Gotcha," Patrick agreed with a knowing smile.

"With one exception."

"And that is?"

"The kid's gonna trust me," Downes said as he parked the car. "I got him out of that peeping scrape and treated him right. We can play on that, but I might need some help. That's why I brought along the meanest prick on the force."

Patrick's smile widened. He knew exactly what Downes wanted. They had played this game before.

It was seven-thirty and the living room lights were on in Gary's house. Downes could hear the mindless chatter of the TV set when he rang the bell. A moment later, Gary opened the door. He was barefoot and wearing jeans and a Whitaker football team tee shirt. The presence of four policemen on his doorstep confused and frightened him.

"Hi, Gary, remember me?" Downes asked with a cheerful smile.

Gary's brow furrowed. Then, he remembered Sergeant Downes. He was the nice policeman who helped him the night he . . . Gary's initial relief was replaced by anxiety as he recalled the humiliating circumstances of his arrest for peeping. Had the girl he spied on pressed charges? Were these men here to arrest him?

"What do you want?" Gary asked warily.

"Hey, Gary, there's nothing to worry about. I'm here because I need your help. Can I come in?"

Gary hesitated for a moment, but he remembered the good manners Mom had taught him and stepped aside. Downes led the other policemen inside.

"Nice place you got here," Downes commented.

"Thank you. Do you want to sit down?" he asked, acting just the way his mom told him he should act when company called.

"Sure," Downes said, lowering himself onto the sofa. "Say, Gary, could we turn the TV off? It's a little loud."

Gary turned off the set and sat opposite the burly police officer. Gary noticed that none of the other policemen sat down. One stayed by the front door, one stood near the entrance to the hall and the officer with the greasy hair made Gary uncomfortable by moving out of Gary's line of vision and standing behind his armchair.

"Have you heard about the girl who was murdered in Wishing Well Park?" Downes asked.

Gary nodded. Downes took a snapshot of Sandra Whiley out of his breast pocket and handed it to Gary. Whiley was standing on a lawn in front of the business school dressed in shorts and a tank top, acting silly. She was leaning slightly forward because the camera had caught her while she was laughing.

"She sure was pretty, don't you think?" Downes asked.

Gary nodded noncommittally, even though he did think the girl was pretty. After his problem at the Stallion and his arrest at the dorm, Gary was afraid of expressing too much interest in girls.

"We're talking to anyone who might have seen this woman last night. Did you see her?"

"I don't think so."

"Take another look. You were at the Stallion yesterday evening, weren't you?"

Gary's heart rate increased. They were here about that girl. The one he yelled at.

"Hey, Gary, relax. You look uptight," Downes said.

"No I ain't," Gary answered defensively.

"Well, that's good, then, because there's no reason for you to be worried. This is just a routine inquiry. Now, you were at the Stallion last night, weren't you?"

"Yeah."

"Why don't you tell me what you did there."

Gary felt sick. He did not know what to say. Downes waited patiently.

"I don't remember too much what happened. I was drinking a lot."

"Did you try to pick up a girl at the bar?" Downes prodded.

"I . . . I might have."

Downes lifted his head a fraction of an inch and made eye contact with Bob Patrick.

"Look, Harmon," Patrick barked, "we know you attacked a girl at the bar, so can the shit."

Gary's head swiveled around. Patrick loomed over him. He looked as if he might hit Gary.

"Calm down, Officer Patrick," Downes said firmly. "Mr. Harmon invited us into his home. He's not a suspect and that remark was uncalled for."

Patrick stared hard at Gary, but said nothing more.

"Sorry about that, Gary, but we did talk to the bartender and some other witnesses and they told us about the argument you had with a girl. Were they telling the truth?"

Gary hung his head. He wished Steve or Donna were there to protect him, but they were on their honeymoon.

"Well, Gary?"

"I got a little mad. I shouldn't of."

"What made you mad?"

"I don't know," Gary mumbled.

"You wouldn't be rude to a young lady without a reason. Am I right?"

Gary looked down at the floor. He didn't know what to say. Downes let him sit like that for a while, then he said, "I have a suggestion to make. Why don't we continue our conversation at the station. Is that all right with you?"

Gary's head snapped up. He looked panicky.

"You ain't gonna arrest me?"

Downes laughed a deep, friendly laugh.

"Arrest you? What gave you that idea? I want your help, that's all. We'll drive you home as soon as we're through. You do want to help me, don't you, Gary?"

Gary hunched forward a little and wrung his hands in his lap. He didn't like the police station. He was scared to go there.

Downes leaned close to Gary. "Remember how I helped you out? Remember how I fixed everything for you?"

Gary nodded.

"Do you trust me, Gary? Do you think I'm your friend?"

Gary hesitated.

"I didn't tell your mom about what happened at the college with that girl, did I?"

"No," Gary answered grudgingly.

"Then, will you be my friend and help me solve this terrible case?"

Gary squirmed in his chair. Then, reluctantly, he nodded his head.

"Terrific! Why don't you get dressed and we can go."

Gary went to his bedroom and Downes and the mean policeman followed him. Patrick stood by the door, but Downes went inside the room. The first things he saw were the Stallion football posters and memorabilia.

"You really are a Stallion fan," Downes said while Gary put on his sneakers.

"Yeah," Gary said, brightening. "We're going all the way."

"I sure hope so. I never miss a game."

"Steve bought me season tickets."

"He's a nice guy. Even when he defends his clients in court, he treats us cops with respect. He's a good citizen, just like you."

Gary felt proud that Sergeant Downes thought he was like Steve. He didn't feel so scared now that he understood that he was just being a good citizen and helping the police solve a murder.

"Say, there's one more thing," Downes said as soon as Gary stood up to go. "Would you mind letting these fellas take a look around your place? I'd appreciate that."

"Look around?"

"Yeah. As part of the official investigation. That wouldn't be a problem for you, would it? They'd do it while we were downtown and put everything back real neat."

"Why would they have to look around?"

"We always look around when we're investigating a case, Gary. Good citizens never object. You don't have anything to hide, do you?"

Gary's thoughts turned immediately to the magazines with the pictures of the naked women, but they were hidden so well he was certain no one could find them.

"Well, Gary?"

"I guess it's okay."

"That's great," Downes told him, beaming with good fellowship as he fished a piece of paper out of his pocket and handed it and a pen to Gary.

"Why don't you read this and put your John Hancock at the bottom where I've put the X?"

"What is it?"

"A consent to search form. It's just routine."

Gary looked at the form. He could read, but it took a lot of effort and this paper had a lot of hard words on it. After a minute of struggling, he got tired and signed. Behind Gary, Bob Patrick smiled. Downes saw him, but kept his composure. Everything was going according to plan.

Gary recognized the room right away. It was the same windowless interrogation room where he was questioned the night he was arrested for peeping.

"Can I get you something to drink?" Sergeant Downes asked as soon as Gary was seated. Gary was thirsty, but he shook his head. He did not want to be left alone with the mean policeman, who was lounging in a chair by the door, staring at him.

"Okay, then," Downes said, taking a seat across from Gary. "I don't want to keep you long, so why don't we get down to it. What happened between you and that girl at the Stallion?"

Gary shrugged his shoulders and stared at the tabletop.

"I guess I got mad."

"That's no big thing. If I didn't get mad at you for what you did at the dorm, do you think I'm gonna get bent out of shape because you got mad at some girl? She probably didn't treat you right is what I'm guessing."

"I was trying to get a date with that girl and she said no. That's why I was mad."

Downes shook his head in disbelief and chuckled.

"Is that all? Hell, the way you've been acting, I thought you had some deep, dark secret. So, what happened?"

"Chris said she wanted to go out with me."

"Chris?"

"He's a friend of Kevin Booth. Kevin and Chris was sitting with me."

"So this Chris said this girl was giving you the eye?"

Gary nodded. "Only I don't think she really was. I think Chris was playing a joke on me."

"Why's that?"

"She really didn't seem to like me."

"What made you think she didn't like you?"

"She wouldn't let me buy her a drink and she told me to go away. Then, she . . . she . . ."

"Go on."

"She said I was stupid," Gary blurted out. His cheeks turned scarlet.

"Well, shit, Gary, that girl had no cause to do that, did she, Pat?"

Gary looked at the other policeman to catch his response, but there was none. Bob Patrick continued to stare with his hard, cold eyes.

Downes leaned across the table. "Gary," he asked in a low, sympathetic tone, "what did you do when you got mad at Karen Nix?"

"I . . . I guess I grabbed her."

"What's all this 'guess' shit?" Patrick snapped angrily. "Either you did or you didn't."

Patrick's loud voice startled Gary and he looked to Downes for help.

"Relax, Pat," Downes said.

"I'm getting sick and tired of this little prick, Dennis. He's jerking us around."

"Officer Patrick, my title is Sergeant, and I'm conducting this interview."

Downes stared hard at Patrick. Patrick tried to meet his stare, then backed down. Gary was elated. Downes turned back to Gary.

"I know this is hard for you, but we need your help to catch the killer. So, tell me what you said to Karen Nix when you grabbed her."

Gary hung his head. He felt nauseous.

"I . . . I guess I said something like I would kill her."

"Then, Arnie Block came over, didn't he?" Downes asked.

Gary nodded. Downes looked relaxed, but he wasn't, because they were about to get down to the real nitty-gritty.

"What did you do after you left the bar?" he asked in a casual tone.

"I don't remember so good. I think I just walked around "

"Did you go any special place?"

"I went to see Steve."

"Steve Mancini?"

Gary nodded.

"Did you see him?"

"No. I went by his house, but he wasn't there."

Downes leaned forward expectantly. "What did you do then?"

"I went to the Ponderosa."

Downes's pulse rate jumped. The Ponderosa was a workingman's bar near the Riverview Motel. It was a few blocks from where they were sitting. So was Sandra Whiley's boardinghouse. If Whiley was walking back to her place along High Street and Gary was walking toward the Ponderosa from Steve Mancini's house, they could have met.

"How did you get to the Ponderosa, Gary?"

"I walked down High."

"So you went by the park?"

"Yeah."

"What side of the street did you walk on?"

"Uhm, the other side. Not where the park is."

Downes leaned forward. "This is real important, Gary. The murder could have happened right when you passed by the park, so you could be an eyewitness." Gary looked surprised. "I want you to think real hard. Did you see anything going on in the park when you passed by?"

Gary's brow furrowed as he struggled to concentrate. Then, Gary's face broke into a wide grin.

"I did see something, Sergeant Downes. I did."

"What did you see, Gary?"

"I seen a guy and this girl. They were hugging."

"Where did you see this?"

"By the big park entrance, near where you go down to the wishing well, only closer to the street."

"What did the man look like?"

"I'm not sure. It was dark."

"How tall was the man?"

"I don't know. He was leaning on her."

"Leaning?"

"Yeah. You know. Hugging her. Leaning down."

"Gary, this is important. Think real hard. Could the girl have been Sandy? Could the man be the murderer?"

Gary was quiet for a moment. Downes edged forward

on his seat. When Gary raised his head, he looked apologetic.

"They was just hugging, Sergeant Downes. I'm sorry, but they was just hugging."

An hour later, Downes and Patrick stepped into the hall, leaving Gary alone in the interrogation room.

"What do you think?" Downes asked.

"I don't know. What about you?"

Downes shook his head. "He seems too dumb to lie, but I don't believe in coincidence. He's admitted to being at the park right around the time the murder probably was committed, he threatened to kill a girl who looks a lot like Whiley."

"I think we need to get a D.A. in on this before we go any further," Patrick said.

Downes frowned. Earl Ridgely had instructed Downes to call him if there was a break in the case, but Ridgely was too close to the Harmons. He'd been invited to Donna's wedding and Jesse Harmon had made a sizable contribution to Earl's campaign. Ridgely might insist on getting Gary a lawyer and that would be that.

Becky O'Shay would never suggest getting Harmon a lawyer, but she would try to take the credit if Harmon confessed. Still, she wouldn't interfere with the interrogation and that was the main thing.

"I'm gonna find Becky O'Shay. That will give you some time to soften up Gary."

"How do you want me to work it?" Patrick asked.

Downes thought for a moment. Then, he got an idea. "This probably wouldn't work on most people, but Gary is dumber than a post. Why don't you try the black light?"

After Downes explained what he had in mind, Patrick frowned.

"I don't know, Dennis. That doesn't sound right to me."

"What's the problem?"

107

"It's trickery. It could taint the whole confession, if we get one."

"No it won't. Not if you don't put words in his mouth. Let me tell you how I'd do it."

2

Peter Hale was certain that the bathroom in his rental home had been built for midgets. There was so little space between the tiny tub and the sink that he could only dry himself by standing sideways and the shower-head was so low that Peter had to stoop to catch the water that drizzled out. It sure was a far cry from the walk-in shower in his condo and its four jet-stream nozzles. Still, Peter was in a good mood. He was going out tonight with an attractive, sexy woman and he was certain he was going to have a great time.

Peter wiped away some of the vapor that misted the mirror and combed his hair. He was singing a few bars of "Life in the Fast Lane," one of his favorite Eagles tunes, when the phone rang. Peter wrapped a towel around his waist and rushed into the bedroom.

"Peter?"

"Hi, Becky. I was just getting ready to come over."

"That's why I'm calling. There's an emergency and I have to go to the police station."

"Do you want me to pick you up there?"

"I'm afraid that won't work. This could take all night. I'm going to have to ask for a rain check."

Peter was crushed.

"You've got one," he said jauntily, masking his disappointment. "I know about emergencies. We had them all the time at Hale, Greaves."

"Thanks for taking this so well. Let's talk later in the week."

Becky hung up and a wave of despondency swept over Peter. He flopped onto the bed. He had been really pumped up for this date. He tried to look on the bright side. Having a date cancel at the last minute wasn't the end of the world. He thought of the many times he had been the canceler. Besides, he told himself, there was a gourmet lasagna microwave dinner in the freezer and a Chuck Norris movie on the tube, sustenance for both the body and the mind. He had everything he needed for an exciting evening right at home.

Peter's attempt to kid himself out of his depression failed miserably and only made him more melancholy. He couldn't stay home tonight after getting his hopes up for an evening that would vaguely resemble the good times he used to have. Peter thought about going to the restaurant by himself, but his appetite had disappeared. He contemplated calling Rhonda or picking up a college girl at the Stallion, but his heart wasn't in it. Then, he thought about calling his father.

Peter had been in Whitaker more than a month. Surely that was a long enough exile. Maybe Richard just wanted to scare him. Maybe he wasn't really written out of the will. He would call his father and explain how working for seventeen thousand a year and living in this dump had taught him about the value of money. He would recount a tale or two about the poor unfortunates he was representing. Surely Richard would see that he was a new man with a sense of responsibility. Certainly he would say that all was forgiven and welcome Peter home with open arms.

Peter dialed his father's home number. Richard picked up the phone on the third ring.

"Richard Hale," a strong, confident voice announced.

Peter wanted to say something, but he couldn't speak.

"Hello?" his father said with a tinge of annoyance.

All Peter's energy drained away, leaving him helpless. The receiver at Richard Hale's end dropped angrily onto its cradle.

"Dad, it's Peter," Richard Hale's son whispered into the dead line.

3

Gary looked up anxiously when the door to the interrogation room opened. He had been left alone for almost half an hour and he was getting scared. His anxiety increased when Bob Patrick entered the room.

"Hi, Gary," Patrick said pleasantly, "I brought you a drink."

Before entering the room, Patrick had dried a can of Coke and dusted it with detection powder. Although invisible to the naked eye, the powder would look orange under the ultraviolet light beamed from the tan flashlight Patrick carried. Gary did not want to take the Coke from Patrick, but he was very thirsty. He eyed the officer warily. The fact that Patrick was being nice to him made Gary suspicious.

"Where's Sergeant Downes?"

"He had something to do. He'll be back soon."

Gary took the Coke with his right hand and drank it greedily. Patrick sat down next to Gary and placed the tan flashlight where Gary could see it. Then, Patrick took several crime scene photographs of Sandra Whiley and laid them next to the flashlight. Gary took one quick look at the photos and turned his eyes away.

"What's the matter, Gary?"

"I don't like them p . . . pictures."

"Is it the blood that bothers you?"

"Y . . . yes."

"Most of the killers I've interviewed couldn't look at their victim's blood," Patrick lied. There had been only two homicides in Whitaker County since he had been on the force and he had never interviewed any of the prisoners. "I don't know what it is, but the blood of their victim scared them. Maybe they thought I could see that blood on them even when they had taken great pains to wash it off. What do you think about that, Gary?"

"I don't know," Gary answered, still averting his eyes from the photos.

Patrick gathered up the pictures and put them away. Gary relaxed visibly. Patrick tapped the black light.

"Know what this is?"

Gary shook his head.

"It's a blood machine, a light that can pick up the smallest drop of blood on a killer's hands. Most murderers think that you can wash off the blood of a victim, but you can't. Oh, you can scrub and scrub, but the blood of a murdered person works its way into the skin and no amount of cleaning can make it completely disappear."

Patrick paused to let Gary absorb what he had just said.

"Now you say you didn't kill that girl. Well, I'm open-minded." Patrick picked up the tan flashlight and pointed it at Gary. "Why don't you stick out your hands and we can settle this right now."

Gary wrapped both hands around the Coke can and drew it into his chest.

"What's the matter, Gary? You aren't worried about what the blood machine might show, are you?"

"N . . . no."

"Then open your hands and hold them palm up."

Gary put the can down. He opened his hands and stared at them. There was nothing on them. Very slowly, Gary extended his hands toward Patrick. Patrick pressed the button on the flashlight and directed the ultraviolet beam at Gary's palms. Large iridescent orange splotches appeared on both hands. Gary stared at the orange splotches in horror.

CHAPTER TEN

Dennis Downes and Becky O'Shay conferenced in the small room on the other side of the two-way mirror. Through the glass, Becky could see Gary Harmon. The suspect huddled on his chair, casting frequent frightened looks at Bob Patrick.

"I called Don Bosco from County Mental Health and he's going through his records to see if he has anything on Gary," Downes said.

"Good idea," Becky agreed. "I definitely think you're on to something. Take the magazines." Becky pointed at the pile of sex books the police had found in Gary's house. "We can assume Harmon saved these particular issues for a reason and I've noticed something they have in common. The centerfolds are all blondes like our victim and Karen Nix."

"Good going, Becky. I didn't spot that."

"Were the victim in the gully and the victim in Blaine blond?"

"One was and the girl he peeped on at the college was blond."

"All right!" Becky exclaimed.

"What about the absence of blood on his clothing and in the house?" Downes asked.

"I don't think we should spin our wheels worrying about that. Let the criminalists run their tests. If they don't come up with anything, we can worry about it then. Harmon may have done something as simple as getting rid of his bloody clothes."

"You're right. If he confesses, we'll find out what happened to the blood."

Downes stood up. "It's about time I started questioning Gary again. Do you think I should Mirandize him?"

"You haven't done that yet?"

"I didn't want to spook him. Besides, he's not in custody. I made it clear that he's free to leave whenever he wants to."

"Technically, you may be right, Dennis, but I'd do it now. Harmon's been here for several hours. Some judges would consider him to be in custody."

"Okay. I'm gonna start taping the conversation. You'll be able to hear everything we say in here once I switch on the intercom."

"Good. You know, it might not be a bad idea to have Don Bosco sit in here with me. The observations of a trained psychologist could be useful at trial."

Downes left to get a tape recorder. Becky was really excited. She rarely got a chance to be in on an investigation from the beginning and this was no ordinary investigation. Her date with Peter Hale was forgotten. Dating Richard Hale's son might have been useful, but Peter wasn't going anywhere. She might not need him to get a job, anyway. O'Shay's plans did not include a long stay in Whitaker. She would gain experience here, then try to land a job with the Multnomah County District Attorney's Office in Portland or the more prestigious United States Attorney's Office. After a few years, she planned to parlay that experience into a job in a big firm where she could make some real money. If she could claim credit for breaking a case involving a serial killer she might not have long to wait before she was on her way.

. . .

"What happened with the black light?" Downes asked Patrick. They were in the hall outside the interrogation room.

"Gary freaked. He started moaning and wringing his hands as soon as I turned on the light."

"Did he admit to anything?"

"No, but he's pretty scared. If he's going to crack, it'll be now."

Gary stood up when Dennis Downes preceded Bob Patrick into the room.

"Can I go home now? I don't want to stay here," he pleaded, casting a worried glance at Bob Patrick.

"I have just a few more questions I want to ask you."

"Can I go then?"

"Oh, sure. And don't think I don't appreciate all you're doing to help the police. I wouldn't keep you here if I didn't think you could help the people of this city solve this terrible case."

Downes held up the tape recorder. While Gary looked at it, Downes flashed a quick look at Bob Patrick.

"To make sure I get what you say down right," Downes said, "I'd like to use a tape recorder. My memory ain't what it used to be and this gadget saves me from having to write everything down. Do you mind if I tape-record our conversation?"

"No."

"Great. Before we get started, I'm going to read you your *Miranda* rights."

"What are you doing that for?" Patrick asked angrily. "This punk's just gonna hide behind a lawyer's skirts like every other guilty asshole."

Downes jumped to his feet.

"I've had enough out of you, Officer Patrick. Gary has nothing to hide. If he does want a lawyer that's his right. Now, I expect you to apologize to Mr. Harmon."

"You've got to be kidding?"

"Apologize, then get out."

114

Gary watched Bob Patrick flush with anger, then he heard him mumble an apology and storm out, slamming the door behind him. He felt so relieved that he sagged on his chair.

"Good riddance," Downes said.

"I don't like him."

Downes leaned forward and told Gary, in a confidential tone, "I don't either. The guy has no respect for a good citizen like you. Hell, you'd never hide behind a lawyer, would you?"

"No," Gary answered, shaking his head vigorously.

They smiled at each other. Downes turned on the tape recorder.

"Well, Gary, to business. First, though, I'm going to give you those *Miranda* warnings we talked about."

Downes proceeded to tell Gary that he had a right to remain silent and could have a lawyer present during questioning. Gary said he understood his rights, but wanted to talk to Downes, anyway.

"I want to help catch the guy who killed that girl," Gary said.

"That's great."

Downes had Gary talk about the incident at the Stallion again, so it would be on the tape. Then he drew his chair a little closer.

"Gary, I want to go back to something you told me that I think is really important. Remember you said you were on the way to the Ponderosa after you left Steve's house when you saw a man and woman at the entrance to Wishing Well Park?"

Gary nodded.

"I want you to think about that couple again."

Gary thought real hard. Then, he shook his head.

"I just remember they was hugging, Sergeant Downes."

"Can you remember what they were wearing?"

"No."

"Hair color?"

"Uh uh."

Downes seemed frustrated for a moment. Then, he thought of something.

"Gary, you think you can't remember anything else, but I'm going to tell you a few things I learned in police work. Have you ever heard of the subconscious mind?"

"I think so," Gary answered hesitantly, not wanting to admit that he had no idea what Downes was talking about.

"Right now you're hearing me and seeing me with the conscious mind. That's what you use when you're awake. But you aren't watching those two at the park now, are you?"

"No."

"How could you tell me about them?"

Gary thought for a moment. Then, his face lit up.

"I remembered."

"Absolutely right. But where was that memory stored all this time?"

Gary thought some more. "I don't know," he said, a little dejected that he was not able to answer Sergeant Downes's question.

"Hey, don't feel bad. The answer is tricky. See, you have a subconscious mind that stores stuff when you aren't thinking about it. Not too many people know that. The trick in police work is to help a witness unlock his subconscious mind so he can remember things he thinks he's forgotten."

"How can I do that?" Gary asked eagerly.

"By getting relaxed and concentrating. The more you relax, the easier it becomes to unlock the subconscious. I want you to close your eyes and get real loose and we'll see what we can do together to catch Sandy's killer, because, from what I know, I think there's a good chance you saw Sandy and her killer when you walked by Wishing Well Park."

Gary did as he was told. The two men sat in silence for a few minutes, until Gary opened his eyes.

"It's no use. All I see is them two hugging."

"Hmm," Downes said thoughtfully. "You know,

116

Gary, if those two weren't Sandy and her killer, they probably were hugging, but what if it was Sandy and the murderer?"

"You mean they wouldn't be hugging?"

"I didn't say that. I don't want to put words in your mouth. What I'm saying is that the mind can play tricks. For instance, you wanted to hug Karen Nix, didn't you?"

Gary squirmed in his seat and blushed.

"Come on, Gary," Downes said with a hearty laugh. "Karen Nix is pretty. Any red-blooded American man would want to hug her. Don't tell me it didn't enter your mind."

Gary hesitated.

"Come on now. We've got to be honest with each other here. You did want to hug her, didn't you?"

Gary hung his head and mumbled, "Yeah."

"All right. So, when you saw this boy and girl together, you put them in a romantic situation. But there are other things that look like hugging. What they were really doing could be registered in your subconscious mind."

"What could they be doing if they weren't hugging?"

"You tell me."

Gary puzzled out the problem. It took a while, then he brightened.

"They coulda been wrestling."

"Hey, why didn't I think of that? You're one step ahead of me already, Gary. This is great! Do you see what I mean about the subconscious mind? Your conscious mind saw two people hugging, but they might also have been doing something else. Your subconscious mind will know the truth. What I want you to do is relax, close your eyes and picture that night."

"I'll try," Gary said, closing his eyes and leaning his head back.

"Okay. Now, maybe this will help. Think about what you were wearing. Can you do that?"

Gary nodded.

"What do you see?"

"Uh, I think it was jeans and a short-sleeve shirt."

"Jeans like you've got on now?"

"Yeah. I got four pairs of jeans and it was another one."

"Where is that pair now, Gary?"

"In the closet."

Downes tried not to show his excitement. "Have you done anything to those jeans since you wore them?"

"Oh, yeah. I have to wash them when they're dirty. It's on the list my mom made up. Every Saturday is wash day and I washed everything in the hamper right when I got up, because I was going to the wedding."

Downes's heart sank. Whiley had been murdered Friday night or early Saturday morning. If there was blood on Gary's jeans and shirt, it was gone now. Out loud, Downes said, "Okay, you're doing great. Keep your eyes closed and feel how warm it is. Picture yourself in your jeans and short-sleeve shirt. You're walking by the park. Can you see the park?"

"Yeah."

"Is it warm, Gary?"

"Yeah."

"Hey, that's great. You're cookin'. So, go on. What do you see?"

"I see them stone fences."

"Good. Now slow up a little. What do you see? Relax and let it come."

There was silence in the room. Downes leaned forward expectantly. He could see Gary's features contort with effort. Then, Gary's eyes opened.

"It's no good. I didn't see anything new."

"Not a thing?" Downes said, making no effort to hide his disappointment. Gary felt terrible. Sergeant Downes had so much faith in him and he was letting him down.

"Can I try again?" Gary asked. He closed his eyes and tried to relax. There were the two stone pillars and the path between them. And on the path were the boy and the girl. He was holding her, leaning down, which meant

118

he was taller. And she was . . . what? Leaning into him? No. Gary slowed time in his mind, trying hard to see, because he wanted to help Sergeant Downes.

"She's leaning back, pushing him away."

"You saw that?" Downes asked excitedly.

"Real clear."

"Is it Sandy?"

"I can't say for sure."

"You've got to try, son. You're doing so well and this is so important."

"I am trying, but . . ."

"You know what might help? Why don't you picture a movie screen in your head and watch what's happening on it. That way, you can slow down the movie to make it easier to see."

"That's what I done," Gary said proudly.

"Pictured a movie screen?"

"No, slowed everything down."

"You done that yourself?"

"Yeah."

"Well, I'll be damned. You know, Gary, you might be a natural at this stuff."

Gary blushed at the compliment. "I just want to get this guy."

"I know you do, so let's see if you can tell for sure if it's Sandy."

"Okay," Gary said, letting his head sag back. This time he did what Sergeant Downes had suggested and watched the action on a big movie screen take him back in time. The park appeared, flowing like water at first, then solidifying until only the edges were wavy. As he approached the park entrance the scene slowed to a crawl and the two people started to appear. Who were they? He was taller than she, but his face and body were in shadow. Gary was opposite them now. He willed the picture to grind to a halt and strained to see if the woman's features were the same as . . . as those in the photograph of Sandra Whiley at the college that Sergeant Downes had shown him.

119

"I can see them. She's kind of turning and he grabs her."

"By her shoulders, her shirt?"

"By the shirt. She's making this real fast turn when he grabs her and she whips around and I think they're probably hanging on to each other, kinda . . . you know."

"Go on, Gary. This is great. Can you see her face?"

"Sorta, but it's like . . . I don't know. You probably wouldn't know me if I was on a dark street."

"But you were directly across from her."

"Yeah, when he pulled her back and grabbed her."

"Was it her, Gary? Was it Sandy? Slow the picture. Make it lighter on the screen. You can do it, Gary. You can add some light. What do you say?"

"I'm . . . I think . . ."

"Go ahead. Say it."

"I'm sure it's her. The one that got killed. And . . . and that's the murderer, too, because he jerked her back. They weren't hugging."

"They weren't?"

"No, no. 'Cause he was grabbing her and she was pulling away and he . . ."

"What? Jerked her back?"

"Yeah. Like that. A jerk, so she spinned around. And that's when I seen her."

"Did you see anything shiny, Gary? It would probably have been right then. In that split second."

"Shiny?"

"We know there was a weapon."

"Boy, I don't . . ."

"You don't see a weapon? We haven't found the weapon, yet. We don't know what he used to kill Sandy."

"Oh."

"So, look at his right hand. Most people are right-handed. It would probably be there."

Gary concentrated real hard, running the picture forward and backward while Downes waited quietly. He could see Sandy. She looked scared.

"What have you got, Gary?"

Gary's eyes opened. "Nothing more," he answered groggily. He was getting tired.

"But you know it's the killer and Sandy?"

Gary nodded. "I could see she was scared."

"Really? You didn't say that before. That's good. See, we're making progress. How are you holding up?"

"I'm hungry."

"Do you want a Coke and a burger?"

"A burger would be good."

"Let's take a break. Then, we'll try again."

An hour and a half later, Dennis Downes was frustrated and Gary Harmon looked exhausted. Gary's eyes were bloodshot and his hair was in disarray from the times he had run his fingers through it. The remains of a greasy hamburger, an empty can of Coke and several paper containers for coffee littered the tabletop. They had been over and over Gary's walk by the entrance to Wishing Well Park and Gary still would not give any more details. Downes knew he had reached a dead end with his current approach. He was thinking of giving up when an idea occurred to him.

"Straight across from me," Gary mumbled sleepily. "I know he's taller than she is, but I still can't see enough. I'm sorry, Sergeant."

"It's okay, Gary. Don't apologize. You've given us our first clues and you've also given me an idea. A way to break through to the truth. Would you be willing to try one more thing before you go home?"

"I'm awful tired, but if you think I can help, I'll try."

"Terrific, Gary. Now, let me tell you my idea. If this doesn't work, we'll call it a night. Have you seen people on TV who can predict the future or read minds?"

Gary nodded.

"Those people are called psychics and some of them

121

help the police. If there's a murder, you give them an object that belonged to the murdered person and they can project their supernatural mind into the mind of the killer through this object and find a missing body or see who did the killing through the dead victim's eyes. Based on what I've seen you do, I suspect you have a very developed supernatural mind. I want you to use it to help me out."

"Gee, Sergeant, I've never done anything like that," Gary said. He was beat. All he wanted to do was sleep. He didn't even think he had a supernatural mind.

"I'm not surprised you haven't used your supernatural mind," Downes said. "You didn't even know you had these powers of the subconscious mind, until tonight."

Downes stood and stretched. "We're gonna need something of Sandy's for this. You sit here while I get it. Do you want another burger or some coffee?"

"That would be good."

Downes left the interrogation room and went next door. Becky O'Shay looked as if she was ready to fall asleep. Sitting next to her was Don Bosco, a short, squat man dressed in tan chinos and a short-sleeve shirt. Bosco had monstrously hairy forearms and bushy eyebrows. There was even an extra-thick growth of black hair on the psychologist's ears.

"What was that all about?" Bosco asked when Downes entered the room.

"Just an idea I want to try," Downes said.

After he explained his plan, Downes asked, "What do you think, Becky?"

"I think he's covering up. You've got him admitting he saw the murder. We need to have him slip up on a detail that will prove he committed the murder. I say, go for it."

"Do you see any problems, Don?" Downes asked.

Bosco looked troubled. "I think it could get risky. Harmon is reacting like someone who's mentally handicapped . . ."

122

"He's not that dumb."

"I don't know," Bosco answered hesitantly. "And, even if he's of normal intelligence, he's awfully tired. He's going to be susceptible to suggestion. You have to be very careful not to lead him. Even telling him that he will be able to see things with his psychic powers is suggestion."

"Okay. I'll be extra careful. Don't worry."

Gary held the picture of Sandra Whiley in one hand and her Crusader's Cross in the other. He was leery of holding the dead girl's jewelry, but Downes assured him the object would heighten the psychic forces.

"Okay, Gary, close your eyes and relax like you did before."

Downes waited in silence as Gary tilted his head back. After a moment, his head sagged sideways until his cheek almost touched his shoulder. Gary's head was swimming. Fatigue loosened his grip on the Crusader's Cross and the chain slipped out of his hand and dangled just off the floor.

"Can you feel the cross in your hand?" Downes asked.

"Uh huh."

"Good. Gary, I'm going to teach you a trick you can do with that cross because of your special powers. It's a trick us ordinary folks can't do and it's called 'projection transfer.' That's Sandy's cross. She was wearing it when she was killed. I want you to project your supernatural mind into that cross and tell me what Sandy saw and what the killer saw. Let yourself go."

Gary let his mind run loose but the picture on the screen was scrambled.

"Do you see Sandy?" Downes asked.

"I'm starting to see them more along. You know, after I walked by," Gary said in a voice so heavy with fatigue that his words were slurred. "She . . . she's . . . He's holding her."

"All right," Downes said, suddenly excited. "This is what we want."

"He's hanging on to her."

"Like she's trying to get away?"

"Yeah. It seems like she slapped him."

"Sandy fought back?"

"Uh huh. And then . . ."

"Yes, Gary. Concentrate. Use your powers."

"His right hand. It's like it was going down."

"Dropping or . . . ?"

"Like he was hitting her."

"This is what we want. This is it, Gary. Now, we know he grabbed her and pulled her back and she whipped around. That's what you saw as you passed by. Then she hit him and he hits her with his right hand. Now I want you to look for one more thing. At this point, the unknown man is hitting her. It had to be with something. Something in his right hand. What is he using? It's very important. I want you to look at his right hand through Sandy's eyes and tell me what you see."

Gary concentrated as hard as he could. What would it be? Then he remembered what the two women said at the wedding about the girl's face being chopped up. What was it they said the killer used?

"I'm trying, but I can't picture it."

"If anyone can, you can, Gary. You have a power that no one else has. You are the man with the power."

Gary opened his eyes. "It's almost there, but . . ."

Downes thought about the location of the head wounds. He stood up.

"Picture it, Gary," he said, unconsciously moving his right hand up and down. "Tell me what's in his hand."

Gary closed his eyes and recalled the autopsy photograph that Bob Patrick had shown him, just before he used the black light. Then, he remembered what the lady at the wedding had said.

"It's shiny," he said suddenly.

"Huh?"

"It's metal shiny."

"Like a . . . like what? Shiny like a knife blade?"

"Yeah, shiny."

"You've got knives, Gary. Is it like a knife you own?"

"Not a knife."

"Not a knife?"

"He chopped her up. Chopped her with a . . . a hatchet."

Downes's heart leaped. "What kind of hatchet?"

"I can't see the blade, but it seems like a hatchet."

There was a drawer in the long interrogation table. In it were pens, paper and a ruler. Downes took the picture of Sandy from Gary's right hand and replaced it with the ruler.

"Take hold of this ruler."

Gary did as he was told.

"Gary, you are unbelievable. I've never seen anyone with your powers. Now, to me, this is a ruler, but with your supernatural mind, you can use 'projection transfer' to transfer this ruler to the hatchet. Do you have it? Can you feel the shiny, silver hatchet?"

Gary nodded.

"All right. Here's where you do your thing. I'm gonna stand and so are you. I'm gonna be Sandy, so I'll squat down some, and you're gonna let that hatchet lead you to strike like the killer did, so we can see how Sandy was killed.

"Okay, stand up and keep your eyes closed. I'm right in front of you. Only now I'm Sandy. Are you ready?"

Gary nodded.

"Let it flow, Gary. First hit. Where was it?"

Gary brought his arm up sluggishly. "Top of the head," he said, as his arm slowly descended.

"This is great. Then what?"

Gary saw it all. His arm swung sideways.

"Another to the right side," he said. "And another."

Blood was spraying from Sandy's face as the blade sliced into it. Gary's arm rose and fell. Her face was breaking up as she fell back, flying away like shards from a fractured mirror. Gary stopped.

"What's the matter?" Downes asked.

"I don't like her face like this."

"What do you mean?"

"The blood."

"You can see her face chopped up?"

"Yes."

"Where is the killer, Gary?"

"Over her."

"Can you see his face?"

"No."

"Try hard, Gary."

"I can't see it."

"Okay, guy. You're doing fantastic. Hang in there. I've never met anyone with powers like yours. So, let's use those powers. Let them flow through Sandy's medallion. Let God help you see that hatchet. Can you see it?"

"Yes."

"Okay. The killer took the hatchet away. Where is it now?"

"He . . . he threw it away."

"Where, Gary?"

"He threw it 'cause of the blood. He didn't want to see all that blood."

"But where did he throw it? Help us find it. Project yourself into that hatchet."

Gary's head wobbled. He wet his lips.

"He's running to a dark place because he's scared."

"Someplace dark? But where?"

"Just dark. I don't know."

"Come on, Gary. Don't let me down now. Use your special powers."

"I'm trying, Sergeant, but he's too far from Sandy to see him."

"You mean he's out of the park?"

"Yeah. She can't see him."

"Where is Sandy?"

"By the well."

"How did she get there?"

"She . . . she ran."

126

"Okay."

"Then, after he chopped her, she was by the well."

"You saw that?"

"Yeah."

"Is there much blood on the killer?"

"Yes."

"Did the killer clean off that blood?"

"I can't see. He's too far away."

"Okay. One last try at something. Why did the killer murder Sandy? Do you know why he did it?"

Gary thought about the girl at the dorm and the girl at the Stallion and how he wanted them to love him. Maybe the killer asked Sandy to be his girl and she said no, like the girl at the bar.

"He wanted Sandy to be nice to him, but she said no."

"To be nice?"

"To love him, but she wouldn't love him and he got mad."

"Like you got mad at Karen Nix?"

"Yeah."

Downes should have been exhausted, but he was so elated he did not feel the fatigue.

"Did I help you?" Gary asked.

"Oh, yeah. You've been a big help."

"Can I go home now?"

"Not just yet."

"Why?"

"Gary, I'm gonna be honest with you. We have a problem here."

"What problem?"

"The problem of how you know so much about Sandy's murder."

"I seen it with my powers."

"Well, that's probably it, but that wouldn't explain one thing. Bob Patrick told me what he saw on your hands."

Gary's eyes widened.

"What did you see, Gary?"

"B . . . blood."

"Why do you think you saw the blood?"

"I don't know."

"Blood doesn't just appear on someone's hands. Where did it come from?"

Gary understood what Downes was suggesting and he started to squirm on his chair.

"Oh no, Sergeant. I couldn't of done that."

"Do you know what you just said, Gary? You said 'couldn't.' You didn't say 'I did not kill that girl.' Why didn't you say, flat out, that you did not kill Sandy?"

"I . . . I don't know."

"You were drunk that night, weren't you?"

"Yeah."

"And you told me that you don't remember everything clearly because you had too much to drink."

Gary nodded.

"Think about it. Why did you say 'couldn't' instead of 'didn't'?"

Gary looked at Downes with pleading eyes and asked, "Do . . . do you think I killed that girl?"

"I don't know, Gary. I wasn't there. Only Sandy and her killer were there. But you'd know in your heart, if you did it. Even if you couldn't remember with your conscious mind, because you were so drunk, your subconscious mind would know."

"I . . . I don't remember killing anyone, Sergeant. Honest. If . . . if I did, I don't remember."

Gary licked his lips. Could he have killed Sandy and forgotten? Could he have done the things he saw on the movie screen?

"Well, Gary?"

"I . . . I couldn't have done that," Gary said, desperately. "No, no, I couldn't. Could I?"

"I don't know, Gary. Why don't we talk about that?"

PART FOUR

THE CHANCE
OF A LIFETIME

CHAPTER ELEVEN

1

Peter was so depressed that he did not fall asleep until two-thirty in the morning, giving him a grand total of two hours sack time before he was wrenched out of bed by the ringing of the phone.

"Hello," he rasped as he squinted at the clock.

"Pete, it's Steve Mancini."

"Steve? Aren't you on your honeymoon?"

"I was. Donna and I are on our way back to Whitaker. Gary's been arrested."

"He didn't get arrested for peeping again?" asked Peter. He had told Steve about Gary's arrest and Steve had saved Gary's job. He had also decided to keep the information about the arrest from Donna and Gary's parents.

"Gary is charged with murder, Pete. It's that girl at the wishing well."

"Holy shit!"

"I won't be back in Whitaker until eleven or so. He needs a lawyer, right away. The cops will make mincemeat out of him if they get Gary alone."

"Steve, I'm very sympathetic. I mean, Gary seems like a nice guy, and I was glad to help him out, but I'm not your man. I've been handling criminal cases for . . .

what? Two months? The only case I tried by myself was a suspended license charge, and I lost it."

"I'm not asking you to take the case. I just want you to make certain that Gary doesn't do anything stupid before I talk to him."

"Why don't you call Amos or someone else with more experience?"

"No offense, but I doubt Geary is sober at this hour and the attorneys who practice criminal law in Whitaker make Bozo the Clown look like Perry Mason. You're the only one I can trust to do this the right way."

Peter had met some of the other lawyers who practiced in the Whitaker criminal courts. Mancini was right. They weren't all that swift. And Steve only wanted Peter to baby-sit with his brother-in-law until he got back to town. It was the least he could do for one of the few people in Whitaker he could call a friend.

"What do you want me to tell Gary?" Peter asked.

"You'll do it?"

"Yeah, yeah. Come on. Brief me."

"I owe you big."

"And don't forget it. So, what should I do at the jail?"

Peter stood when Gary stumbled into the room where Peter's abortive interview with Christopher Mammon had taken place. In the weak rays of dawn, Harmon's face seemed drained of color. There were dark circles under his eyes and his uncombed hair was mussed from his brief sleep.

"I'm Peter Hale, Gary. I helped you out when you were arrested at the college. Do you remember me?"

Gary nodded.

"Why don't you sit down."

Peter indicated the metal folding chair on the other side of the wooden table. Gary shuffled forward. A sour odor assailed Peter as soon as Gary drew close. It was a unique combination of fear, sweat and disinfectant that Peter had come to associate with the incarcerated. He pushed himself back from the table to widen the distance between himself and the prisoner.

"Are they treating you all right?" Peter asked.

Gary nodded. "When can I go home?"

"I don't know, Gary. I think you'll have to stay for a while."

"I don't like it here."

"Yeah, well, no one likes jail."

"Can't you get me out?"

"I'm not going to be your lawyer, Gary. Steve Mancini asked me to help out until he comes back. He's driving here from Portland, right now. He should be in Whitaker by noon and I'm sure he'll come see you."

"Sergeant Downes said I was helping to catch the killer. He said I was a good detective. Why won't he let me go?"

"Maybe the sergeant can't let you out. You're charged with a pretty serious crime. I think you'll need a judge's permission."

"Will Steve ask the judge to help me?"

"You bet," Peter answered. Steve had told Peter that bail was not automatic in a murder case. If the state opposed release, there would have to be a hearing. Gary looked so pathetic that Peter did not have the heart to tell him that he might not be able to get out of jail.

"I don't like jail. I'm all locked in. And I don't like the people here. They scare me. They call me names and say things about that girl. They say I'm going to die in the electric chair. They say my brain will boil and melt."

"Gary, there is no electric chair in Oregon. Those men are teasing you. Ignore them."

"I can't. They say it all the time. Please get me out. You got me out when I was arrested before."

"That was different. I just happened to be walking through the campus when you were caught. I really didn't do anything. Sergeant Downes decided not to arrest you. If you'd been charged, I wouldn't have been your lawyer."

Gary looked so sad that Peter asked, "Have you talked to the police?" in an effort to distract him.

133

"Uh-huh."

"How long did you talk to them?"

"A long time."

"An hour? Two hours? Can you tell me the exact time?"

"It was a really long time. I got sleepy. I ate three burgers."

"And you were talking to the cops all that time?"

Gary nodded.

"Why do the police think you killed Sandra Whiley? Did you tell Sergeant Downes you killed her?"

"No. I just seen the girl killed."

"You saw the murder?"

"Part with my eyes and part with my mind."

"I'm not following you. What do you mean, you saw part of the murder with your mind?"

"I got these powers. Supernatural powers. I never knew I had 'em, but I do. Sergeant Downes showed me how to use them to see who killed Sandy. I was real tired, but I did it to help. Now I'll lose my job because I can't go to work. Mom will be so mad."

"I'm sure someone will talk to the college about your job and your mom won't be mad. She loves you. She knows it's not your fault you can't go to work. Now, try to think about why you're locked up. What do you mean you saw Sandy killed?"

"With my powers, I can close my eyes and see what happened in the past."

"You mean you make it up?"

"No, I really see it happen. Only a few people got my powers. Sergeant Downes said I had the best powers of anyone. Better even than those people on TV."

"What did you tell Sergeant Downes you saw using your powers?"

"I seen Sandy being killed."

"Did you see who killed her?"

Gary shook his head. "It was dark. I couldn't see his face. But I seen him do it."

134

"How much of the evening can you remember when you don't use your powers?"

Gary looked sheepish.

"I don't remember a lot of it too well. Everyone was buying me drinks because of the wedding."

"I'm going to ask you a serious question and I want you to try real hard to answer it."

Gary sat up straight and concentrated so he could give Peter the right answer.

"Is it possible that you killed that girl, but you don't remember because you were drinking?"

Gary licked his lips. He looked very frightened.

"I . . . I don't think I killed her."

"You don't think you killed her? That's not the same as being sure."

"I . . . I couldn't have killed that girl," Gary said uncertainly.

"Then how do you know so much about the murder? I don't buy this superpower stuff. I want you to be honest with me. Did you do it?"

Gary swallowed. He was chewing his lip and looking around the narrow room as if trying to find a way out.

"Gary?"

Gary's head swung back slowly toward Peter. There were tears in his eyes.

"I want to go home."

"Try to stay on track, Gary. We were talking about the murder."

"I don't want to talk about that no more. I didn't do nothing bad. I'm a good boy. I want Mama. I want to go home."

2

At eight o'clock Sunday morning Becky O'Shay called District Attorney Earl Ridgely at home and asked him to meet her at his office. When he arrived at nine-thirty, Becky was waiting for him. Ridgely's spacious corner office looked out on Wishing Well Park and the slow meanderings of the Camas River, but O'Shay had no interest in the scenery. She sprang to her feet as soon as her boss walked in.

"We got him," Becky said excitedly. "He confessed. We have motive . . ."

"Slow down, Becky. Who are you talking about?"

"The man who killed Sandra Whiley. We nailed him."

Ridgely flushed with anger. "Why wasn't I informed? I was supposed to be notified if there was a break in the case."

"We weren't certain we had the right man until early this morning. Dennis Downes and I decided against waking you at 4 A.M."

Ridgely's anger disappeared as quickly as it had come. Catching Whiley's killer was the important thing.

"Who is it?"

"Gary Harmon."

"Not Jesse and Alice's boy?"

Becky nodded. Ridgely walked slowly to his chair and sat down. He felt sick.

"I've known Gary since he was born. I was at Donna's wedding, yesterday."

"I know. It's terrible. But there's no doubt he did it."

"What's your evidence?"

Becky started with the peeping incident and explained about the pornography discovered in the search of Gary's home. Then she moved to the attack on Karen Nix and Gary's threat to kill her.

"Nix and Whiley look alike. We think Nix was the intended victim and Harmon attacked Whiley by mistake. It's obvious from the peeping incident, the porno and the way he handled his rejection by Nix that Harmon is weird where women are concerned."

"Do you know anything about Gary?" Ridgely asked.

"I watched part of the interrogation."

"He's mildly retarded. He's like a kid."

"And children have poor impulse control. Besides, we have what amounts to a confession. At first, Harmon claimed he didn't know anything about the murder. Then, he admitted seeing the killer fighting with Whiley at the entrance to Wishing Well Park. The more he talked, the more detail he gave."

"Did he ever admit he killed Whiley?"

"No, but he didn't deny doing it."

"What did he say?"

"He started by claiming he was too drunk to remember anything, but he ended up giving Dennis details about the murder that only the killer would know."

"Such as?"

"He knew the location of the blows that killed Whiley and he said the murder weapon was a hatchet."

"What?!"

"A pretty odd choice for a murder weapon, right? And, coincidentally, the weapon used to kill those other two women."

Ridgely looked stunned. "Did you question Gary about the other murders?"

"No. We wanted to concentrate on Whiley. We were afraid we'd spook him if we started asking about other crimes. But the hatchet did it for me. Dennis says we've been keeping the type of weapon used on the other women a secret as a check against false confessions."

Ridgely swiveled his chair. Morning fog was twisting through the low brown hills across the river. Becky waited expectantly while her boss digested what she had just told him. When he swiveled back, Ridgely looked exhausted.

"Jesse and Alice love that boy. They've sacrificed so

much for him." He shook his head. "There are times when I hate this job."

3

Steve Mancini's office was in a square, earth-brown, single-story building on the outskirts of city center, five blocks from the courthouse. On one side of the building was Pearl Street. On the opposite side, a narrow parking area formed a buffer between the building and a Mexican restaurant. In the back was more parking and a high wooden fence that separated the lot from a residential area of run-down homes. LAW OFFICES OF STEPHEN L. MANCINI was affixed to the building beside the front door in black block letters. Smaller lettering below Mancini's name listed two other sole practitioners who rented from him.

Steve's office was at the rear of the building next to the back door. It was furnished with cheap wood paneling, a large, imitation Persian rug and a battleship-size desk. A month ago, Peter would have thought the office pretentious, but serving time in Amos Geary's rat-trap offices had dulled his senses.

"Did you talk to Gary?" Mancini asked as soon as Peter was seated. Both men looked exhausted from lack of sleep.

"I saw him this morning, right after you called."

"How's he holding up?"

"Not too well. The poor kid kept asking for you."

"I'll see him this afternoon."

"Uh, just how slow is Gary?"

"He's retarded, but he got through high school and he can work. Why?"

"It looks like Dennis Downes played some games with his head."

138

"What do you mean?"

"Downes conned Gary into talking about the case by convincing him he's a detective. He has Gary believing he has supernatural powers and can read minds or some such nonsense."

Mancini looked puzzled. "I know Dennis. He's a good guy. I can't see him taking advantage of Gary like that."

"I don't care how nice Downes has been in the past. This supernatural mind thing sounds like a trick you'd use to take advantage of someone who's not too bright. You better check it out."

Mancini looked uncomfortable. He picked up a pencil and tapped it on his desk.

"I've got a problem, Pete. I had a lot of time to think on the drive back. There's no way I can be lead counsel in this case. Ridgely might go for the death penalty. Think of what it would do to my marriage if I lost. Donna loves that kid. She'd never forgive me."

"I see what you mean. You're going to have to bring in someone from Portland to handle a case like this. Maybe Michael Palmer or Ann Girard?"

Mancini shook his head. "Whitaker juries won't take to an outsider. I've seen what happens when one of those slick big-city types rolls into town. Ridgely eats them for dinner. No, Pete, I was thinking of you."

"Me?" Peter laughed uneasily. "You've got to be kidding. I've lived in Whitaker for barely two months. I'm as much of an outsider as any other Portland lawyer. And I've already explained how little criminal law experience I have."

Mancini looked Peter in the eye.

"You don't have to take this case, but you'll regret it, if you don't. I'm giving you a once in a lifetime opportunity. If you win Gary's case, you'll be the most famous lawyer in the eastern part of the state. You are going to be the 'go to' guy for every farmer and ranch hand who's injured between Whitaker and the California border. I don't have to tell you how much money Ron Sissler, Dave MacAfee and Ernie Petersen make defending claims for the insurance companies. Pete, there's a lawyer on the other side of every claim they defend. That lawyer could be you."

"That would be great, Steve. But I'd only be famous if I won. A murder case is out of my league."

"Don't be ridiculous. It's not as complex as some of the stuff you handled at Hale, Greaves. Besides, I'll help you. I've got plenty of experience with criminal cases."

Mancini had Peter thinking. He had second-chaired several major cases with his father and he had tried a number of smaller matters that were much tougher than any criminal case.

"Don't tell me you can't use the money?" Mancini said.

"Well, sure, but . . . What kind of money are we talking about?"

"You'd have to ask for at least a hundred grand. What with expert witnesses, investigation."

"Do the Harmons have that kind of dough?"

"Jesse Harmon is worth a lot and he doesn't spend a nickel he doesn't have to, but he'd clean out his savings for Gary."

"What about Amos?" Peter asked, suddenly remembering his boss. "He'd never let me defend Gary. We're up to our eyeballs in court-appointed stuff. If I was representing Gary, I wouldn't have time to do any other work."

Mancini leaned back in his chair and held the pencil in both hands. Then, he said, "Fuck Amos Geary."

"What?"

"Fuck him. For Christ's sake, Pete, he's an old, washed-up drunk. I can't believe a guy like you is saddled with that run-down sot."

Mancini leaned forward. He pointed the pencil at Peter.

"Have you seen what passes for the bar in this burg? We're bigger than that, Pete. When Mountain View gets going I'll be a millionaire, but I'm also going to have to spend a lot of time with the project. I could use a partner right now, but there hasn't been a lawyer in the three counties I'd let near one of my files, until you came along.

"Think about it, Pete. You and me and all of those clients who'll want to be represented by the man who won the Wishing Well case. What does Amos pay you? I bet it's not one hundred thousand a year. And that's just one case."

Peter's heart was beating fast. Amos Geary was in Cayuse County trying a robbery case. He'd be there all week. What would he say if he came back and found out that Peter was Gary's attorney? What could he say? With Peter on the case for a week, it would be a *fait accompli*. Geary would have to accept the fact that Peter was representing Gary Harmon.

"It sounds tempting," Peter said, "but I really should think about this."

"Pete, I hate to pressure you, but the Harmons are here, now."

"What?"

"They're in the conference room waiting to meet you."

"They are?"

"I've been building you up as the only guy in Whitaker who is qualified to represent Gary. They're ready to hire you."

"I don't know . . ."

"Jesse wants his boy represented right away. If you don't hop on this, he's going to see it as a sign that you don't think you're big enough to handle the case.

"And I need you to be Gary's lawyer. He's my brother-in-law. The poor kid needs my help. If you're lead counsel, I can work with you. We'll make a great team."

For a nanosecond, it occurred to Peter that Gary Harmon could die if he screwed up the case, but he banished this pang of conscience from his thoughts. With Steve as his partner, Gary would have a great defense.

Peter imagined himself as the most famous attorney in eastern Oregon, rolling in money and picking and choosing from the supplicants who would beg him to take their cases. He conjured an image of his father staring, openmouthed, at a headline in *The Oregonian* that read:

PETER HALE WINS ACQUITTAL IN BIGGEST
DEATH CASE IN EASTERN OREGON HISTORY

Peter had no intention of spending his life trying traffic cases for peanuts. Steve Mancini had confidence in Peter's abilities and he was handing Peter the chance of a lifetime.

"Let's do it!" Peter said.

Mancini grinned at him. "That was the smartest decision you ever made. Let's meet your new clients."

Mancini led Peter down the hall to the conference room. Jesse Harmon was pacing the floor when Steve opened the door. Harmon's fifty-nine years showed in his thatch of white hair and the lines on his tanned, weather-beaten face. He was barrel-chested and broad-shouldered from years of farmwork. Donna was sitting next to Alice Harmon, a tall, rawboned woman with more gray than brown in her hair.

"I've got good news," Mancini said enthusiastically, as soon as the introductions were made. "Pete's going to take the case."

Jesse and Alice Harmon's faces showed none of Steve Mancini's excitement. They were drawn with worry.

"Steve tells us you've got lots of experience in these cases," Jesse Harmon said, getting down to business immediately.

Before Peter could think up an answer that would satisfy Harmon and not be a lie, Mancini said, "Pete's spent the last four years with the most prestigious firm in Portland working with its top litigator, who just happens to be his father. You might say that Pete's got high-level litigation in his genes."

"Did that firm handle criminal cases?" Jesse asked, ignoring Steve's attempt to skirt the issue of Peter's experience.

"Jesse," Mancini interjected, his expression turning somber, "there is something that Peter and I know about Gary that we've kept from you, Alice and Donna. Something that bears very strongly on the suitability of Peter to represent Gary." Donna and Alice cast worried glances at each other and Jesse's features hardened. "A few weeks ago, Gary was arrested when he was caught peeping in a window at the girls' dormitory while a young woman was undressing."

Alice's hand flew to her mouth and Donna said, "Oh, my God."

"Pete just happened to be walking across campus when this happened. He calmed down campus security, accompanied Gary to the police station and convinced the police that Gary should not be charged. Then, he came to me. I squared things with the college so Gary could keep his job.

"Jesse, not only is Pete a top-flight lawyer, but Gary trusts him. In a case like this, trust between a lawyer and his client is essential."

Peter was concerned that Jesse Harmon would become suspicious if Steve kept speaking up for him. He decided it was time for him to say something. Peter knew almost nothing about the state's case, so he had no idea whether Gary was guilty or innocent, but he had a very good idea of what Jesse and Alice wanted to hear.

"Mr. and Mrs. Harmon," he said with as much sincerity as he could muster, "I know how concerned you are about Gary, so I want you to know why I am willing to undertake Gary's defense. I am convinced that the police knew about Gary's mental handicap and took advantage of it to trick him into confessing to something he never did. What the police have done to Gary is wrong and I intend to do something about it."

Jesse Harmon's features softened and a tear trickled down Alice Harmon's cheek.

"We appreciate what you did for our boy," Jesse said, "and we would be grateful if you would help him out now."

CHAPTER TWELVE

1

Peter had not expected to see Becky O'Shay sitting next to Earl Ridgely's desk when the receptionist showed him and Steve Mancini into the district attorney's office. He started to smile, but caught himself. He remembered how reluctant Becky had been to go out with him because of their adversarial position and decided she might not appreciate an outward show of affection in front of her boss.

"How are Jesse and Alice holding up?" Ridgely asked Mancini when everyone was seated.

"As well as can be expected."

"They're awfully good people. I'm sorry they have to go through this ordeal."

"It would be a lot easier on them if you'd agree to let Gary out on bail."

"I can't do that."

"Earl, you've known Gary his whole life. Do you think he murdered that girl?"

"Look, I feel terrible about the arrest. You know how much I respect Jesse and Alice. But the evidence is very strong. We're still investigating, of course, but we have a taped confession . . ."

"He admitted killing her?"

"Not in so many words, but . . ." Ridgely paused. "I'm sorry. I can't discuss this any further. We'll be going before a grand jury tomorrow. If an indictment is returned, I'll give you all the discovery the law allows, but I'm going to play this one by the book."

"Earl, we've known each other how long? I don't understand the problem in letting us know what you've got on Gary."

"The statutes say the defense isn't entitled to discovery until there's an indictment. I know that's not how this office usually does things. We've only got a handful of lawyers in the county and I know every one of them, so I usually bend the rules. But not this time. Not in this case."

Peter put his hand on Mancini's arm.

"I respect that, Mr. Ridgely. We can wait. I'd appreciate it if you'd let us know as soon as the grand jury votes and I'd also appreciate seeing the discovery as soon as possible."

Peter handed Ridgely his business card.

"Steve, why don't we let Mr. Ridgely get back to work?"

Mancini looked like he wanted to say something else, but he held it in. The two men shook hands with Ridgely and nodded at O'Shay. Just before he left, Peter managed to flash a smile at Becky. She was standing so Ridgely could not see her and she returned the smile. Peter's heart soared.

The door closed and Ridgely sat lost in thought. After a moment, he looked over at his deputy and said, "There's no way I can prosecute Gary Harmon. I know the family too well."

O'Shay had been hoping the district attorney would reach this decision. She had been very worried that he would want to prosecute Gary Harmon himself.

"You were at the wedding, weren't you?" he asked after a while.

O'Shay was ready for this. "Yes," she said, "but I

don't know the Harmons and I only know Steve Mancini professionally."

Ridgely was a little put off by O'Shay's eagerness, but he understood it. Prosecuting a murder case was the ultimate challenge for a district attorney and the chance to do it in Whitaker was rare.

"I can ask the Attorney General for assistance. They provide help to small counties in major cases."

Becky knew it was now or never. She pulled her chair up to the desk and leaned toward Ridgely.

"Earl, I can do this. You know I'm good. I'm running a ninety-five percent conviction rate."

"This is a murder case, Becky. What's the most complex case you've tried?"

"*Peck,* and I won. Three weeks, toe to toe with a hired gun from Portland. I kicked his ass around the courtroom and you know it. Ask Judge Kuffel."

"I don't have to. He went out of his way to tell me what a great job you did."

"Then you know I can try *Harmon.* Give me the chance."

Ridgely could not think of a reason to deny O'Shay the case.

"*Harmon* is yours," he said.

"Thank you. I'll never forget this."

"Before you prosecute Gary, I want you to be damn certain he's the right man."

"Definitely." O'Shay paused. She looked a little nervous when she asked, "What about the death penalty?"

Ridgely paled. He started to say something, then he caught himself.

"I can't answer that question for the same reason I can't try the case. If you ask for the death penalty, it must be your decision."

Becky nodded solemnly like a person beset by a moral quandary of epic proportions, but Becky O'Shay had decided she was going for the death penalty as soon as she realized that she had a chance to prosecute Gary Harmon. A lot of doors would open for a lawyer who was tough enough to successfully prosecute a death case.

2

Kevin Booth lived six miles outside of Whitaker at the end of a gravel road in a single-bedroom house that was little better than a shack. The paint on the outside of the house had been scarred by endless waves of windblown debris. A dismantled junker sat on blocks in the yard in front of a small, litter-filled garage. Booth's nearest neighbor was half a mile away. The view was brown flatlands and desolation, broken only by the wavering outline of another shack, a forlorn apparition abandoned long ago that served as a reminder of the inhospitable nature of the desert.

The inside of the house looked no better than the outside. Empty pizza boxes, crumpled cigarette packs and soiled skin magazines lay scattered around. In the kitchen, the rust-stained refrigerator was almost empty and dried soup congealed around the burners on the dilapidated stove.

Booth had staggered in around one and collapsed on his unmade bed. He was in such a deep sleep that the pounding on his front door did not arouse him immediately. When the din finally penetrated, he jerked awake, upsetting the lamp on his end table. It was pitch black in his room and his heart was beating so loudly that he could not distinguish between the two thumping sounds.

"One minute," he called out, but the pounding continued.

Booth swung his legs over the side of the bed. He was wearing boxer shorts and an undershirt. His mouth felt gummy. Awakening suddenly in the dark had disoriented him. The pills he'd taken before he went to sleep did not help. Booth fumbled for the switch on the lamp and had trouble finding it because the lamp was on its side.

"Just a minute," he yelled again.

This time the pounding stopped. Booth found the switch. The light hurt his eyes. He winced and groped around for his jeans, then pulled them on. After slipping into his sneakers, Booth staggered into the front room.

"Who is it?" he called through the door.

"Rafael Vargas," said a voice with a faint trace of Spain.

"Oh, shit," Booth said to himself.

"Open the fucking door," a deeper voice commanded.

The moment Booth opened the door he regretted it, but refusing to let the two men in would have been useless. The first man through the door could have eaten it if he wanted to. He wore a suit jacket over a tight black tee shirt that stretched across corded muscles. When he moved, the jacket flapped back revealing the butt of a large handgun. The man wore his long hair tied back in a ponytail and a gold earring dangled from his left ear. A jagged scar cut across his cheek, his nose was askew and his eyes were wild. As soon as he was inside, he searched the house.

Rafael Vargas was lean, wiry and obviously Latin. His amused smile revealed even, white teeth and there was a pencil-thin mustache over his upper lip.

"Sit down, Kevin," Vargas commanded after he took the most comfortable chair in the shabby living room. Booth sat on the couch across from his visitor.

"There's no one else here," Vargas's bodyguard said when he was finished searching. Vargas nodded, then turned his attention back to Booth.

"Did Chris explain what we want from you?" he asked.

Booth swallowed. He was still groggy from the pills.

"When Mr. Vargas asks a question, he expects an an-

149

swer," the bodyguard said, taking a threatening step forward.

"Yeah," Booth answered quickly. "I'm just sleepy. It's three in the morning."

"Then you must wake up quickly, Kevin," Vargas said. "There are things to do."

"Uh, look, Mr. Vargas," Booth said anxiously, "I told Chris I didn't think I was right for this."

Vargas held up his hand and Booth froze.

"Look, amigo, Chris is hot. DEA is gonna have him under surveillance. He's smart enough to know that."

"I was arrested with Chris. They probably suspect me, too."

Vargas shook his head. "DEA forgot you the minute you left the courtroom."

"Right, but . . ."

"Kevin, wheels are in motion. It's too late to stop them from turning."

Vargas stood up. "I've got twenty kilos of cocaine in a van parked out front. All you have to do is hold it for a few days. Do you think you can do that?"

Booth felt the way he would have if Vargas had asked him to stand at ground zero on the day they dropped the A-bomb on Hiroshima.

"Twenty . . . Mr. Vargas, I really don't want to be around twenty kilos of snow."

"There is nothing to worry about. We don't plan to leave the merchandise here for very long," Vargas said. "Let's go to the van."

Booth got up quickly and Carlos and Vargas followed him outside. There was almost no moon and there was no light in the yard except for the headlights of a brown van and the light that filtered into the yard through the living room curtains. The only sound was Booth's breathing and his sneakers scraping across the dirt. Booth stumbled on his way to the van, but neither man made any effort to catch him. Vargas found a flashlight in the glove compartment while Carlos opened the back of the van revealing two large, black plastic trashbags secured with ties.

"Take them out," Carlos commanded.

Booth grabbed the bags by their necks and pulled them out. As soon as he started for the garage, lights flooded the yard.

"Freeze! Federal agents!" shouted a man in a dark blue windbreaker. Stenciled on the back in yellow letters was DEA. Vargas dropped the flashlight and started to run, but two armed men appeared from the side of the garage. Carlos held his hands away from his body. Booth froze.

"Drop the bags," commanded the man in the windbreaker. Booth complied instantly. One of the garbage bags broke and a fine white powder seeped out of the tear. Booth was slammed against the side of the van. Rough hands frisked him, then his arms were wrenched behind him and metal cuffs were snapped on his wrists. When he was jerked around, Booth found himself standing next to Vargas. The slender Hispanic said nothing until they were left alone for a moment while their captors conferred. As soon as the agents were far enough away, Vargas turned to Booth and whispered, "You are a dead man."

3

Kevin Booth looked worse than Steve Mancini had ever seen him. Not only was his acne acting up and his body odor more repulsive, but he appeared to be on the brink of a psychotic break. Sweat was pouring off Booth, he jerked around constantly and Mancini could swear that his client had not blinked once since he sat down.

"Kevin, Kevin. You've got to get ahold of yourself," Mancini cautioned.

"Ahold? What are you talking about? I was arrested with ten kilos of cocaine in each hand and Rafael Vargas, the executioner for one of Colombia's biggest drug cartels, has personally threatened to kill me. How can I get ahold of myself? You tell me."

"I admit you're in some serious shit here, but Vargas was probably venting his anger at you. These threats are made all the time and rarely carried out. And as far as the dope goes, you said you were forced to carry the bags. I'll explain that to the feds, we'll agree to cooperate in the prosecution of Vargas and . . ."

"No. No way will I testify against Rafael Vargas. And, besides," Booth said in a suddenly subdued voice, "the feds aren't interested."

"How do you know?"

Booth ran his tongue across his lips. "I tried. When I was arrested, I begged them to let me cooperate. They said they didn't need me. They . . . they said they were going to send me away forever and . . . and nothing I could say would help."

"What happened exactly?" Mancini asked.

Booth told him. Mancini digested this information. He looked at the case from the feds' point of view. The DEA must have been onto Vargas all along and followed him to Booth's home. Carlos and Vargas had probably been photographed loading the cocaine into the van and the three men had been caught red-handed. The case was open and shut. No search-and-seizure problems, no statements to be suppressed. Just three amigos standing around with enough cocaine to get every man, woman, child and household pet in the state high.

Mancini shook his head solemnly. "This is going to be tough, Kevin. I'm going to have to work overtime to save your butt."

"You think you can win, Steve?" Booth pleaded, looking so pathetic that Mancini had to choke back a laugh.

"Didn't I take care of you the last time?"

"Yes. Yes you did," Booth responded eagerly.

"Now, with a case this big, I'll need twenty thousand up front," Mancini continued.

"Twenty . . . The last time you only charged me seventy-five hundred."

"The last time we were in state court and you weren't caught with twenty kilos of snow. Fighting the feds is expensive. They have the resources of the entire government. I'm fighting Washington, D.C., not some small-town D.A."

"I don't have twenty thousand dollars," Booth said desperately.

"What about your parents?"

"My father ran off when I was two. I don't even remember him. And my mother," Booth said bitterly, "she's dead."

"Where did you get the dough last time?"

"Chris Mammon lent it to me."

"Well?" Mancini said with a shrug. "From what you've told me, you're in this scrape because of Mammon. Ask him to go your fee."

Booth hung his head. "I already called him. He won't talk to me."

Mancini sighed. "I want to help you, Kevin, but I can't work for free. Not on a case this big. You understand that, don't you?"

"You won so easy the last time. Can't you give me some credit? If you get me off I'll pay you double."

"No can do. Sorry, but I have an ironclad rule about fees in criminal cases."

Mancini looked at his watch. "Hey, I'm going to have to break this off. I'm due in court."

"Wait a minute. You can't just walk out on me."

"I'm afraid I have other clients, Kevin."

"Don't do this to me, man," Booth whined, "you gotta help."

"I really am due in court."

Mancini started to rap for the guard, but Booth grabbed him by the arm.

"I'll . . . I'll tell the cops about you," Booth threatened.

Mancini did not move his arm. Instead he turned until his face was inches from Booth's.

"Oh, really?" Mancini said. "What exactly will you tell them?"

The former quarterback's bicep felt like steel through his suit jacket and Booth knew he had made a mistake.

"You . . . you know," Booth stuttered.

"Let go of my arm, Kevin," Mancini said softly.

Booth's grip loosened. Mancini still did not move. Finally, Booth's eyes dropped and he released Mancini's arm. Mancini slowly lowered it.

"Never touch me again, Kevin. And never, ever threaten me. But if you feel compelled to talk, remember that two can play that game. Would you like me to visit Rafael Vargas and confirm his suspicions about you?"

Booth swallowed. Mancini smiled coldly, then made a point of turning his back on Booth. Booth sank back on his chair, shaking with terror at the thought of a life in prison, if he was fortunate enough to escape the vengeance of Rafael Vargas.

CHAPTER THIRTEEN

1

Reporters from the *Clarion,* several other eastern Oregon papers and the local TV station were waiting for Peter outside the courtroom where Gary was to be arraigned. Peter made a brief statement expressing his total belief in his client's innocence. During the statement, Peter made numerous references to the Bill of Rights, the Constitution and the American System of Justice. He loved every moment in the spotlight.

Donna, Jesse and Alice Harmon were sitting with Steve Mancini in the front row of spectator seats. Peter stopped briefly to say hello, then walked through the low wooden gate that separated the spectators from the court. There were several defendants waiting to be arraigned and Gary was last on the list. Peter expected Earl Ridgely to handle Gary's arraignment, but Becky O'Shay was handling all the arraignments today and she called the case.

A guard brought Gary into the courtroom. He was used to his status as a prisoner by now and looked more confused than afraid. Gary spotted his parents. He started toward them, but the guard grabbed Gary by the elbow and pointed him toward Peter.

The clerk presented Peter and Gary with copies of an

indictment charging Gary with aggravated murder, the most serious degree of homicide in Oregon and the only charge that carried the death penalty. The judge explained the charge and his rights to Gary, then the judge asked Gary what plea he wanted to enter. Peter told him to say, "Not guilty," and Gary said the words in a nervous whisper that could be heard easily only by those within the bar of the court. Peter and Becky discussed scheduling with the judge for a few minutes; then the arraignment was over.

"Hold up, will you?" Peter asked Becky. She waited patiently at her counsel table while Peter told Gary he would see him later in the afternoon, after he had a chance to read the discovery. As soon as Gary was led out, Peter smiled and asked O'Shay, "How've you been?"

"Great. Sorry about the other night."

"Me, too. Maybe I can collect on that rain check soon?"

"The Harmon case is a real plum for you," Becky said, skillfully avoiding Peter's question. Peter tried to look modest.

"A death penalty case is a big responsibility," he answered solemnly. "Where's Earl? I thought he'd want to handle Gary's arraignment personally."

"Earl isn't prosecuting Gary."

"He isn't? Then, who . . ."

O'Shay smiled.

"You? You're going to prosecute?"

O'Shay nodded and looked suddenly somber. "Unfortunately, Peter, that means that we won't be able to see each other for a while, except, of course, in the courtroom."

Peter had been looking forward to going out with Becky. He felt a little depressed. Gary's case was going to put a damper on his social life.

O'Shay touched Peter lightly on the arm. "Come up to my office and I'll give you the discovery. And don't look so glum. We can make up for lost time when the trial is over."

After court, to his delight, Peter was interviewed by the press again, then Jesse Harmon gave him a twenty-five-thousand-dollar installment of the retainer. The money and the rush from being the center of attention put Peter in a very good mood.

Peter was so excited about the prospect of being the lead counsel in a major case that he had not given much thought to whether Gary had killed Sandra Whiley. Gary's claim that he did not have a clear memory of the hours when the killing occurred and his evasive answers when asked point-blank if he had killed Sandra Whiley had aroused Peter's suspicions, but he had little basis for forming an opinion until he read the police reports.

When he returned to his office, Peter dumped the stack of police reports and the box of tapes O'Shay had given him onto his desk and hunted up a tape recorder so he could hear Gary's interrogation. As he listened, Peter's mood changed from excitement to confusion to concern. Something was not right. Peter could see that Gary knew a lot about the murder, but what was this "projection transfer" and "supernatural mind" stuff? It sounded to Peter as if Sergeant Downes had tricked Gary into making many of the statements that were incriminating. What if Gary was repeating what Downes said and not remembering it? What if Gary was innocent?

2

Several hours after the arraignment, a guard let Gary into the attorney-client interview room at the jail.

"Can I go home now?" Gary asked as soon as he saw Peter.

"No, Gary. I've explained this all to you before. You're charged with murder, so there isn't any way you can get out of jail for a while."

Gary looked agitated. "How will I do my job?"

"Gary, you've got to focus on what's important. Okay? We're talking about your life here. That job at the college is just a janitor's job. That job isn't important."

"Oh no, my job is important," Gary told Peter with great seriousness. "Mom says every job is important and my job is very important. There are germs. They are very small. You can't see them. They make people sick. I scrub and scrub. I clean away the germs. I make the floor shine so you can see your face. I take out the garbage so the room won't smell bad. If I don't do my job people will be sick, the room will smell."

Gary grew more agitated as he spoke. Peter was surprised by how serious Gary was about his work. He felt a little bad about putting down his job.

"Look, Gary," Peter said gently, "I'm sure they have someone filling in for you. Someone to clean away the germs and take out the garbage until you can come back."

"Is someone taking my job?" Gary asked. He was pacing back and forth. "I want my job."

"No, no. No one is taking your job. Listen to me. Did I help you when you were arrested for looking at that girl?"

Gary nodded, but his eyes were darting back and forth with worry.

"Did Steve and I make sure you kept your job?"

Gary stopped pacing. He looked less worried.

"Gary, do you think Steve and I will let them take your job?"

"You helped me keep my job," Gary said, relaxing a little.

"Right. Your job is important, Gary. It's very important. The college needs you to do that job. They won't let anyone take your job because you're so good at it. Okay? But you won't be able to go back at all unless you help me."

Gary's breathing settled. He stopped pacing.

"Now, why don't you sit down and we'll take that first step toward getting you out of here so you can work." Peter indicated one of the metal chairs on the other side of the wooden table. Gary sat down obediently. He wiped the palms of his hands on his jumpsuit and waited for Peter to continue. Peter sighed with relief then pointed to several tape cassettes and the stack of police reports he had reviewed over the past few hours.

"I've received some discovery from the district attorney and I wanted to go over it with you. I've read a summary of the statement you made to Sergeant Downes and I've listened to a few of the tapes of your interrogation. I want you to tell me again how you know so much about this murder."

"It's my powers."

"Your supernatural and subconscious minds?"

Gary nodded. Peter shifted uncomfortably on the metal chair as he searched for the words he wanted to say. Gary watched him hopefully. Peter felt sorry for his client. He wondered what it must be like to go through life with the mind of a very slow child. What did Gary think about? Did he think at all without a stimulus? Was Gary nothing more than a machine with malfunctioning circuits? Were the rich patterns of life mere shadows for him? Or was there more to Gary than was apparent at first? According to the police reports, Gary had flown into a rage when Karen Nix insulted his intelligence. Would a machine care what a person thought of its capabilities?

Peter had thought a lot about the fame and fortune Gary's case could bring him, but very little about Gary Harmon. At first, he was even put off by his client. Peter liked to be around intelligent, well-educated and presentable people. People on the go. People like himself before the Elliot case. Peter would never associate with someone like Gary under normal circumstances, but Peter found Gary's childlike dependence on him endearing as well as flattering. After the way he had been treated at Hale, Greaves, it was nice being appreciated.

Peter stopped musing and looked directly at Gary. Gary met his eye without wavering.

"Gary, I want you to listen carefully to what I'm going to say." Gary leaned forward expectantly. "You do not have any special powers."

Peter waited for a response. Gary looked confused. When he didn't reply, Peter pushed on.

"Do you understand what Sergeant Downes did to you?"

Gary shook his head. Peter tried to think of a diplomatic way of breaking the bad news to Gary.

"I'm your friend, Gary. Do you trust me?"

"Yeah."

"And you know if I say something that hurts your feelings, I'm saying it because I have to in order to save you?"

Gary nodded, again.

"Okay. Do you understand that you aren't as smart as some other people?"

Gary flushed, but he nodded.

"Do mean people take advantage of you sometimes? Play tricks on you or try to fool you?"

"Yeah. I don't like them mean people. They hurt my feelings."

"Gary, Sergeant Downes played a trick on you. He took advantage of you. He said you have supernatural powers, but you don't."

Gary's expression was blank for a moment. Then his brow furrowed.

"How did I see the murder if I don't have powers?"

"There are only two explanations I can think of, Gary. Either you murdered Sandra Whiley . . ."

"Oh no, Mr. Hale. I couldn't do that."

". . . or you made up what you said."

"No. I didn't make it up. I seen it."

"Sergeant Downes told you to imagine what you saw in your head, didn't he?"

"Yeah."

"That's all it was, Gary. Your imagination."

"But it seemed so real."

"Do me a favor. Close your eyes."

Gary obeyed Peter's request.

"Now imagine this room. Do you have it?"

Gary nodded.

"What time of year is it?"

"Summer."

"In your mind, imagine it's winter." Peter waited a few seconds. "Can you see snow on the window? Is it cold?"

"Yeah."

"Now, imagine Santa Claus is in this room with us. Do you see him? Can you see the icicles hanging from his beard? Can you see the twinkle in his eye?"

Gary smiled.

"Gary, have you ever seen Santa in this jail?"

"No."

"But you're seeing him in the jail now."

"That ain't . . ."

Gary stopped. His eyes opened slowly. The smile faded to a look of puzzlement.

"Do you see what Sergeant Downes did to you? Do you understand it now?"

"I . . . I know I seen something. I know I seen two people in the park when I passed by."

"Can you swear you saw Sandra Whiley?"

Gary shook his head. He looked dejected. Peter's heart went out to him.

"This is our job, then. To find out what you really saw and what you made up. It's going to be a hard job, but we're going to work together and we're going to do it. Will you work with me, Gary? Will you help me?"

"Yes I will, Mr. Hale. I'll try real hard."

"Good, Gary. That's a start."

3

It was almost five o'clock when Peter left the jail. Working with Gary was exhausting. He was so open to suggestion that Peter had to watch every word, and he could never be certain if Gary really understood him or was nodding to be polite. Representing Gary Harmon was going to be very frustrating and very time consuming.

As he walked up the stairs to Geary's office, Peter checked his watch. He was going to Steve's house after dinner to discuss strategy. There were all sorts of technical defenses, like diminished capacity, they might employ with a guilty client with Gary's intelligence. After today's session with Gary, Peter was wondering if they shouldn't dispense with them and go with a straight not guilty on the grounds that Gary did not commit the crime.

The autopsy report described the carnage to Sandra Whiley in graphic detail. The person who inflicted those wounds was in a rage. Gary had been in a rage when he attacked Karen Nix, but Gary's rage was a spontaneous response to Nix's insult. The hatchet screamed premeditation. Who walks around with a hatchet? No, the killer carried the hatchet with him to use on the victim and that meant the killer planned his moves. Peter had a hard time picturing Gary Harmon planning breakfast.

"Mr. Geary wants to speak to you," Clara said as soon as Peter opened the office door.

"He's here?" Peter asked nervously.

"Nope," Clara answered without looking up from her typing. "He's at the Bunkhouse Motel in Cayuse County. Said to have you call the minute you walked in." Clara stopped typing and looked at Peter. "Those were his exact words. 'The minute he walks in the door.'"

"Do you know why he wants to talk to me?"

"That's none of my business, Mr. Hale. I'm just a secretary. But he did seem a mite annoyed."

Peter wondered if Geary knew he was on the case already. He had hoped for more time to cement his position as Gary's attorney before having to confront his boss.

"Mr. Geary," Peter said as soon as he was put through by the motel clerk, "Clara said you wanted to talk to me."

"Yes. Yes I do. I was sitting in Judge Gilroy's chambers after court and he jokingly offered me condolences on getting stuck with the Harmon case. I told him I didn't know what he was talking about, because our office doesn't handle death penalty cases. With all the work in the office, we would never be able to commit the time we would have to commit in order to do a competent job. Not to mention that no one in my office is qualified to handle a death case, which, I'm sure you know, is a case that requires a specialist.

"The judge said he could be mistaken, but Judge Kuffel had phoned him during a break in our trial and he thought Kuffel said that my young associate had appeared at the arraignment for Mr. Harmon. That isn't true, is it, Peter?"

"Well, uh, yes it is. I mean, the judge is right. But you don't have to worry. This isn't a court appointment. The Harmons are going to pay us one hundred thousand dollars and expenses."

Peter held his breath as he waited for Geary to absorb the amount of the fee. Peter assumed that one hundred thousand dollars would allay any qualms his boss might have. There was silence on the line for a moment. When Geary spoke again, he sounded as if he was fighting to keep himself under control.

"Peter, I want you to call Jesse Harmon and tell him you made a mistake when you accepted his son's case without consulting me. Then, you march down to Judge Kuffel's office and resign as quickly as you can. First thing in the morning is fine, but tonight would be better, if you can catch him in. You might want to call as soon as I hang up."

"But, Mr. Geary . . ."

"No buts, Peter. You and this office are off the Harmon case as of now. Do you understand me?"

"Well, no, I don't understand. How much do we make on one of your crummy court appointments? What, a few hundred bucks? I just brought in a one-hundred-thousand-dollar fee and you're acting like I did something wrong."

"You did do something wrong, Peter," Geary said in a tone that had Peter picturing swelling blood vessels and tightly clenched teeth. "First, you took this case without consulting me, your boss.

"Second, our firm has a contract to represent indigent defendants in three counties. A contract is a binding promise between two or more parties to undertake particular tasks. In order to honor my part of the contract I need to have you available to represent the indigent accused, no matter how crummy they may be. You will not be available if you are in court on one case for two to four months.

"Third, and most important, this is not some shoplifting case. If you fuck up, Gary Harmon will have lethal chemicals injected into his veins. And you will fuck up, Peter, because *you* are a fuck-up. Did you forget that your father exiled you to this intellectual Devil's Island because of your gross incompetence? Are you so shallow that you want to compound your felony by risking Gary Harmon's life for money?"

"I resent the implications that I took this case for the money," Peter said indignantly.

"I don't give a shit what you resent," Geary shouted. "You either march down to the courthouse and resign the minute I hang up or clear out of your office."

The line went dead. Peter's hand was shaking. He hung up and slumped in his chair. What was he going to do? If he didn't resign from Gary's case, his last chance to get back in his father's good graces would be gone. But if he did resign, a golden opportunity to make a name for himself on his own would disappear. A chance like this might never come his way again.

Peter had rationalized his banishment to this dust bowl as a temporary inconvenience. He always believed that his father would welcome him back after he had done his penance as a low-paid advocate of the indigent accused. What Peter pondered long and hard was his father's reaction to a call from Amos Geary telling him that Peter had lasted barely two months before he had to can him.

Before *Elliot,* Peter would never have believed his father would punish him for anything he did. When he was suspended from high school after tearing up the football field with his jeep in a drunken frenzy, Richard paid for the damage and somehow kept the suspension off his record. When there was that unfortunate problem with the sorority girl in college, Richard fumed and hollered, then paid for the abortion. And what about law school? To this day, Peter had no idea how he would have gained admission with his grades, if Richard had not stepped in. That was why it had been such a shock when his father lowered the boom after his fiasco in *Elliot* and it was the reason why he could not dismiss the possibility that Richard would cast him out forever if he failed him again.

The thought of quitting Geary's firm made Peter feel like a kid getting ready to make a high dive for the first time. He could edge back along the board to safety by dropping Gary Harmon or he could take a frightening plunge into the unknown by staying on the case. Was he willing to trade his freedom for security? Did he want to stay a child his whole life, totally dependent on his father, or did he want to become a man who could stand on his own two feet?

Then, Peter remembered Steve Mancini's advice. "Fuck Amos Geary," Mancini had said. Mancini was right. With one hundred thousand dollars he could say "Fuck you" to a lot of people. And there was the partnership waiting. When Peter thought about it, the choice wasn't all that hard.

4

"What are you going to do?" Steve Mancini asked as soon as Peter finished his account of his phone conversation with Amos Geary. They were seated on the couch in Mancini's living room. Police reports and tape cassettes were stacked next to a tape recorder in front of them on the coffee table. Donna was in the kitchen brewing coffee and slicing a coffee cake.

"I know what I'd like to do, but I have one huge practical problem. If I stay on as Gary's lawyer, I've got to clear out of my office."

"That's no problem, at all. I have an extra office at my place you can rent. You'd have a receptionist and you can pay one of my secretaries by the hour to type your stuff. My place is a hell of a lot nicer than Geary's mausoleum. What do you say?"

"Are you still serious about going into partnership?"

"You bet. Of course, we can't do it right now, because I've got to get Mountain View squared away and you've got Gary's case to try."

"Right."

"But I'm definitely interested."

"That's terrific, because I think it could work."

"Okay. So, we'll talk."

Peter shook Steve's hand and smiled bravely, but his insides were churning with fear.

"Now that we've got that settled, let's get to work," Steve said.

"I want you to read this report." Peter handed a thick, stapled stack of paper to Mancini. "It's a summary of Downes's interrogation. Then I want you to listen to sections of these tapes. The whole interrogation is about seven hours. I only had time to listen to two tapes, but the parts I'm going to play will give you some idea of what's going on."

Donna came out of the kitchen carrying a tray shortly after Peter started playing the tapes. She gave Peter and her husband cups of coffee and a slice of cake. Then, she sat on the couch next to Steve and listened as Dennis Downes explained to Gary the marvelous powers he possessed.

"Are Gary's statements the reason he was arrested?" Donna asked Peter when the tapes were finished.

"They're a big part of it."

"But that's so unfair. Gary thought he was being a detective. He thought he was helping Downes. Gary wouldn't understand that Downes was fooling him. No jury is going to believe that what Gary said was a confession."

"It would if Gary knows something that only the killer could know," Mancini said, "and I'm betting that somewhere on these tapes is something like that."

"Keeping Gary's statement out of evidence is definitely the key to winning the case," Peter said. "The question is how to do it."

"Doesn't the fact that Downes lied to Gary mean anything?" Donna asked.

"I seem to remember reading some cases in law school that held that a confession that is elicited by deceit won't hold up," Peter said.

"Maybe I can help find them," Donna volunteered. "When I was studying to be a legal secretary I took a course on how to do legal research. Mr. Willoughby lets me do research for him, every once in a while."

"I can use all the help I can get," Peter said.

Mancini frowned. "When would you fit it in, honey? You're pretty busy at work."

"I could do the research after work or on the weekend. Please, Steve. I want to do something more to help Gary than make coffee."

167

"Well . . . I guess if it's okay with Pete . . ."

Donna leaned over and kissed her husband on the cheek. Then, she stood up.

"I'll let you two get back to work while I clean up. Holler if you need anything. And, Peter, let me know what you want me to do."

Donna almost skipped out of the room. There was a big smile on her face.

"You did okay, Steve. Donna's terrific."

"Why thanks," Mancini answered with a self-satisfied smile. "One thing, though. Don't count on Donna for much help. She's a good legal secretary, but legal research . . . ?" Mancini flashed Peter a patronizing smile. "Still, if you can find a make-work project for her, she'll be happy as a clam."

"She seems pretty sharp to me," Peter said, surprised to hear his friend put down his wife. "Let's see what she can do."

"Sure," Mancini said. He took a sip of coffee. "Let's get back to the confession. We should make a list of possible attacks on it. I noticed that Don Bosco observed a lot of the questioning. Why don't I talk to him and see what he has to say about it."

"Good idea."

"I'll do it first thing in the morning."

"I'm going to need a good investigator. Can you suggest someone?"

"There aren't many in this area. Ralph Cotton is pretty good. He does some work for the Sissler firm. And Mike Compton does some investigation."

Mancini thought for a moment. "You know, there's a guy I've used, Barney Pullen. He works as a mechanic at his brother's garage, but he used to be a cop. You might check to see if he's available."

Peter jotted down the names Steve had given him. Then, he said, "There are a few other things we have to go over. Becky included a police report about the peeping incident. Another report mentions some pornographic magazines that were found in the closet in

168

Gary's bedroom. I think Becky is going to try and have the porno stuff and evidence of the peeping incident admitted. What can we do about that?"

"We have to file a motion to keep that out. The jurors are going to believe Gary's a pervert if they hear it."

"I agree. Why don't I concentrate on this issue."

"Okay."

"There's something else," Peter said.

Mancini noticed a change in Peter's voice. Whatever this new thing was, it had Peter worried.

"What's the problem?"

Peter handed Mancini a stack of police reports.

"I'm hoping these reports are in here by mistake. If they're not, Gary may be in big trouble."

Mancini skimmed the first report. His features clouded.

"Did Becky mention anything about this?"

"No."

Mancini laid the stack of reports on his desk.

"She can't think Gary was also involved in these cases."

"She must. Why would she give me police reports about the murders of two other women if she didn't think Gary committed them?"

CHAPTER FOURTEEN

1

The prisoners in the Whitaker jail were allowed an hour a day to exercise in the yard. Gary waited for that hour like a marooned sailor longing for rescue. Inside, the jail was musty gray and the air was heavy. Outside, there was the sun, birds in flight and air sweet with reminders of the way his life used to be. This afternoon, Gary leaned against the chain-link fence and watched several prisoners pumping iron on the far side of the yard. Gary wanted to lift weights, but he was afraid to go near them. Besides, he wasn't feeling so good. The meeting with Peter Hale had left him confused. Peter said he did not have supernatural powers, but he was certain he did. If he didn't have those powers, how did he know so much about the murder? How had he seen Sandra Whiley die?

"Hey, Gary?" a familiar voice said. Gary turned around and saw Kevin Booth. Booth was sweating and he could not stand still. He had been using so many drugs that his system was having trouble adjusting to the deprivations jail imposed. Gary did not notice. All he knew was that he finally had a friend to talk to.

"Hi, Kevin! Are you arrested too?"

"Yeah. I got busted a few days ago."

"What did you do?" Gary asked with concern.

"I fucked up, big time. Federal stuff."

Booth's shoulders twitched a little.

"I don't like it here," Gary confided.

"Why is that?"

"Some of the men pick on me. They say mean things."

"You've got to learn how to deal with those mother-fuckers," Booth responded with false bravado. He wanted Gary to think he was not afraid of being in jail, but he had barely slept during the short stint he had spent when he was arrested at Whitaker State and last night had been hell. "If anyone messes with you, you mess them up first or you won't get any respect."

"My mom says I shouldn't fight," Gary said nervously.

"Yeah? Well, your mom isn't in jail."

Just as he said this, Booth noticed Rafael Vargas sitting in the bleachers near the body builders. Not far away, his bodyguard, Carlos Rivera, was completing a set of curls with weights that were the size of car tires. Every time he brought the bar to his chest, his body would swell up like a balloon. Booth felt his bowels loosen and he looked away quickly.

"So, man," Booth said, moving so Gary's body blocked Vargas's view of him, "I read about you. You're a fuckin' media star. Front page! Murder! That's heavy."

"I didn't do anything to that girl," Gary assured his friend. "I just seen it."

"Seen what?"

"My lawyer doesn't want me to talk about the case to anyone."

An idea suddenly occurred to Booth. He shot a quick look at Vargas. When he turned back to Gary, he was wearing an ingratiating smile.

"Hey, Gary, this is me. We've been buddies since high school. What do you think I'm gonna do, rat you out?"

"Oh no," Gary said, coloring with embarrassment.

"Your lawyers probably don't want you talking to

171

someone you don't know. Now, that makes sense. But I'm your friend, right?"

"Oh, sure," Gary agreed.

"So, what gives?"

Gary hesitated. Peter was emphatic about not talking to anyone about his case. He said that some people in jail would tell the D.A. he had confessed to them so they could get a deal on their own case. Then, they would testify against him in court and tell lies. Peter had warned him to look out for those men, but he couldn't have meant Kevin. Peter probably meant he shouldn't talk to strangers, like Mom had always warned him. Kevin Booth wasn't a stranger. He was a friend. So, Gary proceeded to tell him everything about his case.

2

It was late afternoon when Steve Mancini returned to his office. He picked up his message slips at the reception desk and glanced through them as he walked down the hall. One of the messages was from Harold Prescott. Mancini's mouth went dry and the hand holding the message shook. He closed his office door. As he dialed Whitaker Savings and Loan, he shut his eyes and said a little prayer.

The United States Olympic ski team trained at Mount Bachelor near Bend, Oregon. Three years ago, the state of Oregon had launched a campaign to bring the Olympics to Bend. Shortly after, Mancini had joined a group of investors to form Mountain View, Inc., with the goal of building a ski lodge and condominiums near Bend. Harold Prescott had engineered a construction loan at his bank. The loan was used to start work on the lodge and the first condo units, but the weather, labor problems and escalating costs had eaten up most of the loan and slowed progress on the project. The loan was due soon. Mountain View was trying to get a long-term loan from the bank to pay off the construction loan and complete the first phase of the project. Mancini had invested heavily in the project. If it failed, he would be ruined.

"I'm afraid I have bad news, Steve," Prescott said as soon as they were connected. "The committee met this afternoon. It voted against authorizing the loan."

Mancini felt as if he was going to throw up. He squeezed his eyes shut and fought the nausea.

"Steve?"

"I don't get it," Mancini managed.

"I argued for it, but there was too much opposition."

"What's the problem?" Mancini asked desperately. "We've been dealing with Whitaker Savings and Loan since the project started. Nothing's changed."

"Steve, I warned you about this potential problem two years ago. The Federal National Mortgage Association would not approve the project. Without their approval we can't sell the loan on the New York market. I tried to persuade the others to take a chance, but it was no go."

"Fannie Mae wouldn't approve because it's a resort area and we don't have earnest money for fifty percent of the units. That will change as soon as Bend wins the bid for the Winter Olympics."

"The problem is that there's no assurance Bend will get the games. The rumor we're hearing is that one of the European countries has the edge. The committee was unwilling to take the risk."

"Harold, I don't know who you've been talking to. Roger Dunn told me his sources say we've got a terrific shot. Once the announcement is made, those condos will sell like hotcakes."

"That wasn't the only problem. There aren't enough liquid assets in your group. Most of the land is only optioned. The feeling was that there wasn't enough hard equity in the project."

The rest of the conversation went by in a dull hum.

Mancini responded automatically as a sharp throbbing pain filled his head. After a few more minutes, he hung up and stared at the wall. He knew he should call the other partners, but he could not move. All he could think about was his financial ruin.

Mancini told his secretary to hold his calls. Then he took a glass and a half-filled bottle of scotch out of his bottom drawer. He poured a stiff drink, downed it and poured another. The whiskey burned and the numb feeling wore off and was replaced by rage.

It was Shari, his first wife, who had talked him into investing in Mountain View, filling him with tales of the millions they would make. Then, the bitch bailed out, leaving him to face financial destruction. She'd probably known this would happen all along. He could imagine her laughing at him when she read about the collapse of Mountain View. Mancini's stomach knotted and pain ripped through his skull. His hands squeezed together and the whiskey glass shattered, spraying scotch and blood onto the carpet.

3

"Donna Harmon is here to see you, Mr. Hale," Clara said over the intercom.

"Send her back," Peter answered, relieved that Clara had not buzzed him to say that Amos Geary was on the line. Peter had spent the day in torment as he pondered his decision to leave Amos Geary. He had come to work late, timing his arrival to coincide with the start of court in Cayuse County, and had been out of the office during every conceivable time that Geary could call. Clara had given him several messages from his boss, each longer and more threatening, but Peter had returned none of them.

"Hi," Peter said when Donna stuck her head in the door. She looked excited.

"I think I found some good cases about tricking people into confessing," Donna said, thrusting a manila envelope at Peter.

"Sit down. Let me take a look."

Peter pulled out copies of the cases and articles Donna had photocopied for him.

"There's a great sentence in *Miranda v. Arizona,*" Donna told him, referring to her copy of the famous United States Supreme Court case that established the rule that police had to warn suspects about their constitutional rights to remain silent and to have counsel before questioning them. "It says that even a voluntary waiver of your rights is no good if the accused was threatened, tricked or cajoled into giving the waiver. And listen to this from a University of Pennsylvania *Law Review* article about 'Police Trickery in Inducing Confessions.'

"The author says that 'A form of deception that totally undermines the Fifth and Sixth Amendment protections available to an individual occurs when the police deceive a suspect about whether an interrogation is taking place.' That's what Downes did. He made Gary think there was no interrogation. He made him believe he was a detective."

"You're pretty good," Peter said with genuine admiration after he skimmed the material. The cases were old and the *Law Review* article had been written in 1979, but they would make it easier for him to zero in on more recent cases.

"Thanks," Donna answered, blushing from the compliment.

"When did you do this?"

"During lunch."

"Well, I couldn't have done better in that amount of time. This will really help."

"You think so?" Donna asked hopefully.

"Definitely."

Donna's features clouded. "Have you talked to Gary?" she asked.

"Not since yesterday. He's doing pretty well, under the circumstances. He seems to have accepted the jail."

"He would. Gary never complains about anything."

"You really love your brother, don't you?"

"I love him very much. We all do."

"It must be hard with his being, uh . . . so slow."

Donna smiled. "You mean 'retarded'?"

Peter flushed. "I didn't mean . . ."

"No, that's okay. I'm used to it. People always think that a person who's 'retarded' is harder to love, but that's not true. When Gary was small, he was so much fun. You know how handsome he is. Well, he was a beautiful little boy. Always running and laughing. It wasn't until he was older that we realized how dreadfully slow he was and how hard it was for him to learn. One day Mom came back from school. It had never been official before. Just something we knew, but never admitted. Mom told us what Gary's teacher had said about a special class with other 'slow learners.' Then, Mom said that Gary was God's child like everybody else and that was all she was interested in. If Gary needed extra help he would get it, but she was not going to treat Gary differently because of his intelligence. As far as she was concerned, Gary was a kind and moral boy and that was all that mattered.

"I never loved Mom more than I loved her when she said that. It shaped Gary's life. We never made him feel like a freak or demanded less than he could accomplish."

Donna paused. Her features were set in stone.

"He is a good boy, Peter. A good, simple boy, just like Mom said. He's always been like that. He couldn't do what they're saying."

Peter wanted to say something to reassure Donna, but he knew that anything he said would sound wrong. Donna took a deep breath and stood up. She was embarrassed by her sudden display of emotion.

"I . . . I'd better go. I have to shop for dinner."

"Thanks for the cases."

"I hope they help," Donna said as she left the office.

Peter closed the door behind Donna and wandered back to his desk, lost in thought. Donna really trusted him, so did Gary. They believed that he would set Gary free. Was their faith misplaced? Peter remembered his phone conversation of the day before with Amos Geary. His boss had told him bluntly that he was not competent to try an aggravated murder case. Was Steve Mancini mistaken in his belief that Peter had the tools to handle a capital murder? Was Peter fooling himself? What if a death case was too complicated for him at this stage of his career? What did he really know about trying a charge of aggravated murder? It occurred to Peter that he should talk to someone with a little experience in this area in order to get some idea of what he was getting into.

Peter looked up the phone number for the Oregon Criminal Defense Lawyers Association. The secretary at the OCDLA gave him the names of three experienced death penalty attorneys. Peter decided not to call the first two names on the list. They practiced in Portland and he was afraid they would know who he was. Sam Levine was a Eugene attorney and he was in.

"So this is your first death case," Levine said after Peter explained why he was calling.

"First one."

"I remember my first. I'd tried about seven, eight murder cases and I thought I was a hotshot." Levine chuckled. "I had no idea what I was getting myself into."

"Why is that?" Peter asked nervously.

"No other case is like a death case. They're unique. The biggest difference is that you have to prepare for two trials from the get-go. The first trial is on guilt and innocence. If your guy is convicted of aggravated murder, there is a whole second trial on what penalty he should receive.

"With your usual case, you don't think about sentencing until your client is convicted. With a capital case, you have to assume he's going to be convicted even if you're personally convinced you're going to win, because the penalty phase starts almost immediately after a conviction in front of the same jury that found your client guilty and you won't have time to prepare for the penalty phase if you wait until the last minute."

Peter asked question after question and felt more and more insecure with each answer. Levine explained the special jury selection procedure he should request and told Peter that there was an entire body of law peculiar to capital murder cases. After three quarters of an hour, Levine said that he had to meet a client, but he told Peter he would be glad to speak to him again.

"Thanks. I really appreciate the time you've taken."

"You'll learn that there's a real fraternity among death penalty lawyers. I always call other attorneys for help. You've got to. When you try a driving while suspended, you can afford to fuck up. What are they going to do to your client, give him a weekend in jail? But with a death case, you have to be perfect. If you make one small mistake, the state eats your client."

4

Donna Harmon's arms were loaded with groceries, so she backed through the front door, then pushed it shut with her foot.

"Steve, I'm home," she shouted cheerfully, as she deposited her packages on the counter next to the sink. The house was dark. Donna turned on the kitchen light. It was late and Donna assumed Steve would be home by now. She called out his name again as she walked down the hall to the living room. When the lights went on,

Donna was startled to see her husband sitting silently by the fireplace.

"Why didn't you answer me?" she asked, still smiling. But the smile faded as her husband looked up at her. Mancini's eyes were bloodshot and his clothing was rumpled. He was holding a drink and it was obvious that it wasn't his first. The hand holding the glass was bandaged.

"What happened to your hand?"

"I cut it."

"How?" she asked, crossing to him.

"If you were concerned about me, you would have been here when I needed you."

The anger in Steve's voice made Donna stop.

"I had no idea you were hurt, but I have something that will make you feel better. Veal and spinach pasta with a sauce I read about in *Gourmet* magazine."

"Do you know what time it is?"

"I lost track of time. I was meeting with Peter about some research I did in Gary's case. I'm sorry if I'm late."

"I'm sorry," Mancini mimicked. "Is that supposed to make everything better? I bust my ass all day for you and all I ask is that you have my dinner ready when I get home."

Mancini stood up slowly and walked over to Donna. He was speaking in a monotone. The muscles in his neck stood out and his face was flushed. For the first time since she'd known him, Donna was frightened of her husband. Mancini stopped in front of her. She could smell the thick odor of alcohol when he spoke.

"Now, let's get one thing straight here. You are not a lawyer and I don't expect you to pretend to be one. You're a goddamned secretary and my wife. You work from eight to five, then you get your ass home. Is that clear?"

Donna was so hurt it was hard for her to speak. Tears welled up.

"I . . . I said I'm sorry. I appreciate how hard you work . . ."

Mancini stared at his wife with what looked, unbelievably to her, like contempt.

"I would like a little less appreciation," Steve said between clenched teeth, "and some food. Do you think you can manage that?"

"You . . . You're not being fair," Donna stuttered. "I was trying to help Gary. I . . . I know I'm not as smart as you, but I can do research. I . . . I can be useful."

"What did I just say, you cunt?" Mancini shouted.

The first blow was backhand and rattled her teeth. The second was openhanded and sent her stumbling backward. Donna was in shock. She gaped at her husband, unable to accept what was happening even though she could see Steve's fist moving toward her. The blow struck her in the solar plexus, driving all the air from her. Donna sank to her knees, then crumpled onto her side, flailing for oxygen. Mancini kicked her in the ribs and watched her writhe on the floor.

Mouth open, Donna sucked in air. She could not breathe and she thought she would die. Nothing but air mattered. Her lungs filled and a sob escaped from her. As her breath returned, she was gripped by terror. Donna rolled on her side and saw her husband put on his jacket. By the time she could speak, he was gone.

Had Steve really hit her? It seemed incredible, even though she knew it was true. Donna curled up on the floor and tried to piece together what had happened from the moment she opened the front door. What had she done to deserve a beating? She was late, but that was because she was helping Gary and Peter. She was sorry she was late. She was sorry dinner wasn't ready. Sorry, sorry, sorry. But did she deserve to be beaten because she was late with Steve's dinner? There must be something else, but what could she have done that was so awful that it had driven her husband to hit her? Donna asked that question over and over as she lay sobbing on the living room floor.

CHAPTER FIFTEEN

1

When Donna awoke, it was to the scent of roses. The pungent smell confused her, because there hadn't been any roses in her bedroom when she had finally passed out from exhaustion, alone, in the early hours of the morning. Donna sat up to find every inch of the bed, the floor and the furniture covered by roses of every color and her husband sitting in a corner of the room watching her. Memories of the night before flooded in. Donna shrank back against the headboard.

Steve was unshaven. His clothes appeared to have been slept in. There was no anger in him. Only contrition. He walked over to Donna and knelt by the side of the bed on a carpet of red and yellow roses. His head hung down.

"I have no excuse for what I did to you. All I can do is explain why it happened and pray for your forgiveness."

The rose fragrance was overpowering in the closed room. The memory of her husband looming above her as his blows rained on her body was vivid and frightening. But Steve seemed so chastened that Donna let him try to explain his savage attack.

"I'd been drinking. I started in the afternoon and never stopped." Mancini paused and took a deep breath before continuing. "The bank turned down the Mountain View loan." There were tears in Steve's eyes, but Donna was still too frightened of him to move. "I didn't know what to do," he sobbed, and Donna's heart began to break. "We could be ruined. I sank everything I had into that project."

Her husband raised his eyes to hers. He looked so sad.

"Can you ever forgive me? I was so full of anger and so afraid, but I should never have taken it out on you. Please, Donna, I don't want to lose you."

"Where . . . where have you been?" Donna asked, as she tried to sort out her jumbled thoughts and emotions.

"I drove around for hours thinking about what I'd done. When I was too tired to drive anymore I pulled into the first motel I saw, but I couldn't sleep. I felt so bad about . . . about hurting you. God, how could I have hit you?"

Mancini's face crumpled. Kneeling by the bed, his head down, framed in the multihued bouquets of roses, Steve looked like a little boy. Donna reached out and touched him on the cheek. He took her hand and pressed his lips to the palm, then pressed it against his cheek again.

"I'm sorry about the loan," Donna said, "but we'll pull through. You have your practice and your brains and you have me."

Steve looked at Donna with the rapt glow of a supplicant whose prayers have been answered. Then, he squeezed her hand and wiped away the tears that had clouded his vision.

"Thank you, Donna. I should have known you'd stand by me. But I was so depressed. I wanted Mountain View to succeed so much."

"I love you, Steve. I don't need Mountain View to be happy."

"You don't understand. I want to do things for you that I can't do now. I wanted us to be important, not just in Whitaker, but everywhere. If Mountain View is successful, we'll be rich. But now . . ." Mancini shook his head slowly. "I don't think we can make it. I'm tapped out and I can't think of any place to turn for money, now that the bank's turned us down."

"Maybe . . ." Donna started. Mancini looked up at her. "I could talk to my father . . ."

"Oh no, Donna, I couldn't ask you to do that."

"How much money do you need?"

"I'd have to talk to my partners," Mancini answered excitedly. "If we could buy some of the property instead of having it on option, we might get Whitaker Savings to rethink the loan."

Mancini stood up and sat next to Donna on the bed. They fell into each other's arms and Steve hugged her to his chest.

"I don't deserve you, Donna. What I did can't be excused. I must have been out of my mind."

"Just hold me," Donna said, not wanting to think about the horror of the past evening.

"I will. I'll hold you forever. And I swear to you that I will never, ever hurt you again."

2

"I don't think this is important," Eric Polk told Dennis Downes, "but I figured, better safe than sorry, so I had Wilma come down."

Eric was also on the Whitaker police force, but he was several years older than Downes and was not working on the Harmon case.

"How you doin', Wilma," Downes said, smiling at Eric's wife.

"Just fine. How are Jill and Todd?"

"Damn kid of mine runs me ragged. He's only ten and he's almost as big as me."

"I heard he's tearing up Little League," Eric said.

"Don't get me started on Todd or I'll chew off your ear. So, what do you have for me, Wilma?"

Wilma Polk was a heavyset woman in her mid-fifties with curly gray hair and a round, pleasant face, who was not used to being the center of attention.

"It's probably nothing. I'd even forgotten about it until Eric said something about Donna Harmon's wedding and, well, it just popped into my head."

"Go ahead, Wilma," her husband said.

"Mabel Dawes and I were over by the food table at Donna Harmon's wedding reception. We were talking about the murder because Eric had been at the scene that morning. Gary was nearby and he must have overheard us. He came over and started talking about the murder, too."

"What did he say?" Downes asked.

"I've tried to remember exactly, but it's been a while, and I wasn't really interested at the time."

"Just give me the gist, if you can't remember the exact words."

"He didn't get to say much, because Eric came up and interrupted us."

"We were due at Mary's at two and it was one-thirty, so we had to get moving," Eric explained. "It was Kenny's third birthday."

"So, go ahead," Downes prodded as he jotted down some notes about the time of the conversation.

"As I remember, I was saying something about Eric being at the crime scene. I believe I had just explained about the horrible wounds when Gary walked over. He said he had seen the girl at the Stallion, the night before. I was about to ask him some more about the girl when Eric reminded me of the time."

"How did Gary seem? Was he nervous, excited?"

"He didn't seem nervous. Maybe a little excited, but we all were. The murder is very frightening."

"Okay," Downes said, smiling at Wilma as he scribbled some more notes. "Thanks for dropping by. I'll write a report about the conversation for the D.A."

Eric Polk escorted his wife out of Downes's office. Downes looked at his watch. It was time for a coffee break. He decided to dictate his report on his interview with Wilma Polk, then see if anyone wanted to go over to Mel's Café for a piece of pie and a cup of coffee. He was finishing the dictation when the phone rang.

"Dennis, are you busy?" Becky O'Shay asked.

"I was going out for a cup of coffee. Why?"

"Put the coffee on hold. I just received a call from the jail. One of the prisoners claims Gary Harmon confessed to him. I want you to come along with me. If this pans out, I'll buy the coffee and treat you to lunch."

3

"The last time you escaped justice by a nose, Mr. Booth," Becky O'Shay said with a smirk, "but your luck seems to have run out."

Booth flushed with anger and looked at the floor, afraid to let O'Shay see the hatred in his eyes. He could not stand being humiliated by a woman, but he was in no position to do anything about it.

"I understand you have something for us."

"Yeah, I got something. What I want to know is what I get in return."

"What do you want?"

Booth licked his lips. His right foot could not stop tapping and Booth could not sit still. Withdrawal, O'Shay thought immediately. She bet every nerve in Booth's body felt like a live wire. When he looked up, O'Shay read stark terror on Booth's face.

"I want witness protection. I want to go somewhere Rafael Vargas and Chris Mammon can't get me."

"That's asking a lot. Your beef's federal. I don't know if they'll go along, even if I wanted to."

"Hey," Booth pleaded, "I'm small potatoes. I'm nothing. The feds don't want me. I'm an undersize catch. But I can deliver Mammon or Vargas and I can ice Gary Harmon."

"Tell me about Harmon."

Booth shook his head vigorously from side to side.

"Uh uh. What do you take me for? I'm not giving up anything until I know I'm going to be protected."

O'Shay turned to Dennis Downes. "Can we transfer Mr. Booth to the jail in Stark?"

"We've done that before. Sheriff Tyler will keep you warm and comfy, Kevin. They got a nice security wing. Real modern."

"I don't care where I go, as long as it's away from anyone connected with Rafael Vargas."

"I'll check to see if any of his people are incarcerated in Stark. If there's a problem, I've got another couple ideas."

"So, Mr. Booth?" O'Shay asked.

"What about my deal? If I talk, what do I get?"

"Let me explain something to you. If we make a deal before you testify it will affect the value of your evidence. The first thing Peter Hale will ask you on cross-examination is what reward you're getting for your testimony. If you can say that you are testifying as a service to humanity, it will make you much more believable."

"You want me to testify for nothing?"

"I didn't say that, did I?"

"No, but . . ."

"Do you think I'll let you down if you come through for me?"

Booth licked his lips. O'Shay made him very nervous and she was so sexy it was distracting.

"How do I know you won't screw me? What if I testify and you lose anyway? I need a guarantee."

"You need help, Mr. Booth, and the only person in the galaxy who can help you is sitting in front of you in this room. Do you want my help?"

"Yeah. That's why I'm here."

"Good. Then we'll do things my way or not at all. If you ask for anything in return for your testimony, I'll walk out of here. If you want to be a good citizen and help me out, I'll be very receptive to any pleas for assistance you might make after Harmon's trial."

"Man, I don't know. I don't like this."

"You don't have to like it, Mr. Booth. You only have to accept the fact that you have no choice but to do as I say. Right now, I would appreciate hearing a summary of what you can tell me about Harmon."

Booth didn't trust O'Shay, but he realized he had no choice.

"Gary confessed to me. He told me he done it."

"Why would he do that?"

"I've known Gary since high school. He thinks I'm his friend. He's so fuckin' dumb, it was easy. At first, he denied doin' it, but I told him it took balls to commit murder. I built him up. Gary's such a retard, he never figured out what I was doin'. Soon, I had him bragging about how good it felt to snuff Whiley."

"That's certainly interesting, but how do we know you're not making up this whole story? You're facing a long sentence in a federal prison, you have some very scary people mad at you. That's a lot of motivation to lie."

Booth looked wild-eyed. He felt his only chance at safety and freedom slipping away.

"I ain't lying. This is the truth. He spilled his guts to me."

"Maybe he did, but I only have your word for that. Unless you can give me something concrete, something that proves Harmon killed Sandra Whiley, your testimony will be useless."

Booth put his hands to his head. He closed his eyes and shifted on his seat.

"Let me think," he begged.

O'Shay felt disgust for Booth, but she did not let it show. If Harmon really had confessed to Booth, Booth's

187

testimony would be very important to her case. Now that the first flush of excitement had faded, she realized that her case was not as strong as she first imagined. Although she would argue that Harmon's statements to Downes contained so much detail that he had to be the killer, Harmon had not really confessed to killing Whiley. And there was the problem of the blood, or lack of it. Police technicians had not found any of Whiley's blood on Harmon's clothes or in his house. And the murder weapon was still missing.

Suddenly, Booth's face lit up. "I got it," he said. "I got something solid. Something that will prove I'm not lying."

4

Peter watched Clara Schoen leave Amos Geary's office from the coffee shop across the street. Geary had left half an hour before. Peter gave it fifteen minutes more to be certain Clara would not return before scurrying across to the law office.

Peter felt a little bit like a thief, though he had convinced himself that there was nothing wrong with clearing out his own belongings from his own office after everyone was gone. He wasn't taking anything that wasn't his and coming in when Geary wasn't there would prevent a nasty scene. Everyone was better off this way.

Peter had brought an empty liquor carton with him. He set it on the desk and was filling it with law books and personal items when he looked up to find Amos Geary watching him from the doorway.

"He . . . hello, Mr. Geary," Peter said with an uneasy smile.

Geary shook his head slowly.

"You are some piece of work." Geary's voice was filled more with sadness than anger. "How are you going to defend a man's life when you don't even have the guts to leave my office in broad daylight?"

"I . . . Uh, I was, uh, going to drop in tomorrow to, uh, thank you for . . ." Peter started, but Geary cut him off with a sound that was half laugh, half bark.

"You really don't have any pride, do you? It's beyond me how a man like your father could sire someone as worthless as you."

Peter flushed, but he was too embarrassed at being caught to reply.

"Where are you sneaking off to?" Geary asked.

"I'm not sneaking anywhere. These are my things," Peter said, tilting the carton to show Geary the contents. Geary kept his eyes on Peter's face and didn't look down. Peter was able to keep eye contact for only a moment before he lost his nerve.

"I'm moving to Steve Mancini's offices," he answered. His voice quivered a little.

Geary nodded slowly. "You and Mancini should get along just fine."

Peter straightened up. He realized that he had packed all his things and there was no more need to stay, but Geary was blocking the doorway.

"I, uh, I really do appreciate the chance you gave me. I learned a lot these past weeks," Peter said, hoping that he sounded suitably grateful.

"You didn't learn a thing, Peter. You're the same sorry son of a bitch you were when you cheated that poor woman in Portland. Is it going to take the death of Gary Harmon to make you see how truly pathetic you are?"

It suddenly occurred to Peter that Geary might be angry enough to try to talk Jesse Harmon into firing him.

"What are you going to do?" he asked nervously.

Geary made no effort to hide his contempt.

"Don't worry. I won't interfere with your precious

189

case. You've been admitted to practice law in this state, so you're entitled to try any type of case you want to, and the Constitution gives Gary Harmon the right to be represented by the counsel of his choice, no matter how sorry a son of a bitch that lawyer may be. But I will leave you with a thought. Gary Harmon is a living, breathing human being. If you continue with this farce and he is executed, you will be as much a murderer as the bastard who killed that poor girl in the park."

PART
FIVE

—

DEATH
CASE

——

CHAPTER SIXTEEN

1

There were no fancy decorations in the Whitaker County Circuit Court. The county could not afford them and the penny-conscious rural constituents did not want them. They wanted justice, fast and without frills. So, the benches for the spectators were hard, the judge's dais was unadorned and the only dashes of color were in the flags of Oregon and the United States that flanked Circuit Court Judge Harry Kuffel's high-backed chair.

Judge Kuffel was someone you could easily picture in a bow tie, vest and bowler hat tap-dancing across a vaudeville stage. He was five six with a dancer's slender, but compact, build. He wore his gray hair slicked down and his mustache was neatly trimmed. Kuffel's suits were expensive and conservative, but the judge had a ready smile and tried to keep the atmosphere in his courtroom from being overly stuffy.

"The state calls Don Bosco, Your Honor," Becky O'Shay said.

As the psychologist walked to the front of the packed courtroom to take the oath, Judge Kuffel sneaked a look at the clock. It was four-thirty. In one half hour, he would recess for the night. Kuffel looked interested, but was secretly bored. He had decided how he would rule on the defendant's motion to suppress Gary Harmon's statements to Dennis Downes hours ago.

"Will this be your last witness?"

"Yes, Your Honor."

"Very well."

Peter had been relieved when Steve Mancini volunteered to handle the pretrial motion. He knew very little about the law of confessions and was only too glad to let Mancini do the research, write the brief and examine the witnesses.

Peter barely listened while Bosco explained his academic and professional credentials and gave the court a brief outline of his duties as Director of Mental Health for the county. This testimony was strictly for the record, since Bosco was well known to the court.

Peter glanced at Gary. Poor kid. Peter had to admire him. He really tried. Mancini had told Gary to take notes when witnesses were testifying. They had to train Gary now, so he would know how to fake it when there was a jury in the room. Peter and Steve agreed that subjecting Gary to cross-examination would lead to disaster. Since he would probably not take the stand, it was important to create the illusion that Gary was involved in his defense.

Gary had taken the note writing to heart and scribbled constantly, even though he understood little of what he heard. Peter had glanced at Gary's notes and they were gibberish. Still, he looked great writing. Very intense. Thank God for his good looks.

"Mr. Bosco," O'Shay asked, "were you summoned to the Whitaker police station on the evening of Sandra Whiley's murder?"

"I was."

"Do you remember when you arrived?"

"Not exactly, but I'm certain it was sometime between nine and ten."

"Where did you go when you arrived at the station?"

"Into a small room next to the room where Mr. Harmon was being questioned."

"Could you see and hear the defendant?"

"Yes. There was a two-way mirror and an intercom that let me hear what was said."

"Was Mr. Harmon's interrogation under way when you arrived?"

"Yes."

"How much of it did you hear?"

"Several hours. Maybe five. The interrogation went on for some time."

"Did Sergeant Downes make any promises in exchange for Mr. Harmon's cooperation?"

"No."

"Did you ever hear Sergeant Downes threaten the defendant?"

"No."

"Did it sound like Mr. Harmon was being coerced into talking to Sergeant Downes?"

Bosco hesitated before answering and looked at Steve Mancini. Peter caught the look, but Mancini did not react at all.

"No," Bosco said.

Becky O'Shay checked her notes. Then, she smiled at the witness.

"No further questions."

"Mr. Mancini?" Judge Kuffel asked.

"No questions."

Bosco frowned. He tilted his head slightly, as if he was attempting to signal Mancini, but Steve was absorbed in his notes. Bosco stood slowly, as if trying to give Mancini extra time to act. Mancini saw Bosco staring at him and smiled. Bosco's brow knitted, but he walked out of the courtroom. Peter noticed the psychologist's confusion and leaned over to Steve.

"Bosco hesitated when Becky asked whether Gary seemed to be coerced. I think he wanted to say something. Why didn't you follow up?"

"I already interviewed Bosco. He can't help us," Mancini whispered.

"Do you have any rebuttal witnesses, Mr. Mancini?" Judge Kuffel asked.

"No, sir."

"Then, we'll recess for the day and I'll hear argument in the morning."

Judge Kuffel left the bench quickly and the reporters surged forward. Peter walked over to them, but Becky O'Shay intercepted him.

"Drop by my office before you leave the courthouse," she said.

Steve Mancini talked to Gary while the guards handcuffed him. Mancini patted Gary on the shoulder and said something that made Gary smile. While Peter and Becky talked to the reporters, Mancini gathered up his notes and law books.

"Becky wants to see us," Peter told Steve when he returned to the table.

"What for?"

Peter shrugged. The two attorneys hefted their briefcases and books and headed upstairs.

"What's up?" Peter asked the deputy D.A. when they were all in her office. O'Shay handed Peter copies of a police report.

"We received this information last week, but we've been checking it out. Now that I've decided to use this witness, I'm obligated to give you his statement."

The two defense lawyers read the police report. When Mancini finished it, he shook his head and chuckled.

"You're not serious about using Kevin as a witness, are you?"

"Dead serious," Becky answered.

"Come on. You can't believe a thing Kevin says. You know he's just trying to weasel out of this federal drug bust."

"I'm sure that's what you'll argue to the jury."

"We've got a problem," Steve Mancini told Peter as soon as they were outside the courthouse. "I've got to get off Gary's case."

"Why?"

"I've got a conflict of interest. I can't represent a client if another client is going to be a key witness against him."

"What if I cross-examine Booth?"

Mancini shook his head. "If I know something about Booth that will help Gary and I don't tell you, I'm violating my duty to Gary. But if I use confidential information I obtained from Booth to help Gary, I'm violating my duty to Booth. Even staying on as co-counsel presents the appearance of impropriety. I have no choice. I've got to get off the case."

"Jesus, Steve. How am I supposed to try this case alone?"

"Hey, I'm sympathetic. I feel bad about talking you into taking the case. If you don't think you can do it, you can resign."

But Peter knew that resigning was not an option. He had cut himself off from his father and quit his job. If he tried to get a position anywhere, he would receive references from Hale, Greaves and Amos Geary that would make Saddam Hussein look like a better job candidate. Without the Harmons' retainer he would be dead broke. A victory for Gary Harmon was his only way out of the hole he'd dug for himself.

"No, I can't let Gary down," Peter said.

Mancini clapped Peter on the back. "That's what I wanted to hear. Besides, I have confidence in you. You're a quick study, Peter. This criminal stuff is a cinch. This might even work out better for you in the long run. When you win, you won't have to share the credit."

2

The Ponderosa was on the opposite side of Whitaker from the Stallion. It catered to workingmen and solitary drinkers. Its jukebox played country and the waitresses were older women who had lost a few rounds to life. Most of the time it was a place where a man could get totally sloshed in peace and quiet. Occasionally, it was the scene of violent barroom brawls.

Barney Pullen fit right in with the Ponderosa regulars. He had a beer gut, a bushy black beard and a don't-fuck-with-me attitude he had picked up in the Marines. He liked to fish, hunt and drink beer. NFL football was as intellectual as he got. After the Marines, Pullen worked as a cop in Eugene, Oregon, until an incident with a suspect occurred. Pullen wasn't exactly fired, but he didn't exactly quit the force, either. The whole affair was left murky and Pullen moved to Whitaker, where he worked in his brother's body shop.

One day, Pullen was assigned the job of figuring out what caused the knocking sound that Steve Mancini heard whenever his Cadillac went over fifty. In between discussions of car engines and pro football, Pullen mentioned his police background. Mancini needed an investigator with a knowledge of cars for a personal injury case and Pullen agreed to work on the case. He had done spot investigation for Mancini ever since and Peter had hired him for the Harmon case on Mancini's recommendation when the other investigators Mancini had mentioned turned out to be unavailable.

Jake Cataldo was tending bar when Pullen stepped in out of the late afternoon sun. Pullen blinked a few times and waited for his eyes to adjust to the dark.

"Hi, Jake," Pullen said, as he hoisted himself onto a bar stool next to a couple of regulars.

Cataldo was a big man with short, curly black hair and the pale complexion of someone who is indoors during the day.

198

"Hi, Barney. What can I do you for?"

Pullen ordered a beer. Cataldo turned to get it for him.

"What are you doin' with yourself lately?" the bartender asked, when he placed the glass of beer in front of Pullen.

"You been reading about the girl who was murdered in the park?"

Cataldo nodded.

"I'm still working at the garage and I'm doing a little investigating for the guy who's trying the case."

"No shit? You know, that Harmon kid was in here the night that girl was killed. Sat right here at the bar. I served him myself."

"Is Harmon a regular?"

"Not really. I mean, he's stopped in once or twice."

"Then why do you remember him?"

"He was picked up the next day for the murder. It was on the news. His picture was in the paper."

"You don't happen to remember what time he came in, do you?"

"Actually, I do. It was around eleven fifty-five."

"How do you remember that?"

"There was a Mariners game on and the damn thing was still going after seventeen innings. Then, Griffey hits this shot and the game's over. I glanced at my watch. It was eleven fifty-three, eleven fifty-four. Something like that, but not exactly midnight. That's when the Harmon kid sat down and asked for coffee. I didn't hear him, because I turned away to switch the channel. I told him to hang on. I remember that clear as day."

"How'd he look?"

"A little rocky." Cataldo shrugged. "He was quiet. He had the coffee and something to eat. Then, he had a few drinks. When he left, he was weaving, but I thought he'd make it home okay."

"What did he eat?"

"Some biscuits and gravy."

"Biscuits and gravy?" Pullen repeated, while thinking

199

that this wouldn't be his dish of choice if he'd just slaughtered a woman. "Did you notice anything unusual about Harmon's clothes?"

The bartender considered the question for a moment, then shook his head.

"No blood?" Pullen asked.

Cataldo thought about that. "You see how the lighting is in here. There coulda been something I didn't see. But I didn't notice blood."

CHAPTER SEVENTEEN

1

Carmen Polinsky was a forty-six-year-old mother of two who was married to an accountant. For twenty years, she had been a housewife. Before that she worked in a bookstore. Nothing in her past had prepared her for a job interview for the position of assassin for the state of Oregon. This job interview was technically called "voir dire" and it denoted the process by which a jury was selected in Gary Harmon's trial.

Judge Kuffel had denied the motion to suppress Gary's statements, but he had granted Peter's motion for individual voir dire because of the unusual nature of a death case. None of the other jurors were in the courtroom to witness Carmen Polinsky's distress when Becky O'Shay asked her if she had an attitude concerning the death penalty that would make it impossible for her to vote for a death sentence if Gary Harmon was convicted of aggravated murder. Whenever anyone mentioned the death penalty, Mrs. Polinsky gripped her purse so tightly that her knuckles turned white. It was obvious that she would rather be in Zaire during an Ebola outbreak than in this courtroom in Whitaker. It was equally obvious that Mrs. Polinsky would never, ever condemn anyone to death.

"To tell the truth . . ." Mrs. Polinsky started.

O'Shay leaned forward, praying that Polinsky would confess her inability to kill for the state. Normally, O'Shay would have gotten rid of her with a peremptory challenge, which can be used to excuse a juror without stating a reason, but it was near the end of the second week of jury selection and the prosecutor had used all of her peremptories. Now, she could get rid of Mrs. Polinsky only by convincing the judge that she could not be fair to the state.

Polinsky shook her head. "I honestly don't know," she concluded.

O'Shay went at Mrs. Polinsky from a different angle. Her job was to manipulate the woman into saying that she could never condemn someone to death. If O'Shay succeeded, it would be Peter's job to rehabilitate the woman by convincing her that she could vote to kill Gary Harmon, because that was the only way he would be able to keep her on the jury. The absurdity of the position in which he found himself was not lost on Peter.

Mrs. Polinsky vacillated again. Judge Kuffel glanced at the clock and said, "It's almost five. I'm going to stop for the day. Mrs. Polinsky, I want you to think about Ms. O'Shay's question. When we reconvene tomorrow morning, I'll expect a decisive answer from you. A 'yes' or 'no' answer. Understood?"

Mrs. Polinsky sped out of the courtroom.

"I'll see you two in chambers," the judge commanded as he left the bench. Peter gave a few words of encouragement to Gary as the guards cuffed him and led him away. While he was gathering up his paperwork, Peter noticed Becky in an animated discussion with Dennis Downes at the rear of the courtroom. Downes was nodding his head vigorously in response to something O'Shay had asked and Becky was grinning broadly.

The court reporter was not present when Peter and O'Shay walked into chambers, and Judge Kuffel was puffing on a smelly cigar in violation of a no-smoking ordinance he stubbornly chose to ignore, so Peter knew the conference was off the record.

"For Christ's sake, Peter," the judge said, "let that woman off the jury."

"It's up to Becky to lay a foundation if she wants to kick her off," Peter answered stubbornly, dropping onto an overstuffed couch that stretched along a wall covered with diplomas, certificates of appreciation from community organizations and pictures of Kuffel holding up fish of various sizes.

"Be reasonable, Peter," O'Shay said. "Even if she gets on, she won't last a day. She's already a wreck and she hasn't even seen the autopsy pictures."

"You might be right," Peter answered with a condescending smile, "but there's still no legal basis for excusing her. Being nervous doesn't do it. Everyone on that jury is going to be nervous."

Judge Kuffel shook his head in disgust. Hale was right to fight O'Shay on this. Gary Harmon would be better off with Polinsky on the jury and O'Shay would have to give him a legal basis for kicking her off or the reluctant housewife would become one of Gary Harmon's judges.

"I have something I wanted to mention," O'Shay said. "Several weeks ago, we interviewed an inmate at the jail who claimed that the defendant confessed to him."

"Did you notify the defense?" the judge asked.

"Oh yes. Mr. Booth is awaiting trial on a serious drug charge and has a reason to try to ingratiate himself with our office, so I asked him for some corroboration for his story. We just got it."

O'Shay handed Peter and the judge a copy of a document.

"What the hell is this?" Peter asked, as soon as he scanned it.

"It's a report from the FBI laboratory in Washington, D.C. We sent them a hatchet we found in a storm drain on the Whitaker campus. It was right where Mr. Harmon told Kevin Booth he threw it after he hacked Sandra Whiley to death. The handle was wiped clean of fingerprints, but Sandra Whiley's blood and hair are on the blade."

When Peter found his voice, he said, "I move to have this evidence suppressed. This is a clear violation of the discovery statutes. This should have been revealed to the defense as soon as it was discovered so we could have our own experts test the blood and hair."

O'Shay smiled sweetly at Peter. "I don't think we violated the discovery statutes. They only require the prosecution to reveal the existence of evidence we intend to introduce at trial. I had no intention of introducing this hatchet until I was certain it had some connection with this case and I did not become convinced until I read the FBI report. After all, Peter, Kevin Booth is a criminal. We weren't sure he was telling the truth about your client's confession. Until now, that is."

2

"Move it, Booth," the guard commanded as Kevin Booth lathered up for the second time. "This ain't a resort."

Booth thought of some choice retorts, but he didn't dare make them to the six-five, two-hundred-and-fifty-pound corrections officer who was lounging just outside the bars next to the shower. Inmates in the security block of the jail in Stark were allowed only two showers a week and these were precious moments for Booth.

A minute later, the guard cut off Booth's hot water and he screamed. The guard doubled over laughing and Booth choked back a "motherfucker" that surely would have led to some diabolical punishment.

"I warned you to move your ass. Now, finish up. We got other guests in this hotel."

Booth dodged in and out of the freezing water until all the soap was off. His clean clothes were in his cell at the other end of the security tank. He wrapped as much of his shivering body as he could in a towel that barely covered his private parts and huddled his shoulders as he walked past the fags, psychos and snitches who shared the security block with him.

Booth hated his new situation. At least he had human beings to talk to in Whitaker. The security block was for prisoners who could not be allowed to live in the normal jail population: escape risks, homosexuals, ultraviolent prisoners and informants. Booth hated queers, was scared to death of psychos and considered himself different from the other snitches, but he was going to have to stay in this madhouse if he expected to live long enough to trade Gary Harmon's freedom for his own.

Booth's cell was long and narrow and contained a sink, a flush toilet and two bunks, but he was the sole occupant. As soon as the guard saw that his prisoner was inside, he closed the moving bars electronically. The guard never entered the security block unless there was an emergency. He patrolled the long corridor on the other side of the bars occasionally, but when it was shower time, he stayed in his chair and used the controls to open and close the bars of each cell as each prisoner's turn to shower arrived.

"How you doin', Kevin?" a voice asked as Booth was getting into his underpants. Booth paused with one leg raised and looked through the bars. The prisoner who had spoken to him was a slender young man with pale skin and a blond crew cut. The only distinguishing mark on his body was a swastika tattoo on his right forearm. Booth noticed the tattoo at the same time he noticed the milk container concealed under the prisoner's bath towel. The young man kept his easy smile as he tossed the contents of the milk container over Booth's naked body. Lighter fluid, Booth thought as a lighted match followed the liquid through the bars and transformed him into a human torch.

3

Peter ran as fast as he could along the jogging trails in Wishing Well Park, pushing himself to exhaustion in the hope that his brain would be too busy working on his oxygen supply to concern itself with Gary Harmon. But Peter's brain would not cooperate and images of blood-encrusted hatchets dominated his thoughts.

The feds used a system for determining sentences that allowed judges almost no discretion. If he was convicted under the Federal Sentencing Guidelines, Kevin Booth would do a lot of federal time without the possibility of parole. There was, however, a motion for reduction of sentence that the prosecutor could make if a defendant turned in someone. In cases like Booth's, this system created tremendous pressure to lie about the criminal involvement of an innocent person.

What troubled Peter was the possibility that Gary might be guilty. Gary would not state unequivocally that he did not kill Sandra Whiley. He claimed he drank so much that he did not have a clear memory for the hour or so when the murder was probably committed. Did he kill Whiley and repress the memory or was he simply lying? Peter could not believe Gary was capable of sustaining a lie for this long, but Peter had read about repressed memory. He had a hard time buying into the idea that someone could witness a murder or be sexually abused and have no memory of the event, but he knew it happened. Maybe a person with Gary's IQ was more susceptible to that kind of thing. If he had not killed Whiley, how was he able to tell Dennis Downes that the killer used a hatchet and how was he able to tell Kevin Booth where the murder weapon could be found?

There was no endorphin rush during his run and Peter reached his house depressed and exhausted. He had barely caught his breath when the phone rang.

"Mr. Hale?" a shaky voice asked.

"Gary? You sound upset. Has something happened? Why are you calling?"

"I said I had to talk to you. I said I wanted to call my lawyer."

"That's good, Gary. You did just what I told you to do, if you were in trouble. Are you in trouble?"

"They say I burned up Kevin. I didn't burn him. Please tell them I didn't burn him."

"Calm down, Gary. Who says you burned someone?"

"That lady lawyer and Sergeant Downes," Gary gulped in a voice close to tears.

"Are Sergeant Downes and Becky O'Shay with you?"

"Yeah."

"Put Ms. O'Shay on the phone."

There was dead air for a moment. Peter heard Gary saying something he could not make out. As soon as O'Shay took the phone, Peter said, "What's going on? Why are you questioning Gary?"

"Kevin Booth was set on fire in his cell in the Stark jail," O'Shay answered, her rage barely under control. "Unfortunately for your client, there was a fuck-up. Booth's still alive."

"You don't think Gary was involved, do you?" Peter asked incredulously. "He's not bright enough to plan something like that."

"We'll soon find out."

"How will you do that?"

"Sergeant Downes and I are going to question Gary."

"I can't let you do that. You two shouldn't be anywhere near Gary without my permission."

"This is a totally different crime, Peter. You don't represent Gary on this."

"The hell I don't," Peter said, losing his patience. "Now, listen, Becky. I want you and Downes out of there."

"Don't tell me what to do," Becky answered angrily.

Peter did not want to upset O'Shay. He still had hopes of going out with her. But protecting Gary was crucial.

"Damn it, Becky. I'm Gary's lawyer. I *can* tell you what to do in this case."

"Why are you afraid to let Gary talk to us?"

"Are you nuts? You're prosecuting him. Downes arrested him. I don't want either of you within a mile of him. Now, get Gary back to his cell immediately and don't you dare ask him any questions. If I find you have, I'll move for a mistrial. You know what you're doing isn't ethical."

"I don't think you're in any position to discuss ethics, Hale."

"What . . . what do you mean?"

"Do you think I believed for one moment that story about quitting Hale, Greaves to get out of the rat race? I called a few friends in Portland. They knew all about the way you lied to Judge Pruitt and lost that case for that crippled woman. You're pretty famous."

Peter felt sick. "Look, Becky . . ." he started, but O'Shay had already hung up.

4

Donna's doorbell rang at nine-thirty. She wondered who was calling so late. She smiled when she found Peter on her doorstep, but the smile faded as soon as she saw the expression on his face. Peter usually looked as if he had just stepped out of the pages of a menswear catalog, but tonight his suit was rumpled, his tie was askew and his hair was a mess.

"What's wrong?" she asked as she stepped aside to let him in.

"Everything. Where's Steve?"

"He's staying overnight in Salem. He has a business meeting there about Mountain View, tomorrow."

"Damn! That's right. I forgot."

208

"Is this about Gary? Has something happened?"

Peter nodded. "You know the inmate who's going to say Gary confessed?"

"Yes."

"Another prisoner set him on fire this afternoon."

"They can't think Gary's involved."

"Becky and Downes tried to question Gary without me, but he remembered what I told him about demanding a call to his lawyer if any policeman tried to talk to him. I went down to the jail and they backed off. They're grasping at straws on the torching, but something else has come up. That's what I really wanted to talk to Steve about."

"What happened?"

"They found the murder weapon and they've linked it to Gary."

"Oh no."

Donna's hand flew to her mouth. She looked stricken.

"Don't cry," Peter said when he saw Donna's shoulders start to shake. She tried to control herself, but she couldn't.

"I'm sorry," she sobbed. "It's just too much."

Peter didn't know what to do. He wanted to hold Donna, but he felt awkward. Donna was Steve's wife and this was Steve's house. He settled for handing her a handkerchief and stood red-faced while she dabbed at her eyes and tried to stop crying.

"It just seems like it's one thing after another." Then she was in Peter's arms, her body trembling as she sobbed into his shoulder. He let her lean against him, but he was afraid to hold her. He could smell Donna's hair and feel her breasts pushing against him. Peter held his breath and ended by giving her a few feeble pats on the back.

"I'm sorry," Donna managed, suddenly pulling away.

"Everything will be okay," he replied lamely.

"I've got to get ahold of myself," Donna answered, as she wiped at her eyes. Then she stopped and took Peter's hand.

"I want you to know I appreciate how hard you're working for Gary. He really trusts you."

Donna squeezed Peter's hand and held it for a moment before releasing it. Her hand felt warm and her proximity evoked in him a combination of embarrassment and sexual desire. Peter felt himself flush. They both looked down. Donna stepped back.

"Tell Steve what happened," Peter said. "I need to see him as soon as he gets back."

"I'll call him at his motel."

The Mancinis only lived a short distance from Peter and he had walked over. It had cooled down since his run and the air was pleasant. It took a few blocks to shake off his sexual excitement and refocus on Gary's problem, but every so often Peter's thoughts would drift back to Donna.

CHAPTER EIGHTEEN

1

"What did he say?" Earl Ridgely asked the man in the gray pinstripe suit.

"What did you expect, Mr. Ridgely?" Frank Ketchell answered. Ketchell, an investigator with the State Department of Justice, was tall and gray-haired with a square jaw and bright blue eyes that wowed the ladies, but his good looks had not done him a bit of good with Elmer Maddox. After spending Saturday morning talking to the man who had set Kevin Booth on fire, Ketchell had driven to Whitaker for this late afternoon meeting.

"Maddox thought the whole thing was a big joke. He kept cracking up when he described the way Booth hopped around and rolled on the floor while he was burning."

"Jesus," Becky O'Shay said, shaking her head with disgust.

"The only thing that upset Maddox was that the guard shoved him back in his cell before helping Booth. They found a shiv when they searched him. I guess he was going to finish off Booth when the guard went into the cell to put out the fire."

"How did he expect to get away with this?" O'Shay asked in disbelief.

"I don't think it occurred to him. Like he said to me when I offered him a deal, 'What are you gonna do if I don't cooperate? Give me more time?' Maddox and a buddy were on a spree for over a year, running around the country knocking off banks and killing people. He's already serving three consecutive life terms in Tennessee, he's got a consecutive federal bank robbery for a job in Idaho, he's facing the death penalty for a robbery-murder in Stark and there are four other states waiting in line to get their hands on him."

"Why did he do it, then?"

Ketchell shrugged. "He's got a wife and family in Washington State. I hear he loves his kid. Maybe someone promised to take care of them."

"Who?"

"I've got no idea. I know you want Gary Harmon to be involved. The feds would love to hear that it was someone in the organization that Rafael Vargas works for. But I've got to tell you that there's no evidence connecting anyone other than Maddox to this right now."

"Someone smuggled in the lighter fluid and the matches."

"Oh, yeah. But Maddox could have set Booth on fire for his own amusement or for some real or imagined slight."

"How did he get the lighter fluid, matches and shiv into the security block? What kind of security do they have in Stark?" O'Shay asked.

"Human security."

Ridgely sighed. "I guess finding out who gave Maddox the stuff would help."

"And we're looking into it. There are only a few guards who could have done it, and a few prisoners, but we haven't cracked anyone yet."

"How is Booth doing?" Ridgely asked.

Ketchell consulted a small notebook before answering.

"He was flown to the burn center in Portland as soon as possible. I talked to Dr. Leonard Farber, who's treating Booth. Farber says he's in critical condition with burns over thirty-five percent of his body. Seventy-five percent of the burns are full thickness, which means he'll need skin grafts. Additionally, Booth's bedding caught on fire and he suffered minor smoke inhalation injuries."

"Will he be able to testify?" Becky asked.

"Farber thinks he might be up to it, but not right away. Booth will be operated on about three times in the first three to four days. They use as much of his skin as they can for the grafts and pigskin for the rest. Two weeks later, they'll use more of his skin to replace the pigskin. He can't be moved back to Whitaker for at least four weeks because they're afraid of losing the grafts."

"Damn," O'Shay swore angrily. "I need Booth. He's my key witness."

"You can always ask for a continuance," Ridgely suggested.

"I know I can, but I don't want to if there's any chance Booth can testify now. Think of the sympathy he'll evoke in his condition."

Ridgely was taken aback by O'Shay's callousness, but she did not notice because she was lost in thought.

"Frank," she said, "as I understand it, Booth can't be moved back to Whitaker because they're afraid of endangering the skin grafts."

"Right."

"Call Dr. Farber for me and ask him how soon Booth could testify if we held court in Portland."

2

Peter was at the office on Sunday afternoon when he heard the front door open. He walked into the corridor and saw Steve Mancini checking his messages at the reception desk.

"Am I glad to see you," Peter said.

For a moment, Mancini looked as if he was not happy to see Peter. Then, his face changed rapidly and he smiled.

"How's the trial going?"

"We've got our jury and Becky's putting on her first witness on Monday."

"Donna called and told me about Booth."

"Then you know what's going on. Can we talk?"

Mancini looked at his watch. "I'm really pressed for time. I haven't even been home yet. I drove right here from Salem."

"Please, Steve. I'm afraid I'm getting in over my head and I need your advice."

Mancini clapped Peter on the back and started for his office. "You have any coffee up?" he asked.

During the next half hour, Peter brought Mancini up to speed on the torching of Kevin Booth and the discovery of the hatchet. When he finished, Mancini said, "There's no way Gary was involved with setting Booth on fire. He doesn't have the brains to think up a scheme like that. This sounds more like something Rafael Vargas would do. What did Becky say about that?"

Peter flushed. "She didn't say much. In fact, she's been really hostile since Booth was attacked."

"Oh?"

Peter hesitated before speaking again, but he decided it was best for his friend to hear about his real reason for leaving Portland from him. It was bad enough that he had misrepresented his reason for moving to Whitaker. If Steve heard about the Elliot case from someone else, he might decide not to go through with the partnership.

"There's another reason why Becky is upset. I, uh, haven't been straight with you about why I left Portland. When we met that night at the Stallion . . . Well, I

214

hadn't seen you for years and, uh . . . This is a little embarrassing . . ."

"Are you going to tell me about that personal injury case you tried for Hale, Greaves?"

Peter was stunned. "You know about that?"

"No one gives up a job with Hale, Greaves to go to work for Amos Geary. I was suspicious from the start."

"Who told you what happened?"

"Becky."

"When did she tell you?" Peter asked, wondering how long Becky had known about his disgrace.

"I don't remember exactly, but it's been a few weeks. It was sometime after the arraignment. I figured you'd get around to telling me when you decided you wanted me to know."

Peter suddenly realized something. "You knew about *Elliot* and you still wanted me to go into partnership with you."

"Everyone fucks up, Pete. I'm not going to judge you by one case. You're a sharp guy and we get along. That's what's important."

Peter felt an immense rush of gratitude. After so much disapproval, Steve's words were lifesavers.

"Thanks. You don't know how much I appreciate the vote of confidence."

"Hey, I say what I mean. Now, let's get back to Gary's case. Have you talked to Becky about a plea?"

"A plea? No."

"You should look into it after these new developments."

"You don't think Gary is guilty, do you?"

"I don't know what to think. I wouldn't have believed he was a Peeping Tom, either. And look at the way he jumped on that girl in the Stallion. Gary doesn't think the way we do. He's impulsive."

"Gee, Steve, I don't know . . ."

"I'm not saying you should plead him out. I'm suggesting you explore the possibility with Becky. From

215

what you tell me, the case isn't going all that well. You don't want to see Gary executed, do you?"

"I've got to think about this."

"Of course. I don't expect you to decide this minute," Mancini said as he hoisted his briefcase onto the desk.

Peter stood up. "Thanks for talking to me. And thanks for being in my corner."

"Get out of here," Mancini answered with a laugh.

"Oh, one other thing. This investigator, Barney Pullen, is he any good?"

"Why do you ask?"

"He doesn't seem to be doing anything. Whenever I've been able to get him on the phone, which isn't often, he says he's investigating, but I've only received a few reports, and they weren't worth much. I'm getting worried."

"If you're dissatisfied, why don't you fire him and hire one of the other guys I told you about?"

"They're not available. The one who works for the Sissler firm said he's been working for them exclusively since February."

"I didn't know that."

"Yeah. And the other one . . ."

"Mike Compton?"

"Right. He moved to Pendleton."

"No kidding?"

"It's too late to switch investigators, anyway. It would take someone new too long to get familiar with the case. By the time he was up to speed, the trial would be over."

"You're right. Look, why don't you let me give Barney a call."

"That would be great."

Peter shut Steve's door and went back to his office. He was depressed about Gary's chances, but he was not going to approach Becky about a plea just yet. If things got much worse though, he might have to consider the possibility.

CHAPTER NINETEEN

1

Each morning, the guards waited to take Gary out of the holding cell until all of the jurors were in the jury room, so they would not see him in manacles. The Harmons had purchased a conservative blue suit and a conservative gray suit for their son and he looked very handsome in them. Lawyer and client had fallen into a routine. As soon as Gary was seated, Peter would tell him how good he looked in the suit. Gary would beam and Peter would ask Gary how he was feeling. Gary would answer that he was feeling good. Finally, Peter would remind Gary about sitting up straight, listening to the witnesses and taking notes and Gary would grow very serious and turn his yellow pad to a blank page.

Becky O'Shay was presenting her case in chronological order. On the first day of testimony, she led off with Karen Nix, who told the jury about Gary's attack and his threat to kill her. Several people who were present at the Stallion that night corroborated Nix's version of the events. Marjorie Dooling testified that Sandra Whiley had been at the Stallion on the evening of the fight. After Dooling described how Whiley was dressed, the blood-stained clothing was introduced into evidence. A photograph of the jeans and the Whitaker State tee shirt Nix was wearing was shown to the jurors so they could compare the similarities between her clothing and the victim's.

Arnie Block gave his account of the fight and told about Gary's flight from the bar. Dave Thorne established that Sandra Whiley left the Stallion around eleven-twenty, about twenty minutes after Gary ran outside.

On the second day of Gary's trial, Oscar Watts told the jury about discovering Whiley's body. Then, several police officers and forensic technicians described the crime scene investigation and the gathering of evidence.

On the morning of the trial's third day, Becky O'Shay called Harold Guisti's name. The hall door opened to admit the doctor and Peter turned toward the back of the courtroom. His attention was momentarily diverted from the witness by Christopher Mammon, who was watching the proceedings from a seat near the back wall. Peter could not imagine why the gargantuan drug dealer would be interested enough in Gary's case to spend his morning in the tightly packed and overheated courtroom. But Peter did not have much time to spend worrying about Mammon because Dr. Guisti had been sworn and was about to begin his testimony.

After establishing the doctor's credentials, O'Shay asked him, "In your official capacity as a pathologist did you perform an autopsy on Sandra Whiley?"

Dr. Guisti turned to the jurors and answered the question as if they had asked it.

"Yes I did."

"When was this?"

"Around 5 P.M. on the day Miss Whiley was murdered."

"Why did you wait so long?"

"We held off until the body was identified. That was between three and four in the afternoon, if I remember correctly."

"Where did the autopsy take place?"

"Parson's Mortuary."

"Please describe what you found when you performed your autopsy on Sandra Whiley."

"I found several bruises on the left side of the jaw and above the left cheekbone. More important, there were eight cutting or chopping types of wounds on the body. Seven of them were located on the head. The eighth was located on the top of the left hand and was consistent with a defensive wound."

"What is a defensive wound?"

"That is a wound inflicted when the victim interposes her hand defensively between the weapon wielded by the killer and the object of the murderer's attack."

"Please describe the head wounds."

"Five produced skull fractures. Of these five, three were severe enough to produce injuries to the underlying brain. There was another wound which was in the region of the right eye that also produced extensive fracturing of the bones between the eyes and a considerable amount of bleeding with the blood present in the air passages as well as swallowed blood in the stomach. The remaining wounds produced a variable amount of soft-tissue injury or injury to the skin or muscles that did not fracture bone or involve the brain."

"Do you have an opinion, Dr. Guisti, after looking at these injuries and conducting your investigation, as to the type of instrument that might have been used to inflict these wounds?"

"I do."

"What is that opinion?"

"Either an ax or a hatchet would cause the type of wounds inflicted on the deceased."

Becky O'Shay bent down and reached into a large cardboard box containing many items, most of which were enclosed in plastic evidence bags. She rummaged around in the box until she found what she wanted. O'Shay carried the item to the witness.

"Dr. Guisti, I hand you what has been marked as State's Exhibit 23 and I ask you if the wounds on the victim could have been inflicted with this exhibit?"

Dr. Guisti opened the plastic bag. It contained a small hatchet. He turned it around a few times, all for show since he had examined the hatchet on several occasions.

"The blows could have been inflicted by this weapon."

"Thank you," O'Shay said, taking the hatchet from the doctor and slowly returning it to the plastic bag while standing directly in front of the jury. She placed the hatchet on the rail of the jury box and turned back to the witness. Several jurors had trouble moving their eyes away from the weapon.

"Dr. Guisti, do you have an opinion as to the cause of death of Sandra Whiley?"

"Yes. I think the eventual cause of death was hemorrhaging caused by the wounds I have described."

"In other words, Sandra Whiley bled to death through the hatchet wounds inflicted by her killer?"

"That is correct."

"Dr. Guisti, do you have an opinion as to the direction in which the deadly hatchet blows were struck?"

"Yes, but only as to the blow to the top of the skull. I believe that blow was struck in an up-to-down direction because of the way the wound slants. As to the others, I cannot say."

"Do you have an opinion as to whether the blow to the top of the skull was the first blow struck to the head?"

"In my opinion it was."

O'Shay checked her notes then turned the witness over to Peter.

"Dr. Guisti, what side of the head were the wounds on?"

"As I said, one was to the top of the head. It's difficult to say right or left side because the wound is midway. One blow was to the right eye. The rest were delivered to the left side of the victim's head."

"Thank you, Doctor. I have no further questions."

2

The red paint on the gas tanks in front of Art's Garage was barely holding its own against the ravages of rust and wind and the old wooden garage was not doing much better. The elements had eaten away at an advertisement for Coca-Cola that covered one outer wall and the once blue garage now looked a weathered gray. Barney Pullen was bent under the hood of an old Buick when Peter entered the garage during the lunch recess. Peter called out twice before he got Pullen's attention. When Pullen turned around, he looked annoyed, then his features morphed into a brownnosing smile when he remembered that Peter was the one who paid him for investigating the Harmon case.

"Afternoon, Mr. Hale," Pullen said, wiping his hands on a greasy rag.

"Good afternoon, Barney. I've had trouble reaching you, so I thought I'd drop by the garage to see how the investigation's been going."

Barney shook his head ruefully. "It's real slow. I've been talking to lots of people, but nobody seems to know anything helpful."

"Who have you talked to?"

"Uh, well, I don't have my notes right here. Family, of course. I do have a lot of good information for you for the penalty phase from the mother, the father and Steve's wife. Lots of good stuff."

Peter recalled receiving several poorly typed reports rife with misspellings that were accompanied by a bill claiming hours way out of proportion to the information Pullen had collected.

"I have the family interviews, but that's all. You have been doing more than just talking to family?"

"Uh, let's see, there's the bartender at the Ponderosa. You have his statement, right?"

"No, I don't. What about Kevin Booth? Have you found out anything I can use there?"

"Not yet. His father split a long time ago and the mother died last year. She was an alcoholic. Got drunk and fell down the stairs."

"Did you talk to Booth's neighbors, run a rap sheet?"

"Rap sheet's the first thing I thought of. That arrest for drugs he beat is the only thing I could find. There aren't any neighbors. Booth lives way the hell out of town."

"What about school records, his mother's neighbors?"

"I'll get right on it."

"You mean you haven't done that already? We talked about this two weeks ago."

"Yeah. And I'm sorry. I really did mean to get on it, but Art's kept me hoppin' at the shop here."

"Barney, you have to get moving on this. If you don't come up with something on Booth soon, we'll be facing a penalty phase for sure."

"I am investigating, Mr. Hale. As soon as I'm done with this car, I'm gonna get right on it."

"Look, Barney, you're going to have to give this case priority until it's over. Tell your brother you can't work at the shop until it's done."

"Okay," Pullen answered agreeably.

Peter was going to say something else, but there wasn't anything more to say. He was just going to have to hope that Pullen would come through for him.

3

Trying a death penalty case was incredibly exhausting. While Peter was in court, he was so focused that he did not know where the day went. Most of the time, he was coasting on pure adrenaline because no person could concentrate on every word that was said for hours at a time without it. As soon as the case ended for the day, he felt instantly like someone who had gone for days without sleep.

After a fast dinner, Peter went to his new office in Steve Mancini's building and completed his preparations for the next day of trial. It was a little after eight-thirty when Peter opened the front door of his house. The phone was ringing. He raced to it in the dark, stumbling over an ottoman and almost knocking over a floor lamp.

"Mr. Hale?" an unfamiliar voice asked.

"Yes."

"I've been calling all night. I'm glad I caught you."

"Who is this?"

"Don Bosco. I'm the Director of Mental Health for the county. I was a witness at the pretrial hearing."

"Right. I remember you. You were present when Gary was questioned by Dennis Downes. What's up?"

"I know I shouldn't be disturbing you at home, but I've been wondering since that pretrial hearing why no one from the defense asked me any questions on cross and why you haven't gotten in touch with me about my trial testimony."

"Do you know something that might help Gary?"

"Didn't Steve Mancini tell you about our conversation?"

"All Steve said was that he didn't think you could help us."

"You're kidding. Do you mean to say he didn't tell you that I believe Gary Harmon was inadvertently hypnotized by Dennis Downes during the interrogation?"

Peter blinked. "No. He never told me anything about hypnotism."

"That really surprises me. I told Miss O'Shay that she shouldn't be using Harmon's statements to convict him, but she won't listen to me."

"I want to make sure I'm understanding you. You're saying that you told the D.A. there was something wrong with Gary's interrogation?"

"Yes."

"And you also told Steve Mancini about this?"

"I told him over a month ago. I thought you'd be interested."

Peter was dazed. Gary's statements were the basis for the state's case. Without them . . .

"Can we get together tonight? This is very important and Steve never mentioned a thing to me about what you're saying."

"Okay. There's an all-night restaurant near the turnoff to the interstate. The Jolly Roger. Can you be there in half an hour?"

"No problem."

"Boy, I can't understand why Mr. Mancini didn't say anything to you," Bosco said right before he hung up.

"Neither can I," Peter said to the dead phone. He had been standing during the phone conversation, but he sank into an easy chair as soon as he hung up. Peter didn't know what to think. He remembered the look Bosco had given Mancini during his testimony at the motion to suppress. Peter had even commented on it to Steve. He reached for the phone to call Mancini, but he stopped in mid-dial. It would be better if he waited until he heard what Bosco had to say.

"How did you get involved in this case?" Peter asked as soon as he and Don Bosco were seated in a booth in the rear of the Jolly Roger with two cups of coffee.

"Dennis Downes called me at home around eight-thirty, nine. He wanted me to check my records to see if we had anything on Harmon. You know, a history of mental health problems. Something like that."

"Did you find anything?"

"No."

"What did you do after that?"

"I went over to the station house to tell him. He'd already said that the inquiry concerned the girl who was killed in the park, so I thought it was important enough to tell him in person and see if there was any other way I could help out.

"When I arrived, Becky O'Shay asked me to watch the interrogation with her through a two-way mirror. She brought me up to date and showed me pictures of the victim." Bosco shuddered. "Pretty gruesome."

"Yeah, I've seen them. But why did Becky want you to observe the questioning?"

"She wanted my take on Harmon."

"Were you there when Downes gave Gary his *Miranda* warnings?"

"No. That must have been earlier. I got the impression that Dennis had been going at Harmon for a while by the time I started watching."

"Was there anything unusual about the way Gary was responding to Downes?"

"I didn't like the way Dennis conducted the interview. Not one bit. I even told him to be careful, but he didn't pay any attention to my suggestions."

"What was the problem?"

Bosco took a sip of coffee and thought carefully about what he was about to say.

"The first thing I noticed was all the leading. You know, asking a question that suggests the answer. I mean, Dennis was feeding him everything. And Harmon would go along with every suggestion. I think he really trusted Dennis and wanted to please him. So, Dennis would ask him a question and Harmon would parrot back the answer Downes had fed him."

"And you warned Downes about this?"

"During the breaks. Harmon was exhausted by the end and the more tired you are, the more open you are to suggestion. I told that to Dennis, but he and Becky didn't seem to care. They were too excited about cracking the case. In my opinion, most of what Harmon said is worthless. Especially the last third or so of the interview."

"Why is that?"

"Well, this is only my opinion, but I think Downes

225

induced a trance state and anything Harmon said then, well . . ."

Bosco shrugged.

"Wait a minute," Peter said, "what's a 'trance state'? Do you mean he was in a trance? Like hypnotized?"

"He could have been. I think he was."

"How could that happen? I listened to the tape of the interrogation and I didn't hear Downes saying anything about putting Gary in a trance."

"He wouldn't have to do it intentionally. Dennis could have hypnotized Harmon without either of them knowing."

"Explain that to me."

"Okay. 'Hypnosis' and 'trance' are words that make people think about magicians or Svengali, but hypnotizing a person isn't all that mysterious. All you're really doing when you induce a trance is getting a person relaxed and focused enough to block out exterior noises and influences, so they can go into a quiet, inner space. We all do that when we drop off to sleep at night or when we're so engrossed in a book that we don't hear someone ask us a question, even though they're right next to us.

"If someone is tired and under a lot of stress, like Harmon was that night, they will tend to focus their attention narrowly. Dennis helped Harmon along when he told him to shut his eyes and imagine he was watching events on a movie screen. That's a fairly common technique that hypnotists use when they're trying to intentionally induce a trance."

"What would be the consequences of Gary being in a trance?"

"The big problem is reliability. If he was in a trance, it would be difficult, if not impossible, to tell what Harmon was really remembering and what he was repeating as a result of Downes's suggestions, or just plain making up. See, a person in a trance is not only wide open to suggestion, they also fantasize in order to please the

226

questioner or to fill in gaps in their memory, in order to give the interrogator a complete picture."

"I'm not certain I understand what you mean about the fantasizing."

"Okay. Let me give you an example. A month ago, you got up at seven in the morning, you dressed in a blue suit, a white shirt and a red tie. Then, you ate a breakfast of cornflakes. I hypnotize you and ask you to tell me what you did that morning. You remember everything except the color of your tie and what you ate. I tell you to really concentrate, but you still can't remember. So, I help you a little. 'Peter,' I say, 'you usually eat Raisin Bran, don't you? Did you eat Raisin Bran that morning?' Now, a person in a trance is likely to say he ate Raisin Bran in order to please the questioner. He knows the questioner wants some answer and seems to be happy with that answer being Raisin Bran, so the person in the trance accommodates those wishes.

"Now, the questioner asks you to think about the tie without making a specific suggestion about color. Again, you know an answer is expected, so your subconscious imagines a green tie and fills in the blank with that color. By the time you're through, you'll believe the tie was green, so you will appear to be telling the truth on the witness stand and you will pass a polygraph test."

"And you didn't warn Sergeant Downes or Becky about this?"

Bosco looked embarrassed. "I mentioned it to both of them, but I really didn't catch on to what was happening until I'd been there awhile. By then, the questioning was pretty far along. And, remember, I was only there as an observer. I mean, I wasn't supposed to take part in the interrogation. I guess I should have been more forceful, but most of the harm had already been done by then and I didn't think it was my place to interfere because the case was so important. I didn't do anything wrong, did I?"

4

Peter drove directly to Steve Mancini's house from the Jolly Roger. At first, Bosco's information elated him. Then he realized how much Steve had cost them by failing to use the information at the pretrial hearing. By the time Peter rang Steve Mancini's doorbell at a little before eleven, he was in an emotional quandary. Mancini was his best friend in Whitaker and he was holding out the possibility of a lucrative partnership that would help Peter climb out of the hole he had dug for himself. But Steve might have ruined Gary Harmon's best chance to win his freedom by concealing information from Peter that explained away Gary Harmon's so-called confession, the basis for all of the charges against Gary.

As soon as Steve opened the door, Peter asked, "Why didn't you tell me about Don Bosco?"

Mancini looked confused. Donna walked out of the living room. She was wearing a bathrobe over a nightgown. Mancini glanced at his wife, then back to Peter. When he answered, he sounded nervous.

"We're getting ready to go to bed, Pete. Can't this wait until tomorrow?"

"You know it can't. If Gary was in some kind of trance when he was questioned by Downes, the interrogation was no good. We could have gotten the whole thing thrown out before the trial. There wouldn't have been a trial. Without Gary's statements, the state doesn't have a case. Don't tell me you didn't know that?"

"What's this about, Peter?" Donna asked, confused by his intensity and her husband's obvious discomfort.

"Tell her, Steve."

"Tell her what? I still don't know what you're talking about."

"I just came from the Jolly Roger where Don Bosco, the county's Director of Mental Health, a man with expertise in hypnosis, told me how he explained to you that he believed Gary was in a trance state during most of the interrogation. He called me at home because he was surprised that you never brought that out during the hearing on the motion to suppress. He was also surprised that you never told me about your conversation with him. Quite frankly, Steve, so am I."

"I didn't tell you about the conversation because I didn't buy into what Bosco said. You heard the tape. Downes didn't say anything about trying to hypnotize Gary."

Peter looked astonished. "What Downes did or did not say is irrelevant. We have a witness who would have testified that Gary was hypnotized during the most important part of his interrogation. Didn't you know that there is a statute that forbids the use of hypnotized testimony unless the most stringent precautions are taken? There are cases from around the country that exclude the testimony of hypnotized witnesses. Bosco knew all about them and he's not even a lawyer."

Mancini looked surprised. "I didn't know about the statute. You have to believe me. I've never had anything like this come up in one of my cases."

"Did you know about this and keep it from Peter?" Donna asked her husband.

Mancini turned on Donna. "I can handle this, thank you. Bring us some coffee. Come on, Pete. Let's discuss this calmly."

"It's hard to be calm when I'm busting my ass day and night only to find out that you fucked up on the single most important issue in the case."

"Peter . . ." Donna started, but her husband barked, "The coffee, please."

When Steve turned back to Peter he looked concerned, but calm.

"I can see why you're upset. I'm upset too. Especially if you think I may have screwed up Gary's case. Come on. Let's sit down and talk this out."

The anger drained out of Peter in the face of Man-

229

cini's calm demeanor. He walked into the living room and sat down on the couch.

"I just don't understand this, Steve. Can you explain it to me? Even Bosco saw the problem. He called me tonight because he could not figure out why you didn't ask him about the trance state at the hearing. I can't believe you didn't see the significance of what Bosco told you."

"It's the truth. I didn't know about the statute. I thought the issues were whether Downes gave Gary his *Miranda* rights and whether he coerced him into talking."

"Can't you reopen the hearing?" Donna asked as she lowered a serving tray onto the coffee table.

"I'll try, but Becky has a very legitimate ground for objecting."

"What's that?" Donna asked.

"Steve was Gary's lawyer. He knew all about this evidence at the time of the suppression hearing."

"But I didn't understand the significance of what Bosco told me," Mancini protested.

"That doesn't matter. You should have known it was important. That's the point. I wish there was some way to sugarcoat this, but there isn't."

"Isn't there anything you can do?" Donna asked.

"There might be," Peter said cautiously. "I read a little about confessions for this case before Steve said he would handle the motion to suppress. A defendant can always argue to a jury that they should not accept a defendant's statements because they are involuntary. The problem is that there's no appeal from a jury's decision like there is from a pretrial decision by a judge, because appellate courts won't review the factual finding of a jury."

"If Gary was hypnotized, he wouldn't be responsible for what he told Downes!" Mancini said. "That's great thinking, Pete."

"Yeah, but I've got to convince the jury that Gary was hypnotized. That may mean hiring experts and that's expensive." Peter looked at Donna. "Can your folks afford it?"

"Don't worry about the money, Peter," Donna said. "If my folks can't do it, Steve and I will pay."

Peter did not see Mancini's sudden anger, but Donna did. She was shocked by its intensity and she remembered what happened the last time he was angry with her.

"I think you've come up with a potential solution," Mancini said quickly, "and I also think we should all get some rest. Don't forget, you have to be in court tomorrow."

Peter suddenly realized how much today's court session and this evening's events had taken out of him.

"You're right," he said as he stood up. "Sorry I came down on you so hard."

"I understand completely. I deserve it if I screwed up as badly as it seems."

As soon as the door closed, Mancini returned to the living room. Donna was bent over the coffee table gathering up the coffee cups and the creamer.

"What was that about our paying for Gary's experts?" Mancini demanded angrily.

Donna straightened up with the tray in her hands.

"If Gary needs our help . . ."

"Gary made his own mess. We cannot afford to bail him out. Didn't you understand a thing I said about Mountain View? I'll bet you haven't even talked to your father about helping with it."

"I haven't had the chance," Donna answered, feeling guilty about letting down her husband.

"That's great. You can't take the time to help your own husband and you expect me to spend my money on some Portland shrink."

"The experts can't be that expensive."

"They could be dirt cheap, Donna. I've got to work like a slave at my practice just to keep our heads above water. What are we going to pay them with?"

"Gary is my brother."

231

"That's right, Donna. He's your brother. Not mine."

Steve's cold and cruel reply shocked Donna. She had always believed that her husband liked Gary.

"We wouldn't need the money for experts if you hadn't made a mistake," Donna said angrily.

The open-hand slap spun Donna's head to the right and the tray went flying. Donna watched the cups and spraying cream sail away in slow motion as Steve grabbed the lapels of her robe and used them to fling her to the ground.

"You cunt!" Steve screamed as she hit the floor.

Donna tried to crawl away, but the pain from two strong kicks to her ribs stopped her. Another kick landed on her leg and she straightened in pain. Then, as swiftly as it started, the assault stopped. When she dared to look up, Mancini was pacing back and forth. Donna started to crawl across the floor toward the hall. Steve saw her and dropped next to her on the floor. Donna curled into a ball with her hands protecting her head.

"No, baby, no. You don't have to be afraid. I'm sorry. Please. I'm sorry."

Donna looked up and Mancini saw the blood. The blow to Donna's face had split her lip.

"Oh, God! What have I done?"

Mancini jumped up and sprinted to the bathroom. He ran cold water over a towel. When he returned to the living room, the front door was open. Donna was gone. Mancini threw the towel on the floor and raced out of the house. The car was parked in front. He looked right and left. Where was she? He couldn't call out. He could not let anyone know what had happened. Mancini ran down the street and stopped on the corner. Where had she gone? He had to find her. Without the car, she couldn't get far. He ran inside and grabbed the car keys. He would find her. He had to find her.

Donna waited for the car to drive away before pulling herself to her feet by hanging on to the bushes behind which she had been hiding. A sharp pain in her ribs doubled her over. She gritted her teeth and eased into a standing position. Tears and blood mixed on her face. She loved Steve, but how could he beat her if he really loved her?

Donna wanted to change into her clothes, but she was afraid to go back to the house. Her parents' house was too far to walk. Besides, they were worrying so much about Gary that she could not let them know that her marriage was failing.

Then she thought of Peter. He lived nearby. She could keep to backyards and Steve would not see her from his car. Donna checked the street for any sign of her husband, then she crossed the road and hobbled behind a house. She wanted to run, but the pain in her ribs was so intense that she had to walk hunched over.

A dog barked and Donna's stomach tightened. She kept moving, gasping for air when a sudden bolt of pain knifed through her. Donna waited for the pain to pass before going on. The next street was Elm and cars drove by frequently. Donna waited for a break and crossed the street as quickly as she could manage, paying in pain for speed. "Just a few more blocks," she repeated over and over until, moments later, she was ringing Peter's doorbell.

Headlights turned onto Peter's street just as his porch light came on. When Peter opened his door, Donna was crouched down, looking over her shoulder with terrified eyes.

"Please, let me in," Donna begged.

Peter took one look at her tearstained and bleeding face and he had her through the door.

"What happened to you?" he asked. Then Donna was sobbing in his arms and Peter was too startled to say anything. Peter led her to the living room. She clung to him. As he lowered her to the couch, she spasmed and gripped her side.

"Are you hurt?" he asked stupidly.

"He hit me, Peter. He hit me."

"Who hit you? Is Steve all right?" Peter asked, confused by Donna's sudden, dramatic appearance and thinking that the couple had been attacked.

Donna shook her head. "You don't understand. It was Steve. Steve hit me."

"Steve?" Peter repeated inanely. Donna dissolved into tears and pressed herself against Peter's chest.

"Has . . . has he done this before?" Peter asked.

Donna managed a nod. She got her crying under control and wiped an arm across her eyes.

"How long has this been going on?"

Donna did not answer right away and Peter touched her shoulder.

"I want to help. You and Steve are my friends."

Donna looked at the rug.

"I know this is hard for you, but you have to talk about it. If Steve is doing this . . . You can't let him keep hurting you, Donna."

"It's been a nightmare, Peter." She started to cry again. "I never know what will set him off. He's so kind to me, so loving. Then, all of a sudden . . . I can't take it anymore."

Donna was too exhausted to go on. Peter stared at her. Her hair was in disarray and her robe was open. She was wearing a short nightgown because of the heat. Peter could not help noticing her slim, tanned legs and the swell of her breasts as she breathed deeply. Peter raised his eyes to Donna's face, embarrassed.

"How badly are you hurt?" he asked.

"He kicked me in the ribs. He . . . It was a hard kick. It really hurts if I move quickly."

"I'll drive you to a hospital."

"No! No hospital. They'd have to report Steve."

Peter thought for a moment. Then he got an idea.

"I have a friend. A nurse. Rhonda Kates. She works at the hospital. Let me call her. I'll explain what happened. Maybe she can check you out to make sure you don't have any internal injuries. If there's a problem, we'll make up a story and I'll drive you to the nearest hospital outside of Whitaker."

Peter made the call and Rhonda told him to bring Donna to her place immediately. She even said that Donna could spend the night with her. While Peter talked on the phone, Donna tried to find a comfortable position on the couch and closed her eyes. She was so ashamed that her marriage was a failure and she felt she must be partly to blame, but she could not figure out what she had done wrong. She wanted to talk to someone but the Harmons were not a family that discussed their domestic troubles.

"Let's get going," Peter said, as soon as he hung up.

"Thank you, Peter. You're a good friend."

CHAPTER TWENTY

1

"Mr. Hale," Judge Kuffel said, addressing Peter formally because they were in court and on the record, "your former co-counsel, Mr. Mancini, conducted the hearing on the motion to suppress Mr. Harmon's statements. You've conceded that he was fully aware at the time of the hearing of the evidence you argue is grounds for reopening. Now, there is no question that Mr. Bosco's evidence favors the defense, but Mr. Mancini made a decision not to use it. I have no idea why he made that choice, but it doesn't really matter. Since he was aware of the evidence at the time of the hearing, I have to deny your motion to reopen the motion to suppress."

If Peter were the judge, he would have ruled exactly the way Judge Kuffel ruled, but his failure to win his hastily fashioned motion still depressed him. Peter closed his eyes briefly while he tried to regain his composure. This was a mistake. Suddenly he was half asleep and it took all his willpower to raise his eyelids and return to full consciousness.

It had been two-thirty in the morning when Peter had returned home after leaving Donna with Rhonda Kates. He was totally exhausted, but Don Bosco's revelation and Donna's dramatic appearance filled his head with so many disturbing thoughts that he had as much of a chance of dozing off in the privacy of his room as he had of sleeping at a rock concert. Peter had moved through the morning in court in a sleep-deprived fog.

"I've given a lot of thought to the matter of testimony about the peeping incident, the pornographic magazines found in Mr. Harmon's bedroom and evidence concerning the other two murders," Judge Kuffel continued.

"I will permit the state to introduce evidence concerning the peeping incident on the Whitaker campus and the pornographic magazines. This evidence may make Mr. Harmon look bad to the jury, but it is relevant to the state's theory that Mr. Harmon had a sexual obsession with women with physical characteristics very similar to the victim."

Peter sat forward to hear the judge's ruling on the other murders. He had battled very hard to keep any reference to them out of the trial.

"Miss O'Shay, you have made a very persuasive argument that the murder of Sandra Whiley is part of a series of murders, but I am not going to permit you to put that theory to the jury. A few factors led me to this decision.

"First, there is no evidence connecting Mr. Harmon to the other killings. Second, there are substantial differences between the murder of Miss Whiley and the other murders. The other women were sexually assaulted and blood tests revealed the presence of cocaine in their systems, whereas Miss Whiley's blood did not reveal the presence of cocaine and the autopsy found no evidence of sexual assault . . ."

"Your Honor," Becky interrupted, "Wishing Well Park is a public place. We believe Mr. Harmon was frightened away by other individuals in the park before he could have sex with Miss Whiley."

"Your theory may be correct, but I have to make my ruling based on the evidence."

"There's the hatchet," O'Shay argued. "The weapon is a trademark of this killer. It is very unusual."

"Not in a farming community, Ms. O'Shay. Without

something more I have no choice but to bar you from mentioning the other murders. Introduction of that evidence would lead to speculation by the jury and deprive Mr. Harmon of a fair trial."

The judge's ruling snapped Peter out of his funk. He was concerned about the introduction of evidence about the peeping incident and the magazines, but he had been scared to death that Judge Kuffel would admit evidence about the other murders. If the judge had let O'Shay argue that Gary was a serial killer, there was no way Peter could have won an acquittal.

"Do you have an update on Kevin Booth's condition?" the judge asked. Peter leaned forward. If Booth was too ill to testify, Peter's day would be complete.

"I spoke with Mr. Booth's surgeon this morning," O'Shay said as she consulted her notes. "Dr. Farber says that Mr. Booth cannot be transported to Whitaker without endangering the success of the skin grafts. However, Mr. Booth is metabolically more stable. His fever is down, he's gaining weight and he requires less pain medication, which makes him more coherent.

"According to the doctor, Mr. Booth will be able to testify in his hospital room in Portland by Monday. Dr. Farber is willing to postpone further skin grafts so the trial will not be delayed. It's my intention to examine Mr. Booth in Portland, if the court is agreeable."

"I object, Your Honor," Peter said.

"What are your grounds, Mr. Hale?"

"Booth's testimony is crucial to the state's case. If the jury sees him in a hospital room it's going to generate a lot of sympathy. Booth has been burned to a crisp. I'm going to look like an ogre if I go after him.

"And how am I going to cross-examine effectively? What happens to Mr. Harmon's right of confrontation if Dr. Farber says that I shouldn't excite Booth? And he's on pain medication. He'll be sedated. That means the jury won't be seeing the way he would normally react to questions."

"Your concerns are valid, Mr. Hale, but it seems to

me that they are theoretical. It may be that you will be able to carry on a vigorous cross of the witness without any medical problems occurring. We'll deal with confrontation problems if the doctor tries to restrict you. Of course, we could have a mistrial or Mr. Booth's testimony may be struck, if you are foreclosed from examining Booth because of medical problems, but that's a risk the state runs.

"As to the prejudice caused by Booth's appearance and the location where he will be examined, I plan on instructing the jurors that they may not let any sympathy caused by Booth's appearance affect their decision. I'll draft a jury instruction to that effect and I'll give it to you to review tonight. Let me know if you want any changes by tomorrow morning, before court.

"With that in mind, I'll have a bus meet us here at seven o'clock on Monday morning. Ms. O'Shay, please notify the hospital that I plan on taking testimony at two in the afternoon.

"If there's nothing further, we'll take a short recess. Then I'll have the clerk bring in the jury."

Judge Kuffel left the bench and the guards took Gary to the holding cell so he could use the rest room. Steve Mancini walked to Peter's side as soon as Gary was out of earshot. There were dark circles under his eyes and Peter noticed nicks on his face where he had cut himself shaving. It was obvious that Mancini had not slept last night either.

"I really fucked up, didn't I?"

"What's done is done," Peter answered resignedly. "I'll just have to call Bosco as a witness and hope that the jury buys his theory."

"I wonder what else will go wrong."

"What do you mean?"

Mancini hesitated. Then, he said, "Donna left me."

"What!" Peter responded, hoping that he looked suitably surprised.

"We had a fight after you went home because I didn't tell you about Bosco."

"Jeez, I'm sorry. I shouldn't have barged in like that. I feel awful."

"It's not your fault. I don't even know why I'm burdening you with this. I guess I just needed someone to talk to."

"How serious is this?"

"Pretty serious. I feel really bad. I love her so much." Mancini's voice caught and Peter was afraid he was going to cry. If he did, Peter didn't know if he could keep lying.

"Hey, it'll work out. It's just a newlywed spat. She loves you, too. She'll come back."

"I hope so, Pete. I can't stand being away from her. If you run into Donna, tell her I love her, will you? Ask her to call me. I'm sure everything would be all right if we could just talk."

"You bet," Peter said, but he did not mean it. He felt terrible about deceiving his friend, but he remembered Donna's pain and terror too vividly to help Mancini find his wife.

"I shouldn't have bothered you in the middle of trial."

"It's no trouble," Peter answered guiltily. "Maybe we should go out for dinner tonight . . ."

"No. This was selfish of me. You've got to prepare your case. Gary's life is at stake. I'm just feeling sorry for myself. I'll be okay."

2

During the rest of the morning session, witnesses told the jury about the peeping incident and the pornographic magazines. Becky O'Shay started the afternoon session of court by calling Sergeant Dennis Downes to the stand. Just before he started to testify, Christopher Mammon entered the courtroom. This was the second time Mammon had been a spectator at Gary's trial and Peter remained puzzled by his interest.

Downes testified calmly and professionally about the history of his investigation and the evidence that led him to Gary Harmon. He emphasized the courtesy shown to the defendant and explained how Gary had agreed to come to the station house. When his narrative reached the point where the taping began, Becky introduced the tapes of Gary's interrogation into evidence and supplied everyone with a transcript of the five-hour interrogation. Then, Becky played a two-hour, edited version of the interrogation to the jury. The day's session of court ended with a recitation by Downes of his part in finding the hatchet in a storm drain near the Whitaker State College campus.

After court, Peter went directly to his office to finish the work on his cross-examination of Sergeant Downes. He hoped Steve Mancini would not be working late, because he felt a little guilty about helping Donna hide from her husband. Fortunately, Mancini was not in the building.

Peter tried to work on the case, but he kept thinking about his encounter at the courthouse with Steve. Mancini seemed so sad. Maybe Donna had exaggerated when she described her beating. Mancini had definitely hit her, but based on how contrite he seemed, it was hard to believe that Steve had really meant to hurt her.

Peter was also troubled by his part in the Mancinis' marital problems. He should never have barged into their house the way he did, throwing accusations at his friend in front of Donna. He had made it sound as if Steve was intentionally sabotaging Gary's case. The more Peter thought about it, the more he decided that he owed it to Steve to tell Donna how sorry he seemed in court.

As soon as he wrapped up his work, Peter drove across town. Rhonda Kates lived near the hospital in a garden apartment on the other side of the Whitaker campus from city center. Peter rang the doorbell and noticed the curtain that covered the kitchen window move. Donna looked apprehensive when she opened the door. She had been afraid to go back to her house for her own clothes, so she was wearing shorts and a green tank top that belonged to Rhonda.

"I thought I'd drop by to see how you're doing."

Donna's apprehensive look turned into a smile of relief and she ushered him in.

"You all alone?" Peter asked.

"Rhonda has an evening shift at the hospital."

"How are your ribs?"

"Nothing's broken. I'm still sore, but it could have been worse."

They sat down in the living room.

"I was too upset to thank you last night," Donna said.

"Oh, hey . . ."

"No. Some men wouldn't have wanted to get involved. Especially with the wife of a friend." She paused. "You haven't said anything to Steve, have you? About where I am."

"No. He doesn't know I helped you. I was afraid if I said anything, he'd want to know where you are. That would have put me in the middle. I like both of you and I . . . Well, I really find it hard to believe that Steve hit you like that."

"I know what you mean," Donna answered bitterly.

"Actually, Steve did talk to me today at the courthouse. He's a mess. I think he's really sorry for what he did."

"Sorry isn't good enough. I am not going to be Steve's punching bag. If you love someone . . ."

Donna left the thought unfinished. They sat quietly for a moment. Then, Donna asked, "Are you hungry? I'm fixing some dinner for myself."

"I'm starved."

Peter followed Donna into a kitchen separated from the living room by an L-shaped, waist-high counter. Tomatoes, lettuce, an avocado and pods of fresh green peas were spread out near a large salad bowl on a counter next to the sink.

"I was going to make myself a steak and salad. I've got another steak. Is that okay?"

"Great."

"Do you want a drink?"

"Does Rhonda have the fixings for a gin and tonic?"

"Let me check," she answered as she looked in a cabinet over the stove. "You're on," she said, handing a bottle to Peter. "I saw the tonic in the refrigerator. Why don't you fix me one, too."

Peter found the ice and fixed the drinks. When he set down Donna's glass on the counter, she asked, "How did the trial go today?"

Peter told Donna about Judge Kuffel's decision to keep out evidence of the other murders. Then he recounted the testimony concerning the sex magazines and the peeping incident and Gary's reaction to it. The heat in the apartment caused sweat to bead on Donna's body. While Peter talked, she picked up the cold glass of gin and touched it to her forehead. With her hair in casual disarray, she looked attractive even with her split lip and bruises. The cruel reminders of Steve's beating made Peter want to protect her from any further harm. When he realized that he was staring, Peter averted his eyes, hoping that Donna had not noticed.

"Poor kid," Peter finished. "Here he is facing a death sentence and all he can think about is your mom knowing he's been reading *Playboy*."

"How do you think the jury reacted to the books and the peeping?"

"Tough to say. A couple of them looked upset about the peeping. I don't know what they thought about the magazines. I did see a couple of kindly looks when Gary started bawling."

"Give Gary my love, will you. Tell him . . . tell him I have to go out of town for a few days so he won't wonder why I'm not in court."

"I will."

243

Donna paused. She looked worried.

"If I ask you a question, will you give me an honest answer?"

"Of course," Peter said.

"Is Gary going to be convicted?"

Peter's first thought was to assure Donna that he would win Gary's case, but he found that he could not lie to her.

"I don't know, Donna. I wish I could assure you that he'll be okay, but I just don't know."

CHAPTER TWENTY-ONE

Peter began his cross-examination of Dennis Downes by asking, "How well do you know the Harmon family, Sergeant?"

"Not all that well. I know them to say hello to, but we don't socialize."

"Have you met Gary Harmon in a social setting?"

"No."

"Are you aware that Gary is mildly retarded?"

"I never heard that."

"But you knew he was slow?"

"Well, I knew he wasn't a scholar."

"That's obviously true," Peter said, "because you would have had some trouble convincing a scholar that he had supernatural powers, wouldn't you?"

Downes shrugged uneasily and Peter did not press him for a verbal answer.

"In fact, you had a pretty easy time convincing Gary that he had psychic powers, didn't you?"

"I guess."

"That's because he trusted you, didn't he, Sergeant?"

"I suppose he did."

"There's no doubt in your mind about that, is there?

After all, when he was arrested for peeping at that girl at the college, you fixed it so he wasn't charged."

"I did."

"You must not have felt Gary was very dangerous, or you wouldn't have let him go, would you?"

Downes suddenly saw where Peter had led him. He hesitated before answering "No" and Peter noted with satisfaction that several of the jurors took notes when they saw Downes hesitate.

"Let's discuss Gary's supernatural powers, Sergeant. Until you came up with that idea, didn't Gary insist that he knew nothing about the murder of Sandra Whiley?"

"No, that's not true. He said he saw her and the killer by the park entrance."

"That's not really accurate, is it?" Peter asked as he walked across the courtroom and handed the witness a two-volume transcript of the interrogation. Sticking out of several pages were yellow Post-its with numbers on them. Peter carried his own copy of the transcript with similarly marked Post-its.

"Let me direct your attention to the page marked by the Post-it labeled number one. Have you got that?"

Downes nodded.

"What Gary told you initially was that he had seen a man and a woman hugging in the park, did he not?"

"Yes, but later . . ."

"I'm not concerned with 'later,' Sergeant. I'm concerned with what Gary told you at first. And that was simply that he had seen a man and a woman hugging."

"I guess he did."

"He had no idea who they were?"

Downes scanned the page, then agreed.

"He did not say the man was killing the woman?"

"No."

"Not until you started this business about the subconscious mind."

Downes did not answer.

"In fact, it took you a long time to convince Gary that he had seen Sandra Whiley in the park."

246

"I didn't convince him of anything."

"Oh, didn't you? Look at number five. What is Mr. Harmon's response when you tell him 'There's a good chance that you saw Sandy and her killer when you walked by Wishing Well Park'?"

Downes scanned the page until he found the question and answer.

"He said, 'All I see is them two hugging,'" Downes answered reluctantly.

"And at nine, when you tell him to relax and let it come, doesn't Mr. Harmon tell you, 'It's no good, I didn't see anything new'?"

"Yes."

"And at ten, what does Mr. Harmon tell you when you ask, 'Is it Sandy?'?"

"He says, 'I can't say for sure.'"

"That's right. Now, you had Mr. Harmon believing he was some kind of detective, didn't you?"

"What do you mean?"

"Look again at ten. I'm quoting. 'You know, Gary, you might be a natural at this stuff.' And Gary says, 'I just want to get this guy.' He thinks he's helping the police, doesn't he?"

"Or fooling the police."

"He figured that out with an IQ of sixty-five?"

"Objection," O'Shay said. "Sergeant Downes has no way of knowing what was going on in the defendant's head during this interview."

"Sustained," Judge Kuffel said.

"Very well, Your Honor," Peter answered. "Sergeant Downes, isn't it true that you told Mr. Harmon to guess at what happened in the park?"

"They were pretty good guesses."

"Oh, really? Like the guesses about where the blows fell on Miss Whiley's head?"

"That was accurate."

"It was?"

"Yes, sir. He described right where the wounds were."

"Let's look at twenty-two. Read that to the jury, if you please, starting at line thirteen."

"I said, 'Let it flow, Gary. First hit. Where was it?' and he said, 'Top of the head,' which is where the first hit was."

"Go on."

"I said, 'This is great. Then what?' and he started swinging his arm and said, 'Another to the right side. And another.'"

"Stop there, Sergeant. You are aware, are you not, that Dr. Guisti testified that the killer struck his blows to the left side of Miss Whiley's head?"

"Yes, but . . ."

"Yes or no?"

"Yes."

Peter did not let the jury see how elated he felt. If he could convince the jurors that Downes had taken advantage of Gary's low intelligence to trick him, he would destroy a major part of the state's case.

"When you questioned Mr. Harmon, did he appear sleepy to you?"

"We were both tired by the end."

"How long did the interrogation last?"

"About seven hours from the time we got him to the station house."

"So, there are two hours of interrogation that are not on the tape?"

"Yes."

"It was during that part of the interrogation that you had Officer Robert Patrick play a little trick on Mr. Harmon, wasn't it?"

"I don't understand the question."

"What is a black light, Sergeant?"

Downes colored. "A, uh, black light is like a flashlight, but it shoots out an ultraviolet light beam."

"Did you have Officer Patrick dust a Coke can with an invisible powder that shows up orange under ultraviolet light?"

"Yes."

"After Gary handled the can, did Officer Patrick, on your orders, shine the black light on Gary's hands?"

"Yes," Downes answered uncomfortably.

"Did Officer Patrick then tell this young man, who has an IQ of sixty-five, that the orange splotches on his hands were the blood of Sandra Whiley?"

"Yes."

"That was a lie, wasn't it?"

Downes looked as if he was going to say something else at first, but ended by simply agreeing.

"Where did you learn your 'projection transfer' technique, Sergeant?"

"Nowhere," Downes answered proudly. "I made it up."

"Made it up?" Peter responded incredulously.

"Yes, sir."

"Are you aware that the technique you used on Mr. Harmon is identical to the technique used by hypnotists to induce a trance?"

"Objection," O'Shay said. "That question assumes facts that are not in evidence."

"We intend to offer such evidence, Your Honor," Peter told the judge.

"Very well. With that assurance, I will order the witness to answer."

"I don't know what technique a hypnotist would use, Mr. Hale."

"Whether you knew or not, isn't it true that you led Mr. Harmon to give those answers that you wanted to hear?"

"No, sir. That's not true."

"Look at marker seventeen. Don't you suggest that the man and woman Mr. Harmon said he saw kissing in the park might be doing something other than kissing, despite the fact that Mr. Harmon told you several times that was the activity in which they were involved?"

"I suggested that they would not have been kissing if the couple was Whiley and her killer."

"Thus planting that suggestion in a mind susceptible

to suggestion both because of Mr. Harmon's fatigue and IQ."

"Objection," O'Shay said. "Mr. Hale is making a speech."

"Sustained. Save the oratory for closing, Mr. Hale."

"Sergeant Downes, did you not lead Mr. Harmon to say that the man he saw in the park was holding a weapon after Mr. Harmon repeatedly told you that he had not seen a weapon in the man's hand?"

"Gary brought up the hatchet."

"Look at marker twenty-nine. Read the top few lines on that page, please."

"I ask, 'Did you see anything shiny, Gary? It would probably have been right then. In that split second.' And he says, 'Shiny?' and I say . . .'"

"Stop there. You were the first person to mention the word 'shiny,' weren't you?"

"Yes," Downes said, after a moment's hesitation.

"And it is you who mentioned that the weapon would probably be in the killer's right hand?"

Downes read the page, stopping to reread one sentence.

"I . . . I may have mentioned that first."

"You put those words in Mr. Harmon's mouth."

"No, sir. I just asked the questions and he supplied the answers."

"Only some of them were your answers, weren't they?

"Nothing further, Your Honor," Peter said before O'Shay could object.

"I only have a few questions on redirect, Sergeant." The deputy district attorney sounded undisturbed by Peter's cross. "Mr. Hale pointed out that the defendant described the hatchet wounds the killer inflicted as being on the right side of Miss Whiley's face, whereas the wounds were actually on the left side."

"Yes."

"When Mr. Harmon was describing these wounds verbally, was he also demonstrating the strikes?"

"Yes, ma'am. I gave him a ruler to hold and I told him to pretend this was the weapon. Then I stood in front of him and dipped down a little, so I would be more like Miss Whiley's height. Then I asked him to act out the blows."

"Were the defendant's physical actions consistent with what he said?"

"No, ma'am, they were not. See, while he was talking I stood opposite him. Now Mr. Harmon had that ruler in his right hand and he was saying the blows were landing on my right side, but really, with me facing him, it was on his right, but the left side of my face. See what I mean."

"I'm certain the jurors understand," O'Shay said. Peter also understood with sickening clarity that he had lost one of his major points.

"Mr. Hale asked you if you had Officer Patrick shine a black light on the defendant's hands after a powder had been transferred to Mr. Harmon's hands from a Coke can," O'Shay said.

"Yes."

"This powder then showed up orange on Mr. Harmon's hands under the ultraviolet light, is that correct?"

"Yes."

"What did Mr. Harmon do when Officer Patrick told him that the orange glow was Sandra Whiley's blood?"

"He stared at his hands and began wringing them in an effort to scrape off the blood."

"Now, Mr. Hale asked you if you led the defendant to say that the man in the park had a weapon."

"Yes."

"Did you ever suggest that the weapon used by the person who murdered Sandra Whiley was a hatchet?"

"No, ma'am. When I was talking to Gary we didn't know what was used to kill her, other than it was a sharp-bladed instrument."

"Who is the first person to say that the murder weapon was a hatchet?"

"Gary. The defendant."

"And, lo and behold, the murder weapon did turn out to be a hatchet, didn't it, Sergeant?"

"Yes, ma'am. Much to my surprise, it certainly did."

CHAPTER TWENTY-TWO

1

Dr. Leonard Farber, Kevin Booth's treating physician, had thinning brown hair, clear blue eyes and an easy smile. His cheerful disposition seemed odd when you considered that he spent his days with people who were often in horrible pain. While he walked with Becky O'Shay, Farber explained that his patient had recovered enough to be moved out of isolation in the burn ward to a regular hospital room. O'Shay showed no emotion when the doctor described Booth's injuries and the process of grafting human skin and pigskin onto areas that had been horribly burned, but listening to a scientific explanation of the effect of ignited lighter fluid on human skin was not the same as seeing a person who had been set on fire.

Dr. Farber had arranged for Booth to be temporarily placed in a hospital room that was big enough for the judge, the court reporter, the attorneys and the jury. A policeman stationed outside Booth's door looked up as the doctor and the D.A. approached.

"We're set for two, right?" Farber asked.

"You should probably be here a little before two. Say, one forty-five. Just in case the judge or Harmon's attorney has any questions."

"See you then," Farber said and he headed back to his office.

The police guard opened the door to Booth's room as soon as he checked Becky's ID. Booth was sitting up in a hospital bed that had been elevated so he could watch television. The set was showing a game show. As soon as the door opened, Booth turned off the set.

O'Shay kept her poise when Booth turned his head toward her. His face was covered with silver sulfadiazine, a white, greasy cream. The right side of the face looked normal, but O'Shay could see bright red circles and blobs of healing outer skin through the cream that covered the left side. In addition, Booth had an eighth-of-an-inch tube in his right nostril through which supplemental nutrition was administered. O'Shay also noticed that Booth's left eyebrow was gone.

Booth was wearing a short-sleeve hospital gown. The gown bulged in numerous places where bandages covered the grafts. On the back of Booth's left arm and hand were square patches of pinkish-purplish skin. A clear yellow serum oozed out of numerous perforations in the skin. O'Shay felt light-headed, even though Booth did not look as bad as she had imagined.

"How are you feeling, Mr. Booth?" O'Shay asked as she sat next to the bed on a gray metal chair.

"Bad," Booth managed. His speech had a harsh, rasping quality that startled O'Shay. The word was said so softly that she had to strain to hear it. Dr. Farber had explained that Booth had suffered a minor inhalation injury when he breathed in smoke from the bedding that burned in his cell. Booth's pain medication had also been withheld so he would be clearheaded for his testimony.

"You'll feel better when you're through testifying and I let the U.S. Attorney know how much I appreciate your help."

O'Shay could see that Booth was frightened.

"Don't worry, Kevin. This won't take long. The doctor will be here. The judge will let you take breaks, if you need to. You'll do fine.

"We don't start for a while. I'm here because I want to tell you the questions I'm going to ask you, so you won't be surprised by them. Okay?"

Booth nodded and O'Shay rewarded him with a smile. For the next half hour, O'Shay went through her direct examination with Booth. For the most part, O'Shay let Booth answer without comment, but every once in a while, she would advise Booth to phrase an answer differently so it would have a greater impact on the jurors. By the end of the half hour, Booth seemed to be flagging, so O'Shay decided to wind up their meeting.

"That was great, Kevin. I wanted to go over one more thing, then I'll let you get some rest. Do you think you can hang in there for a few minutes more?"

Booth nodded slowly. His eyelids fluttered with fatigue.

"Jurors are impressed by details. Little things that lend authenticity to what a witness says. There are a lot of good details in your account of Harmon's confession, but there's one thing I realize we've never talked about. Something Gary Harmon may have told you that only the killer would know."

"What . . . thing?"

"You told me that Harmon said that Sandra Whiley wore a good luck piece around her neck. A small, silver medallion on a chain. Did Harmon ever mention anything else about this necklace to you?"

"What . . . would he . . . have said?"

"The necklace was found in some bushes near the entrance to the park. By those stone pillars. We think that the killer tore it off of her neck while they were struggling. Did Harmon ever mention anything about that?"

"I . . . I'm not sure."

"Try and remember. I don't want you to testify about anything Harmon didn't tell you. I don't want you to make up anything. But it would be important, if Harmon did say it. Why don't you think about it while you rest."

Booth nodded. O'Shay stood up.

"I'll come by before everyone else arrives and you can tell me if you remember anything about the necklace or anything else of importance."

2

Peter Hale and Becky O'Shay sat on either side of Judge Kuffel on the left side of Kevin Booth's bed. Behind them, against the wall, sat the jurors. Dr. Farber and the court reporter sat on the right side of the bed. Gary Harmon sat behind Peter. Two guards stood against the wall. Another policeman was stationed outside the room in the hospital corridor.

Peter had his back to the jurors, but he had stolen a glance at them when he was setting up his notes on the bridge table the hospital provided. They seemed uneasy so close to a person who had been horribly burned. Peter appreciated how the jurors felt. He remembered his temporary feeling of disorientation when he saw his father in intensive care for the first time. Hospitals were unpleasant places and patients were graphic reminders of human frailty.

"Mr. Booth, are you feeling well enough to talk to the jury?" Becky O'Shay asked with unctuous concern.

Booth nodded. It had been agreed that he could respond with a nod or shake of the head to questions that could be answered yes or no.

"Good. If you want to rest for a while, please let me know and I'll ask the judge for a recess. Dr. Farber will also be here during the questioning. Do you understand that you can talk to him at any time, if you need to?"

Again, Booth nodded.

"Okay. Now, even though you are recuperating from your terrible burns in this hospital in Portland, you are technically a prisoner awaiting trial in jail on various charges relating to narcotics, are you not?"

Booth nodded.

"After your arrest, were you placed in the Whitaker County Jail?"

Booth nodded.

"Was Gary Harmon in the same jail?"

Booth's head turned slowly until he was staring directly at Gary. Then he turned back toward the prosecutor. Though it took only seconds, the action seemed to take forever.

"Yes," Booth rasped. Several jurors seemed disturbed by the way Booth's voice sounded.

"How long have you known Mr. Harmon?"

"High . . . school."

"Can you estimate the number of years?"

"Six . . . seven years."

"Were you friends in high school?"

Booth nodded.

"So, Mr. Harmon would trust you."

"Objection," Peter said. "Leading."

"That is a leading question, Mr. Hale. Now, I am going to permit more leading than I normally would because of Mr. Booth's condition, but I think this is too important an area to permit it. Why don't you rephrase the question, Ms. O'Shay."

"Very well, Your Honor. Mr. Booth, describe your relationship with Mr. Harmon."

"Gary . . . was my . . . friend."

The effort to get out this halting sentence seemed to exhaust Booth. He closed his eyes and rested while O'Shay asked the next question.

"Did Mr. Harmon appear to have other friends when he was in jail in Whitaker?"

"No," Booth answered, his eyes still shut. "Seemed lonely. Gary . . . stayed by self."

"Did you talk to Mr. Harmon in jail?"

Booth nodded.

"In the course of these conversations did he ever discuss his case?"

Booth nodded.

"Tell the jury how that happened."

Booth took a deep breath. His eyes opened and he slowly turned his head toward the jurors.

"First time I saw Gary in yard, he seemed . . . glad to see me. Excited. We just talked. When I asked about murder . . . he said he didn't . . . didn't kill girl . . ."

Booth paused and sipped from a straw in a plastic water bottle. The jury waited. Booth turned back to them.

"I was . . . a friend. He could trust me. He was nervous. Scared. Later, he told me the truth. He said . . . he killed her."

"Did he just come out and confess?"

"No. It wasn't . . . first time. First time we talked, he said he didn't. Next day . . . he was upset. I told him he didn't have to be afraid. If . . . he wanted to get something . . . off chest . . ." Booth took a deep breath. "Gary was scared . . . He needed to tell . . . someone."

"What did he need to talk about?"

"Mistake. Girl at bar insulted Gary. He was confused. He attacked wrong girl. Then . . . too late."

"So, the defendant thought Sandra Whiley was another girl who had insulted him in a bar and he told you he killed her by mistake."

Booth nodded.

"Tell the jury the defendant's description of the murder."

Booth drank some more water and gathered himself. His testimony was obviously exhausting him. Booth was generating so much sympathy that Gary would be dead and buried by the end of the hospital session if something dramatic did not happen.

"Gary tried to get date with . . . girl at Stallion. She said no. Gary . . . kept after her. She called him stupid . . . Made him angry. Gary grabbed her. Yelled at her.

"Gary said he . . . ran away. Still mad. Ran to his . . . house. Got hatchet. Went back to Stallion."

"Did the defendant say that anything happened on his way back to the Stallion?"

"He saw girl. Thought she was . . . girl from bar."

"The one who insulted him?"

Booth nodded.

"Where did he see her?"

"Near entrance to . . . park."

"Was this the main entrance to Wishing Well Park that leads to the Wishing Well Memorial?"

Booth nodded again.

"What did the defendant say he did after spotting this woman?"

"He threatened her. She backed into the park." Booth paused and took a sip of water. "Gary grabbed her. They struggled. She had . . . necklace. Gary . . . grabbed her . . . by the necklace. It came off. She broke away." Booth paused again. "Ran to the well."

"Who ran to the well?"

"The girl."

"Then what happened?"

"Gary threw away . . . the necklace. Ran after her. Caught her."

"Did he say what he did after catching her?"

Booth nodded. He stared at the jury.

"He killed her."

"Did he say how many times he struck her or where?"

Booth shook his head. "He was . . . upset. Crying. Gary just said he . . . hit her. More than once."

"What happened after the defendant hit Miss Whiley with the hatchet?"

"She was . . . dead. He stood over her. That's when he saw he killed the wrong one."

"What did the defendant do then?"

Booth sipped some water before continuing his testimony.

"He was scared. Ran away."

"What did the defendant do with the hatchet?"

"Put it in storm drain . . . near college."

"And after that?"

"Gary went to the Ponderosa."

"That's a bar?"

Booth nodded.

"Did the defendant ever express remorse for killing Sandra Whiley?"

"He was sorry."

"Sorry?"

Booth looked at the jury and waited a beat before saying, "Sorry he killed the wrong girl."

"Was anyone else present during these conversations between Mr. Harmon and yourself?" Peter Hale asked, when court resumed after a twenty-minute recess.

Booth shook his head.

"So, the jury has only your word that Mr. Harmon made this confession."

Booth did not answer.

"You stand to benefit greatly from your testimony, don't you?"

"I don't . . . understand."

"Well, let's start with the drug charges you're facing. You were arrested holding two garbage bags containing a total of twenty kilos of cocaine, weren't you?"

"I . . . didn't . . . know . . ."

"Your Honor, will you instruct Mr. Booth to answer the question, please?"

"Yes, Mr. Booth. You must answer yes or no, if you can."

Booth ran his tongue across his lips, then nodded.

"And you had just been given the twenty kilos by Rafael Vargas, an enforcer for a Colombian drug cartel?"

Again, Booth nodded.

"Agents of the federal Drug Enforcement Administration made the arrest, did they not?"

Booth nodded.

"Which means you're facing charges in federal court?"

Booth nodded again.

"Has your lawyer told you that under the Federal Sentencing Guidelines you will most likely be sentenced to more than ten years in prison if you are convicted for possession of that much cocaine?"

"I . . . don't have . . . a lawyer."

"I see. But you know the possible sentence?"

"Yes."

"Did Ms. O'Shay tell you about that sentence?"

The question caught Booth off guard and he could not help looking at the prosecutor.

"Don't . . . remember."

"That's interesting. You would think you would remember the person who told you that you were going to spend ten years in prison."

Peter paused and Booth said nothing.

"You're not worried about spending any time in prison, are you, Mr. Booth?"

"What do . . . you mean?"

"Why don't you tell the jury about the deal you're going to receive for testifying?"

"No deal."

"Are you telling this jury that you're not going to receive any benefit from the prosecutor or the federal government for testifying against Gary Harmon?"

"No deal."

"Are you going to trial to contest the narcotics charge?"

"Don't know."

"If you plead guilty or go to trial and are found guilty, do you think Ms. O'Shay will put in a good word for you with the judge at sentencing?"

"I hope so."

"You know so, don't you, Mr. Booth, because you and Ms. O'Shay have a deal worked out already."

"Asked and answered, Your Honor," Becky said

quickly. "Mr. Booth has already explained that he is testifying without any promise of assistance from my office or the federal prosecutor."

Peter could not believe this. There was obviously a deal. O'Shay and Booth had to be lying.

"Do you want this jury to believe that you are testifying out of the goodness of your heart?"

"Didn't want to," Booth managed. "Gary is my friend. But . . ." Booth shook his head slowly. "That girl. To kill her like that. What if Gary was free . . . and killed again?" Booth paused. "Couldn't have that . . . on conscience."

"Did it bother your conscience when you lied to Mr. Harmon at the Stallion by telling him that Karen Nix wanted to go out on a date with him?"

"Not me. Chris Mammon told Gary . . . about girl."

"But you went along with it?"

Booth nodded.

"You've known Mr. Harmon since high school?"

Booth nodded again.

"Then you know he's mentally handicapped?"

Booth hesitated before nodding.

"And knowing this, you went along with Mammon's cruel joke?"

Booth ran a tongue over his lips. "Didn't want to. Felt bad."

"Oh? Does that mean that the witnesses who said you were laughing hysterically at Gary's discomfort were mistaken?"

Booth did not answer.

"You enjoyed tricking and teasing Mr. Harmon, didn't you?"

"No," Booth rasped, but he did not sound convincing.

"And you had no difficulty lying to Gary to gain your ends at the Stallion, just like you have no trouble lying to this jury about what Gary said to you to save yourself from a federal prison sentence?"

"Objection," O'Shay shouted.

"Sustained," Judge Kuffel said.

"Then I have no further questions, Your Honor."

3

Peter replayed Kevin Booth's testimony over and over during the five-hour ride from Portland to Whitaker and he always came to the same conclusion. Booth sounded as if he was telling the truth and Peter's cross-examination had not given the jury any reason to disbelieve him. His cross-examination of Booth had been as disheartening as his cross-examination of Dennis Downes. Neither witness had been broken because Peter was not sure how to cross-examine effectively. He'd had few chances to examine witnesses and his inexperience in court was killing him.

Peter considered going to the office and working on the case, but he was too depressed and tired. Then, he thought about going home, but he did not want to be alone. Finally, he decided to visit Donna and he felt better immediately. He had really enjoyed being with Donna the other night. It had been one of the few times since the trial started that he had been able to relax. Donna was attractive, but Peter tried not to think of her in that way because she was Steve's wife. He tried to think of her as a friend. Someone he could talk to. Someone he just enjoyed being around.

Peter hoped he would find Donna alone, but Rhonda Kates opened the door when he knocked. Rhonda had also proved to be a good friend. She had been great about helping Donna. When he saw her, Peter smiled warmly.

"Hi, Rhonda. Is Donna here?"

"She's freshening up."

Peter noticed that Rhonda looked as though she was getting ready to go out.

"What's up?"

"Donna's moving back to her folks' house. I was going to drive her."

"I'll do it. I have some stuff I have to go over with her about the trial."

"Okay. How is the trial going?"

Peter stopped smiling. "Not good," he said.

The bathroom door opened and Donna walked out. She looked surprised to see Peter. Then, the look of surprise changed to a welcoming smile.

"Rhonda tells me you're going to your folks."

Donna sobered. "I'm sick of hiding. I didn't do anything wrong. Steve did. My brother is on trial for his life and Steve is not going to keep me from being in court to support him."

"Are you going to tell your folks what happened?" Peter asked.

"Yes. I've decided that I have no reason to feel ashamed."

"Good for you. If you want me to, I'll take you to the farm. I can fill you in on the case while we're driving."

Donna hugged Rhonda and thanked her for putting her up.

"What happened at the hospital?" Donna asked as soon as they were on the road. Peter recounted Booth's testimony.

"Do you think the jurors believed him?"

"I don't know. What scares me is that he seemed to be telling the truth. And he was so pathetic." Peter shook his head. "The poor bastard could hardly talk."

"Didn't your investigator find anything you could use against Booth?"

"Pullen has been a disaster."

"I thought he was supposed to be good."

"That's what Steve said, but I haven't seen any evidence of it. I can never find the guy. His reports are useless. The few times I have gotten in touch with him, he's been working at his brother's body shop instead of working on the case."

"Why don't you fire him and hire someone new?"

"It's too late. We're in the middle of the trial."

The road to the Harmon farm followed the river. It was a pretty stretch lined with elm and maple trees. Donna had lapsed into silence so Peter rolled down the driver's window and enjoyed the rich summer air until she said, "I have an idea. I've lived in Whitaker my whole life. I know a lot of people here. Why don't you let me help with the investigation?"

"What?"

"I know I can do it. If . . . if we do go to a penalty phase, I can line up a million witnesses with good things to say about Gary. It would take another investigator weeks to make up a list of people I could remember in an afternoon."

"You've never done any investigation, Donna. You wouldn't know how to go about it. You need a police background or training."

"Barney Pullen has a police background. How much good has he done for Gary?"

"It wouldn't work."

"Maybe not, but I can't do worse than Pullen, from what you've said, and I might do a hell of a lot better. At least you'd know I wasn't going to quit on you."

Peter dropped Donna off at the Harmons' and headed back to town. During the drive, he thought over Donna's offer to act as his investigator. She meant well, but she had no experience and he needed someone who knew what he was doing. One thing she said had made sense, though. If Gary was convicted, the penalty phase would start after a short break. In the penalty phase, the defense told the defendant's life story to humanize him. Donna would not only know what people would be of use at trial, but those people would trust her and talk to her.

The phone was ringing when Peter walked in the door of his house. He answered on the third ring.

"Is this Peter Hale, the lawyer who's defending that guy who's supposed to have killed the girl in the park?"

"Right. Who's this?"

"Zack Howell. I'm a student. I go to Whitaker."

"What's up, Zack?"

"I, uh, read the ad. The one you put in the *Clarion* asking anyone who was near Wishing Well Park when Sandy Whiley was murdered to call you."

"Yes?"

"Well, uh, I didn't want to call, at first. But the guy is charged with murder. So, I talked it over with Jessie, my girlfriend, and she said we had to call."

"You were near the park on the evening of the murder?"

"Yeah, we were."

CHAPTER TWENTY-THREE

After talking to Zack Howell, Peter called Barney Pullen's house. A woman answered and told him that Pullen wasn't in. Peter left a message for the investigator, telling him to bring his reports to the courthouse at eight o'clock the next morning.

Peter was in front of the courthouse at eight sharp. At eight-twenty, Pullen showed up, looking annoyed.

"You're late," Peter said.

"Sorry," Pullen mumbled, but it was obvious that he didn't mean it.

"Where are your reports?"

"I haven't found a lot of useful stuff yet, Mr. Hale," Pullen said, handing Peter a thin stack of paper, "but I think I'm close to some good information."

Peter thumbed through the reports quickly, because there was so little to read. He was stunned at first, then furious. When he looked up at Pullen, the investigator would not meet his eye.

"I can't believe this is everything you've done."

Pullen shrugged.

"Have you walked off the distances between the Stallion, the Ponderosa and Gary's house, like I asked? I don't see a report on it in here."

"I haven't had a chance to get to it, yet."

"I asked you to do that weeks ago."

"Yeah, I know. I was going to do that on the week-end, but something came up."

"What was that, Barney?"

Pullen looked very uncomfortable. "I promised my brother I'd take his kid fishing. I thought I'd have plenty of time to walk off the distances when we got back to town, but my car broke down. By the time I fixed it and got the kid back to his folks, I was beat. I should be able to get to it today."

"Barney, this isn't working out."

"What do you mean?"

"I mean that I'm getting someone else to take over the investigation. I just don't think you're doing a professional job and there's too much at stake."

"What are you talking about? I've been busting my ass on this case."

"We've got a difference of opinion on that. Send me a bill for your time. I've got to get to court."

A reporter from the *Clarion* spotted Donna and her parents in the corridor outside Judge Kuffel's courtroom. Before they could get inside, the reporter cornered Jesse and asked him for a comment. While her father talked to the reporter, Donna took a step back, hoping she would be left alone.

"Hi, Donna."

She turned. Steve was standing next to her. Her breath caught and fear froze her.

"I have an appearance in Judge Staley's court. I was heading there when I saw you."

"I don't want to talk to you, Steve. Please go away."

"You have every right to be angry. I just wanted to find out how you're doing."

"I'm doing fine, now that you can't hit me."

Mancini looked down. He seemed contrite.

"You don't deserve what I did. I'm . . . I don't know

what I am. But I know that I love you and I want our marriage to work. I'm willing to go to counseling, if you think that's what I need."

"I don't trust you, Steve, and this isn't the time."

"I understand. I don't expect you to come back to me right away, but I want you to know that I still love you very much and I feel sick about what I've done to our marriage. I just want to know if we have a chance."

"I don't know if we do," Donna answered firmly.

Jesse Harmon turned away from the reporter and saw Steve. He flushed with anger and took a step forward. Donna put a hand on his arm.

"It's all right, Dad."

Jesse glowered at Mancini, but held his tongue.

"Now isn't a good time," Donna told Steve.

"Will you at least agree to talk this over."

"I have to think."

"Let's go, Donna," Jesse said and Donna followed her parents into the courtroom.

Peter and Gary were already at their counsel table. Gary noticed Donna and grinned. He had been upset when she was not in court. Peter walked over to the bar of the court and motioned toward Donna.

"I thought over your idea about investigating for me. There are a few things I'd like you to do."

"Oh, Peter," Donna said excitedly.

"Look, I don't have any time now, but Becky told Judge Kuffel that she only has one short witness before she rests her case. Kuffel will send the jurors home when she rests, then hear motions. I think I'll be done by noon. Why don't I drive out to the farm after lunch. I'll make copies of all the investigative reports. You can read them over and we can talk about it tonight."

"That would be great."

The bailiff called the court to order and Donna and Peter took their seats just as Becky O'Shay recalled Dennis Downes to the stand.

"I have one more matter I want to discuss with you, Sergeant Downes," O'Shay said, after the judge reminded the policeman that he was still under oath. O'Shay handed Downes a plastic evidence bag.

"Do you recognize the item of evidence marked State's Exhibit 76 that is contained in this plastic bag?"

"Yes."

"What is it?"

"It's a Crusader's Cross on a chain."

"A necklace?"

"Yes, ma'am."

"Who owned this necklace?"

"We established that this medallion was Sandra Whiley's good luck charm. She was last seen wearing it by one of the bartenders at the Stallion shortly before she left the bar around eleven-twenty."

"Was she still wearing the necklace when her body was discovered?"

"No. There was a bruise on Miss Whiley's neck that was consistent with a narrow object like the chain on the necklace being torn off forcefully."

"Where was the necklace found?"

"In a bush near the entrance to Wishing Well Park."

"Was the necklace damaged in any way when it was found?"

"The clasp had been broken in a manner consistent with the necklace having been jerked off of the victim while she was wearing it."

"How many people knew that Miss Whiley was not wearing the necklace when she was found?"

"Not many. It would only be the police at the scene, the medical examiner. Not all of the officers saw the body or learned about the discovery of the necklace."

"So very few people would know that the necklace had been ripped from Miss Whiley's neck when she was killed as opposed to being removed from her neck by the police when her body was discovered at the well?"

"Yes, ma'am."

"What conclusion would you draw as an experienced law enforcement officer, if you learned that Gary Harmon told someone that Sandra Whiley's killer had ripped a necklace from her just before he murdered her?"

Peter objected to the question and Judge Kuffel sustained his objection, but Downes's answer did not matter. The jury had heard Kevin Booth's account of Gary's confession and they were going to wonder how Gary could possibly have known that Sandra Whiley's Crusader's Cross had been ripped from her neck just before she was killed. Peter was wondering about that too when Becky O'Shay told the judge that the state was resting its case.

CHAPTER TWENTY-FOUR

1

The defense case was short and that worried Peter. He wondered if the jury would hold it against Gary that he was able to muster so few witnesses to speak on his behalf after so much testimony from the prosecution.

During the morning session of court Peter called several of the policemen who searched Gary's house to establish that no blood had been found on Gary's clothes. He also called the bartender from the Ponderosa, who testified that he saw Gary around midnight on the evening of the murder and did not notice any blood on his clothes. Then, he called Elmore Brock, whose shaggy brown hair, smooth skin and blue blazer made him look like a student in a parochial school. Gary's face lit up when he saw Brock and he waved at the witness. Brock looked unsure about smiling back, but he did when Gary started to look upset.

"That's Mr. Brock," Gary told Peter excitedly.

"How are you employed, Mr. Brock?" Peter asked after getting Gary to quiet down.

"I'm the school psychologist at Eisenhower High School here in Whitaker."

"Can you tell the jury your educational and professional background?"

Brock hunched over a little. He looked uncomfortable talking to the jury.

"I graduated from Portland State University with a B.A. in psychology. Then, I obtained a master's degree from the University of Oregon in special education. After I received my master's, I spent one year in Portland at the Allen Center, a treatment facility with programs for preschool through adolescence. When the school psychologist position at Eisenhower High opened up six years ago, I applied for it and I've been there since then."

"Mr. Brock, did you work with mentally handicapped children at the Allen Center?"

"Yes I did."

"Does Eisenhower High have classes for the mentally handicapped?"

"It does."

"What is the definition of 'mentally handicapped'?"

"Uh, I'd say it means that a person has diminished capacity to take in and organize new information and diminished ability to use the information. The negative effects of this condition can be seen in all aspects of the handicapped person's life and it affects his educational, social and vocational functions."

"Did you know Gary Harmon when he was a student at Eisenhower?"

"Yes, I did," Brock said, turning toward Gary and smiling at him warmly. Gary smiled back.

"Was he classified as mentally handicapped?"

"Yes."

"What is Gary's IQ?"

"Somewhere between 65 and 70."

"What is the IQ of an average, normal person?"

"One hundred."

"Would a person with an average IQ do well in college?"

"No. Most college students have IQ's in the range of 120."

"Mr. Brock, what is the difference between Gary and someone with an average IQ?"

"Well, if you looked at a photograph, it wouldn't show any difference, but if you talked to Gary you would notice several things after a while. Gary's speech is going to be slower and less distinct. His vocabulary will be significantly smaller. His coordination and fine motor skills will also be more awkward and less developed.

"Gary also functions in the here and now. He doesn't have the ability to make plans that extend very far into the future and the plans he does make are going to be vague and may be unrealistic."

Peter shot a quick look at Gary, but he showed no reaction during this clinical discussion of his intelligence level.

"What classes did Gary take in school?"

"They were special education classes designed to give Gary living skills and vocational skills. He also received some very basic education in mathematics, English and other subjects that normal children study."

"Did Gary have an individualized education plan?"

"Yes. He trained to be a janitor and he worked at the college with the janitorial staff while in high school."

"Was his work as a janitor satisfactory?"

"Definitely," Brock answered enthusiastically. Gary sat up straight and smiled proudly. "Gary works very hard at any task you give him. It took him a while to catch on, but Gary never stops trying to learn a skill."

"Did Gary do any work for you?"

"Yes. He was always asking me if he could help me around the office. I usually told him no, because most of the work was too complicated for him, but I did have him Xerox items on occasion and he was great at stuffing envelopes."

"I did good work for Mr. Brock," Gary said.

"May I have a moment, Your Honor?" Peter asked.

Judge Kuffel nodded. Peter turned toward his client and put a hand on his shoulder.

274

"Gary, we talked about this," Peter said quietly. "You can't talk while a witness is testifying. Okay? You write down anything you think is important and we'll talk about it. But don't talk now."

"I'm sorry," Gary said.

"Mr. Brock, do you have Gary's school records?" Peter continued.

"Yes," Brock said, holding up a manila folder.

"Was Gary a discipline problem at Eisenhower?"

"No, sir. In fact, there are very few negative comments in Gary's folder."

"Do children with Gary's handicap tend to fight?"

"No. To the contrary. Mentally handicapped children tend to shy away from fights, even if they are big and strong like Gary, unless they come from a dysfunctional family and have developed antisocial traits."

"Why is that?"

"They feel inadequate compared to so-called normal people. They get frightened easily and believe they need permission to do things."

"Was Gary a mean or aggressive young man while at Eisenhower?"

"Definitely not. He was usually docile and very sensitive to other people's feelings. Let me give you an example. Gary loves football. I remember one game where a teammate was injured. Mentally handicapped kids have feelings like everyone else, but they have a harder time controlling them. They sort of wear their heart on their sleeves. I remember Gary being in tears while the coaches attended to this kid."

"As an expert in mental retardation and as someone who knows Gary personally, were you surprised to learn that Gary was charged with this murder?"

"Yes I was. Nothing I know about Gary would have prepared me for this. The amount of violence involved . . . Just the idea of Gary inflicting that kind of pain on another person is inconsistent with Gary's personality and the way someone of his intelligence would function."

"No further questions."

Becky O'Shay glanced through the copy of Gary's school records she had received weeks ago with Peter's discovery material. When she was done, she smiled warmly at Elmore Brock. Brock's shoulders hunched a little more, but he flashed back a brief, nervous smile.

"It's Mr. Brock, not Dr. Brock?" O'Shay asked sweetly.

"Yes."

"So, *Mr.* Brock, you don't have a Ph.D.?"

"No."

"Am I correct that your master's is not in psychology?"

"Yes."

"In fact, you are not a licensed psychologist, are you?"

"No."

"A licensed psychologist has to complete a one-year residency where he performs two thousand hours of therapy assessment in the area of his specialization while under the supervision of a licensed psychologist, doesn't he?"

"Yes."

"You didn't do that, did you?"

Brock flushed.

"No," he said.

"And a licensed psychologist has to take national written exams and an oral examination given to him by the Oregon State Board of Psychologist Examiners, doesn't he?"

"Yes."

"But you didn't do that, did you?"

"No," he answered tersely.

"Now, you've explained that the defendant is not as bright as normal folks, is that correct?"

"Yes."

"Could you tell the jurors what Gary's high school average was?"

"That doesn't mean . . ."

276

"Your Honor . . . ?" O'Shay asked the judge.

"Yes, Mr. Brock. Please answer the question. If there is something Mr. Hale wants you to explain, he'll get a chance after Ms. O'Shay is done asking her questions."

Brock ducked his head a little and said, "Sorry."

"That's okay, Mr. Brock," the prosecutor said pleasantly. "This is all new to you. Do you want the question read back?"

"No, I remember it. Gary had a 3.20 grade average."

"A 4.00 is straight A's, isn't it?"

"Yes."

"And a 3.50 is honor roll?"

"Yes."

"Now, I believe you said that someone like Mr. Harmon would have poor coordination?"

"Yes."

"Didn't the defendant earn a varsity letter in football his senior year?"

Brock started to say something, then choked it back.

"Yes," he answered tersely.

"You talked about things that the defendant can't do. I'd like to ask you about some things he can do. For instance, can Gary Harmon lie?"

"Well, yes. Gary could learn how to lie."

"If he murdered a young girl would he be frightened?"

"Yes."

"Would fear motivate a person with even an IQ of 65 to 70 to lie?"

"Yes."

"Now, you told a touching story about the defendant weeping when he saw a teammate injured during a football game."

"Yes."

"Then, I believe you testified that Mr. Harmon wept because mentally handicapped people have the same emotions as normal people but they have a harder time controlling their feelings."

"Yes."

277

"Anger is an emotion, isn't it?"

Brock saw the trap into which he had fallen, but he had no choice but to respond affirmatively.

"Mr. Brock, if someone with an IQ of 65 to 70 was drinking and very frightened because he had just butchered a young girl with a hatchet while in an uncontrollable rage, might he not block out the memory of what he had done?"

"That's . . . that's possible."

"Mentally handicapped people are capable of persevering at tasks, are they not?"

"Yes, they can be very single-minded."

"So, if Mr. Harmon committed a particularly bloody and violent murder, fear might spur him to lie and he would be capable of sticking to that lie?"

"Yes."

"What effect would being drunk have on this scenario?"

"Alcohol might make it more likely that Gary would not remember killing someone, if he did kill anyone," Brock answered reluctantly.

"I didn't kill that girl," Gary said.

"Your Honor," O'Shay said, staring at the defendant.

"Mr. Harmon, you may not speak out in court," Judge Kuffel admonished Gary. "Do you understand me?"

Gary nodded. He looked upset. Peter whispered something in his ear and Gary looked down at the tabletop.

"You said that planning is more difficult for someone with Mr. Harmon's IQ, did you not?" O'Shay continued.

"Yes."

"But he could plan a killing, couldn't he?"

"What type of killing are you talking about?"

"Let's say he was told that a woman at a bar wanted to go out with him by someone who was playing a practical joke. When Mr. Harmon asks the woman if she wants a beer, she not only rejects him, but insults his intelligence, a subject about which he is very sensitive. Let's say further that Mr. Harmon physically assaults this woman. My question, Doctor . . . Pardon me. *Mr. Brock*, is whether Mr. Harmon is intelligent enough to make a plan that involves going to his house to obtain a weapon, returning to the area of the bar, following a woman from the bar, killing her and getting rid of the murder weapon?"

"He . . . he could carry out that plan."

O'Shay smiled. "Thank you. I have no further questions."

"Mr. Brock, you aren't a Ph.D., but you are a specialist in dealing with the mentally handicapped, are you not?" Peter asked the witness.

"Yes. That's where my training lies."

"What does Gary Harmon's 3.20 grade point average mean?"

"Not much. His grades are only relative to his ability to perform the tasks he's given. Gary does not have an A in advanced physics. He has an A in life skills, which means he knows how to make his bed, tie his shoes and things of that sort. The grades are given to make the students feel good about themselves, not to reflect real academic merit."

"Ms. O'Shay pointed out that Gary was on the varsity football team at Eisenhower. Tell the jury about that."

Gary looked up at the mention of his favorite sport.

"Gary loves football. He went out for the team in ninth grade. The coach let him work out with the other boys, but he did not have the ability to really play. Learning all but the simplest plays would be beyond him. So, the coach let him suit up. Every once in a while, if the team was really behind or really ahead, Gary would go in for a play or two. He would be told to block a specific person.

"His senior year, the coach put Gary on varsity, but he was only in five or so plays all year. They gave him a varsity letter because he tried so hard, not because he did the things the other kids did to earn the letter."

"I have one final series of questions, Mr. Brock. How easy would it be to fool Gary into believing that he had supernatural powers that would enable him to project himself into the mind of a dead woman and see how she was killed?"

"It would be very easy. Gary wants very much to please people. He would do or say anything for approval."

"Would he invent a story to make a person in authority happy?"

"Most definitely. Gary has a very limited imagination, but he would pick up cues if the person talking to him suggested what he wanted to hear."

"What effect would there be on Gary if the person questioning him was a policeman?"

"That would have a big effect. Someone with Gary's IQ will follow people in authority without question. If a policeman made suggestions to someone like Gary, there would be no way of telling if the mentally handicapped person was remembering something or making it up to please the policeman."

2

After lunch, Peter called Don Bosco, who voiced his opinion that Dennis Downes had unwittingly placed Gary Harmon in a trance state during the interrogation, thus making any statement he made unreliable for evidentiary purposes. Bosco told the jury that Sergeant Downes's "projection transfer" technique would invite someone of Gary's limited intelligence to fantasize in order to please his interrogator. He pointed out many sections of the transcript where leading and suggestive questions had elicited answers from Gary that echoed suggestions made by Downes.

"Mr. Bosco," Becky O'Shay said, when it was her turn to cross-examine, "if I understand you correctly, you are concerned that the defendant's statements may be unreliable because he may have parroted back suggestions made by Sergeant Downes instead of relating incidents in which he was actually involved."

"That's right."

"You weren't at Wishing Well Park when the murder was committed, were you?" O'Shay asked with a kind smile.

"No."

"So you don't know whether Gary Harmon committed this murder and was telling Sergeant Downes about an incident he remembers or whether he was not present during the murder and is making up a story?"

"That's true."

"Would one way of telling whether the defendant was making up what he told the officer be to see if he knew things about Sandra Whiley's murder that were not common knowledge and were not suggested to him by Sergeant Downes?"

"Yes."

"Thank you. No further questions."

Peter had saved his final witness for late in the day, so his testimony would be the last thing the jurors heard. He wanted the jurors to think about that testimony all night.

"Mr. Harmon calls Zachary Howell," Peter said.

A slender young man with curly brown hair entered the courtroom and walked to the witness stand.

"Mr. Howell," Peter asked, "are you a freshman at Whitaker State College?"

"Yes, sir."

"What are you studying?"

"Uh, I haven't settled on a major, yet. I'm thinking, maybe, biology."

"Do you have a girlfriend, Mr. Howell?"

"Yes."

"What's her name?"

281

"Jessie Freeman."

"How did you come to be a witness in this case?"

"There was an ad in the school paper. It asked anyone with any information about the murder to call you."

"Was the ad more specific?"

"You wanted to talk to anyone who'd been around Wishing Well Park from 11 P.M. to 2:30 A.M. on the evening that Sandra Whiley was killed."

"Do you remember what you were doing on the evening that Sandra Whiley was murdered?"

"I was on a date with Jessie. We went to a late movie. Afterward, we went to Wishing Well Park and, uh, we were in the park for a while."

Peter did not press Howell for more detailed testimony. He could tell from the amused looks of some of the jurors that they were well aware of what a young couple would be doing in the park on a romantic summer evening.

"When did you start to leave the park?"

"A little before eleven-thirty."

"How can you be certain of the time?"

"We were going white-water rafting the next day and we had to get up early, so I looked at my watch to see what time it was."

"What path did you take to get out of Wishing Well Park?"

"We walked along the river until we reached the wishing well. Then we walked up the path and left through the main entrance."

"Did you see a dead body next to the well when you passed by?"

"No, sir."

"Would you have noticed a body?"

"Yes, sir. Jessie made a wish at the well and threw in a penny. We were standing there looking down."

"Do you know what Jessie wished for?"

"Yes, sir," Howell smiled.

"Tell the jury how you figured out Jessie's wish?"

"When we reached the place where the stone pillars are, Jessie kissed me."

"And did you kiss her back?"

"Yes, sir."

"What happened then?"

"Jessie was holding on to my hand and she swung away from me and said, 'See, wishes do come true.' "

"She swung away," Peter repeated.

"Yes."

"Why do you remember all this so well, Mr. Howell?"

"The girl who was murdered, Sandy, she was in one of my classes. Everyone was talking about it the next day when we got back from rafting. I realized that we must have been right where the murder took place, right before it happened. That really scared me."

"Mr. Howell, how long did it take between the time you decided to leave the park at a little before eleven-thirty and the time you actually left the park?"

"Not long. We were pretty near the well. Then, we stopped so Jessie could make her wish. That wasn't much time. I'd say no more than five minutes."

"So, it was around eleven thirty-five when you were at the entrance to the park?"

"Yes."

"How was Jessie dressed?"

"Jeans and a tee shirt."

"Mr. Howell, are you taller or shorter than Jessie?"

"Taller. She's only about five four, five five."

"One last question. What is the color of Jessie Freeman's hair and does she wear it short or long?"

"Jessie's hair is blond. She has long blond hair."

"Are you telling me that you didn't know a thing about this witness?" Becky O'Shay shouted at Dennis Downes.

"Calm down, Becky."

"Don't you realize that our whole case depends on the theory that Harmon made up his story about seeing two people kissing at the entrance to Wishing Well Park? Didn't you hear me tell the jury during opening statement that there were never two people kissing at the park entrance, that the two people at the entrance were Sandra Whiley and the murderer, Gary Harmon? Now, we've got two cute teenagers smooching at the pillars at eleven thirty-five. He is taller than she is, just as Harmon said. She swings away from him, just as Harmon said. And the girl has blond hair and was wearing jeans and a tee shirt, just like Sandra Whiley. Finally, we have Harmon eating biscuits and gravy at the Ponderosa without a drop of blood on him at midnight. The case is falling apart."

Downes shrugged his shoulders. "I don't know what to tell you. No one knew about Howell until he called Hale. It's just a bad break."

O'Shay clenched her fists in frustration. Then she sank onto her chair and sagged.

"I'm sorry I yelled, Dennis. I'm just tired. You go and interview Howell for me. See if you can get me something I can use on cross. Call me at home if you come up with anything."

Downes left and O'Shay stared at the stacks of police reports that covered her desk. Each one dealt with some aspect of the Harmon case. She had read through them countless times, but she vowed to go through them again in hopes of finding anything that would help her deal with Zack Howell's testimony.

Becky missed it her first time through because the clues were scattered around. A report here, a fragment of remembered conversation there. In fact, O'Shay did not put it all together until she caught sight of that afternoon's edition of the *Clarion* lying unread on top of her filing cabinet.

Becky sat up, openmouthed. Then she rummaged through the police reports until she found the one she wanted. A surge of energy coursed through her as she reread it. When she was done she placed several calls. The people with whom she spoke confirmed her conclusion. Zack Howell and Jessie Freeman may have been kissing at the entrance to Wishing Well Park and Gary Harmon may have been sitting in the Ponderosa at midnight eating biscuits and gravy, but Harmon had also murdered Sandra Whiley and Becky could prove it.

CHAPTER TWENTY-FIVE

1

The next day, Peter rested the defense case as soon as court convened, and Becky O'Shay called Dennis Downes as her first rebuttal witness.

"Sergeant Downes, you are aware that Dr. Guisti places Sandra Whiley's time of death sometime between 11:30 P.M. and 2:30 A.M.?"

"Yes, ma'am."

"And the body was discovered early on Saturday morning?"

"Yes."

"Did the authorities know Miss Whiley's identity immediately?"

"No. We couldn't find a wallet or purse, so it took a while to identify Miss Whiley."

"When was the identification made?"

"After four that afternoon."

"How did you discover the identity of the victim?"

"Marjorie Dooling, Miss Whiley's roommate, saw a sketch of the victim in the afternoon edition of the *Clarion* and came down to the station house."

"No further questions."

"Any cross, Mr. Hale?" Judge Kuffel asked.

Peter had no idea why Becky had asked Downes about the time of the identification so he shook his head.

"The state calls Martin Renzler."

Martin Renzler raised his hand and took the oath. He was tall and slender with wavy gray hair. Wire-rimmed glasses made him look studious. Renzler adjusted his suit jacket when he took the stand.

"How are you employed, Mr. Renzler?"

"I'm the managing editor of the *Whitaker Clarion*."

"Is the *Clarion* the only daily paper in Whitaker County?"

"Yes."

"On the morning of the day that Sandra Whiley's body was found did you receive a request from Sergeant Dennis Downes of the Whitaker police?"

"Yes."

"What was the request?"

"He told me that the body of an unidentified female had been found in Wishing Well Park. Sergeant Downes asked if the paper would publish an artist's sketch of the woman because the police could not establish her identity."

"Did the *Clarion* publish the sketch?"

"We ran the sketch on the front page."

"When does the paper hit the streets?"

"I checked our records. The earliest the edition would have been out in the community is 2:30 P.M."

"Nothing further," O'Shay said.

Something Peter had read in a police report began to nag him. It had been a short report. Something about . . . about . . .

"The state calls Harry Diets."

As Peter thumbed through the huge stack of reports, an overweight, thirtyish man in a business suit walked quickly up the aisle and was sworn. O'Shay established that he was the manager of KLPN, the local television station. Diets had also been contacted by Dennis Downes.

"Mr. Diets, did you broadcast the police sketch of the murdered girl?"

"We did. In fact, we made it part of a special bulletin and slipped it in at 3 P.M., because our next regular newscast is at 5."

Peter found the report he was looking for just as O'Shay called her next witness. As Wilma Polk walked to the witness stand, Peter read her statement to the police. By the time she had sworn to tell the whole truth and nothing but the truth, the reason she, Diets, Renzler and Downes had been called to testify dawned on Peter. As she testified to her recollections of the Harmon-Mancini wedding reception, Peter felt a sick, swirling feeling in the pit of his stomach.

"Did you learn about anything unusual that had occurred in Whitaker on the morning of the wedding?" the prosecutor asked.

"My husband, Eric, is a policeman. He was called out early. When he came back, he told me that a young woman had been murdered in Wishing Well Park."

"Did you discuss the murder with Mabel Dawes, a friend of yours, at the wedding reception?"

"Yes, I did."

"Please tell the jury what happened while you were talking to your friend."

"We were at the food table. Gary Harmon walked over. He had a plate of food. I remember that, because it was piled very high and I was afraid some of the food might fall off.

"Gary seemed very interested in the murder. I remember Mabel saying that she would hate to be the person who had to break the news to the parents."

"Did the defendant say anything to you at that point?"

"Yes. Yes he did."

"What did he say?"

"He told us that the girl had been at the Stallion the night of the murder."

Peter paled as he anticipated Becky O'Shay's next

question and the answer he knew Wilma Polk would give.

"Do you remember when this converation with Gary Harmon took place?"

"Oh yes," Wilma Polk answered with a vigorous nod. "We were due at my daughter's house at two. My grandson, Kenny, was having a birthday party. He's three."

"And the time?" O'Shay prodded.

"It was one-thirty. Eric said we had to hurry because the birthday was at two and it was already one-thirty."

"One-thirty," O'Shay repeated. "And you're certain of that?"

"Oh yes, because I looked at my watch. Eric said it was one-thirty and that was exactly what my watch said."

2

Donna had stayed up until after midnight going through the investigative reports again, after Peter left the Harmon farm. The first job Peter gave her was to use a stopwatch while tracing the possible paths Gary could have followed on the evening of the murder so Peter could set up a time chart of Gary's movements. While she was making a list of all the routes she would have to walk, she noticed that she would be near the house where Sandra Whiley had lived with Marjorie Dooling.

The boardinghouse was a yellow, two-story Victorian with white trim. The lawn was neatly tended, but the front porch needed painting. A middle-aged woman answered the doorbell.

"Good afternoon," Donna said nervously. "Is Marjorie Dooling in?"

"I believe so," the woman answered pleasantly. "Who should I tell her is calling?"

Donna hesitated before identifying herself. She wondered if Dooling would recognize her last name and refuse to see her. After a moment's reflection, she decided that it was best to be honest.

Donna looked around the entry hall while the landlady went upstairs. After a minute, Donna heard the landlady knock on a door on the second floor and call out "Marge." A few minutes later, the landlady descended the stairs followed by a girl wearing a Grateful Dead concert tee shirt and cut-off jeans. Her brown hair was cut short. Donna recognized her because she had seen Marjorie Dooling testify.

"Ms. Dooling, I'm a private investigator working for Peter Hale."

Dooling looked surprised. "You're an investigator?"

"Just for this case," Donna explained nervously. "Most of the time, I'm a legal secretary."

Suddenly, Dooling's brow furrowed. "Isn't Hale the lawyer representing the . . . the man who killed . . . ?"

"We don't think he killed anyone."

"I've already talked to the cops. They know your client killed Sandy. They told me he confessed."

"The police can make mistakes. They're making a big one in this case."

"Right."

"Look, all I'd like to do is ask you a few questions about your friend. If it wasn't important, I wouldn't take up your time."

Dooling worried her lower lip for a minute. Then she said, "All right, but can you make it quick? I'm studying for a test."

"I promise I won't be too long."

"Come on up to my room."

Dooling's apartment consisted of a large living room, a bathroom and two bedrooms. The living room walls were decorated with framed posters. Dooling sat on an old couch. In front of her was a low coffee table covered with textbooks and an open loose-leaf notebook. Across from the couch was a TV and a CD player. Two old armchairs made up the rest of the furniture in the living room. Donna took one of the armchairs and opened her notebook. She noticed that the door to one of the bedrooms was closed.

"Was that Sandra Whiley's room?"

"Yeah," Dooling answered quietly.

"Do you miss her?" she asked.

Dooling gave the question a lot of thought.

"We weren't super close, but she was nice. I guess I do miss her."

"Can you tell me a little about her?"

"She was quiet. She was a good listener, too. I could talk to her, if I had a problem."

"Did she date?"

"A little."

"Do you think she might have been killed by someone she dated?"

"The police asked me the same question. I only met a few of the guys she dated. None of them seemed like the type who would . . . You know."

"How did you two meet?"

"Both of us were working our way through school by waitressing at Clark's. We got friendly and decided it would be cheaper for both of us to share my place."

"Marjorie, can you think of anything unusual that happened around the time Sandy was killed?"

Dooling looked a little nervous. Then, she sighed.

"I guess it can't hurt now, and I already told the D.A. Sandy used drugs. A few months before she was killed, I started worrying that she was getting in too deep, but she wouldn't listen to me."

"What drugs are we talking about?"

"Cocaine."

"What did you mean when you said she was getting in too deep?"

"She didn't always use coke. Not when I met her. I mean, she may have experimented with it, but mostly it was grass. I started getting worried when the coke became a regular thing. I think she was seeing someone who turned her on to it. She was staying in her room a lot and skipping classes. She said everything was okay, but I didn't believe her."

"Was this around the time of her death?"

"Actually, right around the murder I began thinking maybe she was trying to quit. She was acting different. She seemed scared of something, too. She was locking the door and not going out at night as much."

"Did Sandy have family? Someone she might have talked to if something was bothering her?"

"I don't think she was close with her folks. They're divorced and she didn't see them much."

"What about at school? Did she have friends other than you?"

"There was a girl in some of her classes. Annie something."

"Do you have a phone number or address for this Annie?"

"No."

"You mentioned that Sandy seemed scared. Was it of anyone in particular?"

Dooling hesitated. "There was a guy."

"Do you have a name?"

"No. But I know he scared her."

"Can you describe him?"

"I only saw him once from the upstairs window. He came to pick her up and he stayed in his car."

Donna asked her some more questions about Whiley's interests, her courses and her personal life. When Donna noticed that Dooling was glancing at the clock and her schoolwork, she stood up.

"Thanks for talking to me. I'm sorry I bothered you, but this has been helpful." Donna handed Dooling the business card of the lawyer for whom she worked with her name handwritten on it. "If you remember anything else, please give me a call."

Donna waited until she was outside before taking a

deep breath. She was nervous, but she decided that her first interview as an investigator had not gone too badly. She just didn't know if anything Dooling said would be of use to Peter.

3

The guard closed the door to the interview room and Gary sat down across from Peter. There was a dull smile on Gary's face. He started playing with the end of his tie. Peter shook his head. His client was totally oblivious to the havoc that had been wreaked on their case by the state's witnesses, but Wilma Polk's testimony had put Peter into a state of shock.

"I want you to listen up, Gary."

"Okay."

"I have a very important question for you and I want you to think before you answer it. Can you do that for me?"

"Sure."

Gary sat up straight and stopped smiling.

"Sandy was murdered between eleven-thirty on Friday night and two-thirty on Saturday morning. You got that?"

"Uh huh," Gary answered with a nod.

"Good. When Sandy's body was found early Saturday, she didn't have any identification on her. No one knew her name. So, the police asked the newspaper and the TV to show her picture and ask for help in finding out who she was. Are you following me?"

"Yeah, Pete. They didn't know Sandy's name."

"Right. Good. Okay. Now the newspaper came out around two-thirty in the afternoon and the TV showed Sandy's picture at three. Sandy's roommate told the police Sandy's name around four. Two-thirty in the afternoon is the earliest anyone could have known who Sandy was because that's when the paper came out with her picture. Do you see that?"

"They coulda seen the picture," Gary said with a smile.

"Right. But there was no picture before two-thirty."

"No one coulda seen it before two-thirty."

"Right. Now listen up. Here's my question, Gary. Mrs. Polk says that at one-thirty, at the wedding reception, you told her the dead girl was at the Stallion on Friday evening. Do you remember her saying that?"

"Who's Mrs. Polk?" Gary asked.

"The last witness. That lady with the gray hair."

Gary looked down at the table. He was embarrassed.

"I didn't listen to her too good. I was hungry."

Peter calmed himself with a deep breath. He did not want to get upset. He did not want to yell at Gary.

"That's okay. I was hungry too. Do you remember Mrs. Polk from the wedding?"

Gary's brow furrowed as he tried to remember Mrs. Polk. Finally, he shook his head.

"I don't remember that lady."

"Do you remember telling anyone that the girl was at the Stallion?"

"No."

"Well, you did. That's what Mrs. Polk said. So, how could you do that? If no one else knew who was killed at one-thirty, how did you know the girl had been at the Stallion?"

"I don't know."

"Well, think."

Gary started to look worried. He shifted in his seat.

"Maybe it was my powers. Maybe I seen it with my mind," Gary said, anxious to please Peter.

"We've been over this already, Gary. You do not have powers. No one has those powers. Sergeant Downes fooled you."

Gary thought hard for a moment. Then he looked confused. Finally he turned to Peter and asked, "If I don't have those powers, how did I do it, Pete? How did I know who that girl was?"

4

"Shit! Shit! Shit!" Peter screamed as soon as he was safely locked in his car with the music cranked up. The session with Gary had driven him insane. Tomorrow, he would have to give his closing argument. What was he going to say? How was he going to explain all of the facts that Gary knew about this case that only the murderer could possibly know?

Peter wanted to believe that Gary was innocent, but he was starting to wonder. Gary was capable of physical violence. He had attacked Karen Nix. Elmore Brock had testified that Gary was intelligent enough to plan the murder of Sandra Whiley. Gary seemed so gentle, so childlike, but he had been drinking on the night of the murder.

How could Gary fool him for this long if he was guilty? Brock said Gary could lie and stick to a lie. Mentally handicapped individuals could persevere at a task. If Gary was frightened of exposure could he maintain a lie for this long? What if he did not need to lie? That was the most frightening possibility. What if Gary murdered Sandra Whiley and did not even know it? What if the combination of alcohol and fear had erased the horrible deed from Gary's memory?

The Harmons lived in a white, two-story colonial farmhouse. There was a large front lawn bounded by a white board fence. Donna came onto the front porch as soon as she heard Peter's car chewing up the gravel on the circular driveway. She was dying to tell him all of the things she had done on her first day as his investigator. Her smile disappeared as soon as she saw Peter's face.

"What's wrong?"

"That's what I have to talk to you about."

Donna ushered Peter into the large front room. Jesse and Alice were at a church function, so they were alone. As soon as they were seated, Peter related the testimony that established that Gary knew the victim had been at the Stallion before anyone else knew her identity. Donna looked more and more troubled as Peter spoke.

"Where was Gary before he went to the Stallion Friday night?"

"With us. Mom cooked a meal for Steve and the family. Steve had to leave early to work on his cases so he could go on our honeymoon. He gave Gary a lift into town."

"Did Steve tell you where he dropped off Gary?"

"I think it was at home. Gary must have walked to the Stallion on his own. It's not that far from his house."

"Gary says he went to Steve's house from the bar. When he didn't find him home, he walked to the Ponderosa. Gary ate there, but he also did some more drinking. The bartender at the Ponderosa says he was pretty tipsy when he left around 2 A.M. Gary doesn't remember going to bed, but he does remember getting up early and doing his wash. When did you see him next?"

"When he and Steve arrived at the church. Steve picked up Gary and drove him over. I asked him to do it in case Gary was having any trouble with his tuxedo."

"Was Gary home when Steve arrived?"

"Steve said he was."

Peter thought for a minute. Then, he asked, "Did Gary say anything to you at the church or the reception that relates to the murder?"

"Gary did say there were police cars at the park. You pass it on the way to the church. I remember that he was excited. But I had the impression that he just saw them as they drove by."

"You know Gary better than anyone. Could he have killed that girl?"

"I'll never believe Gary could be so cruel."

Peter shook his head. He looked exhausted and thoroughly dejected.

"I'm afraid that he's going to be convicted. He knew Whiley was at the Stallion before anyone else knew who she was. He told Booth about the necklace. He knew the killer used a hatchet and where it was hidden. How can you explain all that?"

"I can't," Donna answered softly. "I just know Gary."

"I don't think he killed Whiley, either, but I don't think I can save him, Donna. I . . . I probably shouldn't have taken the case in the first place. Maybe with another lawyer . . ."

Donna put a hand on Peter's shoulder. "You're doing a great job. You can't blame yourself because the state's witnesses are saying things that hurt Gary."

Peter felt awful. Donna had so much faith in him, but she wasn't a lawyer who would know how poor a job he was really doing. He could no longer hide the truth from himself.

"I can blame myself. I had no business taking on this case. Amos Geary was right. He said I would screw it up and I have. I'm no criminal lawyer. I'm no lawyer at all."

"That's not true. You've worked harder than anyone. You've done a wonderful job."

Donna was so trusting. Peter felt sick.

"There's something I have to tell you. It's about why I came to Whitaker. I . . . I didn't choose to leave Hale, Greaves. I was fired. I was helping out in a big personal injury case my father was trying. Right before we went to court, he had a heart attack. Dad told me to ask for a mistrial, but I wanted to show him and everyone at the firm that I was a great trial attorney, so I lied to the judge and said that Dad wanted me to finish the trial.

"The case was so easy that a first-year law student

could have won it. It took a real genius to screw it up, but I did and . . . and this poor woman . . ." Peter shook his head. "You should have seen her, Donna. She had nothing. She was dirt poor with five kids to raise by herself and then she became this cripple. Then, the worst thing happened. She got me for her attorney and I destroyed any hope she and her kids had in one afternoon. And now I'm doing the same thing to Gary."

"You're being too hard on yourself."

Peter looked directly at Donna.

"When I took your brother's case, I didn't even think about him. All I was thinking about was how famous I'd be if I won. I didn't care enough about him to think of what might happen if I screwed up his case the way I did Mrs. Elliot's."

"You care for him now, though, don't you?" Donna asked quietly.

"I do. I admire Gary. He's a much better person than I am. I don't think he would ever intentionally hurt anyone. He thinks about the feelings of other people. When he has to do a job, he tries to do his very best. He's not like me at all and I wish I could be a little more like him."

Donna reached up and touched Peter's cheek.

"I don't know what kind of person you were in Portland. I just know you now. I can see how much you care for Gary." Donna paused and looked down. "I know what you did for me."

Peter wanted to take Donna in his arms, but he couldn't take advantage of her when she was so vulnerable. Donna must have realized how close they were to doing something they would regret, because she pulled her hand back. For a moment, they sat on the couch in an awkward silence, then, Donna said, "I . . . I paced off those distances for you this afternoon."

"Great," Peter answered in a shaky voice, relieved that the danger was over. "What did you find out?"

"I started at the Stallion and walked to Gary's house. It's a little over three quarters of a mile and it took me about twelve minutes. Then, I went back to the bar and continued to the park entrance. It's one-quarter mile from the Stallion to the entrance, so it took me sixteen minutes to walk from the house to the park."

"That means Gary got home at about eleven-twelve if he left the Stallion at eleven and walked straight home."

"If he was walking my speed," Donna corrected. "He could have run or walked faster."

"Okay, but he's still got to take some time trying to find a weapon."

Peter worked the numbers in his head.

"Damn. It could still work out. If he leaves his house around eleven-twelve, follows Whiley and gets to the park around eleven thirty-six . . . If Howell and his girl-friend left the park around eleven thirty-five and Whiley passed by a little after . . ."

"I've been thinking about that, Peter. If it's only a quarter mile from the Stallion to the main park entrance, and it takes about fifteen minutes for the average person to walk one mile, it would only take about three minutes to walk a quarter of a mile. If Whiley left the bar around eleven-twenty, she should have reached the entrance to the park before those kids."

"You're right! That would put her there around eleven twenty-five. But Howell said that Jessie made a wish at the well around eleven-thirty and the body wasn't there. Where was Whiley between eleven-twenty, when she left the Stallion, and eleven thirty-five, when Howell and Freeman left the park?"

"Did you ask Howell and his girlfriend if they saw anyone when they were in the park?"

"Yeah. They don't remember spotting anyone, but they were probably too wrapped up in each other to notice anything. Tell me about the rest of your results."

"Gary could have made it to the Ponderosa from the park in fifteen to twenty minutes, so he could have killed Whiley around eleven thirty-seven and made it to the bar by eleven fifty-five."

"Did you go from the park to the storm drain where the hatchet was found and back to the Ponderosa?"

"Yes. The storm drain is near the campus. We're talking a little under two miles. Even if Gary ran it in a seven-minute mile, there's no way he could kill Whiley after eleven thirty-five, ditch the hatchet and make it to the Ponderosa by midnight."

"So he'd have to hide the hatchet somewhere before going to the Ponderosa, then pick it up later. That sounds a little complicated for someone of Gary's intelligence, but I'll have to ask Elmore Brock about that."

Peter stood up. He looked depressed.

"I've got to go back to the office to work on my closing argument. You keep working on character witnesses for the penalty phase. I hope we don't need them, but I'm afraid we will."

CHAPTER TWENTY-SIX

1

They came for Gary just as the sun was setting. His heart fluttered like the wings of a trapped bird. In the back of the police car, the city fading in the gathering darkness, Gary prayed, "Please, God, please, God," over and over. He promised God he would be good. He promised he would never make Mom and Dad ashamed or mad again. Please, God.

The reporters were waiting on the courthouse steps, cigarettes dangling, cameras resting on the concrete slabs, engaged in loose conversation or lost to the stillness of sundown, until someone spotted the police car. All at once, they were up, jerked into action like marionettes. When the car doors opened, the mob pressed in, jabbing at him with microphones and screaming questions at him. Gary cringed in a corner of the backseat. The sheriff's deputies cleared a path as Gary struggled out of the car, the task more difficult because he was handcuffed. He looked for a friendly face and saw Peter pushing through the crowd.

"What did they say?" Gary asked, as Peter helped him up the steps.

"I don't know. They have to read the verdict in court. The jurors are waiting in the jury room."

"Are Mom and Dad here?" Gary asked as they took the elevator up to the courtroom, surrounded by sheriff's deputies.

"Yes. I called them, first thing. Donna is with them."

The guards escorted Peter and Gary to the defense table. As they took off Gary's handcuffs, a stir in the back of the courtroom signaled Becky O'Shay's entrance. She looked grim and intentionally avoided eye contact with Peter and his client. The bailiff scurried into the judge's chamber to tell him that all of the parties were in the courtroom. Moments later, the bailiff emerged from chambers and entered the jury room. When the door to the jury room opened, the undercurrent of noise in the courtroom stopped. There was a rustle of clothing and a tap of heels as the jurors worked their way to their seats in the jury box. Peter searched their faces for a clue to the verdict, but the jurors would not look at him or O'Shay. Beside Peter, Gary twisted anxiously in his seat.

As soon as the jurors were settled, the bailiff pressed a button at the side of his desk to signal the judge. Everyone stood when Judge Kuffel entered the courtroom. When he was seated, the judge turned toward the jury box.

"Ladies and gentlemen, have you reached a verdict?"

Ernest Clayfield, a farmer, stood slowly. He held a folded sheet of paper in his hand.

"We have," Clayfield answered grimly.

"Please hand your verdict to the bailiff," the judge commanded.

Clayfield held out his hand and the bailiff took the verdict form from him and gave it to the judge. Kuffel unfolded it and read it once. Then he looked at Gary.

"Will the defendant please stand," he said in a subdued voice. Gary jumped up, but Peter felt dizzy from tension and his legs were weak. It took an effort to get to his feet.

"Omitting the caption," Judge Kuffel said, "the verdict reads as follows: 'We the jury, being duly impaneled and sworn, find the defendant GUILTY as charged.' "

There was complete silence for a moment, then Peter heard Alice Harmon moan as Donna softly cried out, "No." He was looking down at the courtroom floor and did not see the wide smile of satisfaction on Becky O'Shay's face. A babble of voices filled the air.

Judge Kuffel gaveled for silence, then asked, "Do you want the jury polled, Mr. Hale?"

"Yes," Peter managed. He touched Gary's shoulder and slumped down in his seat as the judge asked each juror if he or she agreed with the verdict.

"What happened?" Gary asked.

"They found you guilty, Gary," Peter said. "They think you killed that girl."

Gary looked stunned. He rose slowly to his feet and stared at the judge. The guards started forward.

"I didn't do it," Gary said. The judge stopped polling the jury and said, "Please sit down, Mr. Harmon."

"I didn't hurt that girl," Gary cried out, his voice breaking.

"Mr. Harmon," the judge repeated as the guards drew closer.

"I'm a good boy," Gary wailed. "I want to go home."

Peter stood and placed a hand on Gary's shoulder. Behind him he could hear Donna's sobs.

"I wanna go home. I want my momma. I don't like that jail. I wanna go home."

Peter wrapped his arms around Gary and held him. Gary's body shook as he took gigantic breaths and wailed like a confused and frightened child.

Gary had been transferred to the security block in the Whitaker jail as soon as the guilty verdict was received. It consisted of a row of fifteen narrow cells. Each cell was wide enough for a bunk and a bunk's width of floor space. At the back of the cell was a toilet. Outside the row of cells was an area where the inmates could take their only exercise by walking back and forth along the bars. A color television was affixed to the bars high up, in the middle. The guards controlled the programs and the viewing hours. Gary hated his narrow cell. It was like a coffin.

Entry to the security block was made through a sally port. Gary heard the grating sound of the sally port door sliding open and strained through the bars of his cell to see the visitor. When Peter was safely inside the sally port, the outer door slid shut and the guard opened the inner door electronically. The other inmates were locked down while Peter visited. They stared as he walked by. Life on the block was so dull that any change in routine was as great a diversion as a Broadway show.

Gary's cell door was operated from the same master control that opened the sally port gates. When Peter was in front of the cell, the guard opened it and Peter stepped inside. He had planned on a cheery greeting but Gary looked so sad that all he could manage was "Hi, Gary" in a voice so subdued that he wasn't certain he had even said the words aloud.

"Can I go home, Peter?"

Peter ignored the question.

"Sit down, Gary. There are some things we have to discuss."

Gary sat on the bunk and Peter joined him. There was no other place to sit in the cell, except the toilet, which had no lid.

"You're going to have to stay in this cell for a while."

"Why? Why can't I go back to my other cell? That cell was bigger."

"That cell was for when you weren't convicted. Now you are. The penalty phase of your trial will start next week and the sheriff is afraid you might try to escape, so he wants you here."

"I won't try to escape, Pete. I promise. Tell the sheriff I won't try to escape."

"I did tell him, but he has rules he has to follow if a person is convicted. You know about rules, right, Gary? If there are rules, you have to follow them."

Gary looked glum. "I guess if it's the rule, he has to follow that rule."

"Right. Now I have something serious we have to talk about, so listen hard."

"Okay, I'm listening."

"Do you know what happens during the penalty phase of your trial?"

"No, Pete. What happens?"

"You . . . you've, uh, been convicted of aggravated murder. That's the most serious crime in Oregon. The jury is going to listen to the D.A. and your lawyer and decide which of three punishments to give you. Two of the punishments are life sentences. One life sentence lets you have a possible parole after thirty years. One life sentence doesn't have parole. That means you can't get out ever."

"I don't like that. I want to get out."

Peter started to explain to Gary that he could not get out of prison, but he stopped himself. It was all so futile.

"There's another punishment, Gary. You could receive a death sentence. The jury could say that you should be execu . . . killed. Do you understand?"

"I don't want that one," Gary said. He sounded scared.

"And I don't want you to get that punishment either," Peter said, his words catching in his throat. "That's why we're having this talk.

"Now pay close attention, Gary. It's very important

305

that you have a really good lawyer in the penalty phase and I don't think I should be your lawyer."

Gary looked surprised, then even more frightened.

"Don't you want to be my lawyer? You're a good lawyer."

"I'm not so sure about that, Gary. I haven't done very well with this case so far. I . . . I've never tried a penalty phase. If I told the judge that I'm not good enough to represent you, he'd get you a good lawyer."

"No, no," Gary said in a panic, "you're my lawyer."

"Yes, Gary, but I think you'd do better with another lawyer."

"Oh no. You're the best lawyer," Gary said with conviction. "And you're my friend. My best friend. You'll save me. I know you won't let them give me those bad punishments."

"Jesus, Gary . . ." Peter started, but he did not have the heart to go on. "Think about it, will you. Really think about it. Because, I don't know . . . Just think about it."

PART
SIX

———

THE
FLATLANDS

———

CHAPTER TWENTY-SEVEN

1

Judge Kuffel set the start of the penalty phase for a week from Monday, which gave Peter very little time to recover from the trial. On Sunday, Peter woke up a little after nine from a restless sleep haunted by unsettling dreams. He did not want to spend the day in his depressing rental house and he did not have the energy for a run, so, after a shower and breakfast, he went to the office.

Peter had no plan to save Gary. He spent the first half hour aimlessly stacking everything in his case files on his desk. He had been through the police reports, the autopsy report and witness statements several times. The only new things were Donna's neatly typed investigative reports. Peter picked them up and went through them without enthusiasm. He found nothing of interest until he read Donna's summary of her interview with Marjorie Dooling. Something she'd written triggered a memory and Peter shuffled through the police reports until he found David Thorne's statement.

As Peter entered the Stallion, a man in a Pittsburgh Steeler uniform spun away from two Oakland Raider defenders and gained five yards before being brought down by another Raider. Several patrons groaned and several more cheered. The bartender turned away from the television when the Steelers called a time-out.

"Dave Thorne?"

"That's me," the bartender answered with a smile.

"I'm Peter Hale, Gary Harmon's lawyer."

The smile disappeared. "Tough loss, man." Thorne shook his head. "I have a hard time believing Gary could do something like that."

"I don't think he did. That's why I'm here. I wanted to ask you about something you told the police. It was in the statement you gave to Dennis Downes."

"I remember that."

"I was interested in what you had to say about Sandra Whiley. She was sitting at the end of the bar farthest from the door, right?"

"Yeah, near my station."

"So you saw her for a while?"

"I wasn't paying that much attention. I was pretty busy."

"Right, but in the report you said that there was a time when she seemed nervous or frightened."

"I did?"

Peter gave him a copy of his statement and Thorne read it carefully. He stopped at a section of the report that Peter had highlighted in Magic Marker. Thorne read it twice, then nodded vigorously.

"I remember now. What do you want to know?"

"You said that she was watching two men who were walking toward the back door and she seemed frightened. Tell me about that."

"It was after I called Steve Mancini. When I turned around, Whiley looked shocked or scared. I thought she was staring at two guys on the level above the dance floor, up there."

Peter looked where Thorne was pointing.

"Did you get a good look at the men?" Peter asked.

"No. It was dark and I only glanced at them. Things were pretty frantic up front."

"Can you describe them at all?"

Thorne thought for a second. Then he brightened.

"One guy made no impression, but the other guy was huge. I remember thinking he looked like a pro wrestler."

Marjorie Dooling had appeared briefly as a witness in the state's case-in-chief. Peter asked her no questions, but he remembered what she looked like. It only took him a few minutes to locate her in the Whitaker State College library, where her landlady said she was studying. Dooling was hunched over a history text at a large table next to a row of book-filled stacks. The seat across from her was empty and Peter took it.

"Miss Dooling, my name is Peter Hale." He handed her a business card. "I represent Gary Harmon. You testified at the trial." Dooling's features clouded. "You were kind enough to talk to my investigator the other day, and there was one small item in her report that I wanted to clear up."

"All right," Dooling sighed. "One question. But that's all. I have a test tomorrow."

Peter showed Dooling the section of Donna's report where she had mentioned the man who came to the house to pick up Sandy.

"You said you thought Sandy was frightened of him."

"She was real nervous all day. When he honked the horn for her, she seemed scared to me."

"Can you remember anything more about the man who picked her up? His hair color, his size?"

Dooling started to shake her head. Then, she stopped as something occurred to her.

"I only saw him from the second-floor window and he was in his car. But there was something. When Sandy came out of the door, his arm was resting on the car window. I only saw it for a second, because he brought it inside as soon as he saw her."

"What about the arm?"

"He was wearing a short-sleeve tee shirt and I could see part of his biceps and his forearm. They were really big, like a weight lifter's, and they were covered by tattoos."

"Can you describe the tattoos?"

Dooling closed her eyes. When they opened, she said, "I'm not certain. Like I said, I was looking from a second-floor window and I only saw his arm for a moment, but I think I saw snakes and a panther."

Peter drove back to his office in a fog. Sandra Whiley knew, and was afraid of, Christopher Mammon. Was Mammon monitoring Gary's trial to make certain that he was not implicated by any of the evidence? Mammon had the opportunity to commit the crime. He left the Stallion around the time that Whiley left the bar. If Peter could show that a monster like Mammon had a reason to harm Whiley, Gary Harmon would cease to be the only viable suspect in her murder.

As Peter parked in front of Mancini's building, he remembered Amos Geary telling him to read Mammon's file before the preliminary hearing, but Peter had only given the documents in the file a cursory glance. Now he wished he had been more thorough. There might have been something in the file that would help Gary. Asking Geary to see the file would be useless. He doubted Geary would even talk to him. Besides, the file was confidential and Peter no longer worked for Geary. However, Steve Mancini represented Kevin Booth in the case involving the Whitaker State bust. He would also have the police reports.

All of the closed files in the office were in a large room behind the secretarial station. Peter turned on the lights. Mancini's files were arranged alphabetically, so Peter found Booth's file quickly. It was not that thick, since the case had not gotten past the preliminary hearing. There was a table with a reading lamp at the front of the file room. Peter sat down and opened the file. He took out the envelope holding the police reports and piled them on the table. He read through the reports slowly, but discovered nothing helpful until he found two reports halfway down that looked strange. They were different in form from the other reports and seemed neater. It did not take Peter long to figure out why the reports looked different. They had not been written by the Whitaker police or the campus police. They were reports written by agents of the DEA, the federal Drug Enforcement Administration.

The first report detailed the activities of an unnamed, confidential, reliable informant, or CRI, who had been busted with cocaine and had agreed to work off the case by setting up Kevin Booth. The report was a chronological history of the contacts between Booth and the CRI in Whitaker. The CRI was to purchase increasingly larger amounts of cocaine from Booth until Booth was unable to supply the CRI's demand and had to agree to put the CRI in touch with someone who could.

The second report detailed the arrest of Kevin Booth and Christopher Mammon on the Whitaker campus, but it contained information about the arrest that was new to Peter. The CRI was supposed to be bringing thirty thousand dollars to Booth for two kilos of cocaine. After the sale went through, the CRI was going to up the ante to a point that would force Booth to use his contacts to supply a very large amount of cocaine. It was hoped that this deal would be handled directly by Booth's supplier. From the report, it appeared that the arrest by campus security had been totally unexpected and neither the DEA nor the Whitaker police wanted the arrest to occur.

Peter was certain he had never seen either of the DEA reports in Geary's file. Why would Mancini have them, but not Geary? Peter reread the reports. A thought occurred to him and he felt himself grow cold. What if Sandra Whiley was not simply an innocent bystander who was murdered by mistake? What if she was working off an arrest for cocaine and had betrayed Christopher Mammon to the DEA? That would give Mammon a huge motive for murder.

Peter put the envelope with the police reports back in the file. He was about to close it when he spotted a telephone message slip that Mancini had clipped into the folder on the left side. The slip was dated the day before the preliminary hearing. The letters ASAP underlined in red and written in capital letters caught Peter's eye.

Peter read the message carefully. It was from Becky O'Shay. She wanted Steve to call as soon as he came in—ASAP—so they could discuss a deal in the Booth case. Peter wondered what the deal had been. Maybe that's what Steve and Becky had been discussing when he saw them in the hall outside the courtroom before the prelim. But the deal had obviously fallen through because Booth had not pled guilty.

Peter replaced the file and was about to leave the file room when another thought struck him. Becky O'Shay must have given Steve Mancini the DEA reports. That meant she knew about the existence of the CRI. Did she also know the identity of the CRI? If Whiley was the CRI and Becky knew it, but kept it a secret, Peter could use that fact as a basis for a motion for a new trial. But before he confronted O'Shay or filed a motion, he had to find out if Sandra Whiley was the CRI and Peter thought he knew how he could do that.

2

"I don't know, Peter. I could get in a lot of trouble," Rhonda Kates said.

"I know that. I wouldn't ask if I wasn't desperate."

"Why don't you just tell the district attorney that you

314

need to talk to Booth. Don't they have to let you talk to witnesses?"

"They do. But the D.A. would insist on coming along or she'd convince Booth to refuse to see me."

"I thought that was illegal."

"The reason I have to sneak into Booth's room is because I think the D.A. has already done something illegal. Becky will do anything to win.

"Look, all you've got to do is get the guard away from Booth's door. I only have one question to ask him. I'll be in and out."

"This is a lot to ask."

"Rhonda, Donna's brother may be innocent. If Kevin Booth says what I think he will, I may be able to set Gary's verdict aside and give the police the real killer. If I don't get in to see Booth, Gary will most probably be on death row by the end of next week."

Kevin Booth had been moved to a room at the Whitaker hospital two days before. A guard sat in front of his door at all times. Peter waited in an alcove a short distance from Booth's room and used his cellular phone to call the hospital. He asked for the extension at the nurses' station farthest from Booth's room. Rhonda picked up on the first ring and pretended to carry on a conversation. Then, she placed the receiver down and told the other nurse to make sure the phone was not hung up.

Peter watched as Rhonda told the guard that there was a call for him. He seemed nervous about leaving his station, but Rhonda said the call was from the station house and the caller had said it was urgent. As soon as the policeman got up, Peter slipped into Booth's room.

Booth's hospital gown covered most of his burns, but here and there Peter saw patches of shiny, bright red and purple skin surrounded by bunches of scars. Booth's face was still covered with cream.

"Hi, Mr. Booth. I'm Peter Hale, Gary Harmon's law-

315

yer," Peter said with what he hoped was a winning smile. "We met in Portland."

"What are you doing here?" Booth asked. His speech was normal now. "I thought the case was over."

"It is. Actually, I had a question about the Whitaker State bust. The one you beat."

"Why do you want to know about that case?"

"Chris Mammon still has to go to trial on it."

"Well, fuck him. I don't give a rat's ass about Mammon."

Peter thought fast.

"This may not help Mr. Mammon. Actually, your answer could really hurt his case. But I've got to know if he's telling us the truth. If he's not, he could end up serving a long prison term."

"What did you want to know?" Booth asked, interested in anything that would keep Christopher Mammon off his back.

"You know when you were busted at Whitaker State. Was Sandra Whiley bringing you thirty thousand dollars or three thousand? It will make a big difference at sentencing. Mammon claims that Whiley was only going to bring three thousand and that he didn't know how much cocaine was in the Ziploc bags."

Booth snorted. "Mammon's lying. He knew exactly how much dope was in the bags. He weighed them himself. And he knew how much dough Whiley was bringing because he told her to bring the thirty grand."

"Sorry to hear that. Say, was Mammon aware that Whiley was working for the feds?"

"Not before we got busted. But after, I said the bitch must have turned us in. Chris was furious. He said he was gonna check it out."

"That's what we heard," Peter said solemnly. "Where'd you meet Whiley?"

Booth tilted his head to the side and looked at Peter suspiciously. "I thought you were interested in Mammon."

"I am. He says he didn't know Whiley well. I thought, if you knew her, you could set the record straight."

"He's lyin' to you. Personally, I think he was screwing her."

"You do?"

"The bitch would do anything for cocaine."

Suddenly Booth laughed.

"What's so funny?"

"If Whiley was working for the feds there's gonna be a lot of nervous people in this burg."

"Why's that?"

"She never had much money, so she had to earn her snow. One way she did that was by making deliveries. She could name a lot of names."

"Like who?"

"'Mr. Football' for one. It would serve the cock-sucker right, the way he left me hanging as soon as I said I didn't have any money."

"Who are you talking about?"

Before Booth could answer, the door opened and the guard walked in. When he saw Peter, he put his hand on his gun.

"Who are you and what are you doing in here?"

"I'm an attorney," Peter said with righteous indignation. "This man is a witness in the Harmon case. I have a constitutional right to talk to him."

"Let's see some identification," the guard said, taking the gun out and pointing it at Peter.

"No problem. I'm just going to get my wallet, see."

Peter pulled the wallet out slowly and handed a business card to the officer. The policeman studied Peter for a minute.

"Yeah, you're Harmon's lawyer. I recognize you now. I don't know what you think you're doing, but sneaking in here on my watch is going to get your ass hauled down to the station."

"You better check before you try that," Peter said with more bravado than he felt. "Whitaker doesn't have enough money to cover the damages I'll win if you arrest me for talking to a witness in a death penalty case."

The guard looked a little uncertain, but he stood his ground. Several people had clustered in the doorway to see what was going on. The officer turned to one of them.

"Nurse, call the station house and ask for one of the sergeants. Tell them we have a situation here."

3

Dennis Downes had no idea whether Peter's shenanigans were legal or illegal. Peter was an attorney and Booth was a key witness. As soon as he learned what Peter had done, he called Becky O'Shay. O'Shay had sworn long and loudly, then told Downes she would be at the station in a few minutes.

"Just what do you think you're doing, Hale?" O'Shay demanded the minute the door to the interrogation room closed behind her.

"My duty under the Constitution of the United States."

"Your duty, my ass. That man is my witness and he's in protective custody. You are in big trouble. The worst you're looking at is a bar complaint and I've got someone checking to see if you've broken any laws."

Peter was furious with O'Shay, but he did not let it show. Instead, he asked in a casual tone, "Do you think what I did was as bad as hiding the fact that your victim, Miss Whiley, was the woman who was bringing the thirty thousand dollars to Christopher Mammon and Kevin Booth on the evening of their arrest?"

Peter noticed, with satisfaction, that O'Shay's normally pale complexion was now thoroughly bleached of color.

"Do you think it's as bad as concealing from me the fact that Miss Whiley was working with the cops, a fact that Mammon suspected and that drove him into a murderous rage, thus making him a very viable suspect in Miss Whiley's murder?"

"What . . . what are you talking about?" O'Shay stuttered.

"I'm talking about a serious violation of your duty as a prosecutor to turn over to the defense *all* exculpatory evidence in your possession. I think the fact that you knew a homicidal maniac like Christopher Mammon had it in for the deceased and failed to mention that little tidbit to me constitutes a gross violation of your duties as a prosecutor, an officer of the court and a human being."

"Mammon didn't kill Whiley, your client did," O'Shay said.

"That's for a jury to decide, not you."

"In case you've forgotten, hotshot, a jury did decide."

"They didn't have all the facts."

"This bullshit about Mammon is just that, bullshit," O'Shay shot back, seemingly over her initial shock. "I gave you all the information you were entitled to."

"We'll see about that. I think it's time to go to Judge Kuffel."

For a brief second, O'Shay looked panicky. Then, she sat down across from Peter and, in a reasonable tone, said, "Listen, Peter, I shouldn't have gotten so angry. I know the pressure you've been under. And there's Harmon's family. This has been tough on everyone. But I can tell you that you're barking up the wrong tree."

"I've seen the DEA reports you sent to Steve Mancini."

"What are you talking about?"

"The reports that mention the CRI who was involved with the drug deal at Whitaker State where Mammon and Booth were arrested."

"I didn't send any DEA reports to Steve Mancini."

"Someone did. They were in with your discovery material."

"Let me see them."

"I don't have them. They're in Steve's file."

"I think you're confused, Peter. If Whiley was working with the government, I would have been told."

O'Shay stood up and headed for the door.

"Where are you going?"

"Home. It's Sunday."

"Are you going to tell Downes to let me go?"

"As soon as I'm certain that you haven't broken any laws."

"And when will that be?"

"When the deputy I've got working on the project lets me know."

"That's fine by me, Becky. You're just increasing the damages I'm going to receive when I sue the Whitaker police, the Whitaker District Attorney's Office and you, personally."

The door to the interrogation room slammed shut and Peter swore.

4

The police held Peter for two more hours, then they let him go. While he was in custody, it occurred to Peter that he should make a copy of the DEA reports to show to the judge when he filed his motion for a new trial. Peter's car was still at the hospital, so he hiked there and picked it up. He arrived at the office a little after eight. All the lights were out. Peter went directly to the file room and took out the envelope with the police reports. He shuffled through them twice before realizing that someone had removed the DEA reports from the file.

Peter's first reaction was anger at Becky O'Shay. She

had to be behind the theft. She was the only person to whom he had mentioned the reports. He felt so stupid for doing that, but he never would have believed she would go this far to hold on to her victory. She must have kept him in custody long enough to send someone to the office to retrieve the reports from the file.

Unfortunately for O'Shay, there was someone else who knew about the reports. Peter walked to his office and dialed Steve Mancini. It was going to look very bad for O'Shay when Steve confirmed the existence of the two documents in front of Judge Kuffel. There would definitely be enough circumstantial evidence to support an inquiry by the Oregon State Bar into O'Shay's behavior.

"Steve, this is Peter," he said as soon as Mancini picked up.

"How are you doing?" Mancini asked. "You didn't look so good after the verdict."

"I didn't feel so good, either, but something has happened that's gotten me excited. I found out that Sandra Whiley was involved with the drug deal that went sour at Whitaker State. The one where Chris Mammon and Kevin Booth were arrested."

"What!"

"Yeah. I think Whiley was working with the police and Mammon found out. It gives him a terrific motive to kill her."

"That's incredible. How did you work that out?"

"I hope you're not mad, but after I learned about the relationship between Mammon and Whiley I looked in your file on Kevin Booth. I couldn't ask Amos Geary to let me see Mammon's file and I remembered that you'd have the same discovery. I should have called you first, but I was so excited I just did it."

"That's okay. You shouldn't have looked at the file. It's confidential. But Gary's life is at stake."

"Thanks, Steve. Anyway, I found two reports in your file from the DEA," Peter went on. Then, he told Steve about his interview with Booth at the hospital, his detention by the police and his discovery that the reports had been removed from the file.

"Becky must have had someone break in here and remove them while I was at the police station," Peter concluded, "but she made one mistake. She forgot that you've seen the reports. You can confirm their existence. Once the judge realizes that I saw the reports around noon, I told her about them around four and they were gone by eight, he's going to reach the same conclusion I have and O'Shay's ass will be grass. Kuffel is going to have to give Gary a new trial, once he determines that Becky failed to turn over key evidence that points to another suspect."

"These reports," Mancini asked hesitantly, "what did they look like?"

"They were typed up. Each one was a couple of pages long. They were written by DEA agents."

"Pete, I honestly don't remember seeing any reports from the DEA in the discovery I received from Becky."

"Well, they were in there."

"I'm sure they were. I mean, you just read the reports a few hours ago. All I'm saying is that I haven't looked at that file in a while and I just don't recall those reports."

"How can that be?"

"Booth's case wasn't that big a deal. I think I read through the reports once, real fast. He told me his version. All the stuff I needed to win at the prelim was in the report that the campus security guy filed. I'm sorry. I'll spend some serious time thinking about it, but right now I don't remember any DEA reports."

Peter hung up in a daze. He had been counting on Steve to support him. If Mancini could not remember the reports, he had nothing. Then, Peter recalled the last thing Kevin Booth said before the guard burst into Booth's hospital room. Something about Whiley making cocaine deliveries to pay for her drugs. Booth had said that several people in Whitaker would have to worry if Whiley was working for the police and she named names. The only person he'd had time to mention before the guard came in was "Mr. Football," who had dropped Booth when he found out Booth did not have any money.

Peter walked to the front door of the law office and inspected it. He did the same with every other door that led into the building. None of them showed signs of forced entry. The person who took the DEA reports had a key to Steve Mancini's law office. Peter did not want to believe it. Could Steve have taken the reports? Peter raced back to the file room and opened the Booth file again. The phone message about the deal offer from O'Shay was also missing. Peter felt sick. Why was Mancini helping Becky O'Shay, and what were they covering up?

Suddenly, Peter recalled Steve's failure to tell him about his interview with Don Bosco. It was Steve who suggested that Peter convince Gary to plead guilty. Mancini had given him the names of three investigators, but the only one who was available was the incompetent Barney Pullen. Peter had assumed that Steve Mancini was his ally from the moment he'd become Gary Harmon's lawyer, but now it appeared that Mancini had a hidden agenda of his own and Peter suspected that it included saddling Gary with the lawyer least qualified to handle his case.

5

Peter parked his car at the edge of the dirt drive that led to the garage and surveyed Amos Geary's house. Like its owner, it was broken down and aging. Weeds had overgrown a front yard that had not seen a mower in recent times, the paint was peeling and faded. Only God knew the original color.

There was a light on behind a worn curtain in the front room. Peter hesitated before getting out of the car. He could drive away, but to what destination?

One of the steps leading to the porch was cracked and Peter stumbled over it. He caught himself by breaking his fall with his hands. This was not an auspicious sign. Peter thought about turning back, but the door opened. When Peter looked up, he found Amos Geary, dressed in a bathrobe and striped pajamas, looking down at him with contempt.

"Jesus, Hale, you are pathetic. Can't you even walk up a flight of stairs without making a mess of it?"

"Good evening, Mr. Geary," Peter stuttered as he stood up awkwardly. His hands stung where they had smacked into the wooden porch.

"What are you doing on my property?" Geary demanded.

"I'm in trouble."

"I'm not interested."

Geary turned to go inside.

"Wait!" Peter shouted. "It's not me. It's Gary. Gary Harmon is in trouble."

Geary paused. He turned back. There was a chill in the evening air. A gust of wind went right through Peter and he shuddered.

"What do you want from me?"

"You're the only person I can turn to."

"What happened to your good buddy Steve?"

"There's something going on and Steve may be part of it."

"Going on?"

"A, uh, cover-up."

Peter said the word hesitantly, knowing that it would make him appear paranoid.

"Something like the Kennedy assassination?" Geary asked with a snort. "Something involving the CIA, perhaps? Go home, Hale. You sound ridiculous."

"Please, Mr. Geary. I know I let you down . . ."

"You didn't let me down. I expected you to fuck up.

In fact, Peter, you've confirmed my faith in my ability to judge the merits of my fellow man."

Geary almost had the door shut. Peter was desperate.

"Goddamn it," he shouted, "this isn't about you or me. It's about Gary. That poor bastard is in jail for a murder he didn't commit."

Geary held on to the screen door and looked at Peter over his shoulder.

"Whose fault is that, Hale?"

"Mine! Are you happy? There, I said it. It's my fault. I'm everything you said I was. I'm a self-centered, shallow asshole and I'm asking for your help because I know I don't have what it takes to save Gary."

"My advice to you is to return the retainer you took under false pretenses to the Harmons, confess your misrepresentations and tell them to hire a real lawyer to represent their son."

"It's not that simple. Please, hear me out. There's more to this than the murder in the park. I think Steve Mancini and Becky O'Shay have been working together to cover up something. I don't know what it is, but it's tied into the arrest of Christopher Mammon and Kevin Booth at Whitaker State."

Peter thought that Geary's eyes suddenly looked clearer and that the old lawyer was standing a little taller. Geary pushed the screen door open.

"Come inside. It's too cold to talk on the porch."

"Thank you," Peter answered.

The inside of Geary's house was in as much disorder as the exterior. The living room couch Geary indicated was covered in a flower pattern that had nothing to do with anything else in the room. It was worn and the springs sagged when Peter sat on it.

"You want a drink?" Geary asked.

"Actually, yes."

Geary shuffled out of the room and returned with a fifth of Johnnie Walker and two moderately clean glasses. He poured a liberal amount of scotch in each glass and handed one of them to Peter.

"Talk," he said after taking a sip.

Peter started at the beginning. He told Geary how Steve Mancini had manipulated him into taking Gary's case and he explained his suspicions about the ways Mancini had sabotaged it. Finally, he told Geary about the day's incidents, ending with his discovery that the reports and the phone message slip were missing and his suspicion that they had been removed by Steve Mancini.

"That's quite a story," Geary said when Peter was finished. "Some people might think that you're inventing excuses to explain why you lost Gary Harmon's trial."

"I can see how someone might think that," Peter answered, his eyes locked on Geary's.

"The way I understand it, with the DEA reports missing and Mancini and O'Shay denying their existence, you have no evidence at all to support your highly unbelievable story of a government cover-up."

"That's true."

"Then why do you think I can help you?"

This was the hard part. Peter took a deep breath.

"When I learned the reports were missing and Steve was most probably the one who'd removed them, I decided that the only thing left was to go to the source. I called the DEA office in Portland. There was only one agent on duty because it's a weekend, but eventually I was put through to Guy Price, the agent in charge. I told him everything and I told him how important it was to get copies of the reports so I could go to Judge Kuffel and ask him to reopen the case. I was certain Price would help me. He isn't some ambitious, small-town D.A. like Becky. He's a federal agent."

Peter paused. He was exhausted and remembering one of the most depressing moments in his day didn't make him feel any better.

"He didn't help, did he?" Geary said.

Peter shook his head. "He told me that he couldn't confirm or deny any ongoing investigation."

"Is that all he said?"

"No," Peter answered with a tired smile. "He wished me good luck."

Geary laughed. "That sounds like your government in action, son. If nothing else, you're certainly learning a lot about the real world here in Whitaker."

"Yeah," Peter answered ruefully.

"You still haven't told me how you think I can help you."

"I almost gave up after my call to Price. Then I remembered that there was one person I knew who had enough clout to make someone like Price talk."

"I hope you don't mean me?" Geary asked incredulously.

"No, Mr. Geary. I . . . I came here tonight to ask you to please call my father and ask him to talk to me."

CHAPTER TWENTY-EIGHT

Peter had not slept well and the five-hour drive from Whitaker should have exhausted him, but he was floating by the time he saw the skyline of downtown Portland and the high green hills that formed its backdrop. He was home and he was welcome once again in his father's house.

The night before, Amos Geary had talked to Richard Hale on the phone in his den for almost half an hour while Peter waited nervously in the living room. When Geary finally told Peter that his father wanted to talk to him, he had hesitated. Now that his opportunity for reconciliation had arrived, he was afraid.

When Peter entered the den, the receiver lay on its side on the edge of an old, rolltop desk. Peter had reached toward it, then stopped just before his fingers touched the plastic. What was he going to say to Richard? He hadn't thought that far ahead. Should he tell his father that he loved him? Should he say how sorry he was for disappointing him so often? Should he ask forgiveness for falling so far below his father's expectations? In the end, all he managed was "Dad?" in a voice choked with emotions he was not yet able to express.

"Amos gave me an outline of your problem, but I'd

like you to tell me everything from the beginning," Richard had responded. It was as if there had never been an Elliot case or the intervening months of exile. One part of Peter was relieved that he was able to avoid the emotional exchange he assumed would precede their discussion of Gary's case, but there was another part of him that longed for a tearful reconciliation in which he confessed his sins and inadequacies and Richard forgave him. Thinking about it during the drive, Peter came to the conclusion that his father was not capable of crushing his son to him in a warm and forgiving hug. Peter knew he would never see tears trickling down his father's cheeks. Richard Hale was simply not the type of man who could express his emotions. This assistance in his hour of greatest need might be all his father was able to give.

The office of the United States Attorney for Oregon was in downtown Portland, a few blocks from the offices of Hale, Greaves. It was a little after five when Peter studied his reflection in the glass at the entrance to the office building. He had worn a charcoal gray pinstripe suit, a Hermès tie and his best silk shirt for the meeting. Sunlight rebounded from the shine on his black wing tips.

When Peter entered the lobby, Richard was standing off to one side. He had put on weight since the day he sent Peter into exile, but Richard was still thinner than Peter's mental image of his father.

"How was the drive?" Richard asked.

"Long and boring."

Richard smiled.

"Thanks for doing this for me," Peter said.

"You're my son," Richard answered simply. Then he turned toward the elevators.

"I don't know what to expect, Peter. There are no guarantees. Katherine probably knows nothing about what's going on in Whitaker. At best, one of the assistant U.S. attorneys is working with the DEA agent in charge of the case. Price might not even know that much about the operation or, if he does, his people may not be involved in this cover-up. That might be the work of the D.A. in Whitaker and your friend, Mancini."

"I know that. I just want to find out if Whiley was working for the DEA and whether O'Shay knew it. And I want copies of any reports that will prove O'Shay knew about the Mammon-Whiley connection."

The elevator doors opened into a reception area. Richard announced their presence to a receptionist who sat behind a window of bulletproof glass. Minutes later, a door opened and a tall, well-dressed woman with glasses and short black hair walked into the waiting area.

Katherine Hickox owed her appointment to the state circuit court bench to Richard Hale and others at Hale, Greaves, and it was to Richard Hale that she had turned when she decided to apply for the position of United States Attorney. Richard had quietly touted her to Oregon's United States senators and had made a phone call to a high-ranking official in the Justice Department with whom he had served on a committee of the American Bar Association. So, it was no surprise when Hickox agreed to meet with Peter's father at five-thirty and to make certain that Guy Price attended the meeting.

"Richard," she said, offering him her hand.

Richard took it, then motioned Peter forward.

"This is my son, Peter. He's just driven in from Whitaker."

"It's nice meeting you," Hickox said warmly. If she knew about Peter's disgrace she hid her feelings well. "Let's go back to my office. Guy is waiting for us there."

Hickox led them along a series of corridors to a corner office with a panoramic view of the city. When they entered, a short, muscular man in a brown sports coat stood up. After she made the introductions, Hickox sat down behind a large oak desk and Price sat beside it.

"Why don't you tell us why you needed to meet?" Hickox suggested.

"Mr. Price," Richard said, looking directly at the

DEA agent, "my son called you from Whitaker yesterday."

When Richard called Hickox to set up the meeting, he had not mentioned that his son would be accompanying him. Price suddenly made the connection. He did not looked pleased.

"For your benefit, Katherine, Peter has been trying a death penalty case in Whitaker. Last week, his client was convicted of murdering a woman named Sandra Whiley. Until yesterday, there did not appear to be anyone else in Whitaker with a motive to murder the young woman. Then, Peter discovered two DEA reports in the files of a Whitaker attorney named Steve Mancini. The reports, coupled with other information, led him to conclude that Whiley had been working as an informant for the DEA in a case in Whitaker involving a very dangerous and violent drug dealer named Christopher Mammon.

"These DEA reports were mixed in with police reports that had been given to Mancini in the drug case by the district attorney who is prosecuting the death penalty case. When Peter asked her about the reports, she denied knowing anything about them. Peter returned to his office to make copies of the reports and found them missing. He called Mr. Price for assistance and was told that it was against policy to confirm or deny the existence of an ongoing investigation. I'm here to ask Mr. Price to tell Peter if Sandra Whiley was working for the DEA in a case involving Christopher Mammon so that Peter can try to avert a miscarriage of justice."

Price looked uncomfortable. "I told your son that I can't discuss ongoing investigations, even to confirm or deny them. I'm afraid that's still my position. I wish you'd called me before having your son drive all the way here from Whitaker for nothing."

"I understand the official position of your office, Mr. Price. What you need to understand is the effect of following it," Richard told the agent coldly. "If Sandra Whiley was working for the DEA and the Whitaker dis-

331

trict attorney intentionally concealed this fact from Peter, she is guilty of a gross violation of the discovery rules. If she conspired to have the reports destroyed to prevent Peter from proving her misconduct, she may be guilty of a crime."

"Mr. Hale, I know you want to help your son, but I'm not going to discuss DEA business with either of you. If this D.A. is violating some law, your son should take it up with the judge who's trying the case."

Hale stared hard enough to make Price break eye contact. Then, in a level tone, he said, "Katherine will tell you that I am not without influence. If I find out that you're aware that Sandra Whiley was an informant for the DEA in the Whitaker case and you kept quiet about it, knowing it could cost a young man his life, I will personally make sure that you wish you were never born."

Price's eyes widened and he leaped to his feet.

"Guy!" Hickox said, holding out her hand in his direction. Price remained standing, but he restrained himself. The U.S. Attorney turned to Richard.

"I won't have you threatening Guy in my office, Richard."

"You're quite right," Richard said, in a tone that let Price know he still meant to keep his promise. "I apologize, Mr. Price. I'm sure you probably don't know what's going on in Whitaker and I'm equally certain that you'll do the right thing, if you discover that an obstruction of justice is occurring there."

Price glared at Richard, but held his tongue.

"Thank you for meeting with Peter and me, Katherine."

"Let me show you out," Hickox answered stiffly.

As soon as they were out of Price's hearing, Hickox said, "How dare you pull a stunt like that? I don't work for you and I won't let you involve me in one of your cases."

Peter's father stopped and looked directly at Katherine Hickox.

"You don't work for me, but you are the chief law enforcement officer for the United States Government in this district. I wanted you to know that something very dirty may be going on in your bailiwick. Something you don't want to be part of. Have a talk with Mr. Price after we're gone. Listen carefully to what he tells you. Price may be clean, but he can find out if someone else is dirty and he can make certain that Peter gets a copy of those reports. I've known you a long time, Katherine, and I know you'll do what is right."

When the elevator doors closed, leaving Peter and his father alone, Peter exhaled with relief.

"Jesus, Dad, are you sure you know what you're doing? Price is a really powerful person."

Richard turned to Peter with a wry smile.

"It's because Price is so powerful that I called him out. I'm sure no one has talked to him like that for some time. As soon as we left the room, I bet he started thinking about what type of person would have the balls to dress him down like I did. And Katherine is going to tell him as soon as he asks her, which should be right about now."

"You might have made him so angry, he won't help out of spite."

"I weighed that risk, but Price is a bureaucrat. He can't afford a scandal. If someone is fucking around with one of his investigations, he won't like it."

"I hope you're right."

"We'll know soon enough."

"Dad, thanks. You put yourself out for me and I really appreciate it."

"I haven't done a thing. You're the one who's going the extra mile for a client and I'm very proud of you."

Peter's chest swelled and he felt a lump in his throat. The elevator doors opened and Peter followed his father into the lobby.

"What are your plans?" Richard asked.

Peter looked at his watch. It was after six.

"It's too late to drive back to Whitaker. I guess I'll get a room at a hotel and head back in the morning."

"Nonsense. We'll have dinner and you'll stay with me. You can sleep in your old room."

"I'd like that," Peter said. He didn't know if his father realized it, but he had just given Peter the best present he had ever received.

CHAPTER TWENTY-NINE

Peter was exhausted but happy when he pulled into his driveway the next evening. He and his father had not talked about the future, but it was obvious that they had one together. Not right away. Peter still had a lot to prove to Richard, but the wall between them had come down.

As soon as he entered his house, Peter slapped together a quick dinner, showered and put on jeans and a sweatshirt. Then, he checked the TV listings for something completely mindless. Tomorrow morning, Peter planned to plunge back into the Harmon case with a vengeance. Tonight, he would relax and get a good night's sleep.

The phone rang during the sitcom he was watching. Peter turned down the sound. The voice on the other end of the phone was soft and indistinct, as if the speaker was trying to disguise it.

"Peter Hale?"

"Yes?"

"I'm only going to say this once, so pay close attention. If you want to find out the truth about Christopher Mammon and Sandra Whiley, take the highway east. Eight point three miles from the WELCOME TO WHITAKER sign, there's a dirt road on the right. Drive down the road until you come to a barn. I'll be waiting. If you're not here by ten-thirty, I'll be gone. And come alone or I won't show."

The flatlands was a desolate stretch of cracked brown earth that began a few miles east of the Whitaker city limits. No one lived in the flatlands. It was a place to drive through, not a place to visit in the dead of night. As soon as the glow of the city lights faded away, Peter felt he was riding through a sea of ink. There was no moon and no other source of illumination but his headlights and the stars, which hid behind a cover of thick clouds. The highway was one lane east and west. The only trace of color was the broken white line that divided it. To the left and right the only variety was provided by an occasional tumbleweed or a patch of sagebrush.

Peter set his odometer as soon as he passed the WELCOME TO WHITAKER sign. When it read eight point one, he slowed down and strained toward the side of the highway. The turnoff was more of a dirt track than a road and he almost missed it. The car started to buck as soon as it began traversing the narrow, rutted trail. Peter stared around nervously. His isolation was complete. There was not even the broken white line to break up the monotonously bleak and barren landscape that loomed up in his headlights, then disappeared as he passed by.

After a while, Peter's headlights settled on a shape in the distance. As he drew closer, he made out the burned and rotting timbers of an abandoned barn. Peter wondered why anyone would have dreamed that farming was possible in this desert, but the thought was fleeting and it was replaced by a feeling of dread when he realized that there were no other cars in sight.

Peter kept the lights on and the motor running. There was a flashlight in the glove compartment. He took it and stepped out of the car. It felt very strange to be out at night in a place where there was no artificial light. Without the headlights, Peter would be in complete darkness.

A wind ripped across the flat, dry ground and knifed through Peter. He used his free hand to zip his windbreaker tight around his neck. Then he took a few steps from his car and stared hard at the barn. No shapes emerged, no lights flickered in its dark recesses.

Peter turned slowly in a circle. He strained for any sound, but there was only the low hum of the wind. Nerves made Peter's stomach tighten. Maybe it would be for the best if no one did show. He was beginning to seriously question the wisdom of coming to this wasteland on the darkest of nights. He remembered the autopsy photographs of Sandra Whiley and the descriptions of the way the other victims had perished. It had to take time to die like that. He imagined the blade biting in, the pain, the terror.

"Have any trouble finding this place?"

Peter's heart streaked through his chest. He spun toward the voice, reflexively raising the flashlight like a weapon, but there was no one to strike. The area around him was black and empty.

Peter looked right and left as he tried to catch his breath. Suddenly, there was a break in the dark curtain that surrounded him. A blur became a vague shape and Christopher Mammon stepped out of the darkness. Peter took a step back. Mammon watched him. Could he get into the car and lock the doors before Mammon got to him? Could he streak away and outdistance Mammon in the stygian darkness of this desert hunting ground?

"I hear you've been telling people that I killed Sandra Whiley."

Peter tried to talk, but he couldn't.

"Not smart. Everyone else thinks Gary Harmon murdered Whiley. If I did kill her, you'd be the only one who suspected it. It would be in my best interest to lure you to an isolated spot like this and get rid of you before you could cause any trouble."

Mammon let Peter think about that for a moment. Then he took a step forward. There was something small and black in his hand. Peter's next step brought him hard against the side of the car. Mammon raised his hand and pointed the object at Peter. "Oh, God," Peter thought. "Don't let me die now. I'm not even thirty." Then part of the object dropped down revealing something shiny.

"You can relax," Mammon said. "I'm not going to kill you. I'm a cop."

It took a moment for the words to register. About the same amount of time it took for Peter's brain to recognize the object in Mammon's hand as a leather carrying case for a badge. Peter sagged against his car. If it had not been there to hold him up, he would have sunk onto the dusty, rock-strewn ground.

"Now listen up," Mammon said. "If you want to learn the truth, I need a guarantee that you will never, ever tell anyone about this meeting."

"What are you talking about?"

"I'm deep cover in an operation that has been going on for two years. As soon as we finish talking, I'm leaving this continent. No one at DEA will acknowledge my existence. You can file subpoena duces tecums until you're old and gray and you won't find a trace of me in any of the files you'll be searching. So you play this by my rules or I'm gone and you'll never know what happened to Sandra Whiley."

"I . . . I've got no choice, then."

"That's right. And there's something else you should know. You and your father really pissed off a couple of people. I've got instructions from the top to stay as far away from you as I can."

"Then, why are you doing this?"

Mammon took a breath. For a moment, his hard features reflected doubt.

"It's Gary. That poor bastard. If it wasn't for me, he

338

wouldn't be in this fix. I was hoping he'd be acquitted. Then I could have forgotten him. But now . . . If he was executed, I would be to blame."

"What do you mean?"

"Kevin Booth lived in Seattle for a while. An acquaintance of his worked for Rafael Vargas, who runs the cocaine in the Pacific Northwest for a Colombian cartel. Kevin got to know Vargas and picked up pin money acting as a mule. When he decided to move back to Whitaker last year, Vargas asked him to set up a distribution network.

"About eight or nine months ago, Sandra Whiley was busted on her way to deliver cocaine to a customer of Booth. The locals had no idea who Booth worked for. Whiley spilled everything. One of the Whitaker cops called the state police and they contacted us. OSP knew we were trying to find a way into the organization Vargas works for. We had been running into a stone wall until we got this break.

"I've been in deep cover for two years building a background and trying to make contacts. I was transferred here to get close to Booth and force him into a position where he had to introduce me to Vargas."

"Did Whiley know who you were?"

"No. We couldn't risk that. She thought I was working for organized crime. Her orders were to assist me so the DEA could bust me and Booth's group. The night Booth and I were arrested at Whitaker State, I was waiting for Whiley to bring me thirty thousand dollars to pay for the two kilos of coke that were found in the car. This buy was going to give me credibility when I negotiated for an amount large enough to bring Vargas into the open.

"Our arrest was bad luck and it came at a really bad time. I had to stay credible in Vargas's eyes, so it was arranged for Booth to win his preliminary hearing and for me to lose mine."

"Wait a minute. What do you mean when you say it was arranged for Booth to win at the prelim?"

"That whole thing was a hoax. O'Shay was contacted by a higher-up in the Justice Department. He asked her to throw the prelim and she did."

Peter was stunned. He'd never heard of anything like this.

"Who was in on the fix?"

"O'Shay, Mancini and the judge."

"What about Earl Ridgely?"

"He was out of town for the week and O'Shay was asked to keep the whole thing from him. He's too much of a straight arrow to go along with fixing a court case. She told the judge that she had Ridgely's approval, but that was a lie. Ridgely still doesn't know why Booth won his prelim. Even Booth didn't know.

"O'Shay, Mancini and the judge worked out a scenario that would provide a legal basis for cutting Booth free. I stayed in jail to make it look like I could be trusted, then I made bail.

"The night of the murder, I was meeting Booth to convince him to take over my part in the final stage of our plan to bring down Vargas. The plan worked. We not only caught him red-handed with twenty kilos of cocaine, but we have wiretaps and other evidence that implicate him in the importation and sale of many times that amount. Vargas knows he's facing life without possibility of parole. We hoped he would cave and give us a way to get to the next level in the cartel. He broke three days ago."

Mammon paused. He looked embarrassed.

"When I arrived at the Stallion on the night of the murder, Harmon was sitting with Booth. I had to get rid of him, so I told him Karen Nix had the hots for him. I'm the one who caused his argument with Nix. If I hadn't taken advantage of him, the poor bastard wouldn't have been convicted for a crime he didn't commit."

"How can you be so certain that Gary is innocent?"

"I know who killed Whiley."

"Who is it?" Peter asked anxiously.

"While Gary was arguing with Nix, I went outside and talked with Booth. While we were talking I saw Whiley follow a man to his car. They argued over something, then they drove off together. The man was a customer of Booth. Someone to whom Whiley had delivered cocaine. Steve Mancini."

"Oh, my God," Peter said. Everything made sense now. Whiley must have threatened Steve. Mancini could not afford a scandal with Mountain View's finances hanging in the balance. When Gary was arrested, it was a godsend, and Mancini did his best to make certain that Gary would be convicted by hooking up Peter with an inept investigator, sabotaging the motion to suppress and making certain that Gary was represented by a self-centered, incompetent fool.

"You've got to testify for Gary."

"No. Not now. Maybe not ever."

"How can you refuse? Gary may die if you don't come forward."

"I'm leaving for South America tomorrow. If I stay and testify, my cover will be destroyed. I'm this close to being accepted by the cartel. If Mancini is going to be caught, you're the one who has to do it. I've risked my career by meeting you. I'm not going to destroy it."

"How am I going to prove any of this?"

"I don't know, Hale, but I hope to God you can."

CHAPTER THIRTY

1

Peter had been sitting in Amos Geary's waiting room for half an hour when the office door opened. During that half hour, Clara Schoen had not spoken one word and the few times she stared in Peter's direction it had been to beam death rays at him. As soon as Geary stepped into the waiting room, Clara's head swiveled in his direction and her thin lips twitched in anticipation of the dressing-down Peter was certain to receive from her boss. So, it was with astonishment that she saw Geary smile at the scoundrel whom he had so recently driven from their offices.

"Come on back," Geary said, as he walked past Peter. Clara's mouth gaped open. Geary was almost out of sight when she remembered to remind him about his first court appearance.

"I know, Clara. Lenny Boudreau at ten-fifteen in Judge Staley's court," Geary said without looking back. Clara's mouth gaped wider. "Hold my calls until Peter and I are finished."

Geary closed the door behind them and went to his filing cabinet while Peter took a chair.

"Clara thinks I can't remember my schedule without her," Geary said as he pawed through his filing cabinet in search of the *Boudreau* file. "I let her keep thinking that way. It makes her feel needed."

Geary lit up as soon as he found the file. "Did Dick save the day?" he asked as he settled in behind his desk.

"No, but there has been a break of sorts in the case."

Geary filled the room with a dense cloud of smoke as Peter told him about the meeting at the U.S. Attorney's office, his encounter with Christopher Mammon and everything he knew about Steve Mancini.

"Mancini, huh?" Geary said thoughtfully when Peter finished. "I wouldn't put it past him."

"My problem is how to prove Steve killed Whiley without Mammon as a witness and how to get Gary a new trial on the grounds that O'Shay concealed exculpatory evidence. The Justice Department has put a lid on this, so there's no way I can get the DEA reports without a major lawsuit, and O'Shay won't admit what she's done. With Mammon gone, I've lost my key witness. There's also a good chance all copies of the reports have been destroyed."

"You definitely have problems," Geary agreed.

Peter sighed. "I've only got a few days before the penalty phase starts. There's got to be some way to show that Whiley was the CRI."

Peter suddenly noticed that Geary had a faraway look in his eyes and the hint of a smile on his lips. The cigarette, forgotten for the moment, dangled from his nicotine-stained fingers, the ash flaking off the tip and falling onto his carpet. Suddenly, Geary chuckled.

"Rebecca fucked up."

"How?" Peter asked eagerly.

"Come on, think. If an old drunk like me can figure it out, a sober young stud like yourself should be able to crack this case in no time. I'll even give you a hint. There's a witness who can bury O'Shay."

Peter went over everything he knew while Geary watched his struggle with glee. Finally, Peter gave up.

"Ah, me. The younger generation," Geary cackled.

"Stuff it, Amos. I've lost my sense of humor."

Geary sat up and blew a plume of smoke across the desk. Peter coughed.

"Lighten up, then listen up and I'll tell you how we're going to bust this case wide open."

2

Earl Ridgely looked surprised when he walked into the chambers of District Court Judge Brett Staley with Becky O'Shay and saw Peter Hale and Amos Geary sitting next to the judge's desk.

"What's up, Brett?" Ridgely asked.

"Something pretty unpleasant, Earl. Why don't you and Miss O'Shay sit down and I'll let Mr. Hale explain."

O'Shay noticed that the judge had avoided eye contact with her. She looked at Peter warily, but said nothing.

"On Sunday, I made a very unsettling discovery, Mr. Ridgely," Peter said. "Almost by accident, I learned that Miss O'Shay has been withholding exculpatory evidence that casts the whole Harmon case in a different light."

"Earl, this is a crock," O'Shay said contemptuously. "What really happened on Sunday is that Mr. Hale snuck into Kevin Booth's room at the hospital and was arrested. I'm preparing a bar complaint. I don't know what story he's concocted, but it's his way of trying to get back at me for reporting his conduct to the ethics committee."

"Why don't we hear what Peter has to say, Becky?" Ridgely said. O'Shay started to protest. Then, it suddenly dawned on her why they were meeting in Judge Staley's chambers instead of Judge Kuffel's and she turned pale.

"Becky has known for several months that Sandra Whiley was working as an informant for the DEA in

344

a case involving Christopher Mammon, Kevin Booth, Rafael Vargas and a very violent Colombian drug cartel and she has intentionally concealed this information from the defense," Peter said.

"Is this true?" Ridgely asked her.

"Earl, this is nonsense," O'Shay answered angrily.

"I suppose I'd also be crazy to suggest that you fixed the Booth-Mammon prelim?" Peter said. "I'm sure your boss will be interested in knowing that you told Judge Staley that he knew all about your deal with the Justice Department."

"What deal?" Ridgely asked O'Shay.

"Miss O'Shay came to me with Steve Mancini and a Justice Department official from Washington, D.C., before the preliminary hearing for Christopher Mammon and Kevin Booth," Judge Staley answered. "She told me that you had approved a plan that involved my dismissal of Kevin Booth's case at the hearing so that a federal undercover operation would not be endangered."

"I what!"

"You did assure me that your scheme had Mr. Ridgely's approval, didn't you, Miss O'Shay?" Judge Staley asked.

"Earl, there was no time to track you down," O'Shay said desperately. "We shouldn't even be discussing this. We could be endangering a major undercover operation."

"Will someone explain what's going on here?" Ridgely asked.

"The feds were monitoring a drug deal that was supposed to go down on the Whitaker State campus," Peter explained. "The deal was being used to help an undercover agent infiltrate a Colombian drug cartel. Then, the campus security guards screwed everything up by arresting Booth and Mammon.

"You were out of town on vacation, so Becky was contacted by the DEA. They wanted her to get Booth back on the street. The feds concocted a plan to fix

Booth's prelim. Becky lied to Judge Staley and said she'd cleared everything with you.

"When Gary was arrested for Whiley's murder, Becky knew Whiley was an informant. She'd been briefed by the DEA and she even sent Steve Mancini two DEA reports about the Whitaker State case when they worked up the hoax. I found out about the reports by accident and she convinced Steve to destroy them and deny he'd ever seen them. She knew Judge Kuffel would have to throw out Gary's conviction if he learned about her cover-up."

"I don't believe this," Ridgely said incredulously.

"There's more and it's worse than what I've told you."

Peter paused and looked directly at O'Shay. He was about to bluff and he hoped O'Shay could not tell how scared he was that he had guessed wrong.

"Steve Mancini has been sabotaging Gary Harmon's defense from the beginning of this case. His last act was destroying the reports, but he had done several other things to make certain Gary was convicted. What I couldn't understand was why he would want to send his brother-in-law to death row. But Becky knows the answer to that riddle, don't you?"

"I . . . I don't know what you're talking about."

"Why would Steve destroy the DEA reports for you, Becky? Why would you trust him to do that instead of running to me with evidence that would win Gary a new trial? You knew that Steve had a reason to want Gary convicted. You knew that Steve had to obey you or risk exposure. You knew that Steve Mancini was with Sandra Whiley right before she was murdered."

"Is this true?" Ridgely demanded.

"What does all this matter?" O'Shay implored Ridgely. "Harmon's guilty. How did he know that the victim had been at the Stallion hours before anyone knew Whiley's identity, if he didn't kill her?"

"I talked with Gary before I set up this meeting to see if I could figure out how he knew some of the things he

346

seemed to know. The morning that the body was found was the morning that Steve was married. He drove Gary to the church. They passed by the park and saw the police cars. Donna remembered that Gary was excited by all the activity. He probably asked Steve why there were police all over the park. I'm betting Steve slipped and said some girl who'd been at the Stallion last night had been murdered.

"I also spoke to Wilma Polk. Her husband was at the crime scene. He told Mrs. Polk that the man who killed Whiley chopped her up with a hatchet. Mrs. Polk told her friend about the killer using a hatchet when they were at the food table at the reception following the wedding. Mrs. Polk remembers Gary standing next to her and listening intently to what she said.

"And the placement of the blows. Before Bob Patrick tricked Gary with the black light, he showed him several autopsy photos of Whiley's head wounds.

"There are reasonable explanations for a lot of the evidence that incriminates Gary, but you weren't interested in the truth, were you, Becky?"

"I . . . I thought it was Gary. I still do. I didn't know that Steve was with Whiley that night until I debriefed Booth. He saw them together at the Stallion."

"And you told Booth to keep his mouth shut," Peter said accusingly.

"I couldn't tell you. The jury would never have convicted if it knew about Whiley being an informant and Steve being with her right before she was killed. There would have been too many other suspects. And Steve swore he didn't kill her."

"You still don't understand what you've done, do you?" Peter asked, amazed by O'Shay's continued defiance. "You still don't see that you've done something terribly wrong. How could you blind yourself to the possibility that Steve killed Whiley when it was right in front of you? How could you . . ."

All of a sudden Peter knew why O'Shay had shielded Steve. He remembered the way Steve and Becky acted when they were together, he recalled a cryptic remark Becky had made at the wedding reception when Peter asked her how she knew Steve.

"Did Steve swear he was innocent while you were having sex or after you were finished screwing?" Peter asked O'Shay.

Becky's eyes widened. "What are you talking about?"

"Are you denying that you've been sleeping with Steve Mancini?"

Earl Ridgely stared at O'Shay with a growing sense of horror.

"If Earl learned that you lied to Judge Staley in order to fix the prelim and that you were secretly sleeping with a defense attorney against whom you've tried cases, he would have fired you on the spot. Did you keep quiet about Mancini because he threatened to expose you?" Peter asked.

"No, no, it wasn't like that. As soon as Kevin Booth told me he had seen Steve with Whiley at the Stallion I confronted Steve. He swore he was innocent. Then, he reminded me of . . . of something I should have remembered. Steve and I . . . Well, uh, we've been together off and on since I moved to Whitaker. And, well . . . We'd made plans to spend the evening before his wedding together."

"What!" Peter said.

"You don't think Steve married Donna Harmon for love, do you?" O'Shay said scornfully. "He was worried about Mountain View and he figured Jesse Harmon would come through with a sizable investment once he was married to Jesse's daughter."

"That son of a bitch," Peter said. Amos Geary put a restraining hand on Peter's arm.

"You were telling us how you knew Mr. Mancini was innocent, Miss O'Shay," Geary prodded. "Why don't you continue."

"Steve was with me the night Whiley was killed. He showed up around midnight. He seemed upset. When I asked, he said it was because Gary had been in some trouble at the Stallion.

"Later, I confronted him about Booth seeing him with Whiley. He admitted it was true. He said Whiley was at the Stallion. When he left, she cornered him. It was in the parking lot. She was almost hysterical. She told him she had to leave town. She was scared to death of Christopher Mammon. Whiley thought he was in jail. Then she saw him in the Stallion. Whiley thought Mammon would suspect her of setting him up at Whitaker State and kill her.

"She was making a scene, so Steve told her to get in his car. They drove around for a while. She demanded money from Steve so she could run away. He tried to reason with her, but she was irrational. She said she would tell everyone Steve was using cocaine if he didn't give her money. She even threatened to crash his wedding.

"Steve told her he had some money at his office. He didn't want to be seen with her so he dropped her at the entrance to Wishing Well Park and said he'd meet her at the well as soon as he got the money."

"When did he say he dropped off Whiley?"

"Eleven-fifty. He checked his watch because he was supposed to come to my place around midnight."

Peter controlled his excitement. The bartender at the Ponderosa had testified that Gary came into the bar at eleven fifty-three or eleven fifty-four. If everyone's times were accurate, it would be impossible for Gary to be the killer.

"What did Steve say happened next?"

"He said he went to his office, picked up every penny he could find, which was about three thousand dollars in cash, and went right back to the park. Steve said he parked on a side street and walked over. He saw someone running away from the well when he approached. At first, he thought it was Whiley. Then, he saw her body."

"When did you learn all this?" Earl Ridgely asked in

a tone that made it clear that he was having trouble believing what he was hearing.

"Right before Booth was set on fire."

"And . . . and you kept this to yourself? You made that poor bastard and his family go through a trial for murder when you knew he wasn't guilty?" Ridgely asked as he looked at O'Shay with disgust.

"I didn't know that. Steve denied killing Whiley and I believed him. I still think Gary committed the murder."

"How could you?" Ridgely demanded. "Whiley was blackmailing Mancini, he was at the park with her at the time of the killing. My God, are you an idiot?"

"No, Earl. I'm sure he didn't kill her. I remembered the suit he was wearing when he came to my house. I'd seen him in it earlier in the day. It was the same suit and the same tie. The same shoes. I confirmed that he was wearing the suit at the Stallion by checking with Karen Nix, the bartenders and some other witnesses."

O'Shay paused and breathed deeply. She stared at the floor when she spoke.

"I . . . I undressed Steve that night. I saw his shirt, his suit. The killer would have had blood all over him and there wasn't a drop of blood on Steve Mancini."

CHAPTER THIRTY-ONE

The Harmons sat in the front row of the courtroom. Peter had told them to come to court, but little else, because he did not want to get their hopes up. Steve Mancini sat in a row behind the Harmons on the other side of the courtroom. A deputy sheriff had served him a subpoena while he was eating breakfast. Mancini wondered why Earl Ridgely was sitting alone at the prosecution table. He was not aware that Becky O'Shay was in a jail cell charged with tampering with a witness and official misconduct.

Gary Harmon looked desperate when the guards led him into Judge Kuffel's courtroom. He was twitching from nerves and had not slept.

"Please get me out of jail, Pete," he begged as soon as he was seated between Peter and Amos Geary, "I'm scared there. I just want to go home."

"Well, you might be doing just that, Gary. So, try to calm down."

While Peter was talking to Gary, Judge Kuffel emerged from chambers carrying the motion for a new trial that Peter had hastily prepared after the meeting in Judge Staley's chambers. He looked perplexed.

"You're joining in this motion, Mr. Ridgely?" the

judge asked to make sure he understood correctly what he had just read.

"Yes, Your Honor. In light of certain matters that have come to my attention, I believe that the interests of justice require the court to set aside the guilty verdict against Mr. Harmon."

The judge still looked puzzled. He wondered where Becky O'Shay was and why Amos Geary was sitting with Peter Hale.

"What's the basis for this motion, Mr. Hale?" Judge Kuffel asked.

"I think my first witness will clear up your confusion, Your Honor."

"Very well, call the witness."

"Mr. Harmon calls Kevin Booth."

Yesterday afternoon, after the meeting in Judge Staley's chambers, Earl Ridgely, Peter Hale, Amos Geary and a detective from the Oregon State Police had interviewed Booth at the hospital. Booth was brought into court in a wheelchair and allowed to testify from it. He was wearing a hospital gown and a bathrobe.

"Mr. Booth," Peter said, after the witness was sworn, "you have already testified in the case of *State v. Harmon*, have you not?"

"Yes."

"Was the testimony that you gave in Portland truthful testimony?"

"One second here, Mr. Hale," Judge Kuffel said. "You're asking this man if he committed perjury. If he says he lied, he's admitting to a crime."

"That's true, Your Honor. But Mr. Booth is also testifying under a grant of immunity from prosecution for any false testimony given in Mr. Harmon's case, a promise that he will not be prosecuted for his part in the incident at Whitaker State College and a promise from state and federal authorities that he will not be prosecuted for his part in the crime that led to his arrest at his home."

Peter did not tell the judge that the cooperation from the feds had been obtained when Earl Ridgely threatened to go public with what he knew about the rigged preliminary hearing and the undercover operation against the Colombian cartel.

"Very well. Proceed."

"Mr. Booth, I repeat, did you testify truthfully in this case?"

"No."

"When you said that Gary Harmon discussed his case with you at the Whitaker jail, was that true?"

"Yes."

"Did Mr. Harmon ever tell you that he murdered Sandra Whiley?"

"No. He said he didn't do it."

"Why did you lie about what Mr. Harmon told you?"

"I was scared I'd go to prison on my federal drug charge, so I had to make a deal. It was my only way out."

"The prosecutor in Mr. Harmon's case is Rebecca O'Shay. Did you worry about her learning that you were lying about Mr. Harmon's guilt?"

"No. She wanted Harmon convicted."

"Mr. Booth, did Ms. O'Shay instruct you to conceal from the defense certain information that would have cast doubt on Mr. Harmon's guilt, if made known to the jury?"

"Yeah."

"What was one thing she didn't want you talking about?"

"Whiley was a cokehead and she bought from me. She didn't have a lot of money, so sometimes she had to work off her debt. On the evening I was busted at Whitaker State with Chris Mammon, Whiley was late bringing thirty thousand dollars to the meet. When we were arrested, Mammon thought Whiley set us up. He told me he was going to kill her, if he found out it was true."

"And you told Ms. O'Shay about the threat?"

"Yeah. She knew Mammon was at the Stallion at the same time as Whiley on the night of the murder. I thought she'd be interested, but she said Harmon did it and I wasn't to tell anyone that Mammon knew Whiley."

"Did Ms. O'Shay tell you to keep quiet about anything else?"

Booth located Steve Mancini and his scarred lips twisted into a malicious grin.

"Yeah. I told her I saw Steve Mancini drive off with Sandra Whiley from the Stallion on the evening that Whiley was killed."

Donna put her hand over her mouth. Jesse Harmon fixed Mancini with a look of pure hatred. Mancini looked around nervously. He started to stand, but stopped when he noticed the armed guards that Earl Ridgely had stationed inside the courtroom doors.

"What happened when you told this information to Ms. O'Shay?"

"She said I'd better forget about it or she'd see I spent the rest of my life in prison."

"Did Mr. Mancini know Sandra Whiley before the evening of the murder?"

"Sure. Mancini bought cocaine from me. Whiley delivered it to him at his office and his house a few times. One time, she told me she had sex with Mancini for some of the blow."

Mancini had broken out in a sweat. His eyes darted around the courtroom, desperately seeking a way out.

"No further questions, Mr. Booth."

"Mr. Ridgely?" the judge asked.

"No questions."

"Do you have another witness, Mr. Hale?"

Peter faced the spectator section and said, "We call Steve Mancini, Your Honor."

"I didn't kill her," Mancini shouted.

Judge Kuffel pounded his gavel. Mancini froze. The judge glared at him, then said, "You've been called as a witness, Mr. Mancini. Please come forward."

Mancini hesitated. He looked around at the accusing eyes that stared at him from every corner of the room. Then, he walked unsteadily to the witness box. Peter looked directly at Mancini, but Steve would not look back.

"On the evening that Sandra Whiley was murdered, did you drive away from the Stallion tavern with her?" Peter asked.

"I'm . . . I want to speak to a lawyer," Mancini said in a trembling voice.

"Mr. Hale, I'm going to have to adjourn this hearing so Mr. Mancini can consult with counsel. From what I've heard here, he may need one."

Peter knew this would happen and he did not object. Mancini started to stand up. Ridgely signaled to two police officers, who approached Mancini.

"I have a warrant for your arrest, Mr. Mancini," Ridgely said.

Steve froze. "Hey, Earl, this isn't true. I didn't kill her."

Ridgely ignored him. "Please bring Mr. Mancini to the jail," he told the officers. "See he's read his *Miranda* rights and is allowed to call an attorney."

"Earl," Mancini begged, but Ridgely turned his back on him and Mancini was led out of the courtroom.

"May Mr. Harmon be released into the custody of his parents, Your Honor?" Peter asked, as soon as the courtroom had quieted down.

"That would be highly unusual. He's been convicted of aggravated murder."

Earl Ridgely stood slowly and addressed the court.

"Rebecca O'Shay is not present today because she is under arrest. Ms. O'Shay intentionally concealed crucial evidence from the defense. Evidence which casts grave doubt on Mr. Harmon's guilt.

"I haven't had time to investigate this case thoroughly in light of the new information that the court has just heard, but I know enough to feel that justice will be served best by releasing Mr. Harmon into the custody of his parents while I sort everything out."

Judge Kuffel pursed his lips and considered the request.

"Very well," he said. "Mr. Harmon, I am ordering your release to the custody of your parents. There will be certain conditions you will have to follow, which I will devise after consultation with counsel. Do you follow what I'm saying?"

Gary looked scared and uncertain. He turned to Peter.

"He's sending you home, Gary," Peter said.

Gary's mouth opened for a moment. Then it formed into a wide smile.

"I'm going home?" he asked as if he could not believe it.

Peter could not help smiling back. "Yeah, Gary, you're going home."

Gary's eyes shone. Then he whooped and threw his arms around Peter.

"You're a good lawyer, Pete. You're the best lawyer. You made them send me home."

Judge Kuffel started to gavel for order. Then he thought better of it and lay the gavel down. Peter stood helpless and speechless in Gary's embrace, blushing wildly.

CHAPTER THIRTY-TWO

1

"Will you have another piece of pie, Peter?" Alice Harmon asked.

"Mrs. Harmon, if I eat one more slice of your apple pie, I'll explode."

"I believe I can fit in another piece somewhere," Amos Geary said.

"Gary, hand me Amos's plate, please," Alice told her son. When Gary picked up the plate his back was to Alice Harmon and he did not see how his mother beamed.

Donna stood up and turned to Peter.

"I'm going to get some fresh air. Do you want to join me?"

"Sure."

Donna opened the screen door and led Peter onto the front porch of her parents' house. It was mid-September, the sun was almost down and the night air was nippy. Donna and Peter both wore sweaters. They walked into the front yard. Donna wrapped her arms around herself as she strolled slowly next to the white board fence that ran along the edge of the Harmons' property.

"It's so great having Gary home," Donna said. "You can't believe the change in Mom and Dad."

"It's not over yet," Peter cautioned. "We still have to get the charges dismissed."

"They won't send him back," Donna said confidently. "They couldn't. Mr. Ridgely is too decent a man."

They walked in silence for a while. Then, Donna said, "It is amazing how everything conspired to make Gary look so guilty. His overhearing Wilma Polk, O'Shay telling Booth about the Crusader's Cross and Steve letting it slip that the dead woman was at the Stallion . . ."

"That's why Earl's going to go slowly before he charges anyone else. He won't want to make another mistake."

"Who do you think killed Sandra Whiley?" Donna asked when they reached the large oak that shaded the front lawn.

"I don't know. I really haven't given it that much thought. In the movies, the defense attorney always saves his client by figuring out who the killer is. In real life, defense attorneys really don't care. I've spent this whole case trying to counter the state's evidence in order to raise a reasonable doubt. I mean, it would be great if I did prove who killed Sandra Whiley, but as long as I can convince Earl that he should set Gary free, I've done my job."

"You must have some idea. What about Christopher Mammon? I heard that he's disappeared."

"Mammon is definitely not the killer."

"How can you be so certain?"

"In order to tell you, I'd have to break a promise I made. Just trust me. I know it's not Mammon."

Donna turned her back to Peter and bowed her head.

"If Christopher Mammon isn't guilty, then Steve probably is."

"I guess that's true," Peter answered thoughtfully. "He's certainly the most likely suspect. We just learned that his first wife left him because he also beat her, so he clearly has a propensity for violence. The problem with the case against Steve is Becky O'Shay's evidence."

Peter caught himself. Donna turned toward him and he turned red.

"I'm sorry . . ." he started, but Donna shook her head.

"Don't be. I'm glad I found out that he screwed her on the night before our wedding. It relieves me of any lingering doubts I may have had about Steve."

They walked on in silence until Donna asked, "Will you be moving back to Portland when you've wrapped up Gary's case?"

"No. I was really thoughtless leaving Amos short-handed, so I'm going back to work for him tomorrow. I don't think I'll stay in criminal law forever, but it is sort of exciting."

"I'm glad you'll be around," Donna said, looking directly into Peter's eyes. Peter hesitated for a second. Then he reached out and took her hand.

"There's another reason I'm sticking around Whitaker."

Peter waited for Donna to pull free. When she didn't, he said, "I don't know if this is the right time to say this. You're going through so much right now and I'm still trying to figure out who I am and what I want. There are a lot of things about me you don't know, too. Things you might not like."

"We don't have to rush, Peter. Now that you're staying in town, we can take our time. Let's just see how things work out. Okay?"

Then Donna kissed him. It was a soft kiss, but it stunned Peter. Donna rested her head on his shoulder and they held each other in the dark. Peter had never made a commitment to a woman before. Even thinking about it was a little scary. Was he capable of being true to one person? He thought he might be able to do it. He had done some pretty amazing things since arriving in Whitaker.

2

"You look pretty satisfied with yourself," Amos Geary said when they were on their way back to town in Peter's car.

"What do you mean?" Peter asked self-consciously. He had been reliving his kiss with Donna.

"She's not someone to play with. Donna's been through a lot. If you're not serious about her, don't start anything."

"Jesus, Amos, give me some credit, will you," Peter protested.

"Given your track record, I decided to be blunt."

"Hey, the old Peter is gone."

"We'll see."

They drove on in silence for a while. Peter drifted back to thoughts of love, but Geary was thinking about something else. After a while, he let out a long breath.

"What?" Peter asked.

"I was thinking about that poor girl. The police have lost so much time that I don't think they'll ever catch Whiley's killer."

"We know it's not Mammon. I haven't ruled out Steve, but it's pretty unlikely that he killed her if O'Shay is telling the truth."

"Which she may not be doing. Just thinking about O'Shay makes me sick."

"Something just occurred to me. Ridgely should check on Steve's alibi for the time when those other two women were killed. With all the excitement, we forgot that the person who killed Whiley probably killed them, too."

"Earl's no dummy. I'm sure he's already thought about seeing if he can tie Mancini into the other killings. I'll say one thing—whoever committed those murders is one sick son of a bitch. Killing someone is bad enough, but butchering a defenseless woman with a hatchet, like she was some kind of farm animal . . ."

Geary lapsed into silence at the thought of such sense-less slaughter. Suddenly, Peter pulled the car over to the side of the road. Geary wasn't wearing a seat belt and he was thrown forward. Fortunately, he caught the dashboard with his hands.

"What the fuck is wrong with you?" Geary shouted.

Peter wasn't listening. He looked stunned.

"Hale, are you having some sort of yuppie fit? Talk to me."

Peter turned slowly. He looked pale.

"The hatchet. My God, I didn't even think . . . We've got to go to the office and look up something in Mammon's file."

"What are you talking about?"

Instead of answering, Peter hit the accelerator and Geary was thrown back into his seat.

"I'll explain on the way," Peter said, as Geary hurriedly fastened his seat belt.

"Is this where we turn?" Peter asked.

"I'm not certain," Geary answered.

"I thought you lived here most of your life."

"I'm a lawyer, not a goddamn surveyor. Now, shut up and give me a minute."

Geary studied a map of Whitaker and the surrounding area while Peter impatiently drummed his fingers on the steering wheel.

"Okay. This is the road that was listed in the police report in Mammon's file."

Peter drove a mile up an unpaved, dirt track. There was a full moon and they soon saw the object of their search. Peter stopped in front of the dilapidated house.

"You're sure this is legal?" Peter asked.

"It's not legal. It's breaking and entering. But we aren't working for the government, so Earl can use any evidence we find at trial while we are serving our sentence for burglary."

"Thanks for clearing that up. I feel much better now,"

Peter said, as he tried the door. It wasn't locked. Peter had brought along a flashlight, but Geary flipped on a light switch and he didn't need it.

"Looks like the electricity is still paid up," Geary commented.

"God! What's that smell?"

Both men winced as a sour and fetid odor assailed them. It was the essence of the decay that permeated the house. Flies buzzed around rotting pizza crusts and decomposing cheese that hung on the sides of oil-stained pizza boxes. Unwashed clothes lay in clumps on the couch.

"This place is a fucking sty," Peter declared.

"Let's search it fast, so we can get out of here," Geary said.

They split up, Peter taking the bedroom and bathroom and Geary searching the living room and kitchen. The search did not take long, since the house was so small.

"Anything?" Peter asked.

"Not a thing," Geary answered when they both finished.

"I was so sure."

"Your reasoning is sound. He probably killed the women somewhere else."

"I guess," Peter answered dejectedly.

Peter walked outside. Geary turned out the lights and shut the door. Peter was about to get in the car when he froze.

"What's that?" he asked.

Geary looked where Peter was pointing. Another house could barely be made out in the moonlight.

"It's worth a look now that we're out here."

The two men turned on their flashlights and walked a dusty quarter mile. It was not until they reached the shack that they could tell it was deserted, but there was a padlock on the door.

"What do we do now?" Peter asked.

Geary raised his foot and kicked the door with all the

force his near three hundred pounds could bring to the task. The rotting door splintered and gave. A second kick and it swung inward. An odor, different and more foul than the one they had smelled in the other house, assailed Peter when he crossed the threshold. He clamped his hand over his mouth and moved the flashlight beam around the interior of the shack.

"Holy shit!" he whispered when the beam found the bloodstained mattress pushed up against the far wall. Geary was speechless. Peter moved his beam around the floor and gagged when he realized that almost every square inch was encrusted with dried blood.

"Peter," Amos called. Peter looked at the corner of the room that Geary's beam was illuminating. He saw piles of women's clothes, a purse and two wallets.

"What do you want to bet that one of those wallets belongs to Sandra Whiley?" Geary asked.

"If you're right, I'm not going to be the one who discovers it. Let's get out of here and call the police."

3

Kevin Booth was asleep when Earl Ridgely entered his hospital room followed by members of the Major Crime Team. He stirred when the nurse turned on the lights, then sat up.

"What's going on?" Booth asked, rubbing his eyes as he searched for the clock. Then he saw how many people were in his room.

"I have a few questions for you, Kevin," Ridgely said.

"It's three in the morning, for Christ's sake. Can't this wait?"

"Actually, no." Ridgely pulled a chair next to Booth's bed. "But I promise not to take up too much of your time. First, though, I'm going to give you your *Miranda* rights."

Ridgely took a laminated card out of his wallet and read Booth his rights. Booth looked at Ridgely as if the D.A. was insane.

"What is this?" Booth asked when Ridgely was through.

"Can you explain why Sandra Whiley's wallet and the clothing of Emily Curran and Diane Fetter were found in a shack less than a quarter mile from your house and why the floor of the shack was covered with blood?"

"What . . . what are you talking about? What shack?"

"Kevin, at this very moment, fingerprint technicians are going over every inch of the shack and forensic experts are combing it for hair, fibers and other trace evidence."

"Well, you won't find anything belonging to me in some fucking blood-covered shack. I don't know what you think you've got, but you ain't got shit connecting me to no murders."

"Actually," Ridgely said, "we've got quite a lot. For instance, Curran and Fetter both had a lot of cocaine in their system when they died. Background checks on both women showed that they used cocaine frequently. I think you supplied both women with cocaine and lured them to your house with promises of free drugs. I think you got them high, then raped and killed them."

"You can think all you want."

"I also think you made one monumental error. Peter Hale explained it to me. It's so obvious that I feel really stupid for missing it."

Ridgely waited for Booth to say something. When he didn't, Ridgely continued.

"You were terrified when you were arrested with Rafael Vargas. Not only were you facing serious federal time, but Vargas threatened to kill you, the feds refused to bargain with you and Steve Mancini wouldn't represent you. That's when you decided to trade testimony against Gary Harmon for a deal that would keep you out of prison. You gained Gary's confidence and tricked him into telling you all of the details of the murder of Sandra Whiley that he told the police. Since you killed Whiley, you were able to add some extra information that made the confession sound real, but that wasn't enough for Becky O'Shay. She knew that no jury would ever buy your story without corroboration, so she told you that you wouldn't get a deal unless you could provide proof that Gary confessed.

"You were in a panic, going through withdrawal and not really thinking straight. O'Shay was about to walk out on you and O'Shay was your last chance, so you told her something that only the killer would know. You told her where to find the hatchet you used to murder Curran, Fetter and Whiley. The hatchet you threw in the storm drain because you were afraid that Steve Mancini might have seen you running from the murder scene.

"Gary Harmon couldn't have told you where the murder weapon was hidden. It was impossible for him to have killed Whiley. He was at the Ponderosa when the murder occurred. If Gary didn't tell you it was in a storm drain near the Whitaker campus, how did you know?"

Booth stared wide-eyed at Ridgely, then scanned the stone-hard faces of the men who ringed his bed.

"I want a lawyer," he said finally. "I want a lawyer."

Ridgely nodded. "I figured that's what you'd want, Mr. Booth, and I think you're wise to ask for one, because if anyone needs a lawyer right now, you do."

EPILOGUE

The scoreboard on top of Stallion Stadium showed that there were fifty-eight seconds remaining in the game between the Whitaker Stallions and Boise State, with Whitaker leading by a touchdown and driving for another. Peter figured that fifty-eight seconds was about as long as he could take the frozen rain that had turned the last game of the season into a mud-wrestling contest. Donna huddled against him, just as miserable as he was. Only Gary seemed oblivious to the ghastly weather conditions. He was on his feet screaming with each play, transported by the very real possibility that the undefeated Whitaker Stallions might actually go all the way.

Many things had happened in the three months since the dramatic termination of the charges against Gary Harmon. Kevin Booth had not been able to hold out for long. Connections between Booth and the three murdered women were easily established once the police started concentrating on Booth as the prime suspect. In order to escape the death penalty, Booth cut a deal that would keep him in prison for the rest of his life without the possibility of parole. Booth had shocked the prosecutors by confessing not only to murdering Sandra

Whiley, Emily Curran and Diane Fetter, but to the murder of his mother, whom he had pushed down the stairs.

Booth told Earl Ridgely that he had watched from his pickup truck as Whiley and Mancini argued. Then, he followed them as they drove aimlessly through Whitaker. Whiley had haunted Booth's sexual fantasies since she began buying cocaine from him, but he had been afraid to touch a woman whom he believed belonged to Christopher Mammon. Booth suspected Whiley of betraying him as soon as he was arrested at Whitaker State and he longed to make her suffer. His humiliation at Mammon's hands had driven Booth into a rage. He was terrified of Mammon, but he thought of Whiley as prey. When Mancini dropped off Whiley at Wishing Well Park, Booth had taken his hatchet from the pickup and followed her with the idea of taking her to his shack where he could torture and rape her, but Whiley had fought Booth and had paid with her life.

As soon as Steve Mancini was certain that he would not be prosecuted for killing Whiley, he confessed his attempts to cover up his involvement with Whiley on the night of the murder. His motive in sabotaging Gary's case was simple cowardice. Mancini was terrified that a competent lawyer and a competent investigator would uncover his meeting with Whiley. He feared an arrest for her murder and he could not afford a scandal involving his use of cocaine with the Mountain View project on the verge of destruction.

"As soon as this game ends, we're heading for my place and a gallon of hot toddies," Peter managed to chatter.

"Two gallons, but we'll have to figure a way to get Gary out of the stadium. He's going to want to run down on the field when the game ends and shake hands with the players."

"Oh, shit. I forgot."

This was Gary's postgame ritual and he always went through it.

"I'll make it up to you," Donna smiled.

"When? It's going to take us a year to thaw out."

The whistle blew and Gary's face lit up.

"All the way, all the way," he shrieked, as his fists pummeled the air. He grabbed Donna and dragged her to her feet, then hugged her so tight she had to tell Gary to stop.

"Pete, Pete," Gary screamed, "all the way, all the way."

Then Gary was scrambling down the icy grandstand and streaking onto the field.

"It looks like the only good thing that asshole husband of yours did was to get Gary these season tickets," Peter joked as he and Donna cautiously made their way out of the stands.

"Soon-to-be ex-husband. Judge Kuffel is hearing the divorce next week. At least Steve had the grace not to contest it."

"He's got a lot more on his mind than the divorce. Ridgely has agreed to dismiss the criminal charges if he resigns from the bar. And Mountain View bankrupted him. I hear he's going to leave town."

"How could he stay here? Everyone in Whitaker knows what he's done."

"I saw Earl at the courthouse yesterday. O'Shay won't plead. She's also fighting disbarment."

"I hope she ends up in prison for what she did to Gary."

Donna and Peter found shelter near the concession stand where they always waited for Gary after a game. Peter bought two cups of hot coffee. They drank in silence for a few minutes, savoring the warmth provided by the steaming hot liquid. After a bit, Peter decided it was time to talk about something he had been meaning to say all day, but had not had the courage to bring up.

"Dad called last night."

"Oh?"

"He asked me to come back to Hale, Greaves. I guess all is forgiven."

"What did you tell him?" Donna asked cautiously.

"I said I couldn't give him an answer right away. I told him my answer depended on the answer to another question."

"What question?"

"Well, uh, my practice is going pretty good. I've picked up a lot of business because of Gary's case. Enough so Amos and I are going to hire an associate to help him handle the indigent criminal cases so I can concentrate on personal injury and retained criminal stuff. So, that's a reason to stick around. But there would be a bigger reason if you'd marry me when your divorce is final."

Donna blinked, then her eyes filled with tears and she threw her arms around Peter. Her half-filled cup of coffee went sailing through the air.

"Does that mean yes?" Peter asked as he broke out laughing.

Before Donna could respond, Gary burst up the concrete ramp and ran toward them. He was holding a jersey that was so covered with mud that the numbers were almost illegible.

"Look, look," he shouted, holding up his prize. "The coach said I could keep it. He said I'm lucky. He said the Stallions couldn't win without me."

"That's great, Gary," Donna managed.

"We did it, Pete. We went all the way and the coach said I helped."

Donna and Peter broke out laughing as they watched Gary bounce up and down with joy. Donna hugged Peter, then she hugged her brother.

"Let's get you home," Donna said to Gary, as they started toward the parking lot. She had to shout to be heard over the blaring horns and raucous shouts from the jubilant Stallion rooters who seemed oblivious to the cold and rain.

"Hey," Peter shouted, "what about my proposal?"

"We're going all the way," Gary shouted at a group of boisterous students.

"My sentiments exactly," Donna told Peter Hale.

THE LAST FAMILY

JOHN RAMSEY MILLER

A harrowing novel of suspense that pits
a former DEA agent against his worst nightmare:
a trained killer whose fury knows no bounds,
whose final target is the agent's own
flesh and blood . . .

"Fast paced, original, and utterly terrifying--true, teeth-grinding tension...Hannibal Lecter eat your heart out!"--Michael Palmer

_____57496-5 $6.99/$8.99